AHAB

A HOCKEY STORY

BRAD HUESTIS

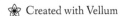

IN PRAISE OF AHAB

Love *AHAB: A Hockey Story*, wonderful job!
Bobby Orr, # 4

Army veteran's hockey novel celebrates sports as rehab for wounded warriors.
Seth Robson, *Stars & Stripes*

AHAB wonderfully captures how hockey in Germany differs from North America—with the outward passion of English Premier League soccer meeting the fervently loyalty of NCAA college football—and reminds us that it's the bond with the "boys in the room" that gives players the connections they'll never forget.
Denny Wolfe, Senior Producer, ESPN Features Unit

AHAB centers on teamwork and belonging—in life, the military and hockey—and what happens when some are left behind. The military themes and Bavarian settings are instantly recognizable and relatable, and you'll find yourself cheering for Will Foley as he battles through rehab to get back to his unit and onto the ice.

Carolyn Warmbold, Editor and Author

Coming of age story? Check. Love interest? Check. Military connection? Check. Foreign setting? Check. All my favorites in one story. Brad Huestis skillfully weaves a coming of age story that checks every box—throw in a good looking woman or two and some Oktoberfest bier, and it's pretty close to perfect. Be prepared for a bit of an emotional roller coaster. A fun read with hidden depths that will stay with you long after you finish the last chapter.

Genie Hughes, Berlin Brigade Judge Advocate

The story's Bavarian settings are vivid and unforgettable. A must read...

MilitaryInGermany.com

Brad Huestis's debut novel is both charming and thought-provoking, combining the emotional freedom of play with the unflinching realities of life and the consequences of our actions. *AHAB* is a compelling story that goes beyond the subject of wartime and examines the human condition, showing we are capable of much more than we believe.

Justin Herzog, author of *First Wave* and *Into the Void*

I recommend *AHAB* to lovers of the beautiful game of hockey and all lovers of fascinating fiction stories.

OnlineBookClub.Org

*In memory of my brother, Clay. His passion
for sport enriched many lives, including mine.*

ONE

I plant my feet, rock back on my chute, and arch my back to lift my frozen butt up off of the icy runway. I exhale and my breath floats up toward one of the airfield's halogen flood-lights. I shiver and think back to a frosty game of childhood hockey.

As my dad bent to tie his skates, I asked him, "What do you like more, real hockey or pond hockey?"

"Outdoor, fresh-air pond hockey," he said. "You gotta love the freedom. No helmet, no shoulder pads, no breezers, no line changes—"

"Breezers?"

"Pants, Silly Willie, hockey pants," he said, "Come on, let's play."

We skated out onto the huge sheet of gray ice. Circling, going from front to back, dipping and turning, passing the puck, we sucked in cold, fresh air. We played without whistles or buzzers to interrupt the ebb and flow of our joy. Cousin Kevin showed up later. Three years older than me, he was a freshman who had just made East Boston's junior varsity team. Tall, lean, and graceful, with a toothy smile, dark hair, and rosy cheeks, he looked like a member of the Kennedy clan. Even today, I'm proud when people say the two of us look like brothers.

Dad and I shoveled away the ice chips our blades had cut from the ice, and Kevin put on his skates. We played two on one. Whoever scored became the defender against the other two. Kevin had the size and strength to beat me, and the youth and speed to beat Dad, so he spent most of his time as the defenseman.

When he scored another easy goal, Dad said, "Okay Willie, we officially suck. Once you pass to me, go straight to the net and stay there with your stick blade hard on the ice. I'll get you the puck for a tap in, okay?"

"Got it."

This time Dad stopped short, did a three-hundred-sixty degree spin-o-rama, and fired a hard pass to me. I deflected it in, beaming.

"Oh, come on, Willie, do a little dance! Show your old man some celly!"

I grinned, raised my stick and did a little jig.

"That's my boy!" Dad smiled. "Now get ready to defend. Here we come!"

And so it went, we free-styled all over the ice like our all-time hockey heroes. On Canadian ponds they might have been Gordie Howe, Wayne Gretzky and Mario Lemieux, but on our New England pond they had to be Bruins. My dad's favorite was always Bobby Orr, Kevin's was Ray Bourque, and mine was Phil Esposito. Ragging with the puck, drawing the defender, and sliding quick passes to the open man—it was pure hockey heaven.

Far-off buzzing brings me back. At night, we always hear the planes before we see them and it's our cue to stand. Not an easy task with chutes on our backs, rucksacks between our knees, and rifles strapped to our sides. Plus the harness always bites into my ass and tonight, carrying a heavy combat load, it's even worse.

Three stubby C-130 airplanes drop out of the sky, land, and circle back to us. They stop and drop their rear ramps. We waddle towards them while the huge propellers send gritty fumes into our camouflage-painted faces. I file in behind my squad leader, Sergeant Duras. My four paratroopers follow me, waddling like green ducklings.

The backwash of fumes isn't strong inside. One after another, we bump into the jumper in front, pivot, and fall into a sitting position. We squeeze into four rows of webbed seats that run lengthwise down the plane's wide cargo area. Once we're packed in facing each other knee-to-knee, the rear ramp rises like a drawbridge. In the inky darkness, I tuck my chin into my chest and withdraw into myself.

Duras punches my shoulder and yells over the engine noise, "First night jump, Foley?"

I straighten up, hoping my soldiers don't hear Duras questioning my experience. "My second, Sergeant!" I bark. My lack of experience relative to those around me reminds me of when I was called up as a sophomore to center the varsity team's third line—I'd succeeded then, and I'll succeed now. Duras smiles and gives me a thumbs up. I return it and hope my guys see us talking and smiling. I want them to be confident in me as we fly from Grafenwöhr to capture a Polish airfield somewhere near the Russian border.

Three bumpy hours later, First Sergeant Robalo stands on the rear ramp and shouts, "Ten minutes!"

I shake my head and slap my helmet. The plane cuts power and drops. On the way down we get a rough ride and my stomach does backflips.

"Stand up! Hook up!" Robalo yells.

My adrenaline rushes. We echo his commands, struggle to rise, and snap our static lines to a steel cable running the length of the dark cabin. The plane bounces and we reach for the walls and center benches to steady ourselves. Bouncing again, my stomach heaves, but I maintain my composure. I can't afford to have my men suspecting all of the fear buzzing in my gut.

"Check equipment!" Robalo yells.

An electric buzz takes over the cabin. Robalo opens the jump door and hurricane-force wind rushes in, adding to the madness. The plane jerks down, then up. Bile fills my mouth and I choke it back down. Behind me, Duras checks my static line for tangles, slaps me on the ass, and shouts, "Okay!" That's my cue to do the same for my soldier. I trace his static line from the steel cable, down over his shoulder, zigzagging across his back, and finally to where the yellow line is sewn to the top of his chute. It's tangle free, so I slap his ass, yelling, "Okay!"

The plane bounces hard and tilts wildly to my right just as the daisy-chain of "Okays!" make it to Robalo. I grab my static line up high where its clip slides along the cable. Shuffling towards Robalo, puke rises again. This time it's too much to choke back, so I pull my t-shirt up over my face and let it go. Robalo signals for the company commander to step forward, turn right, and grip both sides of the door frame. While I watch the wind whip around him, puke slides down my chest and settles in my belt line.

The wind whips around the commander, as he seems to hang there forever. The red light above him flashes to green and Robalo sends him out, knees in the breeze!

There's commotion behind me and I turn to see a silky canopy snaking between legs toward the open door. Some idiot released his reserve chute inside the plane! If it gets sucked out the door, it'll inflate, rip the jumper it's attached to out of the plane and drag everyone between him and the door out in a mass of tangled, broken limbs. Our training kicks in and we surge forward, racing the chute out. I turn to the right and push my static line to Robalo. He ignores me, dropping to his knees to grab the runaway chute. Pushed out by the jumper behind me, I spin and tumble into the night sky.

Snapping into a modified position of attention—with my chin on my chest, hands on both ends of my reserve chute, and feet and knees tight together—I yell, "One-thousand, two-thousand, three...," my stomach is up in my throat when my main chute jerks open, yanking it down somewhere between my aching nuts.

I reach up and grab my risers, which run from each shoulder up to thirty suspension lines and finally connect to my thirty-five-foot-wide canopy. Twenty seconds later, I pull the tab between my legs to release a tether strap and drop my ruck fifteen feet below me. I squeeze my feet and knees together, hoping to hit the ground with the balls of my feet, roll smoothly, and absorb the impact. Instead, the ground reaches up and hits me hard. I execute a half-assed parachute landing fall, keeping my feet and knees pressed together, but my heels hit first, followed by my butt with the back of my head smacking hard against the rocky ground.

Everything is a wild blur, until it all goes still. I exhale, feel frozen ground between my shoulder blades, and stare up into the frigid night sky. Blood rushes in quick beats in my ear drums. I take two deep breaths, stretch, and wiggle my toes. Nothing seems broken, so I enjoy my paratrooper's brief moment with God.

Well-drilled commands learned at Airborne School

interrupt my temporary bliss. "Pull the quick release, you dumb-ass, or your chute will re-inflate and drag you to death!" I reach across my chest and pull a quick-release clip that connects my body harness to the risers. The buckle snaps open. I wiggle out of the harness, roll to my stomach, and do a functions check on my M-4. Staying low, I reel in my parachute and stuff it into a canvas bag that had been secured between my reserve chute and lower abdomen.

I crouch to follow the tether to find my rucksack. I reach forward, stumble, and fall. I rise, stumble, and fall again. Then, everything goes black.

TWO

I blink, turn away from the harsh fluorescent lights, and a wave of nausea hits me. I close my eyes and take three shallow breaths. I open my eyes and see First Sergeant Robalo. With his shaved head and gun-fighter's squint, that's certain—but nothing else is.

"Where are we?" I croak.

"Landstuhl," he says, leaning forward and resting his elbow on my bed's chrome railing. "You've got a broken leg." Holding up his hand, he asks, "How many fingers?"

"Two," I grin.

He smiles back. "What do you remember?"

"Jumping into Poland. Landing. Recovering my gear." Trying to sit up, I ask, "What happened?"

Robalo is built like a bouncer and moves with the fluid control of a bullfighter. He straightens up, looks away and says, almost to himself, "Those idiot jet-jockeys missed the drop zone by half a mile. Then some asshole released his reserve in the plane. And one of your jump buddies probably cut under you and stole your air."

Damn, I'm lucky to be alive.

Robalo catches himself and turns back to me, "That's just my opinion, Foley. Don't worry. Get some rest and leave it to the big-green-machine to go through the entire cluster-fuck and figure it out."

A tall, thin nurse comes in, her steel-wool hair pulled into a tight bun. She looks like a dehydrated version of Nurse Ratched from *One Flew Over the Cuckoo's Nest*, and I immediately dislike her.

Robalo glances over. "He's coming out of it."

"I'll go get the doctor," she snaps.

She returns with a squat, no nonsense Major wearing a starched lab coat over blue hospital scrubs. His stethoscope is tucked into a pocket, rather than hanging around his bull neck. Dr. Dennis tersely introduces himself and reads from his notes, "Patient has several fractures and bone fragments and requires an immediate fasciotomy in his lower right leg using a two-incision technique—"

"Sir, we're paratroopers," Robalo interrupts. "Can you put that in words we can understand?"

The doctor lowers his notes. "His right leg is crushed. He needs surgery to release pressure and get blood flowing again."

Robalo fidgets, "And if it doesn't?"

"Then a transtibial amputation would be in order."

"What?" I gasp.

Nurse Ratched turns her joyless, pinched face towards me and glares.

"We must wait and see," Dr. Dennis says, looking back at his notes and then shaking his head. After an uncomfortable silence, he and the nurse leave.

Robalo says, "Hang in there Foley. You'll be okay."

"Top, can you get me my iPhone?"

"I'm going straight back to Poland, but I'll let Major Manning know you need your stuff sent here."

"Thanks, Top."

Robalo leaves me with my crushed leg and uneasy thoughts.

THE NEXT MORNING, I get my two-incision fasciotomy. Nurse Ratched says it went well. I strain to lift my head high enough off my pillow to look at the swollen hunk of flesh that used to be my foot. I immediately regret it.

An attractive medic comes in with my dinner tray. I sit up, read her nametag, and say, "Thanks, Specialist Leonard."

"No problem," she says, smiling shyly.

"Hey, any idea when I'll be released?"

She shakes her head and smiles. "That's way above my pay-grade."

She leaves. I pick half-heartedly at my red Jell-O and cottage cheese. It's my second day in this sterile, lonely room and I already hate it. Leonard returns with Nurse Ratched, who carries a syringe with an extremely large needle.

"Please tell me you're not going to stick me with that monster," I laugh.

"Please tell me, *Ma'am*," Ratched corrects.

"Sorry, ma'am," I say.

"No such luck, it goes here," she says, injecting the syringe into my IV line, "to help manage your pain."

Leonard picks up my dinner tray, and the two leave together. As the pain killer kicks in, I pull the sheets up over my head. My mind wanders to my dad. He was so proud when I graduated from Airborne school. What will he think about me getting hurt in a stupid training exercise?

Four days later, my swelling goes down enough that my foot looks human again. My prize is another surgery. Dr. Dennis attaches a carbon fiber external fixator with stainless steel pegs into my shattered bones. Three times a day Ratched and Leonard use sterile gauze and tweezers to remove crusting and drainage from around the holes. I look away when they rinse them with an antimicrobial solution. Pain shoots up my leg, and I can't help but wince. Leonard gives me a sympathetic smile, kindly ignoring my tears.

Things settle into a dull routine. Mornings bring light and life, days bring pain and distraction, and nights bring loneliness and self-doubt. For hours on end, I lie in bed and think. Two weeks ago I was camouflaged, weighted down with sixty pounds of combat gear, and squeezed into the cargo area of a C-130 airplane. I *was* happy. Was it a mistake to trade my hockey stick for an M-4 carbine? How stupid was it to give up a comfortable life in Boston for a much rougher one in the Army? But standing to jump was just as exciting as waiting to step out on to the ice for a big game. Sure, the sights and smells couldn't be more different. The rink smells like ice, over-ripe equipment, and testosterone. The plane smells like exhaust fumes, gun oil, and puke. Both get me fired up, but now only rubbing alcohol, stale air, and bland food fill my nose.

A woman's voice interrupts my pity party. She drawls, "You were number twelve?" An athletic, thirty-something lady strides up to me. Her bright-white Adidas track suit contrasts nicely with her cocoa complexion.

"Excuse me, ma'am?"

"Number twelve?" she asks.

Her enthusiasm, dazzling smile, and ponytail reminds

me of a cheerleader. I hesitate a beat, "Um, in high school I wore number twenty-two."

"Oh no, Sugar" she says, bouncing on the balls of her feet. "The twelfth jumper!" She presses a newspaper clipping into my hand. "Here, read this. I saved it, because I figured we'd be working together. Oh, and I'm Jill, your friendly physical therapist!"

Troops Injured in Jump Treated, Released
Stars & Stripes
Thursday, April 4, 2013

Eleven 173rd Airborne Brigade paratroopers injured during a nighttime jump in Poland were treated and released just hours after suffering minor sprains and twisted ankles, a U.S. Army Europe spokesman said late Wednesday. A twelfth soldier injured during the Tuesday night jump is set to be released next week and will return to his battalion's home station in Grafenwöhr, Germany.
"He will need surgery on his leg, and is expected to recover fully," said Major Manning, the unit's Rear Detachment Commander.
More than 570 U.S. and Allied troops took part in the airborne operation. During the jump, part of exercise Saber Shield, the paratroopers conducted an operation to seize an airfield.
"Night jumps are routine, but there is always an increased level of risk because of limited visibility and greater combat-load carrying weight," Manning said.
According to the U.S. Army Europe, about 25,000

troops are taking part in Saber Shield, United States Army Europe's largest exercise of the year.

I STARE AT THE ARTICLE. "Released next week? Is Manning nuts?" I shout.

"Come on, Sugar," she says, touching my arm. "Let's just get to work on that full recovery part." She flashes a bright smile, props me up, and hands me crutches. I swing my legs over the bed and take ten awkward steps toward the toilet. I can barely stand the pain, and my hospital gown keeps opening up in back. It's embarrassing and exhausting, and after Jill helps me back into my bed, she lets me be.

The next morning, Jill wheels me to physical therapy. She insists it's important to begin as soon as possible. I'm not so sure, but shut up and do what I'm told. We start with stretching, bending, and walking with crutches. Jill calls it PT, but it isn't anything like physical training back at my unit. Here, PT must stand for *Pain and Torture.* During our first session, I complain about not having my phone, wallet or clothes.

"Don't worry Sugar, your unit will send them," she drawls.

Damn, I don't know how Jill stays so optimistic in this drab place, and then I realize she is about the same age my mother was when she passed away.

———

I FALL into a dull routine of bland hospital meals, grueling PT sessions, and hours of mind-numbing TV. Then Specialist Leonard rushes in. "You've got a call from Boston."

"Hello, this is Corporal Foley."

"Willie, are yah okay?" my dad asks. "The Army people called and said yah'r wicked hurt."

"I'm okay, Dad, just a broken leg."

"Ah, thank Gahd, what happened?"

I smile. Hearing my dad's booming Boston accent makes it seem like he's in the room with me. "I'm not really sure. It was a night jump—lots of confusion. Something went wrong. I remember landing and trying to recover my chute, but that's it."

"Are they taking good care of yah? Do I need to come over and get 'em in line?" he jokes.

I smile. "Nah, it's all good."

"I tried your cell phone and got voice mail. Later nothing. I was damn worried!"

"Sorry, I wasn't screening you. When we jump, we don't carry anything personal. So my cell phone and wallet are still in the barracks."

"Are yah going' back soon?"

"I hope so..."

To break the silence, he asks, "Catchin' any puck ovah there? The Bruins are looking good, a couple more wins and we'll lock up home ice for the play-offs."

"The games start late here, but I get the highlights in the morning. The NHL cut the season in half, right? And they pushed the play-offs back a few weeks?"

"Yep, it's all a little weird. And now it looks like the original six teams will all make the playoffs. I'm glad for the fans, but those greedy owners sure don't deserve our money after screwing us with their lock-out!"

Dad can talk for hours about hockey, especially when he's upset. So before he can really get going, I ask him, "Are you pulling a bunch of overtime to get ready for Patriots' Day?"

"With the marathon, nobody remembers that the holiday is for the battles at Lexington and Concord. Course everyone is still glad to take the Monday off."

"People here only know about the marathon," I say. "They assume Patriot's Day is set aside to celebrate Tom Brady and another Super Bowl win!"

Dad laughs, "I'll take the ovah-time."

"Okay, Dad, gotta go, they're bringing my dinner now."

"All right, take care."

"You too." I hand the phone back to Leonard, trading it for my cold, gray dinner.

I CAN'T FALL asleep and mind wanders to Leonard. As an enlisted medic, she serves meals, strips and makes beds, and cleans up bodily fluids. She said that she likes her work because it makes her feel useful and tires her out so she can sleep soundly each night, or day, depending which shift she's on. She works under the critical eye of Nurse Ratched, whose real name is Captain Smith. She told Leonard to go back to school while she's still young, but Leonard says she's content here. I don't understand Leonard's lack of drive. Doesn't she want to move up and be in charge? What's wrong with her? I do like her. She spends time with me before and after shifts and gets me double servings of dessert, but it's very awkward when she cleans me. During sponge baths we both blush and don't speak. If I had a vote, I'd rather smell like piss than go through the embarrassment of having her clean me down there.

I still can't sleep and fantasize about fucking Leonard. But she's too sweet. I switch to Jill, but she's too motherly. I even try Ratched, but she's way too grim. I settle on a hot, slutty girl from high school. Just as I start to rub one out, cramping and pain shoots up from my shattered leg. I hit the call button, but then panic. What if it brings Leonard? She can't see me like this! I hit it again, hoping to turn it off. It stays on and my blood pressure surges, flooding my erection and my crushed leg. Pain races up the tendons behind my knee, cramps the back of my thigh, and radiates across my lower back. I struggle to sit up and straighten my leg. Unable to, I lie back and arch my back. Fuck me, the pain is so intense.

Blinking back tears, I pray for my erection, cramping, and pain to go away. The door opens, the lights flash on, and Ratched walks in. She sees my dick pointing skyward, chuckles, and says, "Sorry, soldier, you've got to tame that beast yourself."

"Cramp," I gasp, reaching behind my knee.

"Where's the pain?" she asks, reaching in and massaging my cramped hamstring. As the pain fades, she says, "No more night workouts, okay?"

I nod, silently promising to keep my hands above my waist.

A FEW DAYS LATER, a banner runs across the bottom of the television, "Bombs explode at the Boston Marathon."

Oh my God, Dad's there!

A blond reporter looks sternly at the camera and says, "At approximately 2:49 p.m., two bombs hidden near the finish line exploded within seconds of each other, instantly turning the sun-filled afternoon on Boylston Street into a gruesome scene of bloodshed, destruction and chaos."

I ring the call button for Leonard and ask her to call my father.

Holy shit, I enlisted to fight terrorism overseas, and now my friends and family in Boston aren't safe? I slap my good leg in frustration, and wait for an update. I'm powerless, just another asshole aching to learn more about what happened.

Leonard says my father didn't answer. As the night wears on, CNN recycles the same information: three spectators died, and over two hundred sixty were wounded. My eyes sting from staying up all night, hoping for a meaningful update. The sun rises and breakfast arrives. My appetite is gone, replaced by a headache and a fever. I'm worried sick and there's still no news about Dad. They would tell us if a cop died, right?

THREE

At noon, I ask Leonard to try again. She hands me her personal cell phone to make the call. It's six a.m. in Boston and my dad answers on the second ring.

"Are you okay?" I ask.

"Been better, Willie, but I'm alive if that's what you mean."

"Were you there?"

"Yep, I heard the first one and turned to see it. The second one went off and people went down all ovah the place. Thank Gahd the emergency service boys started helping right away." He pauses, "Did you see they postponed the game? We're making it up tonight. With a win, we'll clinch a playoff spot."

"Will you catch the rat-bastards who did this?"

"Believe it. We've got a thousand federal, state, and local boys on the case. We'll get 'em," he clears his throat. "Hey, I got to go, I've got an, ah, I'm back on the clock soon."

"Go get 'em, Dad."

"Thanks," he says, hanging up.

Damn, I should be there, not here.

———————

FOUR LONG AND lonely days pass as the pale German sun struggles to melt the watery spring snow. The stalled marathon manhunt weighs heavily on me and antibiotics give me diarrhea. The shootout with Tsarnaev breaks things up, but when they lock down Boston to conduct a search for his brother, the hours drag by. Even after they find the younger Tsarnaev hiding in a dry-docked boat, I remain furious about the gutless bastards who ambushed my home town.

Although I know it's wrong, I vent my frustration on the hospital staff. When Dr. Dennis makes his afternoon rounds, I pounce. "Sir, when am I getting out of here? I need to get back to my unit! Please, I just need to know that there's an end in sight."

"Corporal Foley, I'm sorry, I thought you knew," he says.

"Knew what, sir?"

He sits heavily on a chair next to my bed. "Your leg is infected." Staring at the floor, he continues, "To prevent spread, we must amputate."

"What?" my voice catches. "I've gotta get back to my unit."

Dr. Dennis looks up. "You understand, we did everything possible?"

I shake my head, "No, I don't understand!"

"Your infection isn't responding to antibiotics. A below the knee amputation done now will save the rest of your leg."

I sit up and lock eyes with him. "I've done everything

you've asked of me. Everything, sir." I swallow, holding in my anger. "Is there any way to save my leg?"

"No, there isn't."

"What if I object? What if I say no?"

He stands, pushing back the chair. "Normally it would be elective, but it's necessary and will happen tomorrow."

I'm stunned speechless. Then I snap, "Tomorrow! What the fuck? I got up on the damn thing! I walked on the damn thing!"

"As I was saying, if we cut below—"

"Get out!" I sit upright and turning to get out of my bed. "I'm signing out and going back to Graf, right now!" I yell, pushing Dr. Dennis away.

"If we don't do it now, in a few days it could be in your hip. You could be dead in a week," he says.

I fall back in my bed. How the hell did this happen?

Dr. Dennis's voice softens. "Let me assure you, with all the roadside bombs in Afghanistan and Iraq, I've done hundreds of amputations."

"No! Not on me. Fuck no!" I shout.

He ignores my outburst. "Our technology is improving. We use computer scanning and three-dimensional printing to manufacture customized limbs. We also use high-tech materials and motors to mimic natural movements."

The throbbing pain in my leg is back, along with a sharp headache.

"I'm sorry," Dr. Dennis says, turning. He holds the door open for Nurse Ratched. As she passes, he whispers something to her. That sneaky, bull-necked son of a bitch thinks he can push his dirty work off without me hearing!

Ratched gives me a stern look and pulls up the bed's rails, trapping me like a baby in a crib. She briefs me, rapid-fire. "You won't have any food tonight, only liquids. In the morning I'll wake you at zero six hundred hours. You'll be in surgery at zero eight hundred hours. The procedure won't take long, but you'll be under general anesthesia. You'll wake before lunch, probably feeling thirsty and hungry. You'll be able to have water right away. Any questions, Corporal?"

"Fuck you," I say.

She continues, "After surgery, you'll stay here for pre-prosthetic care. Your wound will be swollen and will take time to shrink. Shrinker socks, silicone liners, and elastic wraps will assist the process. Healing takes anywhere between one to four weeks. With your fitness level, and the fact that this is a planned surgery, you'll likely get through it in about ten days. Once your residual limb fully heals, we'll start you with an initial prosthetic. You'll begin gait training and will learn to walk without crutches. Questions?"

Without waiting for an answer, she turns, switches off the light, and closes the heavy door behind her.

This can't be real! It was just a stupid training jump. Nobody loses a leg that way! Twenty minutes later my angel of mercy, Leonard, brings me sleeping pills. I take them and drift off to medicated sleep, dreaming of running in formation on two good feet.

The next morning, I wake at 06:30 to the normal clatter of breakfast carts. Leonard hands me a breakfast tray.

"What's going on?" I ask, wondering about Nurse Ratched's instructions.

"Roadside bomb in Afghanistan," Leonard answers. "It's pretty bad, so you might get a roommate."

"What?"

Leonard shrugs. "When I first got here, we had two or three air ambulances coming in every week. Patients were sometimes tripled up in these rooms."

"Am I going in for surgery?" I ask.

"They told me to feed you, so definitely not today."

I pick at my breakfast and pray for a miracle to save my foot. I think about the wounded soldiers. What is the point of it all, I wonder. Then, I picture the Marathon bombing. I know the point.

Leonard comes in after lunch. "You have a visitor," she says.

A wiry major follows Leonard. I struggle to sit up.

"At ease, Corporal," he says.

What? Did the arrogant little prick think I was going to jump out of bed, stand, and go to the position of attention?

He stops short and waits for Leonard to leave. "I'm Major Manning, here for your command visit. Are you being treated well?"

"No, sir."

"Excuse me?"

"They want to amputate my foot against my will," I say, pointing to my leg and its bulky fixator.

"One second," he says and leaves.

He comes back ten minutes later. "Okay Foley, cut the crap."

"What, sir?"

"Cut the nonsense. You are being disruptive and disrespectful to the staff here, and it will not be tolerated."

"It's my foot," I protest.

"You are a soldier, Foley. You take orders. Stop making this harder than it needs to be. Do you read me?" he says.

I shrug. He glares, forcing an answer from me.

"Yes, sir, I read you loud and clear."

A nearly imperceptible smile twitches at the corner of his mouth. "Since I'm here, I'll take your statement for the jump's safety investigation. Do you understand?"

"Not really," I say.

He freezes me with an icy stop-being-a-smartass stare. "Every time there is a jump injury, like yours, we have to investigate it to see if it was preventable. We also have to do a line of duty investigation. Do you wish to make a statement?"

"Ah, I guess so."

Manning gives me another disapproving look.

"Yes, sir," I answer more formally.

"Do you remember what happened?"

"Yes, sir," I say, and detail the loading at Graf, the jump, and the landing in Poland.

"Did you puke on yourself?"

Embarrassed, I answer, "Yes, sir."

"Why did you leave it out?"

I swear the smug little fucker is enjoying my discomfort. "Sir, I don't know. I guess I didn't think it was important."

"The Army doesn't pay you to think, Corporal," he says. "Did you shit yourself?"

"No, sir."

"Are you sure?"

"Sir?"

"Are you sure?"

"I think—"

"It says here," Manning interrupts, "that you puked and shit all over yourself."

"May I see that?"

"No," he says.

Ratched comes in and stands off to the side.

"Do you know how you broke your leg?" Manning asks.

"Someone stole my air, collapsed my chute, and made me burn in."

"Do you have anything to back up your theory, Corporal?"

"I do not, but… " I stutter, avoiding his accusing eyes.

Setting his notepad down, he takes a sheet of paper from a folder and hands it to me. "Sign this."

"What is it, sir?"

"A statement of charges for the equipment you destroyed."

"I didn't destroy anything—"

Ratched interrupts, "Don't sign it."

Manning turns his attention to her, "Excuse me, *Captain.*"

"Sir, he's my patient and now is not the time for this."

"He puked and shit his gear, and you people disposed of it as a biohazard. He signed for it, and he is responsible to the government for the loss."

"Sir, you know better," Ratched says.

"Excuse me?" Manning says, standing to confront her.

She steps forward, "Please leave now, sir."

Manning blinks, and starts to gather his things.

"Sir," I say, remembering my phone, wallet, and clothes. "Did you bring my stuff from Graf?"

"Excuse me?" he snaps.

"Sir, ah, my phone and—"

"Do I look like a delivery service?"

"No, sir. First Sergeant Robalo, he, ah—"

"Corporal, stop talking. Take it up with Robalo," he says, punctuating it with a tight lipped grin. His statement freezes me. There is something frightening lurking behind his muted expression. It's impossible to know what he hides behind those still, dead eyes.

Manning turns and leaves. Ratched steps forward and takes the statement of charges from me. "Two thousand dollars?" She shakes her head and hands the statement back, "for gear they cut off of you in the air ambulance?"

I nod.

"Go see JAG. Their attorneys can help you with this nonsense."

AFTER DINNER RATCHED TELLS me that my surgery will be on Monday. She then recycles her no-food, no-drink speech.

"No! Get out!" I shout.

"Grow up," she says.

I stare at her, my eyes full of hate.

"You heard right," she says. "Do you think Dr. Dennis wants to amputate? Do you think he gets paid extra for doing it?"

"But, I've done everything—"

"Grow up," she says, shoving the consent form in my face, "and sign it."

I shake my head and turn away. "I'll check with JAG first."

ALL WEEKEND I think about blown-up soldiers, the Marathon bombing, and my leg. If I don't have the surgery, the infection will spread and I'll lose more of my leg. I might even die. But without my foot, they'll kick me out. Then what? What would I do?

Seconds turn to minutes, minutes turn to hours, and no roommate arrives. Ratched returns early Monday, abruptly turns on the lights and jars me awake. I sign her goddamned consent form and ask for some water. She denies me, and preps me like meat for butchery.

Mr. Clean wheels me into a room filled with buzzing machines. Before I get my bearings, someone puts a mask over my nose and mouth. The last thing I remember is hoping that it's all a sick, horrible joke.

FOUR

"Hey Sugar, you awake?" Jill's voice pulls me back to reality.

"Yeah," I answer in a scratchy voice.

She smiles and hands me a cup of water. "Small sips," she says. "How are you doing?"

"My foot hurts like hell."

"Your foot, Sugar?"

"Yeah, Doc must have saved it."

The worry lines on Jill's face reveal more than any word ever could. My chest tightens. "That's ghost pain, Sugar," she says, "Your foot's gone."

"No, my toes are cramping. I can wiggle them, but they keep curling up."

"You'll feel that for a while. The docs call it phantom limb syndrome, but don't fret, it's just your mind playing tricks on you."

"Don't fret? I'm twenty years old and my foot's gone!"

"Your life's not over. Here, I brought you a handout to help explain the grieving process."

"Grieving process?" I ask, ignoring the handout.

Jill looks deep into my eyes. "You've heard about the grieving process when someone passes away?"

I nod.

"You go through the same process losing a foot."

I stare at the ceiling, and refuse to acknowledge her.

"I know it doesn't make much sense now, but here, take the handout and I'll come back tomorrow, okay?" I don't answer and she doesn't budge. Finally I take the paper from her. She nods, her brown eyes shadowed with concern. She speaks slowly and softly, "Just look later. Know that the first phase is denial, and it will take a little while."

I shake my head.

"Tonight go to your happy place. Think of a place that makes you really happy, and imagine being there. Take your time and focus on every little detail. It'll give you a chance to escape from this place."

I stare blankly.

"Want to know a secret? Mine is out on Bourbon Street for Mardi Gras," she whispers conspiratorially, adding a quick wink. "See you tomorrow."

Mr. Clean wheels me back to my room. Just add a gold earring, and he'd be a dead ringer for the cleaning solution guy. Leonard delivers, then takes away my uneaten dinner. Without saying a word, she hands me two pills and a glass of water.

I lie in the dark, wait for the pills to work, and take deep breathes. I'm empty, somehow less than human. I take Jill's advice and go to my happy place. I recall a glorious day of pond hockey with my dad.

At breakfast, he asks me, "Hey Willie, what you got going on today?"

I look up from my Cheerios, "It's Saturday, I'm playing hockey with Kevin."

"Mind if I play?" he asks, with a twinkle in his eye.

I shoot him a skeptical look. "You're working today," I say, pointing at the shiny badge on his chest.

"The weather is wicked good for some old-time pond hockey. I'll put my skates in the squad cah, knock off a little early, and play some puck with my boy."

"I'll see you there!" I exclaim, in my excitement spitting a Cheerio on to the table.

We skate free, under a clear and cold Massachusetts sky. Twenty minutes into our one-on-one game, Kevin joins us. Later, playing two-on-ones, he asks, "Have yah got a hockey nickname yet, Willie?"

"Nope."

"What do you think, Uncle Jimmy? Espo? He's racking up goals down low, just like Phil did with Bobby."

"Ah, numbah four, Bobby Orr," Dad says, in an exaggerated rink announcer's voice. "No, we're Irish, boys. Willie's a little stallion, but not Italian. How about Hands? He's got great hands. Or Scrapper? He's sure got some scrappiness."

"Oh wait, Uncle Jimmy, I've got it! 'B.D.' You know, for balls deep! When Willie's on the crease with the puck's on his stick, he's going balls deep every time."

"Oh yeah, that works!" I shout.

"Not so fast boys," Dad says. "I don't think Will's mother, or any of the Foley women, would approve. So, let's just keep this B.D. business between us. Okay?"

"Yes, Uncle Jimmy." Kevin answers.

"Okay, boys, Kev defends. Here we go," Dad says, lugging the puck up ice.

On cue, I sprint to the goal mouth. Dad sends the puck across to me in a perfectly arched saucer pass. I meet it and send it between our mini-goal shoes and into a distant snow bank.

"Nice goal, B.D.!" Dad and Kevin call out in unison.

I raise both arms and do a joyful shuffle.

When the sun dips below the tops of the pine trees, Dad says, "Okay boys, it's getting dahk. We've got to get home."

"Do we have to?" I whine.

"Yep, and I Hope that Mom's got a big pot of chowdah waitin' on us."

Tired, sweaty, and sunburned, we load our gear into the squad car. We drop Kevin off and slip into our house. After washing up, we feast on Mom's steaming chowder and warm soda bread.

I look over at my exhausted father, and say, "That was the best day evah."

He smiles back, "Me too, Willie, me too."

In the dark hospital room, I no longer notice the throbbing pain in my right leg. The past and present merge. I drift off to sleep with the sound of my father's voice echoing in my ears and the taste of my mother's chowder in my mouth.

THE CLATTER of breakfast wakes me. I finish my green Jell-O and cottage cheese, and see the paper Jill left peeking out from under my tray.

"Dealing with the Grief and Depression of Amputation." *Oh, joy.*

While I'm reading Jill comes in. "How are you doing, Sugar?"

I turn away, trying to hide the stupid handout.

"Oh, you're reading it. That's awesome," She says,

reaching out and touching my arm. "This won't roll through easy, but you'll get through it."

"My foot cramps hurt like hell."

"Look at me," she says, again touching my arm. "You might get a little down, but you can't stay there." I look away, and in her soothing Southern drawl, she continues, "You let me know if you lose your appetite, can't sleep, or can't concentrate. You'll do that for me?"

I nod, but tear up.

"Okay, so here's our plan. First, you get your rest and eat right. Then we'll get back to our physical therapy, and relearning all the things you like to do. How does that sound? Nod if you're with me."

I wipe away a tear, and feel a tremor buzz in my lower lip.

"When you get back to Graf, promise this, keep moving forward. Keep eating healthy and exercising, because that releases endorphins. Do your deep breathing to relax, relieve pain, and focus. And don't you dare self-medicate! Don't start drinking to pass the time, because alcohol is a depressant. Are you with me?"

"Yes, ma'am, tracking. Stay healthy and no substance abuse," I say, giving her a half-hearted salute.

"Very good, Corporal Foley. I see why you made rank so quickly. Even after you go back to Graf, you be sure to let me know if you always want to be alone. Deal?"

"Yes, ma'am."

"What is it that the Army pays you to do? Fall out of airplanes?"

"One super-duper paratrooper at your service," I grin, knowing my fake enthusiasm doesn't begin to hide my sadness and uncertainty.

FOR THE FIRST TIME, I have lots of time to think. I've led mostly a charmed life. I was a happy kid and a good student, but my real passion was always hockey. Like cousin Kevin, I made the varsity a year early and was named captain in my senior year. The coach said that at 5'10" and 170 pounds, I had the perfect frame for college hockey. Man, I guess I should have looked into that a little harder.

When I graduated, going to community college seemed easiest. It gave me time to sort things out, and compared to a four-year college, the price was right. After six months of boredom, I snuck off to see an Army recruiter.

I felt unsure about it, because I knew my dad liked having me around. Money, of course, was an issue. But really it was more of a sense of vague discontent and honest-to-goodness patriotism that drove me to see the recruiter. When Kevin was home for Christmas break, he explained that going to the Academy and then serving was basically the same as serving and then using the G.I. Bill. The only difference was the timing of when the Army paid for your college. I have to admit, when I heard my dad compliment Kevin about how good he looked in his cadet uniform, I was jealous. That sealed it. I decided right then to enlist.

People who knew me weren't that surprised. Signing up for the infantry and volunteering for airborne school was icing on the cake—the harder the better, right? Once in, I was happy. I loved the camaraderie and found a bond of brotherhood that I hadn't felt since hockey. And I was making good money.

I was stunned to see Dad in the stands at graduation from airborne school. He and Kevin had flown down to Fort Benning to surprise me. When I walked off the drop zone after my fifth jump, they found me ten pounds lighter and full of a paratrooper's swagger. I told Dad it was from all the push-ups, but we both knew I had become a man. After taking a little leave back home, I was on my way to Italy to serve in the Army's only overseas Airborne Combat Brigade, but then I got diverted to a subordinate battalion in Germany.

Now I'm here at Landstuhl, with the Poland jump playing on repeat in my head. It's vivid, and I can't shake it. I wake in a cold sweat, look for my missing foot, and can't believe this is real. I turn on my bedside lamp and look for the stupid handout about amputation and grief. "There are five stages of grief," it reads. "First, denial and isolation." Oh, I recognize those two. "Then anger." Check! "The next stage is bargaining." This one's harder to comprehend. If I work hard in rehab, maybe I'll get my old life back? It sure doesn't seem possible now, but hell, who knows? "The last two stages are depression and acceptance." These two are foreign to me, because Foley men are fighters.

FOUR MORNINGS IN A ROW, right after Leonard takes away my breakfast tray and returns to change my dressing, Ratched reads step-by-painful-step instructions from a manual to Leonard. "For trans-tibial amputations, the early postoperative rehabilitation guidelines dictate that the dressing will be covered with figure eight wrappings until sutures are removed."

Leonard slowly unwraps the old bandages and does a washout before re-wrapping. She tries to be gentle, but I can hardly take the pain. I always look away, and when I finally look, I immediately regret it. My right foot is gone. There is only a bright pink stump—so revolting, even after I look away, my stomach heaves and a pitiful yelp escapes me.

Ratched tells Leonard to get Dr. Dennis's permission to use local anesthesia during my washouts.

"I don't need anything from you or the doctor!" I yell.

"Fine," Ratched says. "Then stop whimpering like a dog."

I nod, knowing I must tough it out in silence.

Leonard promises it will be less painful once the sutures come out. Then shrinker socks will replace the figure-eight wrappings, and Dr. Dennis should clear me to bear weight on my hideous stump.

Damn, it can't come fast enough. Still, I have doubts. Can shrinker socks and a plastic leg make me whole? What will Dad think about his peg-legged paratrooper? This never-ending cycle of surgeries and rehab grinds on me. The only constant is pain. It's unrelenting. Damn, I need to stop feeling sorry for myself. I've got to man up and embrace the suck like a bad-ass paratrooper, and paratroopers don't bitch about aches and pains. But what about the worthless feeling that leaves me so hollow? I need to figure that part out, pronto.

MUSCLE-BOUND Mr. Clean says staying in bed isn't an option. He helps me into a wheelchair, and pushes me to my first amputee physical therapy session. The rehab room is basketball court sized, with padded walls and some light gym equipment. Two sets of parallel bars line the far wall.

Jill sees us and waves.

Mr. Clean leaves, and Jill asks me, "What cha' looking at, Sugar?"

I don't realize that she's teasing, and mumble, "Ah, nothing."

"You like my stick?"

"What?" I say, unable to hide my surprise.

"My stick," She holds it up and twirls it like a drum majorette. "You puck-heads always check it out. It never fails."

I smile. "Wow, yeah. I used an Easton stick. You could heat the shaft to switch out the blades. They don't make them like that anymore."

"Light and strong, it's perfect for stretching," she says. "Here, take it and use it to stand up."

I hold it upside down like a staff and stand. I steady myself, turn it over, and push the blade into the floor to flex the shaft. It feels good. Even its right shot blade is perfect for me.

THE NEXT DAY LEONARD ASKS, "Have you ever been to Paris?"

I shake my head.

"It's only a two and a half hour train ride from here. When you're discharged, we should go see the Eiffel Tower."

"We can't go together. I'm a corporal and you're a specialist."

"Come on," she laughs. "We're paid exactly the same."

"But I've got my NCO stripes, so it's fraternization," I say, a little too forcefully.

"You're my patient, that's what makes it off limits!" she says, leaving me to eat my breakfast alone.

TWO DAYS LATER IN REHAB, I sit on the floor wearing a gray Army shirt and black shorts. They are loaners, because Major Manning still hasn't sent my stuff from Graf. A shrinker sock and donning tube lie on the floor between my knees. Seeing my sawed-off leg still freaks me out. It will never seem right, but I suck it up and do a self-washout. I hate it, not for the pain but for having to handle the blunt end of my leg which looks like the dead end of a giant hotdog all pulled together and puckered.

I struggle to pull the shrinker sock over the donning tube. It's like trying to get an extra-small tube sock over an extra-large paint can. Once I have it stretched over the top of the tube, I flip it around and push the bongo end against my stump. I look away and push as far as possible, and then have to look to unroll the sock, like unrolling a giant condom.

Jill watches from across the room. As I set the donning tube aside, she puts down her coffee cup and strides over. "You're doing great, Will."

I look up. "I don't want to be here."

Jill smiles down at me. "You're still in mourning, Sugar. You're still struggling with your internal body image coming in line with your external awareness."

"What?"

"Your mind doesn't want to give up the past and accept the present. That leaves you worn out, but it will pass. Let me look at your shrinker sock."

I hold up my stump for Jill's inspection.

"Perfect. Now, time for some quality PT with your favorite drill sergeant."

"I still feel my toes cramp. When will it stop?" I ask,

wondering if I'll ever be able to jerk off without triggering ghost pain.

"Everyone's different. Just know that it has nothing to do with weakness. Once you start wearing your prosthesis, you'll feel more discomfort but it will be a different kind. Don't worry, we'll go slow and take the time to toughen up your skin."

I nod, and ask, "When will the night cramping—"

"Stop stalling," Jill playfully snaps, "It's time for another round of pain and torture. I've got to get you ready for gait training, soldier!"

"Yes, ma'am," I answer, moving over to the parallel bars. I put down the stick and try to stand on my good leg. Sweat rolls off of my buzz cut and down my face. My leg starts to shake and I fall.

"Don't get so worked up. Everyone's balance is a little off at first," she says. "You just need a little time to learn your new center."

I refuse to get up.

"Come on," Jill says, "get up."

I shake my head. To my surprise, Jill leaves.

I sit on the floor, feeling more and more embarrassed. After twenty minutes crawl by, she comes back and asks, "Are you ready?"

I nod.

Jill helps me up. I put all of my weight over my left leg, saying, "I don't get it. You told me that I will have to break the habit of standing only over my good leg once I start wearing my prosthetic."

"That's true," Jill says, wagging her finger at me. "But you still will need to get outta bed and hop to the bathroom."

I laugh.

"Seriously, Sugar, it'll all come in stages. You'll get your balance back. You'll get your confidence back. We'll work on the parallel bars and get you ready for gait training."

"Crutches? I don't need no stinking crutches," I joke, as I struggle to stay balanced on my left leg.

"Crutches are important. If your skin gets too irritated and needs a break, you'll be glad you learned to crutch from the master."

I stall, taking a slow drink of water.

"On your foot, soldier!" Jill barks. "We've got time for one more set."

IT'S BEEN two weeks since the Marathon bombing and a week since Dr. Dennis took my foot. Leonard comes in and hands me a phone. Somehow I know it's the call from Boston that I've been dreading.

"Hello. Corporal Foley," I say.

"Willie, my boy, how yah doin'?" Hearing my dad's accent makes me homesick.

"Hi Dad, been watching you take down the Tsarnaev brothers. I'm glad you caught those bastards."

"Yeah, it looks like those jack-asses went rogue, but my Gahd did they evah do a lot of damage with their damned pressure cookers."

With his accent going into to full growl mode, I ask, "Hey, what's your take on the playoffs?"

"The boys got a great draw getting the Leafs."

"Oh yeah, and were you ever right about all the original six teams getting in."

"Plus four of the six Canadian teams," he adds.

"I like Boston with home ice against Toronto. Any chance you'll go to any of the games?"

"I put in for it, but who knows? You get to watch the games on ovah there?"

"Yeah, AFN shows a live game at one a.m. and a tape delayed one the next day at lunch. So I should get to see one or two."

"Did yah see the rescheduled game? Its pregame ceremony was pretty damned nice, and we clinched the playoffs by forcing overtime."

"I saw the highlights, but not the ceremony. It is cool when they put a first responder up on the big screen and everyone gives them a standing ovation. Boston Strong, right?"

"Damn right, Boston Strong. I love it! Hey, are you back with your unit yet?"

"No, sir."

"I didn't think so—I can't get you on the phone and your e-mail doesn't work. What's going on? Do bones take longer to heal in Germany?"

"No, my phone is still at Graf."

"When are you getting out?"

"Ah, I've got some bad news," I say, choking up. "They, ah, amputated my foot."

"What? No! Yah gotta be kidding me."

"It was infected. Wouldn't heal."

"Gahd, Willie, I'll come right ovah."

"No, sir, please don't. I'm in rehab and they will give me a bionic leg. I'll be good as new, maybe better."

"I can't believe it," Dad says, and the line goes dead. I know he just didn't know what else to say. In truth, I don't know either. Foley men aren't built to sit around and chat about horrible news—that's why God invented Guinness.

FOR ANOTHER WEEK, I work my ass off pushing through all the required strength and balance training, but Dr. Dennis still won't clear me for gait training. I've always been athletic, and crutching around awkwardly is unbearable. Jill tells me to relax; my progress is amazing. In return I give her the brunt of my frustration.

She finally snaps, "Look here, Sugar, your leg still has some swelling and edema. Your washouts still sting. I bet you still have ghost pain."

I sit on the floor, avoid her eyes and work a shrinker sock on to a donning tube. "So, it's my fault?" I ask, snapping the elastic sock into place.

"No, edema and phantom limb syndrome are nobody's fault. Just trust me. Trust Dr. Dennis. It isn't a race, and we'll keep working on your balance and strength. You'll be miles ahead when your leg is ready to bear weight."

"I'm ready now."

"No, you're not."

"But I'm going crazy in here! I don't have my phone and there's nothing to do," I complain, pushing the bongo end of the tube over my stump.

"Okay, Will, I'm going to give you a little speech. You won't like it one bit, but I have to give it. And you have to listen. You hear?"

I look up and nod.

"Depression and suicide are serious issues for amputees. You have to be kind to yourself. And know, you can always ask for help."

"What? You're crazy!" I glare. "I just want out of here and don't need any psycho-babble from you!"

"Relax, I'm on your side. Once you get through gait

training, you'll switch over to outpatient care. You'll continue your physical therapy back at Grafenwöhr and just return here for checkups and fittings. It'll happen, just be patient. Deal?"

THREE LONG DAYS LATER, Dr. Dennis watches me expertly do a washout. He conducts a detailed examination of my stump and is finally satisfied. After he leaves, Jill lets me peek at the note he put in my medical file: "Patient able to conduct residual limb self-care and physically prepared for prosthetic gait training." We high-five and go down to Landstuhl's small food court to celebrate over Baskin-Robbin's.

Jill says, "You're doing great, and now get to focus on mastering your prosthesis."

"Yep," I say between big spoonfuls of chocolate chip ice cream.

"Gait training is the most frustrating part, Hon. It's back to the parallel bars so you can get the feel of walking on your new leg."

I shrug, "Too easy."

"Seriously," she warns, "you'll have to re-learn the biomechanics of walking."

"Bring it on!" I smile.

Jill laughs, grabs our empty bowls, and throws them away. I grab my crutches and follow her up the long web of hallways to my last round of physical therapy. Next stop, gait training!

AT 08:45 SHARP, I leave for my fitting. The prosthetics lab is one wing over and two floors up, and takes me fifteen minutes to crutch there. I sign in, take a seat in the small waiting room, and fidget restlessly.

A lean man wearing a white lab coat greets me. "Hello, Corporal Foley." He smiles, extending his hand, "I'm Jimmy Newsome, your prosthetics guy." He has a steel-gray flattop and intense blue eyes, and I can tell right away that he's retired military. We shake, and I instantly like him.

Mr. Newsome continues, "I hear that you are way ahead of schedule. That's great!" He waves me back to his small fitting room and hands me the prosthetic. It's basically a metal pole that has a cup for my stump on one end and a ridiculously fake fiberglass foot at the other end. It feels very heavy in my hands.

He helps me put it on. First, he puts a gel liner over my shrinker sock, then helps me fit the cup over the liner, stopping to explain that later my high-tech reactive foot will have a cup custom made to fit the exact contours of my residual leg, but for now my dumb prosthetic just needs a comfortably tight fit.

When it's finally on, it feels much lighter than it did in my hands. It still looks weird down there. The fake foot is flesh-colored, but they really could have used any color, because its only purpose is to hold a shoe. And for that, I finally have a pair of New Balance on my feet!

I crutch over to physical therapy wearing my prosthesis. Jill is thrilled, but I'm bothered by the newness and discomfort, and living up to the prediction that I'll return to duty in record time. How on earth will that work?

Jill tells me that getting used to the new foot will be the biggest hurdle. "You'll see, Sugar, you'll get the hang of it and will run around on two legs soon!"

I FINALLY DO GET the hang of it, a little. On my discharge day, Leonard spends the morning with me. She is nice, but after the Paris thing it's been awkward. She wheels me down to a waiting van, and we're both a little sad. With my prosthetic firmly in place, I stand unsteadily and reach out to shake her hand. She hands me a note and then gives me a full body hug. I close my eyes and breathe her in.

Looking up, I see Jill watching us. She is, of course, wearing one of her colorful Adidas track suits. She's also holding her Easton hockey stick. "Thought you'd get away without a proper goodbye, Sugar?" she says, flashing her dazzling smile. She steps forward waving a listen-to-me-closely finger in my face. "Adjusting will take time. Be gentle with yourself. Don't you dare hide away in the barracks, you hear?"

"Yes, ma'am. I won't let you down."

"Here, I brought you a little something," she says, and hands me the stick.

It feels like she's given me back a piece of myself. I can barely manage a quick thank you. Switching the stick to my left hand, I straighten up and execute a perfect military salute. She smiles and salutes back. I get into a waiting van, and cradle my stick. Finally, I'm on my way back to my unit in Grafenwöhr.

FIVE

Graf's iconic water tower sits well above the tree line. Its enormous tank, hidden behind the façade of a Swiss chalet, floats high in Bavarian sky. Behind it are rows of concrete barracks buildings, five-story replicas of the original stone and half-timbered Bavarian barracks. In the new barracks, lower enlisted soldiers double up, but NCOs like me are assigned single rooms. The design was clearly inspired by college dorms, although here the rooms are all business, well-scrubbed, and ready for inspection.

I go straight to my wall locker, break the plastic band, and open its padlock. I put my iPhone on its charger, empty my pockets, and find Leonard's note. It says, "Congrats! You're not my patient now. Call me!"

I shower and take a quick nap. An hour later, my phone is charged and I'm connected to the world. I spend the night scrolling through hundreds of text and email messages. My dad wrote almost every day. I try to reach him on video chat, but it doesn't work. So, I dial his phone number.

On the second ring, he answers, "Hello, Jim Foley."

"Dad, it's me, I'm back at Graf."

"Oh, that's great news. How you doing?"

"Okay, still getting used to the new foot." Silence. I wonder if our call has disconnected, and ask, "Dad, you there?"

"Yeah, hey, yah catching any games?"

"Mostly highlights," I say, glad we're still connected. "Splitting at home wasn't good, but beating them five to two in Toronto was perfect. We'll close out the series in five".

"I hope so," he says. "Tomorrow's game will be tough. Being down three to one will make the Leafs desperate."

"Will you go?"

"I'll try to, but if not I'll catch the game on TV."

"Me too," I say. "The game starts late here, but I'll stay up."

"Hey,we'll be watching ta'getha! Ah crap, I gotta go." Dad says and hangs up abruptly.

A wave of melancholy hits me. My dad and I both secretly dread the playoffs. When they start, watered down national NBC coverage bumps our local NESN coverage. And here's a dirty family secret—once NBC takes over, we switch to the Canadian feed. The CBC commentators aren't as good as Jack Edwards and Andy Brickley, but they are a hell of a lot better than the clowns on NBC. The bigger problem is the season starts to slip away. Sure, we love cheering for Boston to win it all, but it gets so damn quiet when the season ends.

To cheer myself up, I put on my favorite Bruins T-shirt, go to the Shoppette and get Guinness for the game. The Leafs spoil my night by beating Boston two to one, and that means we'll have to win game six on the road or come home for a winner-take-all game seven. Before going to bed, I text Dad, "You called it. Time for the boys to close it out in Toronto."

At 06:15, Sergeant Duras knocks and asks if I want to go down to formation. Even with only two hours of rack time, I'm in.

"James did his best to fill in," Duras says, "but he wasn't ready."

"Thanks," I say, glad that I was missed.

Outside, most of the main body is back. Some soldiers come over to say hello, and my fire team circles me in a friendly group huddle. Robalo calls us to attention, and I'm thrilled to be back in my old spot next to Duras, with James, Hector, Washington and Lovely on down the line to my left.

It's not just the familiar sights and sounds that are good for my morale, I also like being back in a routine. Our daily battle-rhythm officially starts at 06:15, when everyone gathers outside for first formation and physical training. We assemble and at 06:30 the post's speaker system plays Reveille. On the bugler's first note, everyone comes to attention and salutes Old Glory flying over the headquarters. Then we stretch, do push-ups and sit-ups, and run in formation. Afterwards, we are released for personal hygiene and breakfast. At 09:00 we form up for work call. We form up again just before 17:00 and the post cannon fires signaling 5 p.m. and the end of the duty day. We salute as the colors are lowered, and are free for the night. At 23:00 Taps plays. It's lights out and silence reigns until we get up to do it all over again.

ON A SUNNY WEDNESDAY AFTERNOON, Robalo calls me in to his office. He sits heavily. "Okay, Foley, have a seat. I'm required to counsel you about your medical profile." He reads from a piece of paper, "According to Army policy, you may remain on temporary profile for up to one year during rehabilitation." He stops, drops the paper, and looks at me. "Listen Foley, all bullshit aside, you have a year to return to duty. That just means get off medical profile and pass the damn PT test. Understand?"

"Yes, First Sergeant."

To give you a fighting chance, I'm moving you to the admin section. You won't deploy and can make all of your medical appointments. I know you don't like it, and neither do I," he says. "But make the best of it. Hit the gym every day, take a college course, and steer clear of Major Manning."

AT FRIDAY'S safety briefing and release formation, we learn that our Brigade on alert to deploy to the Ukraine to train with partner units. On the outside, I maintain my bearing. On the inside I'm dying, because the sick, lame and lazy always form the core of the rear detachment. I know that I'm not ready to deploy, but I hate being left behind.

On Monday morning, everything kicks into high gear. The Army has a standard operating procedure for everything and packing is one SOP paratroopers know extremely well. Everyone does their part to prepare for the deployment.

Everyone, except me and Manning's misfits.

We still go out at 06:15 to stand in formation and listen to a scratchy recording of a bugler playing Reveille. We still form up at the end of the duty day, and when the cannon fires at 17:00 sharp, we're released for dinner. At 23:00 when Taps plays, it's still lights out. But for me and the rest of Manning's malingerers, it's all the in-between stuff that is different. Other than going to our appointments, nobody expects us to do anything. For the first time in my life, I'm disposable.

There's no SOP for how to deal with it. While everyone rushes around prepping to go wheels up, I'm off by myself limping around post. There are some lucky fools too deaf and blind to know that the whole world has turned against them. So desperate to fit in and be a part of the action, I'm certainly not one of them.

SIX

I sit alone at the breakfast table I used to share with my squad. An evil thought suddenly hits me like a sledgehammer—because of my leg they no longer trust me! Deployments are about trust. You must trust the guys on your left and right. To ensure everyone gets home, they must be willing to die for you and you must be willing to die for them. Nothing short of that works. Because my team no longer trusts me, I'm no longer welcome in their club. That's why Robalo benched me! The pain of it cuts deep. As if to punctuate it, ghost pain shoots up my leg and stabs into my right ass cheek.

I limp over to the gym right after breakfast. Two tired-looking soldiers in camouflage man the front desk. I recognize them as rotten apples from my unit. The rumor is they're pending courts-martial for drugs. I nod hello and scan the barcode on the back of my ID card. To my left, are two empty basketball courts. The main workout area is on the ground floor. It is filled with Nautilus, cardio machines, and free weights. In the finest military tradition, the machines are lined up precisely. Three rows of cardio machines face out along the panoramic glass wall. Outside there are four baseball diamonds ringed by a jogging trail. Pine and birch trees dot the slope that leads up to the American housing village of Netzaberg. All of it provides a beautiful springtime backdrop for my workouts.

On my way to the locker room, I pass five trophy cases. The middle one is dedicated to the post hockey team. I stop and count seven years' worth of military championship pucks, and trophies from tournaments in Czech, Holland, and Spain. I'm shocked to see First Sergeant Robalo in team photos. I didn't know he played.

Man, I need to play again! I look down at my prosthetic and frown, because there won't be any hockey in my one-legged future.

In the locker room I pull my headphones and padlock from my gym bag, lock up and head downstairs. Jill suggested getting used to my prosthetic on a Cross Trainer, so I pick one in the third row that lines up with a flat screen TV playing the Boston game from the night before. I already know the score, but I plug in my headphones and switch on the sound anyway. While I move my arms and legs on the low-impact machine, the hockey game plays above me.

I zone in and out out of the game and daydream about my glory days at East Boston High. I was a high-scoring forward. Logging tons of minutes, I centered the power play unit and anchored the penalty kill. We made it to the state finals, and in double overtime, we went on a power play. Our coach, Mr. Sheehan, took a timeout to let us rest. The scorekeeper blew the horn to signal resumption of play, and I coasted slowly into the face-off circle.

With the opposing goalie to my front right, I bent forward and gripped my stick down low. The defending center already had his stick on the ice, and I timed my backhand swipe to match the ref's drop. I won cleanly, drawing the puck back to my defenseman. Skating straight to the net to block the goalie's view, I spun just as the puck zipped past my left elbow and beat the goalie high on his stick side. As long as I live, I'll never forget that win!

A year later, I was a paratrooper with orders to report for duty in Italy. Then the Army changed my orders and sent me here. Damn, that changed everything.

I finish my workout just as the game ends. Toronto wins again. "Come on, Bruins! You're gonna have to find some offense to win game seven," I think, vowing to change our luck by getting Sam Adams instead of Guinness for the elimination game.

I LINK up with my old fire team at the chow hall for lunch. We sit together, but it doesn't feel the same. We used to be so close. When I laughed, they laughed. It's not like that anymore.

After lunch they help me move my stuff from the NCO barracks to a small attic room. James asks, "You have a roommate?"

"I guess," I shrug, confused because I should have a single room.

Hector, our hulking SAW gunner, makes a joke about locking the crazies in the attic. Everyone waits to see what I do. I ignore his stupid comment and nobody dares laugh. On our second trip up, Specialist Jack Martin waits at the door.

"Fat Jack's your roomie?" James asks.

I don't know what to say. Maybe in the Rear-D everyone gets a roommate?

"Yep," Jack says, "if you're crashing here, you're my new roomie."

What? I need to fight this! Sticking me in a double room is one thing, but rooming with a lower enlisted soldier is something else.

My guys drop the last boxes and say goodbye. I feel abandoned. I know that it's not their choice to leave me behind, but there's no way around it, that's exactly what's happening.

Two days later, I meet Duras and his squad for lunch at the Kantine. It's a weird farewell, because technically I should be farewelling them; however, it feels more like they are farewelling me. We gorge ourselves on oversized schnitzels.

On the way out, I wish everyone a safe deployment ending with, "Feet and knees together, boys!"

"We're not jumping in," Duras laughs.

"Okay then, stay warm and dry and I'll see you on the backside," I mumble, embarrassed by my gaff and burning with deployment envy.

Duras drops me at the bus stop and I take a twenty-minute bus ride through the training area to Rose Barracks. In the administrative wing of the medical center, I find a small legal office. Standing in its open door, I wait for a large man in a wrinkled suit to look up.

"Sir," I finally say, getting his attention. "Jill from Landstuhl sent me to see you."

He reads my name and rank from my uniform. "Corporal Foley, I'm Jon Hoffmann, the civilian paralegal here." He pauses and reaches for his oversized mug. "It's my job to make sure guys like you get a fair shake." Taking a swig of coffee, he continues with his well-rehearsed spiel, "our discussions are strictly confidential. The important thing to remember is that everyone here works for the clinic commander except me. I don't and no matter what I'm in your corner." He punctuates his speech by raising his mug and taking another swallow of coffee.

"Why is that, sir?" I ask.

He strokes his salt and pepper beard, saying, "There's a complex system in place to figure out if injured soldiers can be retained and returned to duty, assigned to different duties, or medically retired."

"They might kick me out, sir?"

"Don't call me sir. I'm a retired NCO. Go with Mr. Hoffmann, or Jon."

"Okay, Mr. Hoffmann," I nod. "So, they might really kick me out?"

"Let me give you some background before I answer that question."

I don't see any way out of it, and reluctantly take a seat.

Dotting his lecture with legal and medical jargon like "administrative due process", "*ex parte*", and "reasonable accommodation", he gives me a painfully detailed briefing about the process. Every few minutes he looks up and asks, "Tracking?"

"Yes, tracking," I say.

"So let me ask you, why did I bother to tell you all of this?"

I shrug, hoping no response is acceptable.

"Your commanders and the medical folks will try to move your case as quickly as possible. If things slow down, they might take it out on you. That's where I come in. I don't care about how fast your case moves. I only care about fairness. Tracking?"

Pain shoots up my bad leg and forces me to shift, but this time the Hoff waits for an answer. "Tracking," I say, wishing that I was anywhere but here.

"In about a year, your case will go to an evaluation board. They will decide if you stay in the infantry, stay in the Army doing something else, or medically retire."

I sit up, momentarily forgetting my leg. "A year?"

Jon nods. "But if they can keep you in, they will. Your job right now is to follow the doctor's orders and concentrate on rehab. The doctor will determine when you've reached your medical retention determination point. That's when your healing has gone as far as it'll go. Then you'll be assigned a liaison officer. But throughout, you can always see me." Jon says, smiling.

"Um, you were with JAG?"

"Yes, still am."

"Can you help me with a statement of charges my commander gave me?"

"What's it for?"

"The gear they cut off me in the jump," I say, reaching down to knead my leg.

Jon shakes his head in disbelief. "Sure, I'll talk with JAG and they should kill it."

"Could you, ah, also help me with a problem in the barracks?"

"That depends, what's the problem?"

"When my unit moved me to the rear detachment, they moved me from a single NCO room into a double room with a specialist."

"Well, rooms are assigned on a space-available basis," Jon says, "and you and your roommate do share the same pay grade."

"But I'm an NCO," I protest.

"Your unit seems to think it's okay," Jon says and reaches for his coffee. "Hey, I rattled off a lot of information. For now, just be the best soldier that you can be. Don't rock the boat. And for damn sure stay out of trouble because if they can kick you out for misconduct, they don't have to worry about all the medical hurdles and timelines. Tracking?"

"Yes, sir, still tracking," I say, standing up and jarring my stump.

On the ride back to Graf, I stare out the window. All that legal mumbo-jumbo boils down to the medical stuff taking forever and me having a bright-red target on my back. *Nice!*

MY PHONE BUZZES at 04:00, but it's okay because I'm wide awake, wearing my Bruins jersey, and pumped full of adrenaline. I answer and Dad says, "Did you see the game? It's a miracle!" He inhales just long enough for me to answer.

"Heck yeah! When Boston scored first, I was sure we'd win. But when Toronto scored four in a row—"

"Oh, that was the best win evah!" Dad blurts out. "Trailing by three in the third and coming back to win in ovah time, it's exactly what we need!"

I know exactly what he means about needing this game seven win. It's been less than a month since the pressure-cooker bombs went off, killing three and injuring hundreds, and Boston is still in mourning. I also know the Bruins can't fix it, but they are playing with pride and living up to the city's new rallying cry—Boston Strong. "It was amazing!" I agree.

"Amazing only gets you half-way there! Horton scoring, then Lucic with a minute twenty-two left, I almost had a heart attack! Then who comes through with less than a minute, and scores again in overtime? Bergeron!"

"The boys will be super fired up to play the Rangers," I add.

"Oh yeah, we're going all the way to the finals!" he shouts. "Hey, will you get any sleep tonight?"

"Nah, I have a PT formation in about two hours."

"Then I better let you go," he says. "Love you, Willie."

———

WORKING out twice a day can be monotonous, but damned if it doesn't release endorphins. After an afternoon workout and sauna, I walk over to the dining facility to see what's for dinner. Luck is with me. They are serving my favorite: baked cod, boiled potatoes, and corn on the cob. After dinner, I head back to the barracks.

Before the jump, my room was my refuge. Now it's not.

My new roommate has a bad back, shoulders and knee. He also claims to have sleep apnea. I'm no expert, but the dumpy guy can sure snore. Jack is shorter than me and older by five years, and he has packed on weight—going way past husky straight to fat. He gave up on military haircuts and bangs hang over his wide forehead. He's a classic over-the-hill high school jock with nothing too remarkable about him, except his face which is permanently wind-chapped. Only dark sunglasses can hide his sharpshooter's squint, and nothing can conceal the deployment wear-and-tear on his fleshy, weather-beaten face.

There is no way around it, Jack is a disappointment. He shows up to formations and makes it to all of his medical appointments, but that's it. He plans to get even fatter in order to aggravate his sleep apnea. It's all part of his bigger plan—codenamed Operation Fat Jack—to get a higher disability rating. After PT formations, Fat Jack usually goes back to bed. He doesn't get up again until just before noon. Settling in on the couch, he eats microwave pizza, drinks his first beer, and plays Xbox until our 17:00 release formation. The only deviation he has from his barracks-rat life is for medical appointments, like when he rides the bus to Vilseck for his weekly traumatic brain injury appointment. Jack told me he enlisted to get the G.I. Bill, go to college, and get his teaching certificate. He wanted to be a high school football coach. One deployment turned into two, and Jack will now skip college and forsake football to live on a medical retirement which he says, "Uncle Sugar mother-fucking owes me."

I don't know how Fat Jack can live with himself, and to make things worse between us, he routinely gives me unsolicited advice:

"The big green machine broke you; it owes you."

"Dude, keep going to the gym and you ain't never going to get paid."

"Don't fuck yourself. Fuck the Army."

Turning into a slug like Jack is my secret nightmare. Each morning, I go to the gym and push myself until the endorphins kick in. Then I push harder.

On a sunny afternoon I come back and turn on the lights because Jack has the blinds down. He's sitting on the couch clicking wildly on a video controller. He looks up and nods. A half-empty rack of German beer and a pizza box sit on the coffee table.

"Dude, want to play some 'chell?" By 'chell he means NHL hockey on Xbox.

"Come on, Jack, why don't you give it a break?" I say, pointing at the flat screen TV.

"Heck no, Bro. Today I went to the Shoppette and picked up this tasty rack o' beer, and a delicious meat lover's pizza. Oh sorry, the pizza's already gone."

I shake my head.

"Dude, lighten up," he says, setting his controller down. "Want a brewski?"

"Just *one*," I say. "But come on football star, you've got to start coming to the gym with me."

"I knocked up a cheerleader, too," he grins. "Hey, I'm just marking time 'til I get my rating. I'll get fit when I'm back in the real world."

I shake my head and frown.

"Cheers," he says, tapping his bottle against mine. "It's nuts, man. With sleep apnea, the VA gives me fifty percent disability. Add in my bad back and knees, and I could get one hundred percent. That's cash for life! Why would I fuck that up by going to the gym with you?"

"Have some self-respect, Jack. Just come and ride a stationary bike. It'll release some feel-good endorphins."

"Fuck endorphins, they ain't gonna get me paid," he says, shoving his empty beer bottle back in the rack.

"Jack, you need to cut back on boozing and spending so much time alone."

"Shut up, Mother. Are you going to play some 'chell or what? I'll be Pittsburgh and you can be whoever you want. It doesn't matter, 'cuz I'm gonna put a beat down on you, you puck-headed, endorphin-loving motherfucker."

"You're going down," I say, picking up a controller.

THE NEXT MORNING Jack goes back to bed as I leave for the gym. Most mornings I focus on strength, saving cardio for the afternoon. A red, white and blue BMC Ranger jersey hangs over a pair of crossed sticks high above the stairway to the cardio area. It looks like the New York Rangers away Jersey, except with BAYERN in red slashing diagonally across the middle. The bottom of the jersey is accented with blue Bavarian diamonds cutting across in a matching slant. Over the heart, where the captain's C would normally be, is a black and gold Ranger-style tab which reads, U.S. ARMY. Hey, I've got no love for the New York Rangers, but it really is a sharp looking jersey. And man, does it ever makes me want to play again!

AT LUNCH, my iPhone buzzes. It's Dad trying to reach me. I hit cancel and text him, "I'll call back in ten."

Back in my room. Dad pops up on my screen, He says, "Hi there, Willie! You'r looking' good."

"Thanks, Dad, sorry about the cancel. I wanted to use my WiFi to call you back for free."

"Free is good. How's rehab treating you?"

"It's going. I have formations, but then I'm on my own. Mostly, I'm at the gym."

"Good for you! Catching any games?"

"I saw a recap with Marchand's overtime goal. Boy, I'm glad he's a Bruin!"

"Yep, he's our feisty little ball of hate. Did you see game two?"

"Oh, yeah, five different guys scoring to win, that's Boston *very* Strong."

"And your old man was there, in the Gahden!"

"Were you working the game?"

"Nope. Ah, the Bruins gave some tickets to first responders. I was there in uniform, but got to sit and watch the
whole game."

"Wow, that's great!"

"Yep, and the team's grit is inspiring. It's helping us all
recovah from the shock," Dad says, choking up. "It's definitely restorin' a sense of normalcy."

Instead of asking if the images of people bleeding and
missing parts causes him to think about me, I stick with
talking about the game. "Secondary scoring all over the
place! Rask is seeing and stopping everything. We've got a
good chance to win it all."

"Yeah, I like seeing the scoring from the back end. Krug
seems small for a defenseman, especially next to Big Z, but
can he evah shoot the puck."

"Boychuk hammered one home from the point, too."
I add.

"Heck, we may sweep the Rangers."

"AFN is showing game four live and I'm definitely
staying up to watch," I say.

"I'll be watching with you!"

SEVEN

May edges into June and the Bavarian days keep getting longer. The sun is already up when Jack and I go down for our 06:30 PT formation, and the daylight lasts until about 20:00, or eight o'clock. This is much better than winter, when PT started and ended in the dark, and the sun went down fifteen minutes before our 17:00 release formation. Almost everybody loves the warm summer nights, but it's already hot up in the attic. The terra-cotta roof stores heat and radiates it into our room, and the Army didn't bother to spend money on air conditioning.

My biggest problem isn't the heat, it's having too much time. My mind drifts. Maybe that's why I always kept myself busy with school, hockey, and the Army. Maybe that's why community college didn't work out. When I'm in constant motion, there's no time to think and, I realize, I like it that way.

Physical therapy gives me a reason to walk across post a few times a week. The NHL playoffs give me something to look forward to, especially when Boston plays. I don't mind getting up at 01:00 to watch, because I know Dad is watching and that connects us.

Boston wins two at home and beats the Rangers four to three at Madison Square Garden to take a commanding three-game lead. Dad and I both predict a sweep, but then the Rangers fight back, extending the series to a game five back in Boston. At 04:00, I watch the Garden's scoreboard count down to zero. My phone rings. It's Dad.

"Three unanswered goals, Willie. Now that's the way to close out a series!"

"After they avoided the sweep last game, we sure didn't want this game going into overtime."

"You're right. If you let a team hang around long enough it'll bite you. In an elimination game, you've got to put them away early."

"Who do you think we'll get for the conference finals?" I ask.

"Pittsburgh is looking tough. With Crosby and Malkin at center, and Fleury in net, the Pens are pretty strong down the middle."

"Well, bring 'em on," I say. "We'll be rested and ready. With Bergeron and Rask, we're solid down the middle, too. If Tuukka keeps seeing and stopping the puck, we can beat anyone."

UNTIL JILL SUGGESTED IT, I never considered taking college classes on post. Over at the education center, I have no idea how to get started until a grandmotherly lady with kind hazel eyes talks to me. She cautions about jumping in too quickly with an online science class, explaining that most new students do better with "on-ground" classes. She recommends a University of Maryland night class, and registers me for "History of the Grafenwöhr Training Area".

"Do I use my GI Bill to pay?" I ask.

"Heavens no, save it for later," she says. "It's better to use tuition assistance while you're on active duty."

"Okay, thanks."

"Oh wait, one more thing," she says. "Professor Krieger is our most popular instructor, but he goes really fast. Before class starts, check out the GTA's one-hundred year timeline on the internet, and see if the library still has a copy of *Grafenwöhr Training Area, Yesterday & Today.* If not, buy a copy at the PX."

"Thanks," I say, pivoting on my good leg.

I skip the library, buy the book, and graze the chow hall's salad bar for dinner. Then I walk in on Fat Jack. He's sitting on the couch, wearing only boxer shorts, and watching porn. *You can't unsee that.* He looks over, stuffs a handful of Cheetos in his mouth, and between chews he asks, "Want some? They're the spicy kind."

I shake my head, take my GTA history book, and go over to the USO. It isn't the ideal place to study, but it's convenient. Only a two-minute walk from the barracks, recent renovations turned it into a roomy airport-style lounge. They have free sodas and snacks, and offer free long-distance phone calls, computer terminals, and WiFi. I settle into a leather recliner farthest from a big screen TV showing *Argo.* If I'm lucky, my study session will last longer than Jack's porn-a-thon.

The book is easy to follow. It has lots of pictures and diagrams, and the text alternates between German and English. So, it's only half as long as I'd feared. Right away I learn that in 1907 the Kingdom of Bavaria established the training area and used it to conduct maneuvers and fire artillery. Huh, we still do that. The Bavarians completed the fourteen-story, water tower in 1910. Wow, I walk under it every day and it still provides water to main post. I flip through chapters about how Germany absorbed the Free State of Bavaria and elected Adolf Hitler. As Hitler consolidated power, he took direct control over the GTA. Then things moved pretty fast. Hitler reintroduced mandatory military service, doubled the size of the training area, and visited the GTA on June 24, 1938.

I check my watch and realize it's late. Hopefully, late enough to miss Jack's porn and Cheetos fest. I walk back, pausing to look up at the tower bathed in moonlight. Its rooftop spotlight rotates, making it look like a gigantic lighthouse. How in the heck did it survive the Allied bombings in 1945? I hope Krieger covers cool stuff like that in class.

ON A CHILLY WEDNESDAY, I walk to my first class in twilight. Why am I nervous? I was a good student in high school and passed all my classes at community college. Still, going back to class feels strange. My heart pounds as I look for my classroom. When I find it, I see eight students. Five are soldiers; their athletic builds and short haircuts give them away. The other three are the wives or daughters of soldiers. They are young, but they lack the severe looks of female combat soldiers. Plus, they all cluster together and chat as if they have known each other for years. Soldiers normally don't do that, at least not right away.

A shaggy-haired man comes in. Maybe he's an undercover cop? Or a spouse? With that wild hair, he for sure isn't a soldier. I'm still deciding what to think about his mop-top, when he plops himself down next to me. Then a second scruffy guy shuffles in. He wears a tie-dyed t-shirt, baggy cargo shorts, and Birkenstock sandals. My surprise increases when he goes up front and empties his backpack. He takes off his ball cap, and reveals closely cropped salt-and-pepper hair. Then I get it, his wire-rimmed glasses and mostly gray goatee mark him more as an intellectual than a hippie.

He looks up, and the room quiets. "Hello, I'm Professor Krieger. Welcome to class." He hands out copies of his syllabus and explains that most of the class materials are available online. "This is a history class," he says, "but let's start with some basic geography." He points to a map of Europe. "The GTA lies sixty miles east of Nuremberg and one-hundred-forty miles north of Munich. We're near the Czech border and as close geographically to Prague as we are to Munich. There is an ancient east-west trading route that runs between Prague and Paris. Today we call it Auto-bahn 6."

Huh, that's the way to Landstuhl; no wonder Leonard suggested a trip to Paris.

"Graf is the U.S. Army's largest overseas training area. It covers ninety square miles. That's larger than Boston. It's home to one-half of the Army's combat power in Europe, including the 2nd Stryker Cavalry Regiment and parts of the 173rd Airborne Infantry Brigade. How many of you are assigned to these units?"

Counting six raised hands, including mine, Krieger nods and continues, "The training area was originally established to support the Royal Bavarian Army's 3rd Corps. Bavarian and German soldiers trained here in both World Wars, Americans trained here during the Cold War, and now it is home to over twenty-five thousand American soldiers, civilian employees, and their family members." Krieger turns to his syllabus and explains his grading based on weekly quizzes, a research paper, and an oral presentation.

A civilian who has her hair pulled back in a sporty ponytail raises her hand. "Will you approve our paper topics in advance?" she asks in a high-pitched voice.

"A perfect segue," Krieger nods. "There are many lenses through which to view the GTA. Some topics to consider are the economic, ecological, or social impact of the training area. Or you could focus on famous visitors to Grafenwöhr. Or the weapons developed and tested here. Or the geographic importance of the training area to the Kingdom of Bavaria, Nazi Germany, and NATO."

"We select our own topics?" Ms. Ponytail squeaks. Damn, she is really hot and should have a confident and sexy voice. Instead, she sounds like Minnie Mouse!

"Yes, but approved by me within the next three weeks to give you enough time to focus your research. Any other questions?" Krieger asks, pushing his round John Lennon glasses up on his button nose. "No? Then let's turn to the course itself." For the next hour, Krieger regales us with stories about the GTA's early years. He wraps up with: "Each week we'll cover a discrete time period. Next week, we'll cover the GTA's role in the First World War. In our third week, we'll turn to 1936 when the GTA significantly expanded. Can anyone tell me the significance of this time period?"

Squeaky answers, "Hitler took over?"

"That's correct," Krieger smiles. "In week four, we'll cover the Second World War and the bombing raids in the spring of 1945. In week five, we'll focus on the United States' occupation of the GTA. Then, we'll cover the Cold War and NATO plans to defend against Warsaw pact troops. Finally, we'll cover the fall of the Berlin Wall, the training area's role in the global war on terror, and our ongoing missions in Eastern Europe. You'll turn in your research papers and give your in-class presentations at our last session together. Questions?"

Krieger waits and when nobody speaks, he gathers his papers. Mop-top Serpico and I follow Squeaky out. She's wearing black yoga pants and a tight black sweater. And man, does she ever look fit. She notices us and gives me a discreet wave.

"Who's that?" Serpico asks.

"I don't know," I shrug. "Maybe she works out at my gym?"

He laughs, "I need to start going to your gym!"

MOST MORNINGS after reveille the broken soldiers are released, and the fit soldiers stay for unit PT. This morning I stay outside and watch them do push-ups, sit-ups, and leave for their formation run. The whole time, I long for when I led my fire team through the same workout. I walk over to the dining facility while the sweaty soldiers head upstairs to shower and change. In line, I shift my weight and test the stability of my prosthetic. Each day it seems a little better, but it's still not quite right. Moving through the food line on autopilot, I smile at the irony of an ultramodern glass-and-steel dining facility still slinging old-time Army comfort food like biscuits and gravy.

In the oversized dining room, Robalo sits alone enjoying the sunshine. Normally a corporal doesn't eat with a first sergeant, but I was one of his favorites. He even fast-tracked my promotion to corporal. And, I want to talk to him about hockey.

I ask to join him, he smiles, and I sit. Then his face clouds over. We eat in uncomfortable silence, both knowing that Major Manning's mission will be to get me cleared for duty or kicked out of the Army. It's horrible that the Army treats soldiers like meat, but the Big Green Machine needs deployable soldiers to defend America. It can't afford to degrade readiness by keeping non-deployable soldiers like me on the books. But at Landstuhl Robalo kept his poker face, and didn't telegraph any of it. Sitting here now, he seems ashamed.

To break the awkward silence, I ask him about the Rangers' game in Cheb.

His face lights up, "Cheb's in the Czech Republic, but it's only about an hour away. They hosted the game to commemorate the anniversary of the U.S. Army's liberation of their town. Their mayor even dropped the puck for the opening face-off." He turns and points. "Look, there's the game banner underneath those crossed sticks."

"Was the Czech team any good?"

"Yeah, Coach was worried about bringing a team that could compete. So he loaded up with some German ringers. He even brought his son back from college to anchor our defense, and we had a West Pointer who brought a lot of skill and toughness."

"Are they still playing?"

"The Germans are, and Zach still comes back on school breaks. Jeff left for the Q-course. He's hoping to qualify for Special Forces."

"Wow, that's a lot of turn-over."

"Right, we have about forty regular guys and usually dress fifteen for a game. But everyone wanted to play in Cheb."

"I'll bet!"

"Coach took five lines and put the best players on the top three lines. He told us that if we built up a lead, or fell way behind, the fourth and fifth lines would play in the second and third periods."

I lean in, "How'd it go?"

"Our team captain and starting center, Taz, scored ten seconds into the game! At the opening face-off, he chipped the puck forward, split the surprised Czech defensemen, and beat the goalie with a backhand deke high stick side."

"No shit!"

"No shit. Taz seized the momentum, and we built on it. Our goalie, Bill the Cat, was really on his game. His high school hockey coach was Steve Carlson from *Slap Shot*."

"No kidding? That's crazy!"

"After the first period, we led four to one. In the second, Coach rolled lines one, two, three and four. Our puck luck held, and in the third period lines one, two, three and five skated. So everyone played, and we won eight to three."

"That's awesome!"

Robalo leans back and looks over at the Cheb banner. "Wearing my red, white and blue Rangers jersey, with a U.S. Army tab over my heart, and playing for America. I'll never forget it."

Inspired by Robalo's story, I go straight to the PX to look for tennis balls and am thrilled to find a tube of bright yellow Wilsons. Back in the barracks, Jack is dozing on the couch. I push him to the side, open up the vacuum-sealed tube, and stab a ball with the screwdriver tip of my Leatherman.

"What the fuck are you doing?" Jack asks.

"Got to take the air out of it."

"Huh?"

"For hockey, you don't want it to bounce."

"Hockey? You starting a gimp league?"

"Fuck you. Watch this." I drop the dead ball on the floor and stick handle around our spartan room.

"Wow, slick hands," Jack says.

I reward his compliment with a quick flick of my wrists, zinging the ball at his nuts. Bull's-eye! He doubles over in pain.

"Sorry, dude," I say, holding my stick out to him. "Here, try."

Jack takes the stick and bats the ball around a little. He's no Patrick Kane and admits it isn't as easy as it looks. "Damn, you must have been good before you lost your foot," he says.

AT NIGHT I text Dad about the post team.

"Did you see the sweep?" he answers.

I knew the Bruins had swept the Pens, but I'd only caught the highlights from the 1-0 game four win at the Garden. "Defense wins championships!" I send.

"You're damn right! Chara and Seidenberg were awesome! Crosby and Malkin can start making' tee times. Next week we'll be playin' for the Cup!"

I smile. Dad loves the Bruins, and their dominating sweep of the star-studded Penguins will keep him happy, at least until the Chicago series starts.

WITH THE SUN OUT, I look forward to walking to rehab. I step onto a grassy quad ringed by massive five-story buildings, and the paving stone walkways and trimmed lawns remind me of Boston College, only on a much larger and newer scale. I pass rows of gigantic barracks buildings and think about the spoiled frat boys and sorority girls. If they only knew what a Southie has gotta go through to get an education.

I tilt my head up and enjoy the sunshine. I cross the street, leaving the barracks area behind. To my right is a U.S. style shopping mall, complete with a movie theater, car dealer, PX, food court, barbershop and commissary. To my left is an over-sized parade ground. It has a few tanks and artillery pieces scattered around the edges. More than anything, it looks like a driving range, missing only the golfers wacking balls. The most striking scene is on the far side of the parade gound where the commanding general's gingerbread house sits at the base of a matching tower.

Krieger's lecture has makes it more than just post-card pretty. Built on a slight rise, the quarters and tower are elaborately accented in matching blue and white, to remind everyone of Bavaria's Alpine soul. Set back in a grove of pines and birch, the scene contrasts with the military simplicity of the parade ground, like an elaborate Grimm's fairy tale colliding with a stripped-down Pentagon briefing.

I pass the car dealership and shake my head at the over-priced Fords, Jeeps and Harleys. I cross another street, and enter the oldest part of post. I cut between the coin-operated laundry and military clothing sales shop, which Krieger said were originally built as the officers' bathhouse. Next comes block after block of three-story half-timbered buildings which once housed Bavarian soldiers. Now they are used for the 7th Army Training Command's headquarters company, a Military Police Brigade, and the post's education center. Five minutes later, I stand in front of the post's brand-new medical and dental facility.

Krieger said all of these buildings are here because the Bavarians, the Germans, and the Americans needed the surrounding land for large-scale training, mentioning that Rommel prepped his Afrika Korps on Graf's sandy soil. It's crazy to live and work on an installation that's been home to three nations prepping to fight world wars. We won the Cold War and now deploy soldiers to Southwest Asia to fight the Islamic State and to Poland to train on the Russian border.

Huh, maybe the Cold War isn't over yet.

———

COLD, gray weather moves in on Saturday. Thank goodness I have the gym and class to keep me busy during days of steady rain. It surprises me to learn that before Archduke Ferdinand's assassination started the First World War, the Bavarians were testing machine guns, hot air balloons and biplanes at Graf. During the war they imprisoned fifteen thousand French, Russian and Romanian soldiers here. Well, I can relate to how they must have felt.

On Wednesday the clouds finally move on and I enjoy my rain-free walk to class. Once again the shaggy-haired kid plops down next to me. His name isn't Serpico, it's Andy, and his father is the colonel who oversees the military exercises at Graf.

Krieger dives right into his lecture and sparks classroom discussion by calling on Andy. From their give and take, it seems they know each other.

On break, I ask Andy if he's has Krieger before.

"No, we play hockey together."

"What? Where do you play?"

"Mostly Weiden, but sometimes Mitterteich, Amberg and Pegnitz."

Andy reminds me of my hockey friends back home in Boston. It's much harder to imagine tie-dyed Professor Krieger out on the ice. He's on the small side and he's old, but mostly it's because he's so laid back. So it kills me when Andy says Krieger plays defense. I just can't picture him laying anyone out!

After our ten-minute break, Krieger starts back up. I try to concentrate, but hockey keeps seeping back into my mind. Krieger closes out class by reviewing the quiz answers, and not one answer surprises me. He asks who got all ten questions right, and only me and Squeaky raise our hands.

After class, Squeaky comes over. "Hi, I'm Kelli. I see you at the gym all the time, but you never say hi. Why is that?"

"Uh, hi, I'm Will," I say shyly. "This is Andy."

"Nice to meet you," Andy says. "Hey sorry but I've got to go." When he's out the door, past where Squeaky can see him, he stops and gives me a thumbs up.

Squeaky recaptures my attention by touching my hand. "We should meet for coffee and study together."

"Okay," I stammer.

I'm happy as I walk back to the barracks under a cool, clear night sky. Signing up for school was a damn fine idea.

THE NEXT SET of readings bother me. I can't believe how quickly Hitler took control of the GTA and used it to fine-tune his Nazi war machine. In class Squeaky gives me a quick wave, and I wave back. Professor Krieger leads a discussion that closely tracks the readings. He reviews our quiz, and once again I ace it. As I push myself up from my desk and use it to steady myself, Squeaky stops. She asks me if I want to study with her and suggests we meet right after her Zumba class. I agree and go up to talk with Professor Krieger.

He looks up from his papers. "It's Will, right?"

I nod.

He says, "What can I do for you?"

"For my paper, may I write about the weapons and tactics developed here?"

"They're both good," he says. "How about focusing on one or the other?"

"Aren't they kind of the same, sir? If you don't have machine guns, you can't have trench warfare. If you don't have close support aircraft, you can't have the Blitzkrieg."

"Ah, reading ahead, that's good. I do see your point, but for a short paper and a fifteen minute presentation, you need to pare it down. Keep reading and think about how you could focus either on weapons or tactics," Krieger says, holding the door open for me.

"Need a lift?" he asks.

"No thanks, walking is part of my rehab."

As I start to ask him about hockey, he points at my leg and says. "May I ask what happened?"

"I lost it during a jump." I say.

"Oh, sorry," he says.

I never know how to respond to that. It's right up there with, "Thank you for your service." What am I supposed to say? "Thanks," I mumble. "Hey, is it true that the sand on Bunker Drop Zone was shipped from North Africa on Hitler's orders?"

"That's the urban legend," Krieger says. "They say it

was brought for Rommel to train for desert warfare, but I'm not so sure."

"Why not?"

"The local ceramics industry is here because of the high quality sand in the area, but it's a great story. It's right up there with the one about the water tower being built on Hitler's orders so that he could watch Rommel and his men train." Krieger gives me a quick wave and gets into his well-used VW camper.

"See you next week," I say.

A silver Grateful Dead bumper sticker catches the light from a streetlamp as Krieger drives away.

A DAY LATER, Kelli comes up beside me as I'm running on an elliptical machine. Her cheeks are still flushed from her dance class. "You should join us," she says. "It's way more fun than these stupid machines." Noticing her skin-tight sports top and matching pants, I can only agree.

We shower and change at the gym, and then she drives us over to the Java Café. We argue over who gets to pay and agree to go Dutch. Our study session goes really well, until two women come over to join us. Squeaky introduces them, and I realize all three are officers' wives. Specifically, the wives of cavalry lieutenants who are away for field training.

"Holy shit, I've got to get out of here!" I think, grabbing my stuff and scooting out the back door, without even a glance back.

EIGHT

The daily grind at Graf is driving me nuts. If I'm really on a one-year plan, I still have nine months to go! I don't think my physical therapy appointments and night class will be enough to keep me sane. So, I really look forward to my trip back to Landstuhl. It'll give me a small break. Plus, I fit in there.

During the six-hour bus ride, I notice trucks from all over Europe clogging the Prague to Paris trading route. As we come out of the woods and crest a hill, I see the sprawling military hospital's exterior for the first time. The three-story cement structure vaguely resembles the outer rings of the Pentagon, except the Pentagon's walls are perfectly symmetrical and Landstuhl's shoot out in a bizarre pattern that hugs the shallow valley. Inside it's just as I remembered—spotlessly clean, but disorientating. So disorienting, in fact, that I stop to ask for directions twice to find the prosthetics lab.

In his small waiting area, Jimmy Newsome greets me. Then says, "I understand that you're looking to upgrade to a reactive foot and running blade. Is that right?"

"Yes, sir. My unit deployed and all I really have at is a killer gym. So, I've become a gym rat."

"Good for you! With your stump toughened up, I can make you a socket that fits exactly."

"How long will it take?" I ask.

"I can get you into a custom one today. This morning I'll photo scan your leg to get the tightest fit. That will be important for your transition to the advanced prosthetic now and it will provide enhanced stability for sports later on."

"Sounds great!"

"Today you'll get a reactive foot which has a dynamic response forefoot and shock-absorbing heel; later you'll get a specialized foot for sports."

I nod.

"As you continue rehab, your residual limb will continue to undergo—"

"I'm all in," I interrupt. "Jill said the dynamic response foot will make walking and running feel more natural."

"She's right. The dynamic response foot is for walking and jogging. The running blade is for sprinting or for long distances. Plus, you are authorized a third prosthetic for sports—I call it the Ahab package."

"The what package?"

"Ahab, you know, the sea captain who hunts the whale that took his leg? Well anyway, what sports do you play?"

"Hockey."

"Hockey, eh?" Jimmy smiles. "I've never built a prosthetic for skating. We'll have to get an exception to policy to build it, but if your commander concurs I'll give it a shot."

I nod, wondering if Manning will support it. "Will I be able to return to duty?"

"That depends, what do you do?"

"I'm a paratrooper."

"Huh, only time will tell. With your reactive foot you'll be able to do a lot, but the Army might move you to other duties."

Fuck me, I didn't sign up to be a cook. "Can I at least stay in the infantry?"

"Well, the Army puts push-ups, sit-ups, and the two-mile run at the top of the priority list." He notices my frown and he adds, "Hey, make the most of your downtime. Take college classes, go to the gym, get out and see Europe. Don't worry about things you can't control."

After a morning of measurements, scans, and photos, Mr. Newsome feeds it all into his computer, explaining, "It all goes straight to a milling machine which fabricates your socket on the spot. While we wait, why don't you go get lunch?"

I look for Jill, but she's not in. I run into Specialist Leonard and her enlisted friends. She gives me a hug and introduces me as Will Foley. Thankfully, my PT uniform doesn't show my NCO rank, and I don't have to on-the-spot correct her informality and inappropriate hug. Instead I tell her that I'm running late for an appointment and can't stay for lunch. She makes me promise to text her before she lets me go. I duck into the small Shoppette by the food court, grab a packaged sandwich and apple juice, and go straight back to Jimmy's waiting area to eat.

When he comes back, he says, "Ready to try it? Come on!"

Back in the workroom, we switch out my old socket for one that fits exactly right. We also switch out my dumb foot for one with a springy heel and a motorized forefoot. From the very first step, it feels great. I thank Jimmy, and he hands me my old socket and dumb foot, warning me to keep them as spares. On the ride back to Graf, my mind drifts to Leonard and all the fun we should have had together in Paris.

The next morning is beautiful and sunny. I put on my new foot and walk around to experiment with it. Going to chow, working out, and even sitting around—everything feels better!

After dinner, with the sun still high in the sky, I look out over the gym at the rising slope of Netzaberg hill and decide to walk up it. It's further than it looks, and ends up taking a half-hour to crest the hill. On top, I turn my back on the setting sun and look down on the post and its fairy-tale tower. The sun's slanting rays paint everything in golden hues.

Before Krieger's class, it would have been a beautiful scene. Now it's steeped in history. The Bavarians built it for troops training to hold off the Bohemians. The Nazis seized it, and lost it to the Americans. It quenched NATO's thirst as troops trained to contain the Soviet threat. The Warsaw pact is no longer a thing, but the magnificent tower still stands.

ON TUESDAY MORNINGS Major Manning starts making the twenty-two sick, lame and lazy soldiers on profile remain in formation to watch the sixty-five fit ones do their push-ups, sit-ups and go on a formation run. I hate it, and fall in with the able-bodied troops.

Manning sends me back, saying, "Regular PT violates your medical profile."

"Sir, with my new socket and reactive foot, I can hang."

"Not on my watch, Foley," he says.

Embarrassed and upset, I go stand with the broken. When the fit soldiers finish their run, they stretch in place and the first sergeant reads off administrative announcements. He calls my name, but I miss why.

When he calls us to attention and releases us for personal hygiene and breakfast, I approach him. "I'm sorry, First Sergeant, I heard you call my name but didn't catch why."

Checking his notes, he says, "Report to Major Manning at 17:00."

"For night court?"

"For whatever," he snaps. "Just be there."

Tuesday night is night court. That's when Manning has soldiers and their supervisors report to face the music. Sometimes he just chews them out or issues written reprimands. Other times soldiers face extra duty, fines, and reductions in rank for minor infractions. These cases are handled on the spot with Manning serving as judge, jury and executioner. Soldiers may refuse and demand a trial by court-martial, but that raises the stakes and they face criminal convictions and jail time. In the most serious cases, Manning only serves court-martial charges. Then a military judge handles the case.

Manning hates me for sure, but can't think of anything he could use to set me up for punishment. I go through the motions of a routine day, eat breakfast in the chow hall and go to the gym, but my thoughts keep returning to Manning. He's average height, average weight, and looks like every other plain-vanilla, Army-issued commander. His reptilian eyes are his only unusual feature. They are muddy-brown, flat, and joyless. He allows no emotion to creep across his face and punctuates his statements with a crocodile smile that curls only at the corners of his thin lips. It never reaches his eyes, and somehow shuts down all comments and fore-closes any questions. Make no mistake, he is not a brilliant leader. He doesn't inspire loyalty or respect, just unease. Why on earth did the Army put a psycho like him in charge? The secret must lie in his lifeless eyes. For the Army, the icy control they allow him must be enough. But I sure as hell don't trust him; if he's your friend you don't need enemies.

Just before lunch, I stop by the barracks. Jack is hunched over the coffee table working on a gigantic Eiffel Tower puzzle.

"What's up?" I say, sitting down beside him.

"What?" he says, searching for edges that match the piece in his hand.

"Why are you doing a puzzle?"

"Brittany and I used to do them together. I gave her this one because she loved Paris so much."

"Huh," I say.

"Want to play some 'chell?"

"No," I pause. "I made the night court list."

"Dude, what the fuck did you do?"

"Not a clue," I shrug. "I asked First Sergeant and he said, 'shut up and report.'"

"That's fucked up," Jack says, setting a puzzle piece down and picking up a beer.

"You want to grab some lunch at the chow hall?" I ask.

He shakes his head and points at a half-eaten pizza.

I mope through the afternoon, get a haircut, and go study. My thoughts drift to Nazi Germany and Major Manning. I bet those soulless Nazi psychopaths had the same dead eyes. At 16:30, I go to the barracks, change into my uniform and walk over to the headquarters building. I remove my maroon beret and check myself in a mirror.

Satisfied that my uniform and haircut look good, I go upstairs to the Commander's hallway. Three very unhappy soldiers sit in folding chairs lined up along the wall. About ten feet further up, a group of NCOs stand and talk softly.

First Sergeant Jepson steps out of Manning's office. A strutting rooster of a paratrooper, all of his authority is clearly on loan from Manning. "After you report to the Commander, keep it to 'Yes, Sir,'" he instructs. "Remember, the Commander is not keen on any of you profile riders," he says, checking his notepad. "Is Private First Class Washington and his first-line supervisor here?" he asks.

"Yes, First Sergeant," a young, skinny sergeant answers.

Jepson points at the skinny NCO, "You, come with me."

Five minutes later, the sergeant sticks his head out. "Washington," he says, "knock, wait to be called, and report." Private Washington stands and tentatively taps. Someone inside shouts, "Enter!" and Washington goes inside. Twenty minutes later, Washington and his NCO come out. Washington's face is streaked with tears. As they leave, the sergeant turns and says, "Riley is up next. First Sergeant wants his NCO in first."

A short and squat sergeant pops to his feet. This butterball turns back to his soldier and says, "Maintain your military bearing, Riley, and don't make any excuses."

Another twenty minutes go by.

The same scenario plays out twice more. It is now 19:00, or seven o'clock, and I sit alone in the hallway. For some odd reason, Manning has left my sergeant out of whatever he is going to do to me.

Jepson comes out, "Okay Foley, knock and report."

Standing stiffly, I say, "Yes, First Sergeant." I rap twice

on the Commander's door, still having no idea why I've been summoned.

"Enter!" Manning yells.

Military discipline overrides my fight-or-flight reflex. I close the door and go to the front of Manning's desk. I salute and report. With my peripheral vision, I take in the details of Manning's borrowed office. He is seated squarely behind an old-fashioned wooden desk. First Sergeant Jepson stands to Manning's right. On the walls are photos, diplomas and other I-love-me stuff in cheap, mis-matched frames. Remaining at attention, I hold my rigid salute. "Corporal Foley reporting as ordered, sir."

Manning remains seated and casually returns my salute. This allows me to lower my right arm. However, custom requires me to remain at the position of attention with my eyes 'five degrees above the horizon and five thousand miles away' until Manning orders me to parade rest. That doesn't happen, and I'm forced to remain at attention.

Manning reaches for a piece of paper. "William J. Foley, effective immediately you hold the rank of Specialist. Stand at ease." Manning doesn't raise his voice or change its inflection, infusing his order with an unnerving, unnatural authority.

In shock, I go to at ease by stepping out with my left foot into a comfortable stance and moving my hands to the small of my back. I am now free to look around the room. I focus my attention on Manning, looking for any expression or gesture that might offer a glimmer of humanity. I find nothing. Manning passes the paper to the first sergeant who wordlessly hands it to me. I look down at the simple military order which changes my rank back to specialist.

Manning then pushes a second sheet of paper across his desk for Jepson to pass to me. "Go ahead, take it," Manning says. "It's a bill for the two thousand dollars' worth of military gear you turned into biohazard on the drop zone."

"Sir, I—"

"Shut up, Foley," Manning interrupts. "You don't have to say or do anything. Finance will take the money from your pay." For the first time that night, Manning and I make eye contact. His eyes give nothing away, but I see the corners of his mouth turn up.

Overcome by it all, I stand silent.

"You are dismissed," he says.

I come to attention and salute, holding my eyes five degrees above the horizon and five thousand miles away. Still sitting, Manning returns my salute. I about face and exit his office.

I go and sit stunned and alone in the USO. I was promoted just before the jump. I was so excited. So ambitious. So eager to lead. Now, along with my foot, it's all gone. Until tonight, I didn't realize how important symbols of authority were to me. From before I can remember, I was awed by my father's uniform. My eyes were always drawn to the Sergeant's rank on his collar and shiny badge on his chest. On my jersey, I wore the letter C in the same spot on my chest. It showed the whole world that we were in charge.

Back in our room, Jack points out that losing my Corporal stripes won't change my pay.

"So fucking what," I yell, "he demoted me!" It feels shameful and is highly visible, because my stripes have been be replaced by the black chevron of a specialist.

I dread having to correcting the first person who greets me as Corporal Foley. I doubt that I'll be able to do it without sounding like a whiner. When I enlisted, I told my dad it was for the college money. But deep down, I wanted to prove myself. That's why I volunteered for airborne and pressed so hard to make corporal. Despite it all, I still want the chance to prove myself. I want to test the limits of my courage, my endurance, and my leadership. But the amputation took far more than my foot. It took my Army identity.

NINE

I took pride in wearing my combat uniform, but because it shows the world my rank, I now avoid wearing it. Fat Jack is cool and doesn't tease me about it and by spending extra time at the gym, the Java Café, and in the barracks, I'm able to stay in my PT gear the entire day.

Krieger's class starts after the duty day ends, so I can wear civvies without any fear of reprimand. Andy and the Professor are hockey guys, so I pull on a Bruins sweatshirt before heading out for class. I remain silent all evening, and ace another quiz. Along with a few others, I stay after to get my paper topic approved. When it's my turn, Professor Krieger compliments my Bruins sweatshirt, adding that he grew up a Minnesota North Star fan.

"Not Dallas?" I tease.

"Definitely not Dallas," he laughs. "Hey, you were awfully quiet in class. Are you okay?"

"Sure," I shrug. "May I have the post water tower as my project topic?"

"Huh," Krieger says, stroking his beard. "How so?"

"It's been here from the beginning and still gives us our

water. I guess I'd focus on its role as Graf's silent sentinel and water bearer."

"Nobody's picked it as a topic," he says. "So sure, I look forward to it."

As I leave, Squeaky taps my shoulder. "Wait for me outside."

I go outside and imagine the worst. Is she mad because I embarrassed her in front of her friends? Is her husband back and wants a word with me?

She comes out smiling. "Hey stranger."

"Hey."

"Don't you look so very civilian tonight." she giggles. "I like it!"

"Thanks," I blush. "What's up?"

"I heard you explain your paper topic, it's very cool."

"Thanks."

"I've got the water tower's blueprints, history and historical photos," she says.

"You do?"

"The wives' club does tower tours, and I'm a guide," she says. "I could even give you a private tour."

"Really?"

"Sure," she smiles. "Meet me after Zumba tomorrow."

THE NEXT DAY Squeaky steps out of her Zumba class wearing an eye-popping white body suit. "I've got the keys," she says.

"Okay, meet you out front?"

We pull out of the parking lot and she turns right, saying, "They're at home with the blueprints and other stuff."

"Where do you live?" I ask.

"Little America," she frowns. "Netzaberg."

Netzaberg is the Army's knock-off of a suburb. It's sort of pleasant. It sits up on an isolated hilltop, and has an American school, day care, chapel, gas station and convenience store. About eight-hundred houses are loosely arranged on meandering cul-de-sacs, with landscaping and lots of parking. It's like a low-rent gated community, except there are strict rules about where officers, sergeants and enlisted soldiers may live. The streets with single-family homes are reserved for officers. Even the enlisted duplexes offer freedom from the oppressive twenty-four hour supervision that barracks rats like me must endure.

Squeaky pulls into her garage and kills the engine. "Come in, I don't bite."

Her house is big and smells new. From the foyer, I look through the living room to a large, fenced back yard. "Wow, you've got an enormous place."

"Would you like something to drink?" she asks.

"Ah, sure."

"Watch whatever you want," she says, handing me the remote and a Diet Coke.

I sink into a leather coach and wonder what the heck is going on. When I hear the shower, I imagine Kelli wet, soapy, and naked. Did I miss a signal? Before I can decide, the shower stops. She comes down barefoot, in tight jeans and an oversized Arizona State sweatshirt.

Kelli brings over a folder and drops it in my lap. She leans over and shows me blue-prints, old photos and stories about the tower. The scent of shampoo lingering on her damp hair makes it impossible to concentrate. She asks if I want to stay for lunch, and I point to my bad leg, "I can't let sweat dry."

"You could shower here," she suggests.

I shake my head.

"Why not?" she asks. "Are you gay?"

"No," I say, as ghost pain shoots up my leg, forcing to go ridged.

"Oh my God, are you okay?" Kelli asks. She helps me up, gets me to the car, and drives me back on post. On the way, she apologizes and offers me a rain check on the tower tour. "We can go all the way up, and take some great pictures from the top," she promises.

ON SATURDAY, I sleep late and wake up hating life. My paratrooper's swagger is gone. Small, petty stuff bugs me. It wasn't like that when I was jumping. After a jump, nothing fazed me. After you fall through the sky and land in one piece, nothing bothers you. Sure, you might land ass-first and piss blood for a few days, but so what? When you cheat death, everything else is small potatoes.

To break up the monotony, I skip breakfast and go straight to the gym. After my workout, I walk over to the PX, thinking about how unfair it is that single soldiers have meal cards, while married soldiers and officers are paid the cash value of meals in the chow hall. That gives them the option of spending their money on groceries or eating out. For that small freedom, I should have held out and gone to West Point.

There's a big line at Starbucks; besides, I want something different. I take a hard left and stand in line at the Brunner bakery. It's part of a local chain of bakeries. On the surface, it looks like a Dunkin' Donuts, but the glass case at Brunner's holds German sweets and breads. I love their flaky croissants, the crispy apple tarts, and gooey cherry Danishes. I also like the soft pretzels, and the hard rolls called Semmel. They are crusty on the outside; soft and fluffy on the inside. The locals eat them at every meal. At breakfast they serve them with butter and either cheese, cold cuts, honey, chocolate spread, or jelly. They use them as buns for bratwurst at lunch, and as dinner rolls.

I contemplate whether to order a bratwurst or wiener. Then I settle on getting a Leberkäse Semmel. Heck, everyone knows about bratwursts and wieners, but here I discovered Leberkäse. It's an inch-thick slab of baloney-like meat that's heated and served with spicy mustard. The name is very misleading. It translates directly to "liver cheese" which makes no sense, because it isn't made from liver or cheese. On the Brunner menu they translate it to "Bavarian Meatloaf Sandwich" which is also misleading, because the meatloaf part is way off. Just forget it's crazy name. It's warm, juicy, and wonderful.

The girl behind the counter asks, "Ketchup or Senf?"

I go with mustard, and say, "Senf, and I'll eat it here."

She skips packing it in aluminum foil, and hands it to me on a napkin. I stroll out into the food court's seating area and enjoy a much-needed change from Army chow. I hold my juicy sandwich close, breathe in the savory aroma of warm baloney and fresh bread. My mouth waters as I bite through the crunchy crust, hit the sharp mustard, and reach the warm meat. Man, it's so simple and so freaking tasty.

WEEK five of Krieger's class is boring. After the war, the U.S. took over the GTA and started training. The Army hired Germans to rebuild the GTA, thereby contributing to the Marshall Plan's reconstruction goals. Next week's discussion of the Cold War is far more interesting. The simple good-versus-evil story captures my attention. I wasn't alive when Team USA beat the Soviets at Lake Placid, but I've seen the Disney movie a hundred times. Herb Brooks' pregame speech always gives me goosebumps!

Krieger's class on the Cold War doesn't disappoint. Tensions were high and real-life James Bond type spy stuff kept the world on edge. Elvis trained at Graf, and NATO forces conducted grueling exercises and maneuvered across the German countryside preparing for World War III. Of course I knew all that, but what I didn't know was that NATO wasn't established to defend against the Warsaw pact—the Warsaw pact came years later. The Americans and Europeans aimed to bring Germany into NATO so that they would never again become a dominant, destabilizing bully. The first secretary general said NATO's purpose was, "To keep the Soviet Union out, the Americans in, and the Germans down." Krieger says that it all worked perfectly. The Germans took their post-war pacifism seriously and relied on NATO to provide their defense. The USSR collapsed, and the free world celebrated the end of the Cold War.

Squeaky raises her hand, "If we won, why are we still here?"

"Policy makers still view NATO as vital in keeping Germany tightly wound up in its European identity," Krieger says.

"But do we need to keep Graf to do that?" Squeaky presses.

"Maybe not," Krieger concedes. "But no place on earth better represents the German and American commitment to a united Europe."

After class, Squeaky waits for me by her car.

"Damn, Kelli, you really went after the Professor tonight."

She smiles, "I'm more a lover than a fighter."

I laugh.

"Do you want a ride home?" she asks.

"No, I'm supposed to walk on my reactive foot for rehab."

"Reactive, like bionic?" she asks.

"Yeah," I shrug. "I guess so."

"What other super powers do you have?"

TEN

June ends with a heat wave and the gym is one of the few buildings on post with air conditioning. I finish a punishing cardio workout—an hour of interval training on an elliptical machine to simulate taking one-minute shifts in a hockey game.

"Thank goodness for endorphins," I say to myself, wiping down the machine.

Going up the stairs by the rock-climbing wall, I bump into Squeaky. She says we should do our tower tour. "Bring your phone to take photos for your presentation," she adds.

"Thanks, Kelli," I say, being careful not to slip and call her Squeaky. "Can we do it on Wednesday, before class?"

"It'll take at least an hour, so let's meet for lunch," she suggests.

"Uh, I have a meal card," I say. "Can we meet at two?"

"What's a meal card?"

"For the chow hall—"

"You guys eat for free, right?"

"Something like that," I say, holding my tongue.

"Okay," she beams, "then two o'clock at the tower."

CHOW HALL FOOD is mighty boring but healthy, and my body extracts every nutrient, making me leaner, tougher, and fitter. I'm feeling good, until a smart-ass barracks lawyer tells me, "The Army ain't never gonna let you stay airborne. Mark my words, you gonna serve out your enlistment as a cook." All night long his taunt torments me. The next morning I skip my workout and take the bus down to see Jon.

Looking up from his computer, he says, "Hello Corporal, ah, Specialist Foley. Sorry about that."

"It's okay," I snap. "I'm over it."

"Really?"

"No, but what's the point? I won't get my stripes back."

"Why is that?" Jon asks, setting his coffee down.

"My commander hates me."

"Commanders don't hate their troops," Jon says. "They are required to maintain good order and discipline and can be heavy-handed, but it's not personal."

"When Major Manning took my rank, he also took two-thousand dollars for my jump accident."

"Did he give you an article 15?" Jon asks.

"No, it was a short-something for my jump equipment, but forget I said anything about it," I snap, waving him off.

"Have a seat, Will," Jon says. "Has the money come out of your pay yet?"

I shake my head.

"I'll dig into it, and will try to undo it."

"That's what you said last time, but it's not why I'm here," I say, taking a seat in Jon's small, windowless office. "In the barracks I heard that the Army can force finish my enlistment as a cook. Is that true?"

"Yes and no," Jon sighs. "What you heard about is called the Military Occupation Specialty Administrative Retention Review process, or MAR2. It's a reclassification system for wounded, ill and injured soldiers who meet retention standards but cannot fulfill the requirements of their current job. I haven't brought is up, because it's way too early. However, if you want, I can run through it real quick."

I say okay, wondering what other nasty surprises Jon has in store.

"All right, the bottom line is they can't involuntarily turn you into a cook."

"Or fuel handler?" I ask.

"Right, or anything else. Once your rehab is complete, you might tell your doctor that your primary goal is staying on active duty. Then he or she can refer your case to the MAR2 Board. This is all prior to you entering the IDES process. Are you tracking?"

"Got it," I snap.

"During the MAR2, the Army identifies alternative MOS possibilities."

"Cook, fuel hander?" I ask, crossing my arms.

"Or whatever," Jon leans forward, grabbing a pencil and note pad. "If they find a suitable fit, they have the authority to re-assign you to it and send you off to school for retraining. What's your GT score?"

"One-fourteen."

"That's good," Jon scribbles down some notes, then looks up. "You know, one hundred is average. When I was on active duty, it seemed every other court-martial was a Specialist with a GT score either above one-twenty or below eighty. I guess they were all either too smart or too dumb for the Army. Anyway, a GT of over one-ten gets you into Officer Candidate School, and it will get you into any enlisted job."

I shrug.

"Any interest in being a medic or paralegal?" he asks, poised to write down my answer. I remain silent, so he clears his throat and continues, "The other possibility is that the MAR2 doesn't find another suitable MOS. Then they refer your case to the IDES program."

"What does that mean? Will they kick me out? Will I lose my GI Bill?"

"No. You'd just go to a Physical Review Board and then on to a Medical Review Board to find out if they will let you stay in the Army as an infantryman."

"Airborne infantry," I correct him.

"Right," Jon shifts in his seat. "Serving ninety days on active duty vests your benefits and receiving a service-connected discharge will get you one-hundred percent of your educational benefits."

"I have my ninety days." I state flatly.

"Yes, that vests your benefits. Completing your first term gets you one-hundred percent, but you can also get to one-hundred percent if you're boarded out with a service-connected disability."

"So I'm safe?" I ask.

"Yes, just don't get kicked out for misconduct. That would change everything."

Despite the good news from Jon, my mood stays sour. On the way back to the barracks, I stop by the dining facility for lunch and load up on salad. Then, I wander down to the mailroom. It's likely my box will be empty; it usually is. At first glance my pessimism seems justified, but then I spot a yellow package slip and exchange it for a footlocker-sized cardboard box. I open it outside on the sidewalk and pull out my high school hockey bag. I flatten the box and put it in the recycle bin, swing the bag comfortably over my shoulder, and walk back to the barracks.

My dad doesn't answer on FaceTime, so I write, "My gear made it. Thanks a million! Love, Will." Before I hit send, I think about adding something about the Bruins stunning game six loss to Chicago. Two late goals, seventeen seconds apart, ended the Bruins glorious playoff run. Nope, I think, knowing that my words won't help. There's always next season, right? That's really the only cure for the stinging, season ending loss Chicago handed to our Bruins.

I GOOGLE THE BMC RANGERS. They have a public team page and a private player's only group on Facebook. I open the team page and the first thing I see is a team picture. Krieger wears the captain's C on his chest, Andy stands beside him with an enormous smile on his face, and Robalo peeks out from the back row.

I sign out of Facebook and go down to formation for our weekend safety brief. It's always the same, "Don't drink and drive, have safe sex, stay out of trouble, see you back here on Monday morning." After the cannon booms, Sergeant First Class Jones calls me over. A corn-fed Iowa Hawkeye who's pending discharge for a bad back, he's my new platoon sergeant. "Major Manning wants to see you," he says.

"When, Sergeant?" I ask.

"Now," he says, "let's go."

I ask Jones what it's about.

"It can't be good," he says, shaking his head.

We wait twenty minutes before the first sergeant comes

out to get us. As the one summoned, I step forward and formally report.

Manning asks me, "Are you sleeping with a lieutenant's wife?"

"No, sir."

He pauses, narrowing his eyes into slits. "Are you dating anyone, Foley?" His faint trade-mark smirk twitches at the corners of his cruel mouth.

"Ah," I stutter, trying to understand what the hell is going on. "I, ah, I studied with a girl from my history class."

"Stop talking," he says, holding up his palm like a cop directing traffic. "I don't want to read you your rights."

I stare back, unsure about what to do.

"Don't look at me like I owe you money, Foley. I don't owe you anything." His tone stays as flat as if he were reading serial numbers during an arms room inventory.

I snap back to the position of attention. "Yes, sir."

How can he sit there and calmly accuse me of adultery? I want to look into his eyes and make a human connection that somehow vindicates me, but as a well-trained, disciplined soldier, I say at attention with my eyes five degrees above the horizon. I wait for what seems like an eternity for Manning.

"Kelli Peterson is a married woman, and I could charge you with adultery," he hisses. "Break contact."

"Yes, sir!" I answer, wanting to turn and run.

"Dismissed." Manning says, turning back to his computer screen. "Wait," he says, before I can salute and leave.

I stand fast.

"JAG killed the short-survey for the equipment you turned into biohazard."

I stand stone-faced, knowing better than to say thank you.

"Also, I'm issuing you a no-contact order," he says. "You are not to go within one hundred feet of Mrs. Peterson. Do you understand?"

"Yes, sir!" I answer reflexively. Then add, "But sir, we're in the same class."

"Did I approve that?" Manning asks Sergeant First Class Jones.

Jones shrugs, "Sir, I don't know."

"Foley?" Manning asks, "Did I approve it?"

"Sir, you approved my tuition assistance to pay for it."

"Okay, Foley, you may attend class, but no contact with Mrs. Peterson before, during, or afterwards. The one-hundred-foot rule applies everywhere else."

"Sir, at the gym?"

"Don't test me, Foley," Manning says, his eyes narrowing. "You are dismissed."

I salute, turn and leave.

Outside Sergeant Jones says to me, "Holy shit, stepping out with an officer's wife? You've sure got balls."

"We're just friends," I stammer.

"Sure," he laughs. "It's time for you to make some new friends, Foley."

INSTEAD OF A NORMAL MONDAY-TO-FRIDAY SCHEDULE, my life had shifted to a Wednesday-to-Wednesday schedule with Krieger's class anchoring my life. But now with the no-contact order in place, I dread class. And what about the gym? On Monday and Tuesday, I skip my cardio to avoid being within one hundred feet of her Zumba classes.

On Wednesday, I wait under the tower's arched entryway for Kelli. She arrives, almost skipping, wearing the most revealing Zumba outfit yet—a neon blue number that would get attention at a Brazilian beach party. I wave her in with me and explain the situation. At first she's shocked and then gets pissed at her husband. She apologizes and presses the keys into my hand.

"Give them back to me in class."

Back at the barracks, I tell Jack about it.

"Holy shit, player," he laughs. "Getting busy with Mrs. Lieutenant hot-pants!"

I shake my head "It's not like that. She's nice, and there's nothing going on."

He shrugs and grins. "Yeah figures, 'cause she's way out of your league."

I punch him in the shoulder. "I've got to give the tower keys back to Kelli tonight. Will you go up with me and take some photos?"

Jack nods, and we walk over to the tower. The key opens a heavy wooden front door, and a metal gate at top of the stone stairs. It also opens the rooms on the way to the top. We go into each of the three lower rooms which are set up as small museums for the Bavarian, German and American armies. At the top we find a cat-walk circling the gigantic water tank, and a wooden ladder going up to an attic which sits on top of the huge tank.

"Look, Bro', here's another ladder going up to the roof. Maybe it goes to the spotlight," says Jack.

The key works and we are up the open air, surrounded by a few antennas and the big rotating light. The three hundred and sixty degree view is amazing!

"Dude, you miss jumping?" Jack asks.

"A little," I say. "I miss the thrill of standing up, hooking up, and jumping."

"I miss this, Bro."

"What?"

"This," he points out at the horizon. "When you leave the plane it gets so quiet and still. One time my chute opened with me staring back at the plane. It was silent, like a giant whale floating away from me. Man, it was so peaceful."

I nod in silent agreement.

Jack snaps a bunch of photos on top, and more on our way down. At the bottom he says, "Thanks Bro, been here five years and never even knew you could go inside."

"Normally you can't," I say. "Unless you're on a wives' club tour."

"Hah! Leave it to the wives to get their claws into the biggest phallic symbol in Bavaria!"

IN CLASS, I ask Andy to pass Kelli her keys. She looks over and smiles sadly. I give her a thumbs up and her smile brightens a bit.

Krieger moves on from the Cold War and tells us how the fall of the Berlin Wall complicated things. The reunited Germany became an economic engine for both Eastern and Western Europe. To the prosperous Germans, the American military was like a big, ugly guard dog who shouldn't be allowed inside. Reading from his notes, Krieger says, "In 1991, seventy-nine percent of Germans polled preferred Switzerland, Sweden or Japan as their national role model; only two percent chose the United States." Krieger explains that on top of this, Chancellors Kohl, Schroeder, and Merkel knew Germany's continued success on the world stage would depend on not scaring people. By working through the European Union and NATO, Germany boosted its economic and political power without threatening its neighbors.

Then, the September 11th terror attacks changed everything. The U.S. demanded Germany's support in the global war on terror, insisting that they send troops to Afghanistan. Wrapping up his lecture, Krieger says, "In all this turmoil, the troops going into harm's way trained at the GTA, and still do."

That's exactly why I enlisted—to keep the world safe!

ON THE FOURTH of July the Commanding General opens the post for a huge picnic on the parade ground. The CG goes all out with rock bands, hot dogs, apple pie, and ice cream. Soldiers round it out with coolers full of cold beer. Fat Jack and I find shady seats under a huge aircraft maintenance tent which has been converted into a bandstand. We settle in, listen to Gary Sinise and his Lt. Dan Band play an upbeat set of country and rock favorites. It's fun watching the Germans belt out American favorites. Gary thumps away on his bass and chats up the crowd between songs. Sinise was awesome in Forrest Gump and CSI, and my respect for him grows during the concert. Everybody thanks the troops, but how many stars travel to Bavaria to put on a free concert?

The summer sun lasts so long that the fireworks can't start until after ten o'clock. As darkness finally falls, rockets shoot up over the tower bursting and spilling their sound and color across the clear night sky. It's an unforgettable end to a glorious day spent celebrating America's independence.

In the morning, the daily grind starts again. I've got my research paper and presentation to keep me busy. Between Morgenstern's book and Kelli's papers, there's no shortage of information about Graf's hundred-year-old tower. I work hard, learn a lot, and write a damn fine paper. Given the training area's importance to the Nazi war machine, I'm still baffled by how the tower survived the fierce Allied bombings.

ON A MUGGY TUESDAY NIGHT, Jack invites me to go with him to a local dive bar. Graf has nothing like Fort Benning's seedy Victory Drive—a run-down six lane thoroughfare filled with strip clubs, pawnshops, no-tell motels and tattoo parlors. But Graf does have Gate One, with two tattoo parlors and Ed's. All just a five-minute walk from the post.

"Come on, Bro, it's Tittie Tuesday."

"Nah, I've got class tomorrow."

"That's tomorrow, tonight the waitresses are all topless," Jack grins, holding his hands up cupping imaginary Dolly Parton sized breasts. "Sometimes wild chicks just pull out their boobs for the hell of it. Maybe your gal Squeaky will show up and flash us!"

"That's stupid," I say. "What does Brittany think of you hanging out at Ed's?"

"What happens at Ed's, stays at Ed's," Jack says, grabbing his crotch.

"I have to finish my presentation," I say, pointing at my laptop.

"Bookworm pussy," Jack taunts and then leaves me to study in peace.

I'm nervous about my presentation. Up at the very end, following Andy, my nervousness has time to ferment. Andy discusses weapons tested at the GTA, starting with horse-drawn howitzers, early machine guns, and biplanes. He moves on to Nazi rail-mounted super cannons, tanks, and improved automatic weapons. He wraps up with America's multiple launch rocket systems and helicopter-fired hellfire rockets. As he finishes, I'm happy that I switched my topic from weapons to the tower.

Up at the podium, I remember Jack's crack about the wives getting their hands on the phallic monument. I look over at Kelli and grin. She gives me a thumbs up. Then, I begin by showing blueprints and giving a technical description of our post's most famous landmark. I explain that by 1910 the four-teen-story, half-timbered tower provided water to Bavarian troops. I show the photos Jack took, and address the urban legend that Hitler watched Rommel's maneuvers from the top of the tower. "There are meeting rooms in the tower's stem," I explain, "but the half-timber chalet on top houses the enormous water tank. The windows and shutters are decorative and there's nothing but a small catwalk behind them."

I end with a new piece of tower trivia that Professor Krieger shared with me just before class. "In 1945, two devastating Allied bombing raids destroyed rows of stables that sat where the new barracks are today. They were destroyed, but the tower wasn't damaged at all. This wasn't a mistake, because the Allied pilots used it as a landmark and needed it to remain standing." I wrap up my presentation by observing that we don't just live and work under the tower's shadow, we also drink its water and are part of its ongoing history.

Everyone claps, and Kelli winks.

I feel great about my presentation, and stay after to talk with Professor Krieger. "Thanks for teaching a great class," I say.

"Petty flattery won't improve your final grade," he grins. "You did great. Will you take a political science courses next?"

"I'll look into it," I say. Then I turn to the question I really want to ask. "Are you the coach of the BMC Rangers?"

"I can't plead guilty to that, but I play."

I tell him about my experience playing in Boston and he says, "Every year is a rebuilding year for us, and new players are always welcome."

Just before lights out, I send him a friend request and he adds me to the players group. The next morning, I type: "I'm new & need a ride from 173rd barracks. Anyone willing?"

In the afternoon a player named Scrappy answers, "No problem. Meet me out front at four."

ELEVEN

My ride to practice pulls up, pops his trunk, and I stuff in my gear. As we drive away, the post fades from view and it feels great.

John "Scrappy" Dunlap is lanky, and has a quick, hyper smile. Most Army Privates are about twenty, but he looks to be about thirty. He taps the steering wheel with his thumb and fills small silences with chatter, telling me his life story before we get half-way to Weiden. He says his 'Army gig' is only temporary. He'd racked up a pile of student debt, and the Army agreed to repay it at the end of his enlistment. He claims to be a very good goalie, who played high-end hockey in Tacoma with T. J. Oshie.

Tacoma? I guess anywhere they lay down ice, there can be high-end hockey.

Scrappy tells me he bought his fifteen-year-old BMW for $2,500 and hopes to sell to it for $3,000 when he leaves next year. He then launches into a monologue about the greatness of the BMC Rangers. Being around another player, even a goalie, reminds me of how much I miss being part of this rambunctious brotherhood.

"My sergeants are all down on me for being a college-boy, but with the Rangers it's totally different," he says. "There's no rank at the rink." Scrappy explains that privates, colonels, and everybody in between just plays and nobody pulls rank. Still smarting from my demotion, I remain silent.

Scrappy turns left onto Martin Luther Strasse, Weiden's main north-south street. A mile later he turns left into a parking lot which runs the length of a large L-shaped building. Scrappy explains that it houses the city's hockey stadium, practice rink, and spa, and adds that the spa has an indoor/outdoor swimming pool, saunas and salt grotto.

We get out, grab our gear, and walk across the parking lot. Having my bag slung over my shoulder and riding low on my hip is an old, comfortable feeling. I follow Scrappy down wide cement steps through the players' entrance and into the rink. The sights, smells, and sounds are identical to the rinks all over New England. The smell isn't exactly pleasant—like the distinctive oregano smell in an Italian restaurant—but it's every bit as unforgettable and brings back happy memories. Then, the Zamboni rolls onto the ice. The scraping sound it makes as it resurfaces the ice brings me to the edge of sensory overload!

The locker room is full of players taping sticks, putting on gear, and having a good time. Scrappy takes the seat nearest the door, the traditional spot for a goalie. I go deeper into the crowded locker room and squeeze into a spot between Andy and a player using a sharpening stone. Tie-dyed Krieger sits further back, and gives me a wave. I undressing and soak it all in.

The tall guy putting an edge on his blades looks down at my hockey foot and says, "Jeez, we've got gimps playing now?"

"Shut up, McMouth!" Andy shouts.

"No hard feelings," he says, reaching out to shake my hand. "Call me Hands."

I nod, pulling my hand away.

McMouth points at my prosthetic. "You lose it to a roadside bomb?"

"No, a training accident."

"That's fucked up," he grins. "I thought I was sitting next to a war hero."

Krieger jumps to his feet and shouts, "McMouth, last warning."

I flush, but still have enough wits to remember McMouth's jersey number. When we scrimmage, I'll have a little something extra for that loud-mouth.

As McMouth goes into the hallway, Andy says, "Don't worry about that asshole."

Looking down at my prosthetic, I wonder how it will work. Hopefully well enough to drive McMouth through the boards.

More players arrive. Smack-talking and laughter mix with the rattle of equipment. Players pull on protective cups, strap on hard plastic shin pads, pull up thigh-high socks and step into padded shorts which are reinforced with hard plastic thigh and kidney pads. Most slow down and take great care with their skates, testing for a perfect fit while pulling laces tight. Colorful jerseys go on over shoulder and elbow pads. The hard-shelled helmets have either half-glass visors or full-face wire masks. Padded leather gloves go on last.

I fall behind and have to quickly put on my gear. When I get to my skates, my left one feels good. I try the right, and it feels wrong. I open it wide but it still doesn't fit. So I pull the laces completely out, but it's still difficult—like trying to stuff an ugly sister's foot into Cinderella's glass slipper. It finally does go in, but as I work the laces back into my skate it feels dead. I pull on my shoulder and elbow pads half-heartedly, and hope for the best.

An older guy with a white goatee appears in the door-way, and everyone stops talking. With his skates, black sweats, and a baseball cap, he looks a little like Don Cherry.

Andy whispers, "That's Coach."

"Okay boys, listen up," Coach says. "Welcome to a new season of Rangers hockey. The Zamboni is off. Time for warm-ups."

Players grab their sticks and walk across rubber mats to the ice, looking like modern-day gladiators going to battle. The goalies, still struggling to get ready, lag behind. Their protective gear is heavier-duty. Thick leather leg pads go from toes to mid-thigh, and a bulky integrated arm, chest and abdomen protector covers everything but their heads and hands. The back of their stick hand is protected by a stiff rectangular waffle pad, and on their catching hand their glove is a lot like a first baseman's padded mitt. Once dressed, they waddle out with pointy-faced goalie masks pushed up on their heads.

"Sir, what color jersey should I wear?" I ask Coach.

"Go with white and take a dark one to the bench— sometimes I need to even teams up out there."

"Thank you, sir."

"Just call me Coach."

Going from the steamy locker room into the cool rink is bracing and feels great. I step out onto the ice, glide, and take a right turn. Raising my stick over my head, I stretch. Then I bend to touch my toes, gliding past players getting loose along the boards. Skating slowly, I twist my torso from side to side. It would feel good, except for the dead weight below my right knee. My left skate digs into the ice and responds the way it should. My right skate just drags along. I stop. My right skate catches awkwardly and I crash into the boards. Everyone looks. Krieger comes over to check and I wave him off. I take another lap and try to stop on a blue line, fall, and slide helplessly across center ice. I get up, go to the bench, and grab my black jersey.

As I glide towards the locker room, Coach skates up beside me and says. "You're going the wrong way."

I look down at my prosthetic and point, "It doesn't work."

"Give it some time, Foley. You can come back anytime."

As I step off of the ice, I've never felt lower or more alone. While I undress, I realize that I must wait for Scrappy for my ride back to Graf. Damn it, hockey was life and I want it back!

I put on my street clothes, regain a little composure, and go stand at the glass. Players whiz by, set up plays, and take shots. They are professional soldiers, but on the ice they are kids again. Former high school and college players are back in their element. Guys who never played organized hockey finally have a real team to play on. Their joy is visible, and I love it. But in hockey skating is everything, and I can't skate.

Everyone is loose and relaxed after practice. Everyone except me. Krieger goes by with a rack of beer blanketed with six inches of Zamboni snow. As I wait outside, I hear them joke and toast the new season.

THAT NIGHT, in the nearly deserted barracks building, I wake often. Sure, it could be worse. I could have died in Poland. To take my mind off my worries, I imagine Squeaky and touch myself. Right away, pain shoots up from my missing foot. *Holy fuck*, what is wrong with me? My mind jumps to Father Murphy. I miss that guy. He was the only one I could talk to after Mom died. Boy, he'd laugh his ass off about my masturbation problem. I turn my thoughts to safer subjects, like jumping into combat with my brothers-in-arms and playing for the BMC Rangers, and I resolve to keep working to get my old life back.

ON A CLOUDY TUESDAY, just before lunch, I check in to physical therapy. It's in a large, open-bay room in back, behind a hallway flanked by small examination rooms. It's a nice set up, but I don't look forward to like in Landstuhl. Here, we assigned a random therapist each session. They're all nice, but none of them is Jill.

When I arrive, two soldiers are already working with their therapists. Jean waves to me from the far corner. That's good, because she's a tough. Five minutes into our session, she asks, "What's wrong?"

"I tried to skate yesterday," I say, stretching. "It was a complete no-go."

"How so?" she asks, as I start my balance exercises.

"My reactive foot doesn't flex. So, I was basically skating on one leg."

"You should ask Landstuhl to build you a foot for hockey."

"Yeah," I say half-heartedly, recalling what Jimmy Newsome said about needing my commander's approval.

"Seriously, look in to it. If anyone knows how to get it done, it'll be Jon Hoffmann."

I skip lunch and take the bus to Vilseck. Jon is out, and

the man in the next office says he won't be back until Friday. Waiting three days gives me a lot of time to worry. How can I explain to a self-indulgent civilian what hockey means to me? If the Hoff had played, he'd understand that out on the ice there are no deadlines, distractions, or outside obligations. Playing is a complete break from life.

It's also hard. Hockey challenges me more than anything, and I'm good at it. At least I was, when I was whole. Nothing completes me than being on the ice, skating hard, with my mind racing to process all the action. When I read the game, react instinctively, and execute smoothly, I'm in the zone. Deep in it, I can anticipate plays and make the other players struggle to keep up with me. It feels so fluid and magical. How can I explain it to someone who's never played? And what about Manning? That mean little motherfucker might disapprove it just to screw with me.

ON THURSDAY, when I come back from my afternoon strength session, Fat Jack sits on the couch in his underwear —eating pizza, drinking beer, and watching porn. My prized Easton stick rests between his naked thighs.

"Jack, what the fuck?"

"Want some?" he says, motioning towards the pizza.

"What are you doing with my stick?"

"Eatin' pizza and watchin' porn," he grins.

"You pig," I say, grabbing my stick. "It better not be greasy!"

"Greasy is the least of your worries, Bro," he laughs.

"Don't you evah touch my stick!" I shout.

He ignores me and stares at a blond giving some guy a blow-job.

I turn away in disgust, lay my prized Easton on my bed, and slam the door on my way out.

ON FRIDAY, I skip morning cardio to take the bus to Vilseck. I knock on Mr. Hoffmann's door frame, he looks up from his bagel, and says, "What can I do for you, Corporal Foley?"

"Sir, like I said before, I'm a specialist now."

"Oh, sorry. Have a seat," he says, washing his breakfast down with a quick swig of coffee. "What happened?"

"I got moved off of my fire team to the rear detachment, and my new commander took my stripes to free them up for another E-4 team leader, but I'm not here for that," I say. "Jean over at physical therapy said you might be able to help me get a sports prosthetic."

"You're not in trouble at your unit, right?"

"No, sir," I snap, glaring at Jon.

"Like I told you last time, please don't call me sir. But okay, you're not in any trouble. That's good, because to get this approved, your commander must concur."

Jeez, my hockey hopes ride on a guy who breaks a sweat chewing an oversized bagel taking on Manning. I take in a thin, jagged breath and hold it, trying to keep myself together. I breathe out and start talking. "Last week, I tried to use my reactive foot for ice skating, and it didn't work. Jean said maybe you could help me get a foot for hockey. Is that possible?"

"Well, we'll have to put in a specific request for it, and must demonstrate why it has to be for hockey. Why, for example, is hockey better than running, hiking, or skiing? Next, we have to explain why the prosthetics you have doesn't work, and what exactly you'll need to play again."

While he rifles through his messy desk, I check out the framed certificates on his wall. Wow, he served in a Ranger battalion. Finally, he comes up with a notebook. "So, why hockey?" he asks, "Why not biking or tennis?"

I pause a moment, then it all comes rushing out. "It's the skating, passing, and shooting. I'm never as free as when I glide, turning from front to back, swooping like a bird flying low over the ice. It's pure magic."

Jon looks up, smiling. "That's how I felt when my old man took the training wheels off my bike. That crazy sense of rolling effortlessly and then leaning into that first turn, not knowing what exactly keeps you up. Like that?"

"Exactly, except you can make those same effortless turns going forward and backward. And you can do it on one foot, on the other foot, or on both. It's always a rush, and then you add in the passing and shooting, with all of it taking place at top speed," I say, smiling back.

"Tell me about the passing part," Jon says.

"You look over the ice like a quarterback scrambling and looking for receivers. With a flick of my wrist, I can send the puck anywhere I want, and after I give a pass, I normally go to the net looking for a return pass. That's called a give-and-go. It's an amazing feeling to shoot right off of the return pass."

"Okay, tell me about shooting. What's it like?"

"Do you play golf?" I ask.

"Not well."

"Tennis?"

"Even worse."

"Hmm, well, taking a shot is just like taking an easy swing in golf, tennis, and baseball. The ball just explodes away from you and sails through the air, going where you willed it to go. It's weird, because when the puck sails away it's like you aren't a part of it. The puck leaves my stick at seventy miles an hour. And as easily as breathing, I can put it in the top corner—right up where Mama keeps the peanut butter!"

Jon smiles, taking notes furiously. "Keep going," he says.

"For players, shooting drills and scrimmaging are the best part of any practice. With shooting you have lots of options. You can shoot forehand, backhand, take a wrist shot, a quick snapshot, or you can wind up and blast a slap shot. Everyone loves the slap shot. It's not accurate, but the sound and the fury is amazing. It's like hammering a golf ball with a driver, except you've got a crazy guy in pads twenty feet in front of you, and if you drive it past him you score!" I realize that I'm sitting up on the edge of the chair, nearly shouting. I force myself to relax and slide back.

"Okay, this is all great stuff. Anything else you can tell me about hockey being your thing?"

"For sure, hockey's fast. It's faster than any other team sport. And it's not just the speed, there's also hitting. I get a huge adrenaline rush every time I play. First off, I'm a predator looking to hit my opponent. But when I have the puck, I have to keep my head on a swivel. So, you've got the speed of skiing, the violence of football, and the flow of basketball.

Then there's all the teamwork. You're not alone on the ice. The forwards, the defensemen and the goalie all work together to defend, win the puck, pass, shoot, and score." I pause, taking in an excited breath.

"Okay, that's perfect, I can use all of it," Jon says, turning to a blank page. "Can you explain why your reactive foot doesn't work?"

"I got it into my skate, but it was just dead weight. When I pushed off, or tried to stop, it didn't work."

"What does it need to do in order to work?"

I pause, trying to think of something. "Do you ski?"

"I do," he says with a broad smile. "That's my sport."

"Okay, skiing is a lot like skating. When you turn to the right, your weight goes on the inside of your left foot and on the outside of your right foot. When you turn to the left, it's the opposite."

"Yes, exactly."

"But when you ski, gravity does most of the work. With skating, each stride you push your foot out to the side to generate your forward motion. You pump your legs and finish each stride by kicking out your foot. That gives you full extension. On my left side, I'm good. On my right side, I've got nothing. I can't turn very well, and just kind of skid to a sloppy stop. To do those things, I need to be able to dig both blades into the ice."

"You know a lot," Jon says, continuing to jot notes.

"I've been playing my whole life," I say, leaning in.

"So, is there anything written that describes the mechanics of how to skate?"

"I'm not sure," I confess.

"When I send this up, it must describe exactly what you need. Is there anything that describes exactly what your ankle needs to do each stride?"

"In camp we had Laura Stamm's power skating," I answer.

"Okay, tell me about it."

"She was a figure skater who became a power-skating guru. The coaches always talked about her methods and drills. Her basic idea was to get players to skate lower, making them faster and more stable."

"All right, I'll look up more about power skating. Let me draft this and send it to my attorney at Fort Bragg for review. Then it'll send it to your commander for his approval. Check back in a couple of days for an update, okay?"

"Ah, my commander is pretty upset about the gear he ordered me to pay for."

"Don't worry," Jon says, standing to shake my hand. "We've got a good shot."

"Thanks, it means a lot."

On the bus back to Graf, my doubts grow. What will Manning do with my request? Will he punish me for fighting him on the biohazard gear? Does he really believe that I committed adultery? He can't go against the medical folks can he? Well, one thing is clear, the mean little son of a bitch won't go out of his way to do me any favors.

TWELVE

When the Army switched my orders from Italy to Germany, Kevin warned me about Grafenwöhr. He had worked at Graf during cadet summer training, and some of his West Point classmates had much easier duty at the big headquarters in Wiesbaden and Stuttgart. He said field training at the GTA was miserable. Bright-blue Bavarian skies disappeared behind a heavy blanket of clouds. Rain could harden into sleet or snow. Now I know it is all true; last Halloween, it jumped from Indian summer to six inches of snow within a few short hours.

Another big minus is that Graf is way out in the boondocks, and doesn't have a passenger train station. So soldiers who don't have wheels have to bum rides or pay big cab fares to get off post.

Today, the weather cooperates and sunshine pours in through the chow hall's floor-to-ceiling windows. Scrappy joins me for lunch, and we catch up on hockey. He claims Vancouver made some excellent trades and predicts that they'll win the Stanley Cup next season. I tell him he's nuts, because Boston's the team to beat. "Remember Timmy

Thomas and Marchand having their way with the Sedin twins?" I taunt, "Rask is better than Thomas, and Marchand gets better every season."

"Nobody told the Chicago Blackhawks," Scrappy grins.

Ouch, there's no comeback for that, so I ask him how he got his BMW.

"Spend some real money, and get a car that was built to drive on the Autobahn," he says.

His advice makes sense to me, because Scrappy's Autobahn cruiser can really fly.

Back at the barracks, I call home and tell Dad about Scrappy's car. I explain that if I spend $5,000 now, I could sell it for $4,000 or $5,000 when I leave. He seems to agree, until I ask him for a $5,000 loan.

"Willie, money doesn't grow on trees," he says. "Won't the bank lend you the money?"

I admit that I hadn't looked into it yet.

The next day I meet with a loan officer. He says they only loan eighty percent of a used car's Blue Book value. I'm okay with it, and start looking for my dream car. My timing is great, because about a third of the soldiers on post rotate back to the States each summer. So, there should be lots of cars for sale.

There's a week of steady rain, and I check the lemon lot every day. The weather finally changes for the better, and on my way to physical therapy I spot a BMW sports coupe with a 'For Sale' sign. For a nine-year-old car, it looks great. It has less than two-hundred-thousand kilometers, and the asking price is $7,500. I take cellphone pictures of the car and the seller's telephone number. Down through the driver's side windshield, I also snap a picture of the car's VIN number.

For as long as I can remember, BMWs have caught my

eye. In Boston, they were always rare and pricey. I go online and check the Blue Book price. It shows $5,500. Hey, I think, the damn car is overpriced by at least two grand. I call the owner and when we get down to business I say, "Blue Book is $5,000, so the bank will only loan me $4,000." He insists the car is in great shape and he can't go below $7,500. We agree to disagree, but he asks for my contact information anyway.

———————

THAT AFTERNOON, I get a text from Jon Hoffmann. It reads, "Your hockey leg was disapproved." I call to ask why, but Jon doesn't answer. So I go to Brunner's for a mid-after-noon Leberkäse Semmel, and then head to the gym for a punishing cardio session. The whole time I wonder, "Why would they disapprove it?"

The next day, Jon texts me just before lunch saying he's in if I want to call about my hockey foot. I call right away, and he answers. "Soldiers' Counsel Paralegal, Mr. Hoff-mann, may I help you?"

"Hi, it's Will Foley."

"Oh," Jon pauses, and I picture him taking a big swig of coffee. "Hold on, let me open your file."

I wait.

"Are you still there?" he asks.

"Yes," I snap.

"Well, everything was on track. Mr. Newsome can build it by combining the parts from skiing and hiking feet—"

"That's great!"

"—but your commander non-concurred."

"What!"

"Major Manning checked non-concur," Jon says. "He didn't annotate why. Ah, are you pending anything? Maybe an Article 15 or chapter action for minor misconduct?"

"No, sir," I say, wondering if maybe the Squeaky thing is a bigger deal than I thought. Would they court-martial me for meeting her at the tower? "Mr. Hoffmann, what's the penalty for disobeying an order?"

"From an officer?"

"Yes."

"In war the penalty is death, but because Congress hasn't declared war since 1941, the max is five years confinement and a dishonorable discharge."

"You're shitting me," I gasp.

"No," he answers, "did you cross your commander?"

"No, sir," I stammer, "I mean, I don't think so."

"Calm down," he says. "Did your unit hold a urinalysis lately?"

"No, and I'm clean."

"Okay, I'm just trying to figure this out," he says. "I'll scan and send you the non-concurrence. Use your unit's open door policy to ask Major Manning about it."

Fuck me, I'd rather go to jail for five years than confront Manning.

THE CALENDAR CHANGES from August to September, and there's a big drop in the availability of just-past-their-prime sports cars. I had almost forgotten about my dream BMW until its owner calls. "I fly tomorrow," he says. "If you still want it, I'll sell for $5,000."

I've been well-coached by Scrappy and ask, "Will it pass inspection?"

"It passed within the last thirty days," he says. "So it's still good."

The next morning we meet at the vehicle registry office. I have a cashier's check for $5,000 and by nine o'clock I own a blue 2004 BMW with new plates, military registration papers, and an AAFES gas card. The first thing I do is take it for a drive to the rink and back. My new freedom is pure joy!

THAT NIGHT, I wait in the command hallway for Major Manning to finish night court. Even though it's at my request, I hate being here. I formally report. Putting me at parade rest, he asks me what I want. I request permission to approach and hand him the transmittal, asking, "Sir, why did you disapprove my prosthetic?"

He tosses the paper aside. "Are you questioning my judgement?"

"No, sir!" I say, snapping to the position of attention. "My Soldiers Counsel said you might have many reasons to disapprove it and asked me to see you about it." The seconds tick by and a nervous tremor shivers through my lower belly.

Manning looks at the paper, examines it, and finally says, "I didn't disapprove it, I merely non-concurred."

"Sir, my paralegal said everything was good until your non-concur killed it."

Manning again leaves me waiting in a silence which feels like an eternity.

"What does ice skating have to do with soldiering?" he says, punctuating it with an icy don't-you-dare-answer-me stare. "How does it help the United States win its wars?"

This time, he seems to want an answer, so I tentatively say, "Sir, the idea is to make me whole again. I was a hell of a hockey player, and playing will give me a challenge and a chance to prove myself."

"Play where?"

"On the post team, the BMC Rangers," I say, standing rock still waiting for his answer.

He smooths out the paper, grabs a pen, writes something, and hands it to me, saying, "Don't make me regret this."

Outside, where I can once again breathe, I look. Manning crossed out "non-concur" and wrote "CON-CUR" in all caps.

The next morning I call Jon, and he tells me to bring the paperwork to him. When I get there, he calls Landstuhl and then scans and sends them a copy. He tells me, "Go get a haircut or something and come back in an hour."

I go sit in my car, with my joy muted by a nagging pessimism. What will go wrong next?

THIRTEEN

Jon must be a lousy poker player, because before he says even one word I already know we're in the clear. Within minutes of getting the glorious news, I'm on my way back to the barracks for a celebratory beer and pizza lunch with Fat Jack.

A week later, Jon calls to say my foot is ready. Minutes later, I'm cruising down the autobahn. It's empty all the way to Nuremberg and I take full advantage. Even when the traffic gets thicker near Mannheim, I love being at the wheel, listening to German rock stations, and thinking about my hockey foot. After driving four hours, I exit just past K'town and cut through woods to a cluster of metal sheds at the main gate. I roll down my window and hand the security guard my ID card. The guard looks inside the car, checks my photo and scans the barcode on back. After a brief pause, her card reader beeps and she waves me forward. I drive half a mile, park, and go inside the sprawling hospital. Everything is still spotless. The layout is still odd and it's a little too warm—just like my BMW, there's no air conditioning.

Jimmy Newsome sports a freshly cut flat-top. He greets me warmly and says, "We've really knocked it out of the park! Come, I'll show you." Back in his workshop, he has two feet propped up on a workbench. "I did a hockey foot and a running blade. You'll be able to snap off your reactive foot, and snap on either of the other two. What do you think?"

I'm speechless, with an enormous smile plastered across my face.

"Sit down. I'll show you how they work." He holds up my new socket and uses its quick release coupler to attach and detach each foot. "Your foot is the interface between you and the ground. I try to emulate an anatomical foot, but achieving it under varying conditions is pretty much impossible. To make it work, I focus on mimicking anatomical functions for a specific activity."

"That makes sense," I say.

Jimmy has me try the running blade first. It feels weirdly light and springy. In scientific gibberish, he explains, "It has a significant amount of deflection on weight-bearing that adds to its shock absorbing qualities." I examine the running shoe tread glued directly to the bottom. Jimmy notices and says, "Putting tread on the plantar surface eliminates the need for a shoe and reduces weight." That may be true, but it sure looks strange.

Jimmy hands me my hockey foot. It looks like my reactive foot, except the motorized ankle flexes and turns in every direction, instead of just going north and south. Jimmy smiles, "Most athletes leave it in their sport shoe or boot and just snap the entire thing on and off." He points at the sole of his shoe and says, "Others, like downhill skiers, do without a boot altogether. Their prosthetic ends with a binding clip which eliminates the need for a boot, just like your blade."

When Jimmy takes my old socket and reactive foot over to his bench to switch in quick release coupler. I put on the new one and switch out the blade for my hockey foot. I take a few steps. It feels like an awkward version of my reactive foot.

"It's not for walking," he says. "It's built to mimic your ankle when skating."

"Teemu Selanne said that hockey quickness comes from the ankle."

"Who?"

"Selanne, the Finnish Flash?"

Shaking his head, Jimmy says, "You got me there. Anyhow, your new ankle will be as quick as ever, maybe quicker." Jimmy hands me a package of gel liners, explaining that the cushioning and sheer reducing properties make them important for high-impact sports. "Your skin's tolerance is a very important part of this, and these liners have medical grade mineral oil in them to keep your scar from drying out."

I nod along as Jimmy continues. "Use the three-millimeter liners first, but if you need more protection switch to the six or nine-millimeter ones." He stresses that it's critical to limit residual limb motion in my socket, and points out my new socket's airtight sleeve and it's expulsion valve. "Try it," he says. Each step pushes a little air out, creating a vacuum and maintaining a perfect seal. Jimmy points, and says, "It also serves as a vertical shock absorber."

"I'm back, baby! I'm back!" I say, pumping my fists in the air.

Jimmy and I high five, I switch back to my reactive foot, and say goodbye.

I go and meet Jill in the hospital's small dining facility. She's still the brightest person in this drab place, and we hug. After we get our food, I show her my new gear. I tell how hard it's been in the rear detachment. Thank her for recommending night class, saying how much I enjoyed it and how disappointed I am that there aren't any more live classes until spring. I hold back and don't tell her about being demoted or accused of adultery.

"At Graf, hockey is my only positive," I confess.

"Really?" she asks.

"At the rink, I can forget about the bad stuff," I say. "I can't wait to play again."

"I'm glad for you, Sugar," Jill beams. "Hey, when are you gonna call Jesse?"

"Who?" I ask.

"Leonard, you jackass!"

"Ah," I blush. "I never used her first name."

"She still talks about you, and she's at Graf right now."

"Really?"

"Yes," Jill says, flashing her hundred-watt smile.

"What's she doing at Graf?"

"She's at PL-something," Jill says, splashing a spoonful of watery Gumbo back into her soup bowl.

"PLDC?" I ask.

"I think so, but I can never keep Army schools straight. Y'all should just give them normal names."

"She's at the school for new sergeants?"

"Yeah, that's it! She made sergeant last month."

Fuck me, *Specialist* Foley can't date *Sergeant* Leonard! I stab a fish stick and chew on it to keep from saying anything stupid. After dinner, I give Jill a quick hug and promise to score a bunch of goals with the stick she gave me.

On the Autobahn, I blast hockey music—the rock classics by AC/DC, Metallica and Van Halen, and a few newer songs by bands playing with the same driving beat and hard edge. I speed along and hold the left lane against an obnoxious red Porsche who tailgates me and flashes his left blinker. After a minute or two blocking him, I move over to the right lane. He roars by, and I pull out, trying to keep up. In no time, his taillights disappear in the distance. I ease back and settle in to the flow of traffic, and my mind drifts to Leonard; she really was my angel of mercy.

BACK ON POST, I admire the moonlit sky and listen to the wind blowing through the pines. Upstairs I can't fall asleep. So, I fantasize about Leonard. In my imagination she conducts an inspection. I wait comfortably at parade rest, with my right hand resting easily on the barrel of an M-16 and the back of my left hand cradled in the small of my back. She scrutinizes each trooper, working her way down to me. When she finishes inspecting the man to my right, he snaps to order arms and goes back to parade rest. She cross-steps smartly over to me and executes a left face, putting her nose inches from my chin. I immediately move from parade rest to attention, bracing for her close inspection.

She starts at the top, "You need a haircut."

"Yes, Sergeant," I say, remaining locked up with my eyes five degrees above the horizon and five thousand miles away.

She leans in and sniffs my neck on both sides. "When was your last shower?"

"Yesterday, Sergeant," I answer, continuing to hold myself rigid.

"You stink," she says, raking her eyes across my chest

and slowly going down to the shiny cap toes of my paratrooper boots. Finding nothing to gig, her eyes snap back up to mine.

I want to kiss her, but I'm not allowed to even meet her gaze. Being so close to her excites me. Not nervously excited, because I've prepared for her inspection. I'm sexually excited in the extreme.

Her hand shoots out, grabbing me down low. "What's this, soldier?" she asks.

"My balls, Sergeant," I bark, trying to maintain military bearing.

She rubs through my pants, "And this?"

"My cock, Sergeant!"

Suddenly, she's on her knees with my cock in her mouth. She grips my balls with one hand, and grabs my ass cheek with the other.

My hips rock.

She gives my balls a sharp twist, and says, "Lock it up."

"Yes, Sergeant," I say, bracing.

She grabs my ass with both hands and pulls me in deeper. I explode. She stands and wipes the back of her hand across her mouth. "Button yourself up," she orders.

"Yes, Sergeant," I respond.

Drifting off to sleep, I realize it didn't trigger any ghost pain this time. Weird, but hey, I'll take it.

AFTER LUNCH ON SUNDAY, I video chat with Dad, telling him about my hockey foot and BMW. He's happy for me, but seems a little distracted.

"How are you doing?" I ask.

"Ah, you know," he says.

I tell him I miss him, and how my bionic foot should work out on the ice. We share a brief laugh about Mr. Roboto, he hangs up, and we go on about our business on either side of the Atlantic.

It's still two long days until the practice, and I'm just like a little kid waiting for Christmas. This time around, I'm much smarter and test my skate in my room. The new prosthetic fits perfectly. Man, I'm dying to try it out!

―――――――――

I FINALLY GET to pick up Scrappy. Our practice is in Amberg, a medieval walled city about thirty minutes south of Graf. The shortest route is on a two-lane blacktop which has a speed limit. Scrappy suggests we take the long way on the autobahn which has no speed limit. I drive east towards Weiden, and then south on the autobahn towards Regensburg. Trucks, road construction, and speed limits frustrate me, but when I head west towards Nuremberg, I find open road. My speedometer shoots past ninety-nine miles per hour with no sign of topping out. I hit one hundred and ten, and ease back.

"Outstanding!" Scrappy yells over the road noise.

Ten minutes later, I'm driving through Amberg. The Altstadt, or old town, is ringed by a grass-filled moat flanked by a thirty-foot granite walls. It has gothic buildings, cobblestone streets, and a pedestrian-only shopping area. The ice hall is about a mile from the shopping area. It's a big metal barn sitting between the city's indoor pool, tennis park, and fairgrounds. I park and we carry our gear inside.

Hockey players are superstitious by nature, and I'm uneasy because my new hockey foot changes the order of how I put on my gear. With the quick release, I now take off my reactive foot and put on my hockey foot with its skate, shin guard, and hockey sock all already attached. So, skates going on before pants has to be my new ritual. From now on, I must be extra careful pulling my breezers up over sharp skate blades. Huh, I guess it could be a lot worse.

From the bench, players watch the Eismeister drive the Zamboni off the ice, get down and and close the large double doors. They all wait until the doors bang shut before jumping on the ice, because in Germany rules are rules and everything works better when the rules are followed. After everyone else is out, I take a tentative step onto the ice for a slow lap, praying Jimmy's creation will perfectly mimic my skating stride. I accelerate, turn right and left, go from front to back, and make quick stops. It works! The only glitch is that I can't push off quickly in a new direction. *Whatevah!* I'm back, baby! I'm back!

After drills, we divide up to scrimmage. Coach tells me to hang back and play defense. This gives me the chance to make some great passes up ice. I also blast in a clap-bomb from the blue line, scoring a nice goal. Joel, a fellow Bostonian, scores a hat trick on breakaways set up by his new best friend—me! Our chemistry continues into the locker room. He grabs two beers from the case, hands me one, and we toast. Players drink, joke, and change. Steam drifts into the locker room from the back, as players go to and from the showers. I pass my unfinished beer to Scrappy, and put on my running blade to shower. Thankfully, the tread grips the wet tile really well. I put on my street clothes. Elated isn't a powerful enough word, it's something much more. I've rejoined my tribe.

Someone in back shouts, "Anyone want to go to the adult?"

"What's the adult?" I ask Scrappy.

"No, it's Dult. It's like Oktoberfest," Scrappy says. "Remember the Ferris wheel we passed just before the rink?"

"Sure," I reply. "It looked like a carnival."

"There's a big Oktoberfest-style beer tent behind the rides."

We stow our gear in my car and walk past the tennis halls to the fairgrounds. There are signs in German and English saying the Michaeli-Dult will stay open through the third of October. We walk by rides, games and food booths and stop in front of an elaborately decorated fest tent. Inside, hundreds of tables are lined up in long, neat rows. Each table is flanked by matching wooden benches. We join our teammates, who are seated together near the front.

I'd seen men in Lederhosen and women in fairy-tale dresses on TV, but I didn't think real people still wore that stuff. Here the young and old alike are dressed like extras from *The Sound of Music* and it looks great!

The beer comes in two sizes, large and extra-large. The large is served in a narrow glass that's as tall as a quart of milk. The extra-large comes in a heavy glass mug with a fist-sized handle, looking more like a pitcher than a glass. The menu, which comes in German and English, says that the Mass or extra-large mug is, "filled with popular Helles beer from the Kummert Brewery," and the one in the slender glass is, "Weissbier, or wheat beer, made by the Heindl family."

I look up from the menu and see a breathtakingly beautiful woman wearing a traditional dress. She looks straight at me and I blush. With her black hair, red lips and fair skin, she looks like an edgy, über-sexy Snow White. All the guys at the table look, waiting for me to do something. I look to Joel for help.

"She doesn't bite," he teases. "She just wants your drink order."

"I'm driving and...," I stammer.

"He'll have a Spezi," Scrappy says.

"What's that?" I ask.

"It's half-coke and half-orange soda. The little Bavaria kids love it, but don't worry Romeo, Eva won't hold it against you."

"Who?" I ask, playing dumb.

Eva returns with our drinks. We raise our glasses, and with a hearty "Prost!" clank our glasses together. Eva comes back and takes food orders. Everyone is ready, except me.

"Sorry," Joel stage whispers to Eva. "He's a fest virgin,"

"A virgin? Then he must have Schweinshaxe!" she proclaims.

"Schweinshaxe!" the whole table roars and clanks glasses.

A voice at the end calls out, "To our virgin!" Toasting, laughing, and much drinking follows.

When Eva brings my Schweinshaxe and two huge Bavarian dumplings smothered in gravy, it looks like a personal pig roast. The meat and gravy are rich and must match the Mass beer perfectly, but I stick to my Spezi.

I finish my humongous piece of roasted pork and dumplings, I'm stuffed. When everyone else settles their bill, I hang back to pay last.

Eva asks me if I will come back for Friday's fireworks. "It will be beautiful," she says.

I want to tell her, you are beautiful, but instead say, "That's a great idea."

Following Scrappy out into the cool night air, I pat my bulging belly, and say, "Man, I've gained twenty pounds."

Looking back, he says, "Welcome to Bavaria, Bro."

We stroll back to my car and take the long way back to Graf. I enjoy driving on the nearly empty autobahn, but I sure hope he drives next time, so that I can enjoy a Mass bier with Eva.

Before bed, I text Dad. "My hockey foot worked really well, and I had a great practice. I went to a German fest with the team afterwards. Things are looking up!" The next morning he responds, "Good for you!"

ON MONDAY, right after breakfast, I head to the gym for cardio. There, the front page of *The Stars and Stripes* catches my eye:

Short notice in Poland, 173rd Jumps into Combat Drills
Thursday, September 26, 2013

U.S. Paratroopers practiced jumping into combat scenarios and conducted live-fire drills in Poland this past week. Approximately five-hundred soldiers joined their Polish counterparts for the exercise, which concluded Wednesday.

The rapid deployment tested the 173rd's ability to assemble forces, get into a fight fast and maintain cohesive battlefield operations. Troopers parachuted into a mock battlefield to provide an opening for follow-on forces.

"What we did here was to show our ability to conduct a joint forcible entry operation anywhere in the world with limited notice," said unit First Sergeant Mark Robalo. The 173rd is billed as the U.S. Army's contingency response force in Europe,

challenged with quickly projecting forces throughout Europe, Africa and the Middle East.

I can't stomach the fact that my squad, my platoon, and my First Sergeant are training for real-world missions while I rot here in the rear detachment. It's a damn good thing the gym has top of the line machines, because today I will wear them out!

FOURTEEN

Back home, autumns are spectacular. Here, not so much. The locals go to the Alps to see fall on an epic scale, because up in the Oberpfalz, the changes are more subtle and often take place behind a curtain of fog or rain. As the birch trees slowly shed their leaves, emotions that disappeared with my foot slowly return. Hockey reawakens my hunger for adventure. I have new teammates, practices, and games—and it's Scrappy's turn to drive.

We leave through gate six, near the airfield, and pass stubby C-130 airplanes parked side by side on the cement runway. I reach for my stump, grimace, and wonder if the ghost pain radiates from my missing foot, uneasy mind or heavy heart?

"Dude, what's up?" Scrappy asks.

"Nothing, just thinking about all the ways to beat you five-hole."

"Fuck you," Scrappy says, cranking up AC/DC's *Highway to Hell*.

Practice is a joyful blur. In the locker room afterwards,

we pass around bottles of Zoigl beer. I toast Scrappy and down my first one in three smooth gulps.

"Nice skate, Rangers. Impressive speed. Today it's five euro each for the ice," Coach says, taking off his BMC Rangers hat and setting it next to the case of beer. "Just drop it in the hat. Oh, and listen up, Scrappy has something."

Scrappy stands, "Who wants to go to Oktoberfest with me and Basti? We have a three-day weekend next week, and Basti can hook us up with train tickets and a table in the Hacker-Pschorr tent. It'll be about ten euros for the train, and thirty to get a seat at a table, two giant beers, and half a chicken."

"Half a chicken?" asks McMouth.

"Better than two chickens and half a beer," Scrappy shoots back. "I'll post the details in our players group. Sign up tonight, because Basti will make our table reservations tomorrow."

"Oktoberfest is on my bucket list," I say to Scrappy.

"Sweet. Do you have lederhosen?"

"Ah, no. Do I need them?"

"Everyone does," Scrappy says. "They've got 'em at the PX."

"Cool," I say, giving him a thumbs-up despite my fear of exposing my mechanical leg to the whole freaking world.

SCRAPPY DRIVES us to the train station, and cruises the lot looking for parking. It's busy, because Columbus Day is just a normal workday for Germans. I feel a little foolish getting out of the car wearing a long sleeve blue and white checkered shirt, brown leather Lederhosen, knee-high wool socks and hiking boots. However, I'm very happy to have the longer version of Lederhosen which meet my socks just below my knee. Scrappy says the cool kids push their socks down, but I ignore him and keep mine pulled up high, hiding my prosthetic.

Inside, there are groups of young people all decked out in fest clothing waiting for the train to Munich. I spot BMC Rangers by the bakery, and we check in with them.

"We'll wait for everyone to show before getting tickets," Basti says. "If we put five riders on each, the price will come down to ten per rider."

While we wait, Scrappy tells me that Bastian is a plumber's apprentice. Besides working official jobs under his Meister, he also takes side jobs for family and friends. Over to the side, Bastian talks to a girl who really wears her dress well. Her dirndl is pretty traditional, except the skirt is hemmed mini-skirt style and the top has a plunging neckline that comes down to the tight, lace-up vest. I'm taking it all in, then my heart skips when I realize that it's Eva! What is Basti doing chatting her up?

Basti gets our tickets just as the train pulls up. We find seats together in a large, open car. Like the Germans teens at the other end, we have a rack of Helles for our two-hour ride south to Munich. Basti says that Helles translates directly as "light" referring to the tasty Bavarian brew's color, not its strength. He explains that it was Bavaria's answer when Pilsner beer took the world by storm. Basti stresses that Pilsen's famous beer was brewed by a Bavarian who only worked in the Czech city, and that Helles is a much loved newcomer to Bavarian beers, as compared to the old standards Dunkel and Hefeweizen.

We all grab beers and spread out a little. Scrappy and I find spots at a table facing Danny and Derrick. Danny, a lanky defenseman from St. Paul, is extremely relaxed and mellow. Derrick, a compact fast-talker from Boston, is extremely the opposite. As we drink, small farms whiz by.

"D is for Danny," Scrappy announces, taking a healthy swig of his Augustiner Helles. "He always holds his ground and never mishandles the puck. He plays top four, because he's a fucking stud." Danny smiles and raises his bottle to Scrappy, but it's clear that Danny doesn't care if he's top-four. He's just a guy who loves to play.

Derrick is different. He boasts that on the ice he's a shifty, fast skater. As the train rolls on, he tells a story about his breakout performance in last year's tourney. When Coach broke the Rangers into A and B-teams; Derrick landed on the B-team as the top line's center.

Huh, why was that a problem? Center is an excellent fit for a shifty player who likes to carry the puck, and the first line usually gets the most ice time. Derrick interrupts my thoughts, "In the last tourney before Garmisch, we were one win away from the semi-finals. We tied it up with a minute to play and I took a stupid roughing penalty. The Germans turned their power play into a goal, and that was it, we were out. I felt like the biggest Mass-hole evah."

As the train bumps over some rough track, Scrappy rants, "He took shit for his stupid penalty, for his stupid yapping about wanting to play on the A-team, for his stupid white gloves, for his stupid tinted visor, for playing stupid roving defense, for being a stupid *MASS-hole!*" Scrappy hoots and downs the last of his beer. Then it clicks and I remember Derrick. He was the guy with the tinted visor and white gloves in Amberg. He set up behind his own net and dashed end-to-end with the puck on his stick, like Bobby Orr. He was fast, but sadly lacked Orr's vision, hands, and finish.

Derrick glares at Scrappy, and says, "Yeah, the A-team

won it all and the B-team finished second, but it wasn't a great tourney for me."

Scrappy's eyes light up. "We held our team dinner in an eee-nor-mouse Bavarian banquet hall."

Danny jumps in, "We passed our championship cup up and down the tables, chugging Helles and toasting. When the cup finally made it to Derrick he said, 'To next year, when I'm on the A-team.' Can you believe it?" Danny raises his bottle, "You got to give it to ol' Derrick, he ain't never going to sugarcoat it."

I raise my bottle to the grinning Mass-hole sitting across from me.

Scrappy starts in again, "The next season this cocky son of a bitch shows up with his stupid white gloves, ridiculous tinted visor, and me-first attitude—"

"Then," Danny interrupts, "Coach puts him on a line with Bailey and Shane. Bailey was our best center, and Shane was our fastest winger. And Derrick lit it up, scored buckets of goals."

"And what they did in Cheb!" Scrappy says, as the train jerks to a stop.

Hundreds more trachten-clad Bavarians pile on to the train for their annual pilgrimage to Munich. As we pull out of Regensburg, it's standing room only on the train. A blond girl in a red Dirndl, presses against me. As the train bumps along, her breasts bounce inches from my face. I stand and give her my seat. Besides, I need to off-load some Helles and make my way through the crowd of happy people and wait in line for the bathroom. On my way back, the train jerks and I grab a seat back to catch my balance. Someone bumps into me and I turn around. It's Eva!

She narrows her eyes. "You don't come back for fire-works, *Ja?*"

"Ah, I wanted to—"

"Too bad, they were beautiful," she pouts.

"Sorry." I stutter.

She gives me a playful grin.

"Are you here with Basti?"

"No," she smiles. "Why?"

"No reason." I say, looking away. I look back and say, "He set it up for us."

She puts her slender hand on my chest. Her nails, painted shiny black, match her braided hair. "I like your Lederhosen. Are they new?" she asks. The train lurches as I try to think of something clever, but before I can say anything, she says, "We're in Munich. You should go back to your team."

"Thanks," I say, turning and squeezing back through the crowd.

The doors open and hundreds of people spill out onto the busy platform.

The Hauptbahnhof is as big as an NHL arena. It's open end lets in twenty sets of tracks. Beyond the railheads, there is a huge platform running up to a three-story red-brick building. It houses bakeries, bars, restaurants and gambling halls. Two large exits punch through to the outside, and between them an escalator goes to the subway.

We follow the crowd down. Two young women, wearing colorful dirndl, carry a rack of Helles between them. What a sight! Two subway stops later, we ride an escalator up to the Wies'n, Munich's famous fairgrounds. It looks a little like Amberg's Dult, if the Dult was a back-yard barbecue with pony rides and the Wies'n was Disneyland.

Inside, the Hacker-Pschorr tent is full, busy and noisy. It's peaked roof rises fifty-feet above us. Blue banners speckled with white clouds create a shimmering illusion of a perfect blue and white Bavarian sky hovering above.

As we squeeze past the raucous drinking-only section, the smell of baked pretzels and roasting chicken mixes with the white noise of a thousand of partiers. Their chatter drowns out the music, until an Oompa band, sitting high up on a central stage, hits the refrain from John Denver's greatest hit, and a thousand voices belt out in unison, "Take me home, country roads!" Mesmerized by it, I sing along with the world's largest and drunkest chorus. When the song ends, Basti leads us to our tables. We settle in, five on each wooden bench. Next to us there's a group of Australian students, and behind them a row of tables filled with Japanese tourists.

Basti speaks briefly to a waiter wearing a sky-blue shirt over black Lederhosen. Then our waitress, wearing a similar blue and black Dirndl, takes our drink orders—liter mugs of Helles beer for everyone!

"You're a plumber?" I ask Basti.

"Ja, apprentice. Young people here don't want to learn to plumb anymore, so my Meister and I have more work than we can handle. My meister wants to take on more apprentices, but the young only want to work on computers."

"It's the same back home," I say.

"For me, it's great," he laughs. "When there's a broken pipe, I'm the most popular man in Weiden."

Our waitress interrupts us to collect beer coupons, and returns carrying an amazing four Mass of beer in each hand. On a second trip, she serves the rest of our team. Basti stands, raises his glass and yells, "Prost!" Everyone, including the Australians and the Japanese, raise their glasses and yell, "Prost!" We clank the heavy glass mugs together, and drink deeply. The first gulp is always the best, and it goes down very easily. We smile, drink, and sing. The good times roll.

Our waitress collects our meal coupons. The chickens roast on giant rotisseries running down the far side of the tent, and are served with giant soft pretzels. I devour it all and wonder why the Bavarians only hold Oktoberfest once a year. As the waitress clears our plates, Eva walks up, greets Basti, and ignores me.

Hey, what the hell?

The band breaks into the toasting "Prosit" song. Everyone links arms, sways back and forth, and sings along. We butcher the Bavarian words, but nail the ending, shouting, "One, two, three, drink!" We clank our mugs together and take huge gulps. When I lower my glass, I'm facing Eva. She stands, one hand on her hip and the other holding her giant beer. She's way beyond beautiful.

"Having fun at our little party?" she asks.

"You bet," I say, raising my mug to her. "Want to join us?"

The guys shift to make room, and Eva steps over the bench. Before she sits, she raises her mug and shouts, "Prost!"

"Prost!" we all answer, clank, and drink.

Eva sits, and the fun continues. When the band plays Sweet Caroline, everyone in the tent joins in. It reminds me of Red Sox games with my dad. I jump up on the bench and when the crowd breaks into the Diamond's "Sweeeeet Car-o-line—" I lay into the "Oh! Oh! Oh!" part and pump my fist in to air.

I sit back down, and Eva pulls me in close. "Are you a Sweet William, or a Bad Billy?"

I freeze, because she's way out of my league! I struggle

to come up with a snappy response, and am saved by the waitress who brings another round of beers. I shift on the bench. My leg hurts from sitting for too long, but to stay at Eva's side, I put up with it. After a few more sing-alongs, our waitress tells us that out time is up.

How can that be? Where did our two hours go?

On the way out, I detour to the latrine. It's a basketball court-sized room with metal gutters mounted thigh-high along the walls.

Wow, German efficiency in the extreme!

I push back through the crowd to rejoin Eva. She suggests we check out what's happening on the Wies'n. Scrappy peels off to join the Australian students.

He turns and waves, "Don't wait up!"

I wave back, miss a step, and come down wrong on my prosthetic, sending a stab of pain up my bad leg. I keep it to myself and hope Eva doesn't notice my limp as we go see the sights.

We pass beside a wooden roller coaster, and under a four-story spinning tower with people hanging and rotating under it in flimsy swings. Hundreds of smaller rides, games of chance, and food stands dot the massive fair grounds, but the heart of it is the twelve gigantic beer tents. Everything is clean, organized and efficient, and I don't for a minute doubt Eva's claim that seven million cheerful people will eat, drink, and party here during the three-week festival. We pick up the pace walking back through the crowded grounds to link up with the Rangers. My plastic foot swings awkwardly like a dead metronome. Then our fingers brush once, twice, and suddenly we are holding hands. Just as suddenly, I don't feel so awkward.

Eva says, "You were born to wear lederhosen!"

I don't know what to say. I was never good at flirting. As

a hockey player I never had the time to chase girls, besides at our alcohol-fueled team parties the cheerleaders threw themselves at me. If I never learned how to flirt with silly American girls, what chance do I have with this beautiful Bavarian who's making me hum like a tuning fork? At least she doesn't seem to mind my silence.

We make our way back to the Hacker-Pschorr tent and link up with Basti and the Rangers. Eva says goodbye, explaining that because she rode down on a different group ticket, she has to meet her friends for the ride back. Somehow Basti gets us on the right subway, and we make it to our train just in time. On board, the party continues, but my mind goes back to Eva.

As we pull into Regensburg, I realize she could have traveled back with me on Scrappy's ticket.

An hour later, we arrive in Weiden, and exchange Germany-style farewell hugs. Basti asks if I need a ride back to post. I point over to Derrick and Danny, and say, "I'll catch a taxi with them."

During the twenty-minute ride to post, they go on about the hot German girls in their lace-up dresses. "They're called Dirndl," I say, but they're focused on the girls, not learning German.

I look out the window and think about Eva. Damn, I should have kissed her.

FIFTEEN

On the first Sunday in November, the Star Bulls travel north to play Weiden. Bastian says it's an important game, because the Devils are battling with them for position in the middle of the third-league. I'm not concerned about standings, just excited to get off post and see some German semi-pro hockey.

Scrappy looks for a parking spot as the sun sets behind the arena. We had agreed to meet Basti an hour before puck drop, but in the local dialect halb-fünf means four-thirty, not five-thirty, and with all the traffic and activity at the rink it looks like we might be an hour late. Scrappy finally finds parking at a grocery store and we walk back to the rink's crowded parking lot. Luckily, I'm getting better on my reactive foot and can keep up. We spot Basti waiting for us by the players' entrance. He gives us a quick wave and a friendly smile.

"Are we on time?" Scrappy asks.

"Yes," Basti says, "a little early."

"Holy cow, this place is really hopping," I say.

"We love our Devils," Basti says.

More and more people in Ice Devil jerseys arrive on foot. Ushers in team jackets walk past. Basti speaks to them briefly in German, and we follow them to the main entrance. Standing in line, I hear hard rock pulsing from inside and my anticipation builds. While we wait, Basti tells us that the city built the arena in 1987. He claims it's not only the best Eishalle in the Oberpfalz, but the best ice hall in all of Bavaria.

"For the derby games, it always sells out," Basti says.

"What's a derby game?" I ask.

"Games against hated neighbors," Basti says.

"Rivals?" I ask.

"Yes, rival games. Tonight is no Derby. On the radio, they predicted about two thousand fans, not a sell-out."

"Not bad," Scrappy says.

"Half will sit and half will stand the whole game. Our hardest-core fans are in the Fan Zone. There they beat on drums and chant so loud they become part of the game!" Basti adds.

Hundreds of fans line up behind us. The main doors open at five thirty, we pay fifteen euros, and get the tickets Basti had reserved for us online. Security pats us down, and we enter another world. The interior is bright white, with sky-blue trim. Enormous wooden beams run across the ceiling, creating a rustic, Alpine feeling. But, an extra-large scoreboard hangs over center ice, giving the space a modern vibe. On the upper deck, vendors sell bratwurst, beer and pretzels. At ice level, kids wearing Ice Devil jackets press against the glass, watching their hometown heroes up close. The players take passes and fire pucks on net, with near misses cracking loudly off the glass.

The atmosphere is pure magic. Even when I was little, I knew when Dad and I pushed through the turnstiles at the

Garden, we were entering a more vibrant world. We were part of a black and gold tribe, sharing a common purpose, and for a few hours the rest of the world didn't matter. As I grew, and my concerns got bigger, the chance to escape from life's pressures was always a blessing.

Here the same tribal magic exists.

Basti leads us around the far end where the arena opens up over the Fan Curve, which extends from the glass behind the visiting goalie up to the vendors selling draft beer, sodas and snacks on the upper deck. The smell of savory cheddar dogs and freshly baked pretzels fills the air. Our seats are down low on the blue line and just past the Fan Curve. I enjoy the great view of the ice, but my eyes keep drifting back to the Fan Curve. It looks like a stage-front mosh pit with Weiden's rowdiest fans creating havoc right behind the visiting goalie. No wonder they become part of the game!

A horn blares, marking the end of warm-ups. As the players leave the ice, two young skaters wearing blue jeans and team jerseys, come out to pick up the pucks and push the nets off to the side. Speakers blast AC/DC's *Thunderstruck*, and the arena lights dim as the Zamboni cleans the ice. Half the crowd is in line for beers and brats.

Basti leans in to explain more about the league. "The Oberliga Süd has twelve teams in southern Germany playing in the third level of pro hockey, but the winning teams move up and the losing teams move down."

"That's outstanding!" Scrappy says between sips of beer. "How long is the season?"

"It starts in September and ends in April," Basti says. "The teams play each other four times, then the top half playoff to move up, and the bottom half play to avoid relegation."

"I like it," I say. "Bad teams can't just hang around."

"The Oilers would be out!" Scrappy blurts.

The lights go out and three cars, with their head and hazard lights blinking, drive onto the ice. The arena lights come up as the cars make a full circle along the boards. Two are convertibles and have pretty girls dressed Oktoberfest-style waving to the crowd like homecoming queens. Holy cow, one of them is Eva! I wave back, stupidly hoping she can somehow see me. The cars make a tight turn and drive to the middle of the ice. In front of the open Zamboni door, flames shoot twenty-feet in the air.

The music fades out, and an announcer bellows, "Für die Eis Devils, nummer Sieben, Christof..."

In unison the fans yell back, "Hauptman!"

Then the announcer says, "Nummer zehn, Thomas..."

And the crowd finishes, "Kreir!"

"What is going on?" I ask Basti.

"After each player's number and first name is called, the crowd yells out his last name," he explains.

Each player skates out to the center and join the others to form a circle around the cars. This call and response continues until all twenty Ice Devils are on the ice. When the last player joins the circle, the players all turn outward, raise their sticks and salute their cheering fans. The cars drive off the ice, and both teams line up across their blue line. The players raise their sticks and salute each other. Then, they huddle at their respective nets. The horn blares, and the starting players finally line up for the opening face-off.

The same level of pregame energy per fan would blow the freaking roof off of the Garden. But now, as the referee squats to drop the puck, I'm eager to see the quality of the hockey.

The players are small, fast, and agile. Their passes are crisp and accurate, and they fire wild shots on net from all over the ice. But, the game looks a little strange to my American eyes. First, it's played on an Olympic-sized rink, that is wider and longer than the rinks back home. This means the players have more time and space to make plays, and it's harder to hit, defend, and slow down speedy puck-moving teams.

Weiden scores first on a stretch pass breakaway. The announcer calls out the scorer's first name, "Marcel," and pauses. The crowd yells out, "Pal-dow-ski!" Paldi acknowledges the crowd with a quick wave. Rosenheim battles back. On a two-minute power play, they score on a slap shot from the point which ricochets at the goal mouth and goes in. Rosenheim's fans, who stand in a designated area just to the left of Weiden's much bigger Fan Curve, cheer wildly. This creates a wall of back-and-forth noise for the tied game.

I love the atmosphere! I love the run-and-gun hockey! My high school coach would have hated the lack of structure, hitting, and defend-first mentality. But none of it bothers me. This fast, flashy, and flowing hockey reminds me of the free-spirited pond hockey I played growing up.

Between the first and second periods, while the Zamboni lays down a fresh sheet of ice, Basti orders us three Hefeweizen, saying, "This is the only time you can drink Bavarian wheat beer from a plastic cup." I sip my beer, enjoying the bubbly golden brew's distinctive sweetness. No wonder Bavarians like to drink their bread!

Weiden comes out flying in the second period and scores three unanswered goals. Each goal causes the Fan Curve to erupt. Drummers beat on kettle drums, fans chant in unison. Because the teams switch ends in the second period, Rosenheim's goalie is two hundred feet from the heckling. Still, the wall of noise must be unnerving. I've never seen fans so connected to their team. Boston has legions of die-hard fans, but here it's different. Part of it must be having the Fan Curve come right down to the ice. Back home they would be corporate seats which sit empty the first five minutes of each period. Another part of it is definitely the drumming, chanting crowd. We've got nothing like it back home. Still, there's something more to it.

After the second period, I ask Basti about it.

"Growing up my heroes weren't NHL players, they were our players," he says. "I learned to skate with my friends, and we played in the same club as our heroes. I grew up playing with five of the guys playing tonight. They are my Eis Brüder."

"What's that?" I ask.

"A brother," Basti says. "They are my ice brothers."

It reminds me of what my dad says about being a Bruins fan. "It's about supporting the team, Willie. Nevah forget it. Week in and week out, you got to keep the faith." But here, that bond is stronger. It makes me want to go home to root for my Bruins at the Garden; it also turns me into an Ice Devils fan for life.

In the third period, Rosenheim's coach puts their backup goalie in net. When he makes two spectacular saves, it seems like a brilliant move. Then, with fifteen minutes left in the game, Rosenheim scores on a break-away to pull within two goals. Five minutes later, a Rosenheim player goes to the penalty box for tripping, and the Devils really click on their two-minute power play, putting a lot of pressure on the back-up goalie. They finally score with five seconds left in their one-man advantage, and a thousand hostile fans mercilessly jeer the replacement goalie. The Devils score twice more in the next minute.

The Star Bulls coach is furious, and with a little more than a minute left in the game, he pulls his goalie to put an extra attacker on the ice. This backfires, and Paldi scores an empty netter to complete his hat trick. We stand, clap, and cheer, but nobody throws a hat on the ice.

Huh, I guess they don't do that here.

The clock runs down to zero, the buzzer sounds, and the final score stands at eight to two. Our players on the bench spill out onto the ice. Together they wave to the crowd, and take a victory lap, while the announcer wishes everyone a safe trip home. Scrappy and I turn to leave.

"No wait," Basti holds out his arm blocking our way. "You've got to stay and see our Devils dance."

A few minutes later, half-dressed Devils skate back onto the ice. Basti say, "They aren't allowed to do this until after the referees leave."

The players, most in sweat-soaked t-shirts, line up on the face-off circle nearest to the Fan Curve. They form a half- circle facing the silent mob. A drum pounds three steady beats and a lone fan screams out a rhythmic chant. The entire Fan Curve echoes back with rabid passion. I only understand the last part, "Pal-dow-ski!"

Paldi moves out to the face off dot, smiles, and belts out a chant to the crowd. They scream it back. Players clap a beat, and the crowd joins in. Paldi does a little jig. Three times this happens. Each time, the fans get louder and wilder. Raw emotion charges the air. Then the singing and clapping players wave goodbye and leave.

I am blown away. Is this how the German barbarians fired themselves up to fight against the Roman legions?

Back on base, I think about Dad. As long as I live, I'll never forget the feeling of sitting in the Garden next to Dad during warm-ups. The excitement. The electric buzz. Being part of it. Even now, my favorite Bruins games are the ones I watched with my dad.

I text him, focusing on all the strange things: the cars on the ice; the end zone fans standing, beating drums, and chanting; and the players dancing after the win. "I know it all sounds crazy, but it's fun. When you visit, we should go to a game!"

———

ON MONDAY MORNING, a siren jolts me awake. I roll over, jump out of bed and stumble. My naked stump slams painfully against the floor. I stagger forward, grab my crutches and hurry downstairs, the last one to make it down to formation.

I've always been part of a team. Always in the middle, with the team gravitating towards me. But out here in this sad formation, we aren't a team. We're just a collection of broken soldiers standing in ranks and files with no common purpose.

The first sergeant calls us to attention. After getting one-hundred percent accountability, he announces we're having a piss test. *Oh, joy!* My watch reads 05:15, and I have to wait in line for an hour before it's my turn to have someone watch me pee in a bottle.

Back in our room, Jack asks, "Did you study?"

"What?"

"To pass?"

"Pass what?" I snap.

"The urinalysis, genius."

"I'll pass. You?"

"As long as beer and Jack stay legal," he grins, "I'll pass."

After that, it's back to the rear detachment's

monotonous grind. The days blend into weeks, and the weeks blend into months, with soul-crushing sameness.

ON THURSDAY, I have a game. I should be happy; instead, I drive to the rink in silence. Even chatty Scrappy notices my sour mood and stays quiet. I park, and as we grab our bags, my spirits start to lift. Fuck Manning, I won't let him crush my spirit. Out on the ice, I can escape by focusing one-hundred percent on every shift, pass, and shot. At the rink I'm never homesick, because it is my home.

In the locker room, Coach stresses that this is a friendly match, and the final score doesn't matter. Coach puts me on the first line with Joel and Derrick. Normally a center, I defer to Joel and move over to right wing. Just before we hit the ice, Coach reminds us, "Play a clean game. Have fun and we'll get invited to play again."

In warm-ups, my prosthetic feels solid, and all the time in the gym has slimmed me down and hardened me up. When the puck drops, I'm ready. On the first shift, Joel draws the puck back to Danny on defense, Danny fires it up the boards to me, and I hit Derrick cutting across the middle. He streaks in alone and shoots. The puck hits the goalie knee-high and drops between his skates. Before he can find it, I poke it in for an easy goal. By the end of the first period, we're up by four and I already have a hat trick.

Coach calls us together, and says, "I hate to break up Joel's line, but we want to keep it close." Turning to me, he says, "Go switch jerseys with a German." I'm not happy about it, but do as I'm told. The Ice Sharks' coach tells me to trade with their first line center.

When we bend down to take the draw, and Joel sneers, "You fucking traitor."

I chip the puck forward, get it before it reaches Danny, and skate in on Scrappy, firing a snap shot up over his glove into the top corner for a beautiful unassisted goal. I score twice more for the Sharks, and the game ends tied at eight.

Afterwards, I stay out and do a few sprints. I dig into the ice, abruptly stop at the far side, and immediately sprint back. After four times over and back, I lean against the boards catching my breath. I squeeze my stick and enjoy the wet leather sticking to my palms. I lean over, and sweat runs down and stings my eyes. Blinking it away, I adjust my helmet, and push off, speeding away from the boards. My new hockey foot works like a dream—it's perfect!

In the locker room, everyone is loose and happy.

Joel announces, "Hey, Willie's two hat tricks cancel each other out."

"What?" I challenge.

"Yeah," he says, with a twinkle in his eye, "You're plus minus rating is zero, hero. Zero, ha!" Joel is really something. He doesn't have a mean streak, but he's a dangerous man. His day job is cavalry scout, meaning he goes forward as the infantry's eyes and ears. When the enemy hides, he conducts recon by fire, intentionally drawing the enemy's fire to expose their hidden firing positions. Joel centers his line like he lives his life, with extreme abandon. Fore-checking, back-checking, and hunting the puck, he gives his opponents absolutely no time to carry, pass, or shoot. He's an opportunistic, shoot-first player who can, in a blink of an eye, convert a turnover into a scoring chance. He would be an absolute scoring machine if he could put half of his wild shots on net. Oh, but when one of his shots does catch a top corner, the poor goalie never has a chance.

Joel gets up to shower. His upper body is covered with tough looking skull, dagger, and death-themed tattoos except on his left shoulder. There, there's a cute red devil which looks like Tweety-Bird with horns. It has "Horney Little Devil" written underneath it.

Chris, a tough combat engineer who fought in Fallujah, cracks, "Holy Christ, Joel, where'd you get all the tats, in prison?"

Joel shrugs, "What evah."

Chris continues his taunt, "Horny Little Devil? Get that one for your prison roomie?"

Joel stops, giving Chris a hard don't-fuck-with-me stare.

In the stunned silence, Chris shouts, "Hell, if you wanted to get your roomie off, you should've just had a big pair of breasts inked on your shoulder blades!"

Everyone, including Joel, is caught off guard and laughs until tears flow.

During our next practice, Coach asks me how my leg feels.

"On the ice, it's great," I beam.

He glances down at his clipboard, and asks, "Want to practice with the Devils?"

"That's possible?"

"Not normally," he says. "But they have injuries, and are looking for players to fill in. If your leg is good, you'd be a good fit."

"Wow, thanks," I nod. "When's practice?"

"Hold on, let me talk to Peter first," he laughs. "Oh and one tip, Peter's a Czech who speaks pretty good German, but almost no English. If he takes you, find a German player to translate for you, and be the last player in line for drills until you know exactly how they work."

"Got it," I say, flashing an I-got-this smile.

"Listen, I'm serious. If you disrupt the flow of his practice, Peter won't ask you back."

"I got it," I snap, then quickly add, "thanks, Coach."

On the drive back to post, Scrappy says, "Last year a West Pointer practiced with the Devils."

"Cool," I say.

"For us he played center, but the Devils moved him back to defense. It didn't really matter, because they already had three foreigners playing."

"They have a limit?" I ask.

"Yep, in the DEL they can have five. They're mostly older NHL guys playing a few more years or smallish college players who play better on the bigger ice."

I try to hide my disappointment and say nothing.

"Bro, in Weiden they don't get NHL players. They get a few Czech players from across the border," Scrappy says. "If a spot opens up, you've got a good shot."

SIXTEEN

The cold, gloomy weeks on post bleed together. The days get shorter and our first and final formations are held in darkness. I pick up Scrappy for practice as the rain morphs into a dense, icy fog.

"How's your Bavarian princess?" he teases.

"I don't even have her number," I protest.

At first, he doesn't believe me. Then, he calls me a pussy.

Cresting a hill, we see flashing lights. I take my foot off the gas and to see what's going on. A German policeman is using a lighted paddle to wave cars past the first responders working in the middle of the road. As I weave between a fire truck and an ambulance, my chest tightens. I can't breathe.

"You okay?" Scrappy asks.

I try to answer, but only manage two strained breaths.

"Dude?"

"I'm okay," I gasp, holding the steering wheel in a death grip. Clearing the accident zone, I speed away.

How was Dad still able to respond to accidents after

Mom died? Why didn't I catch a ride home with another player? Well, there's no changing it now. I called, she answered, and she died. I don't believe in ghosts, and didn"t ever expected my mom to visit me after we buried her, but she did. At first she visited every day. Sometimes the smell of fresh soda bread triggered a memory and made me smile. The morning after she died was the only time I've ever seen Dad cry. I hope he doesn't think it was his fault. Fuck me, it's time to change the channel, because Foley men don't cry.

"You think we'll scrimmage tonight?" I ask, deliberately thinking about hockey.

Scrappy pauses like he wants to ask me what just happened, but then he lets it go. "Oh yeah, just a few drills and we'll scrimmage."

"I hope we have two goalies, shooting at posts sucks," I say, as my breathing and heartbeat slow towards normal. "Hey, do you know anything about the three-on-three tourney?"

"It's on Veterans Day in Pegnitz, and it's free."

"Really?"

"Yep, the VFW pays for the active-duty players. It's really a cool tourney. The rink is open air, and we play cross-ice hockey all day long."

"You just show up?"

"No, you sign up with your four-player team," Scrappy says, and goes silent.

"Want to play together?" I ask.

"Sorry, I'm on Team Hall Pass," he says. "Just ask around tonight, guys will be looking for a team."

Just as Scrappy predicted, Coach has us do a few drills and then divides us up to scrimmage. I stand by Joel, hoping we end up on the same line. Instead, I end up on a line with

Derrick and Danny. On the first shift, we face off against Joel's line and play to a draw. On the bench, I ask them if they are on a Veterans Day team.

Derrick says they are playing with Joel, and still need a fourth. Last year, they played as "The Grind Line" and this year they'll play as "The Grinders".

I don't care about the team's name. I just want to play.

JACK'S ALARM CLOCK BEEPS, and mine joins in. I roll out of bed and hop straight to the bathroom to piss and shave. I put on my black and gold PT uniform, put a New Balance running shoe on my good foot, and snap on my reactive foot. It's a little backward to do it last, but that's how I did it wearing shorts, and now the zippered bottom of my sweat pants lets me keep doing it the same way. In my pockets, I carry a black knit cap and gloves because I'm not sure if we are switching to the winter PT uniform today.

Everyone gathers outside in the battalion area. Squad leaders drift out to the right, and their squads instinctively line up to their left. When the platoon sergeants take their places out front, everyone shuffles into perfect dress-right-dress ranks and files. I line up third from my squad leader and position myself directly behind the third soldier in front of me. Routine precision like this comforts the type-A people like me, who stand in formations. As the sergeant major calls us to attention, there's a ruckus behind the formation. I want to turn and look, but my military discipline won't allow it.

With my peripheral vision, I see Jack turn, gawk, and choke back laughter.

Before things get too crazy, the sergeant major calls out

"Parade!" and the first sergeants echo it over their right shoulders. The sergeant major completes his order by barking out, "Rest!" His command puts the entire formation in the position of parade rest. That's the classic military pose with feet shoulder width apart, backs of hands resting in the small of the back, elbows out, and eyes locked forward.

Even though the sergeant major's command keeps my eyes forward, I can still hear noises from the rear. The scuffling continues, along with cursing and yelling. The sergeant major calls us back to the position of attention and calls on leaders to report accountability. They salute and report, "All present or accounted for, Sergeant!" The sergeant major then releases the broken soldiers and marches the fit ones off to do push-ups, sit-ups, and formation runs.

Back in our room, I ask Jack what happened.

He laughs, "Man, it was fucking classic. It was Rudeman. His sergeant put out that the PT uniform was hats and gloves. So, Rudeman did exactly that! He fell in wearing only a hat, gloves, and running shoes!"

I snort-laugh, cover my mouth.

"Aren't you glad you weren't drinking milk?"

"What?" I ask.

"It'd be coming out of your nostrils, Einstein. Anyway, Rudeman was buck-ass-naked. The crazy fucker's been trying' to get out for months."

"That should do it," I say.

"Maybe, but Manning knows he wants out. He won't let him go that easy."

"Manning will mess with him," I agree. "But I don't think he'll keep him around just to screw with him."

"Anything's possible, Cuz," Jack says, undressing.

"Back to bed?"

"It's still dark; that means God wants us to sleep."

Jack has a point. With no appointments for the rest of the day, I opt for the extra rack time. Waking at 10:00, I hit the gym before lunch. Huh, not a bad schedule.

SEVENTEEN

Saturday starts out sunny, then the afternoon sky turns slate gray. As night falls, it starts to rain. I check our Grinders' group chat.

Danny writes, "We should wear jerseys with monkey grinders."

"We're not that kind of grinder," Derrick answers, "we're blue-collar grinders who work and play hard." He suggests we wear flannel.

"Flannel?" Joel texts, "Then we'd be the fucking Lumberjacks!"

I don't understand the fuss.

Joel writes, "I can get four road crew vests from the motor pool."

We all agree on Joel's orange vest idea.

Looking through my rain soaked window, I hope our the weather changes before we play on Monday.

AT 06:00 ON MONDAY, Scrappy picks me up for our thirty minute drive to Pegnitz. It's cold and clear—the perfect weather for pond hockey. An hour later, I stand rink side with the frigid air stinging my nose and ears. I skate out onto the empty ice. Free and weightless, I glide around a space normally crowded with ten skaters battling to win a violent game. Out alone, I speed up and enjoy the sensation of flying. I spot a lone puck, stick handle with it, shoot it, and chase it down. It's joyful, primal play. I whiz around, going from front to back, circling with the puck, and sending it ricocheting off the boards with a sharp bang. I don't notice my prosthetic at all. Strangely, I'm now more at home on ice than on land.

Coach calls me to the side to help set up. We drag long four-by-four boards and use them to set up three cross-ice rinks, one in each zone. Heavy-duty plastic beer cases serve as our goals. Teams have gone all out with their jerseys. Krieger's team is called Purple Haze and they wear tie-dyed jerseys. One team has "Duff Beer" jerseys inspired by Homer Simpson. With our orange vests, we fit right in.

The Grinders are ready to play!

We cruise to an easy win in our first game against Krieger and his tie-dyed German friends. We narrowly win our second game against an Air Force team from Ramstein. Our third game pits us against Scrappy. His team is talented, but I'm in the zone, playing fully on instinct. My passes and plays with Derrick, Danny and Joel are automatic. Speeding up to catch a stretch breakout pass, I blow past Scrappy with my muscles running on pure adrenaline.

After lunch, we have five wins and I haven't thought once about my foot, the Marathon bombings, and losing my Corporal's stripes.

In the other pool, an Army team from Wiesbaden is also

undefeated, and Basti's team only has one loss. We face Basti's German team in the semifinals. They're skilled, but can't match our speed. There's no break between semifinals to finals; it's straight in without time to rest. It's an insane amount of hockey to pack into one day, but my time spent doing cardio pays off. We wear the Wiesbaden team out, and I score five straight in the last three minutes to come from behind and win it all!

Coach presents trophies to the top teams. The runners-up from Wiesbaden get bottles of Hefeweizen with BMC Ranger pucks glued on top. As the winners, we get bottles of Zoigl with the same puck crowning them. Coach points out our orange vests and dubs us his "Wrecking Crew" for all the damage we inflicted on our opponents.

In Pegnitz's club room, we celebrate with bottles of helles and big bowls of chili. Basti congratulates me. I thank him and ask for Eva's number.

He sings, "Eva? Eva? Who the fuck is Eva?"

I don't get it, and he tells me it's from the party song about a girl named Alice. I still don't get it, and he gives up promising to text Eva's number to me.

In the locker room, I strip off my wet gear. Danny hands me a Zoigl beer. We pop the flip-tops and toast. I hurt all over, but that's hockey. Players always have some minor injury: a pulled groin, a sprain, or a fractured finger. It's all part of the game. I don't dwell on the regular bumps and bruises. I've learned to ignore the discomfort, a skill that served me well as a paratrooper. The only injuries I really worry about are those that might keep me off of the ice.

As I unlace the skate on my good foot, a stab of pain shoots up from my missing foot. This pain is sharp, and my worry kicks into high gear. I lean forward to attach my running blade and see a dark bruise spreading upwards from the top of my prosthetic. I carefully take off the cup and gel liner, and watch in horror as blood runs out of it onto the floor.

Derrick jumps up to get Scrappy. They come back, help me pack and get to Scrappy's car. I lean my head against the window, concentrating on the cold glass and hoping that the painful cramping in my leg will go away.

It doesn't.

Every player knows hockey demands sacrifices. As a kid it forced me out of bed before dawn, and ate up all my free time. It swallowed all my energy, but I needed it. All the pressures of life outside the rink—like the hard fact that I'd killed my mom—it all went quiet inside the rink. It saved me then.

I can't lose it now.

Scrappy parks and helps me up to my room. Flashes of pain interrupt my worries about Manning and what he'll do when he finds out I've injured myself playing hockey. Scrappy helps me elevate and ice my stump. The next morning I can't believe how much it still hurts. I give myself a gentle washout and am horrified by the damage I've done. It's clear that I'll be back on crutches until my wounds can scab over and heal.

When Manning finds out, will he take hockey away?

That idea stings more than anything. No, Manning cannot find out about my leg.

———

I SKIP PT formation and Jack covers for me by reporting me as accounted for. Two and a half hours later, I hobble down on crutches to stand in the 09:00 formation. Morning fog still blankets the main post, and the tower seems to float above it, like a castle in the sky. Sergeant Major abruptly ends my day-dreaming by calling us to attention. He gets accountability and turns the formation over to Manning.

Manning puts us at parade rest and says, "We've had a casualty in the 173rd, and Colonel Mailman asked me to publish a statement on his behalf." Reading from a card, he continues:

> *No one goes through life without stress and pain.*
> *That is reality. That's why the Army fully resources*
> *programs to address soldiers' spiritual and mental*
> *health needs. I am proud to command tough,*
> *resilient, and mission-focused paratroopers. Taking*
> *care of those assigned to the 173rd is a sacred respon-*
> *sibility. I charge all Sky Soldiers to look out for each*
> *other. If you need help, speak up. If you learn*
> *someone needs help, intervene. Your entire chain of*
> *command will be there for you.*

"Yeah, speak up," Jack says out of the side of his mouth. "And Manning will use it to chapter your ass out of the Army."

I ignore Jack, but deep down know it's true. With my peripheral vision, I watch Manning lower the card. He yells, "Rest!" and this keeps our feet planted but allows us to relax and look around.

"Okay, troopers, here's the real deal," he says, "Specialist Jerome Wilson, an artilleryman in Vicenza, killed himself last night. Somebody there saw something. Somebody there should have intervened. His chain of command failed. That won't happen here. Understood?" Major Manning punctuates his question with his don't-challenge-me grin. He waits a beat, comes to attention, calls us to attention, and then releases us.

As the formation breaks up, soldiers ask each other if they knew Wilson and nobody admits to it.

Back in our room Jack mocks Manning with a dead-on imitation, "That won't happen here, not on my watch," he then really nails Manning's chilling grin with a final, "Understood?" His mocking impression is eerily accurate. So accurate, it makes my skin crawl.

DAD and I haven't talked in a while, so after lunch I try him on video chat. Six hours behind, he picks up during his breakfast. I notice he hasn't shaved for a few days.

"How's it going?" I ask.

"Good, you playing any puck?"

"Well, I was," I stutter. "I mean, I am, but I overdid it at a pond hockey tourney."

"Ovah did it?" he chuckles. "That's easy to believe."

"I'm back on crutches for a while."

"Jeez, that's too bad," he says.

"It felt great to be playing again. My team ran the table and we won it all. I didn't feel anything until the adrenaline wore off."

"Congrats," he says. "Hey, you catching any of the Boston games? The boys are looking good. Even old Iginla looks good skating next to Lucic."

"Wow, that's a tough line!" I say. "Hey, aren't you working today?"

"Sure. Why?" Dad asks.

"I guess I should let you get ready," I say, wondering why he hasn't shaved.

TAPS SOUNDS, and Wilson's suicide keeps running through my mind. I didn't know the poor fucker and can't imagine why he murdered himself. Manning blamed it on poor NCO leadership. Maybe it's true. Maybe it's bullshit.

Maybe the suicide resulted from what the military does right, instead of what it does wrong. The Army excels at connecting people. It integrates individuals into squads and platoons, and teaches them to put their unit before themselves. Deep connections like these are rare. What happens when they are gone?

A painful vacuum can form, that's what.

Hockey fills that gap for me. Could something similar have filled a gap for Wilson? Could it have saved him?

EIGHTEEN

It looks like someone took a belt sander and ground my stump into hamburger meat.

Jack asks if I'm going to rehab.

My watch shows ten o'clock. "Crap, I'm late."

"Blow it off."

"They report missed appointments."

"And?" he shrugs.

"If Manning finds out—"

"Fuck him."

"I've got to go. Will you drive me?"

"I guess so."

I give him my keys and grab my crutches. Five minutes later, we're at physical therapy. Jean checks my stump and gasps. She leaves and comes back with Dr. Noss.

"What happened?" he asks, examining my leg.

"Ah," I stammer.

"Hockey?" he says, probing with his finger.

I wince. "Yes, sir."

"You've really done a number on yourself."

I nod.

He fills out a sick slip, hands it to me, and says, "Crutches for two weeks."

"Two weeks?"

"Then we'll reassess; it might take longer to heal."

Back in the lobby. Jack flirts with a short, heavy-set woman. To cheer me up, he takes us to Burger King's drive through and we eat delicious Whoppers in my car. Back in our room, I text Eva about my rotten luck. She suggests Sunday brunch at Brunner Café.

I send her a smiley face, adding, "What time?"

"Ten," she answers, and sends me the address.

I see it's downtown and smile. Weiden's old town is so peaceful and clean. Plus, I'll get to show Eva my BMW.

ON SUNDAY MORNING, I ignore Dr. Noss's order and put on my reactive foot. With the thickest gel liner in place, the pain isn't too bad and there is no way I'm going to show up for my brunch date missing a foot. Plus, I need both feet to drive. Getting Jack or Scrappy to drive is a definite no go, because I don't want to share Eva's attention.

Driving into town, I struggle to stay under the speed limit. More than anything, it's the German speed trap cameras that keep my lead foot in check. I park in Weiden's large, open-air parking lot. Putting a few Euro coins into a machine, I pay for two hours and put the receipt on my dashboard. I'm a little early, so take my time walking through the old town. Luckily, my stump feels okay.

The downtown is pretty much deserted. Shops are closed on Sundays, refusing to match our hectic American 7/24 pace. I like it here. There's a set time to work, and a set time to relax.

The navigator on my phone tells me I've reached Brunner, but I don't see a Café. I wander around the town's main square and look in a store windows. Eva walks towards me from behind the old city hall. She's wearing black riding boots, black pants and a black blouse, with her hair back in a loose ponytail. When she reaches me, we hug and she waits for air kisses on both cheeks. I nail it, and she steps back to reward me with a beautiful smile. Holding hands, she guides me back and points up to the left. All I see is a fresh fruit and vegetable store.

She enjoys my confusion, and then explains, "Downstairs is the market, and upstairs is the Café." She points again, "The stairs are on the right."

We go up a narrow marble staircase. At the top, we push through a heavy glass door into the Café. It shares its name and baked goods with the simple Brunner Café on post, but they share nothing else. This Brunner is elegant in a friendly, Bavarian sort of way. Lush carpeting, gold railings, fancy marble tables and velvet half-moon booths add to the luxury. And, for a German place it is big, seating at least a hundred. The carved ceiling, however, impresses me the most. There are intricate wood paneled ceilings in castles and churches, but they are always way up high. Here, it is almost low enough to touch. Crystal chandeliers add a warm, golden glow to everything.

Eva takes us to a cozy table next to a window overlooking the main square. Our waitress, in a knee-length Dirndl, asks if we want menus in English.

Eva responds in German. When the waitress leaves, she says. "I ordered in German to surprise you."

"Come on, tell me," I plead, "I promise to act surprised."

She smiles, "I ordered the traditional Bavarian breakfast."

"Nice," I say, thinking the traditional Bavarian breakfast could be horse meat and I'd choke it down smothered in ketchup to impress her.

Our waitress returns with two tall glasses of golden, bubbly wheat beer. Eva picks hers up, holds it high and tilts its heavy glass bottom towards me. "Prost!" She says, flashing her gorgeous smile.

I raise my glass and try to clink its rim against hers. She pulls her glass back and corrects me, "No, like this," and touches the bottom of her glass to mine. "Clinking the thick bottoms together is much safer than the thin tops which could break, spill beer, and create hard feelings. And," she says, "looking away during a toast gets you seven years bad sex."

"Bad sex is better than no sex, right?" I laugh.

Eva ignores my joke and explains that drinking hefeweizen at ten o'clock is not her thing, but she is doing it in honor of my first Bavarian breakfast.

I nod, sip and enjoy the sweet, yeasty, full-bodied flavor.

"A proper breakfast always has two white sausages, one soft pretzel, sweet mustard, and a tall wheat beer." On cue, our waitress brings two extra-large soft pretzels on small plates. Eva doesn't reach for her's, so I sit back, sip my beer, and enjoy the view. "This breakfast comes from olden times. Many men, including my father, still look forward to it every Sunday after church."

Our waitress returns with a large porcelain bowl.

Eva removes the lid, revealing four swollen sausages floating in hot water.

"To avoid bursting them, they are never boiled," she says.

She pulls two sausages out, cuts them apart, and puts one on my plate. "Watch, this is important. Never eat the skin." She puts a big spoonful of brown mustard on the edge of her plate. With her fork, she flips her sausage on its back, cuts it from end to end, and opens it up skin side down. She slices off a bite-sized piece, dips it in mustard, and pops it into her mouth. Making happy chewing sounds, she swallows and says, "What are you waiting for, slowpoke? They're not as good cold."

I fumble with my wurst, and she laughs. Once I finally get a piece into my mouth, it is unbelievably good. The sweet mustard is a perfect match for the mild, bacon-flavored veal sausage.

Eva says, "Süsser senf and weisswurst always go together, and only at breakfast."

After brunch, we stroll through the old town. The wide cobblestone square narrows as we pass under an arch. Even though it is cloudy and gray, many people are out for strolls. At my car, I offer Eva a ride. She sees the parking receipt on my dashboard and teases, "You don't need to pay for parking on Sundays!"

"Now you tell me," I grumble.

Five minutes later, I head north, clearing the last autobahn exit for Weiden. Leaving the speed limits behind, I hit the gas. We rocket forward and cruise at 230 k.p.h., or about 140 m.p.h.! Eva isn't terribly impressed. When I exit at Mitterteich, she asks if she can drive.

"Are you sure you can handle it?" I tease.

"Watch and learn," she says, flashing a cocky grin.

Instead of going back to the autobahn, she takes small highways that loop, curve, and climb toward the Czech border. Man, can she drive! She cuts south and jumps back onto the autobahn. In a flash, she's got us up to 230 and only slows when we approach a 130 k.p.h. speed limit sign.

"Wow, where did you learn to drive like that?"

"I'm German," she smiles. "Getting a license here is difficult and expensive."

"How difficult and expensive?"

"We take a lot of classes and lessons, and pay about two thousand euros."

"Holy cow, that's a lot."

"Yes, but my practice hours were with my dad in his Porsche, so I was very motivated."

Eva pulls up to her house. My goodbye air kisses turn into an embrace and real kisses. I thought Eva's smile was the best thing about her. Now, I know better.

I make the twenty-minute drive back to post with my hormones raging. I limp into the barracks and tell Jack that I've screwed up my leg. That will buy me a few minutes alone in the bathroom. My God, Eva has a grip on me. But now, I've got just enough alone time to get a grip on myself.

THE REST of the week I keep myself under house arrest to stay off of Manning's radar. I can't risk him noticing me gimp around on crutches. For formations, I put on my reactive foot, crutch downstairs and leave the crutches hidden inside the door. After formation, I crutch straight back to our room, take off the gel liner, and air out my scabby stump. The quarantine nearly drives me crazy, but Jack helps by bringing to-go meals from the chow hall. He even shares his pizza and beer with me. He likes the company, but I'm not made for playing Xbox hours on end.

On Wednesday, Eva calls, "Want to watch an FC Bayern game with me?"

"Soccer?" I ask.

"Yes!" she says, "Champions League."

I put on my reactive foot and pick her up. We go to a local bar and grill called Hemingway's to watch. Everyone goes crazy when FC Bayern takes the field to play CSKA Moscow. When FC Bayern's star player Robben falls to the ground and acts like he's dying, I roll my eyes in embarrassment for him, his team, and his sport.

Eva sees, and says, "Don't make faces, FC Bayern is Germany's team, like your Dallas Cowboys, Atlanta Braves and Boston Bruins all in one."

"You mean like the Patriots, Celtics and Red Sox."

She shrugs, knowing better than to argue with a guy who grew up in the greatest sports town on the planet.

FC Bayern wins three to one, and that keeps everyone in a great mood long into the night. It's always fun watching a game with fanatics, but I still can't understand how a hockey girl can get so excited about such a painfully slow sport. At least I know how to answer when she asks if I want to go watch an FC Bayern game in Munich.

"Hell yes!" I say, surprised that my enthusiasm isn't totally faked.

NINETEEN

My luck holds. Dr. Noss clears me to wear my prosthetic before Manning and his lackeys discover my injury. On the way to practice, Scrappy's dashboard clock reads 17:35 instead of 5:35 PM.

"You're so hard core, you've set Army time in your car?" I tease.

"No, dumb-ass, the Krauts also use a twenty-four-hour clock," he laughs.

Whatever, I'm finally skating again. But we're running late, and have only an hour to get there, change and be on the ice. Scrappy cuts through Graf and heads out onto the Landstrasse. The two lane highway is a black slash cutting between dark pines dotted with white-trunked birches. He snags a prime parking spot next to the players' entrance as rain drops start bouncing off his windshield.

"More rain," he says.

"If it ain't raining, it ain't training."

"Who's the Army geek now?" Scrappy laughs.

We grab our gear and rush inside as the rain falls harder. Practice is like ones I've skated in hundreds of times.

Players skate around the edge of the ice. I weave back and forth, testing my socket. It feels okay, so I wind-mill my arms to stretch my shoulders. I skate past players who lie along the boards, stretching their groins. Coach blows his whistle and runs a few easy skating drills to warm us up and break a little sweat. I give one hundred percent on these drills and my leg feels solid. We move on to shooting and passing drills, leaving the last fifteen minutes to scrimmage. The familiar ritual of practice always comforts me, much like weekly Mass which brings the congregation comfort.

The puck drops, and I rush forward on instinct. I hunt the puck, send it to an open winger and streak to the net like a bird of prey. Legs pumping, head up, stick down, ready for the return pass. If the goalie crouches too deep in his net? I'll pick an open corner and shoot. Goal! If he surges out too far? I'll pull the puck in, cut around him, and push it over the goal line as I fly the net. Goal! When they took my foot, I never thought I would feel this way again. Nothing in the world matches it!

Scrappy and I shower, change, and hurry to his car.

"When's next practice?" I ask.

"Next week, but an hour earlier for Coach's chalk talk." Scrappy says, switching his wipers to high.

We ride through the rain with Scrappy going on about Garmisch and the legendary team dinner. He pulls into the flooded barracks parking lot. Getting my sticks and bag out, I get soaked from my Bruins cap all the way down to my running shoes. I wave as Scrappy pulls away. I take off my hat and let the icy rain hit my face. Two-footed life is great!

A WEEK LATER, it's the sad anniversary of my mom's crash. Dad and I talk briefly, like we always do. Neither of us ever says how much we miss her. I don't tell him it was my fault. He doesn't say it was his fault. We each prefer to carry our guilt alone. After we hang up, I pray for Mom to forgive me.

Jack barges in and opens the mini-fridge. "Hey, Dude, want a Brew-ski?" he asks.

"No," I say. "My mom died today."

"Oh, shit. If your dad calls the Red Cross, the Army will send you back."

"No, not today," I say.

"What?"

"When I was twelve," I say, choking up.

"Dude," Jack says, handing me a beer and leaving.

Does Dad drink alone? Does he cry? I sure hope not, because Foley men shouldn't cry.

COACH STANDS in front of a dry-erase board. He raises his hand and the locker room goes silent. "Okay boys, to be successful we need to be on the same sheet of music, so we will play a simple two-one-two system. It is simple, but it's effective. That's why half of the teams in the NHL play it."

He turns and draws a large circle in front of a net, and says, "Ninety percent of all goals are scored the slot. In our end, we want to keep the puck out of the slot."

He draws a large circle in front of the opposite net, saying, "When we attack, it's the opposite, we want to move the puck into the slot, shoot, and score!"

I played the same system in high school. It works when everyone buys in. To score, you've got to get to the slot and shoot, and shoot, and shoot some more. To defend, you've got to box out the other team and keep the puck to the outside.

Coach switches from theory to the specifics of practice. He diagrams a five-man breakout and says we'll repeat it until every line gets it right. Boring, but necessary to ensure moving the puck out of our end is automatic.

Coach doesn't cover it, but another key is to effectively use the boards and the blue lines. You've got to move the puck to the outside, chip it off the boards, and out over the blue line. Then in the neutral zone, you've got to move the puck straight into the attacking zone. Skating it or passing is okay, but once the puck is over the center red line, you can also shoot it in and let the wingers race in to recover it. Back in high school, I played center and stayed high in the slot, ready to take a pass and fire shots on net. As our crusty old Coach always hollered at us, "A shot on net is nevah wrong. Nevah!"

We finish warm-ups and Coach moves on to the breakout drills. He calls out my line and shoots a puck into the left corner. We move quickly in to the defensive zone in a loose two-one-two formation. The left defenseman sprints to the puck and passes it up the boards. Just as the left winger catches it, as I loop in looking for a pass. Breaking up the middle, I send a backhand pass to my right winger, and we sprint into the attacking zone We rush in forming a classic triangle attack, with both wingers crashing deep and me staying high. The right winger slides a pass back to me, and I send a onetimer into Scrappy's outstretched leg. Before he can pounce on it, the left wing taps it in for an easy goal.

"Perfect, men!" Coach yells. He uses his stick to point at the right winger. "He stays wide with the puck." He turns to the left winger, and says, "He's the crashing winger. He goes as fast as he can to the net." Pointing at me, he says, "The center hangs back a little and arrives just in time to take a pass, and you end up with a triangle."

He goes over to the winger with the puck. "Look, he's got three options." Pointing at me, he says, "He can pass to the center up high and go straight to the net for a rebound." Pointing at my left winger, he says, "He can pass the crashing winger down low." He takes the puck from the right winger, takes two quick strides and takes a shot on net. "Okay, let's do it again!" he shouts.

We run through breakouts at a frantic pace for half an hour. Finally, Coach gives us a water break and says, "When each line does it right one more time at full speed, we'll end with a scrimmage." After each line nails it, Coach rewards us with a twenty-minute scrimmage.

Before I get to the locker room, Coach calls me over. "Hey, nice skate. Next practice, I will try you at wing." Coach's heads-up stings. I don't want to try wing, because I'm a fucking center.

I throw my bag in the trunk and wait for Scrappy to load his equipment. Still upset, I run my hand over my buzz cut, sending cold water down my neck and back.

"Want to stop for a Döner on the way back?" Scrappy asks.

"Stop for a what?"

"A hot, flat-bread sandwich," he says. "It's the all-time best drunk food. They're awesome!"

We pull up to a small shop by the train station. Scrappy orders for us. The guy behind the counter shaves meat off of a huge cone rotating in front of a wall-mounted heating element. He loads meat, shredded cabbage, onion, tomato, and some kind of yogurt sauce into the pocket of a pita-type bread. I take a big bite. Holy crap, it is awesome! Driving back on post with a full belly and garlic breath, a heavy mist covers everything making it easy to imagine that the fucked up part world has disappeared.

A WEEK LATER, Coach holds another chalk talk. He stresses the importance of wingers playing deep on attack and high on defense. He looks around the locker room, "Questions?" Getting crickets, he says that after warm-ups we'll run through five-on-zero breakouts again.

In the first twenty minutes, every line does the breakout correctly at least three times. Coach gives us a water break, and then lines us up on the blue line. He puts Scrappy in net, me in one corner, Derrick in the other, and Joel up high as our center.

"Look here, men," he points. "The triangle attack fits our two-one-two system perfectly and does a few other great things. First, two defensemen can't shut down all three passing lanes." He points at Joel, "If we lose control of the puck, it puts our center in position to get back and help the defense." He points at Derrick and me, "Most importantly, it allows both wingers to collapse in on rebounds." Coach passes me a puck. "Show them, guys."

I rifle a pass to Joel and go straight to the net. At the same time, Derrick moves in and blocks Scrappy's view. Joel fires a low shot between Derrick's legs. Scrappy somehow makes the stop, but can't control the rebound. I tip the puck back to Joel, and he shoots it low into the open left corner.

"Magnificent!" Coach says. Turning to the players on the blue line, he says, "It's like having pinball flippers down low. Will should have shot, and is damn lucky Joel scored."

Coach turns, scowling at me and barking, "Down low don't get fancy, shoot!"

He turns back to the guys on the blue line, asking, "Who said, 'You miss one-hundred percent of the shots you don't take?'"

I know the answer, but can't get it out before Joel says, "Wayne Gretzky?"

Spinning around, Coach says, "That's right, the Great One!"

Coach turns back to the blue line, "Shoot first, think later."

Joel grins and sticks his tongue out at me.

"Fuck you," I mouth at him.

"Okay men, our next drill will reinforce our two-one-two play through the neutral zone and into the attacking zone."

He sets up a timing drill where we send a hard, leading pass to a player breaking in across the blue line. The basic idea is to time the pass so it hits the skater in stride, allowing him to break in at full speed. It's simple, but brilliant. After ten minutes, Coach whistles us to a stop for a water break.

"I like the pace, men," he says. "The next drill builds on the last one. Instead of one player breaking, we'll attack with all three in a triangle."

Scrappy shakes his head, sending sweat flying. "Fuck me!" he laughs.

I start at center and send a hard pass to Derrick. Off of the far boards, Basti sprints to the net. Derrick fires a laser pass to him. Scrappy slides over to block Basti's tip in, but is too late.

Basti points back to Derrick, shouting, "Nice pass!"

Coach blows his whistle, and the next set of players bear down on Scrappy.

We run out of time and don't get to scrimmage. I'm still pumped, because the drills reward the aggressive, run-and-gun hockey that I love. Joel and I stay out to move the nets for the Zamboni driver. On the bench, I overhear Coach talking with the Ice Devil coach. He asks Coach if we have any strong goalies this season.

"Sorry, none high-end enough for you. We do have a fantastic forward who's got a great nose for the net," Coach says.

Joel? But Joel's a sniper, not a digger.

"He's got good speed," Coach says. "And he's in rehab, so he doesn't go to the field and won't miss practices."

"Rehab? For what?"

"His foot, but he can skate. He's our best player. Should I ask him if he wants to skate?" Coach asks.

My ego swells, but is burst by the Zamboni honking at me. Startled, I look up into its oncoming headlights. I push the net out of the way and give the driver an embarrassed wave.

Coach calls me over. "You heard me and Peter talking?"

"Who?"

"The Ice Devil's coach."

I look down, embarrassed. "Yes, sorry."

"Do you want to skate with them?"

I look back up, smiling. "Yes, sir!"

"Okay, he's really looking for a goalie, but you'll—"

"What about Scrappy?" I interrupt.

"He doesn't quite have the skill set, plus he rotates to the field. With the Germans, regular attendance is a big deal."

"Oh." I say, thinking about my upcoming medical board.

"Is that a problem?" Coach asks.

"No, I don't think so." I lie.

"Good, because you're invited to tomorrow's practice."

"Really?" I ask.

"Sure, it should be fun."

"Count me in!" I say, wondering how long I can hide practicing with the Germans from Major Manning.

GETTING DRESSED for the Ice Devil's practice, I'm nervous.

All coaches want players who fit in, don't cause problems, and do their job. They want players who play hard, whether they're a first-line star or a fourth-line grinder. I am that kind of player, but I don't know how to show it to Peter. Coach's advice—to go last and watch the flow of the drills—makes perfect sense, but still, I'm damned nervous.

Suiting up, I absentmindedly turn the quick release and switch out my foot for hockey. Self-consciously I scan the room to see if anyone stares. It seems like nobody noticed, and with my shin pad and skate already in place, I look just like any other player.

"Wow," Thomas says, looking at the foot sitting between us. "Can I check it out?"

"Sure," I say, hating the attention.

"It's heavy," he says.

"When I have it on, it's not too bad."

"What does it do?" he asks, looking into the ankle assembly.

"It mimics my ankle by adjusting for uneven ground and transferring energy when I step off."

"Does your other leg do that, too?" he asks, pointing at my skate.

"Basically," I say, "but it's set up to adjust the angle of my blade with each stride, letting me to turn and stop just like before."

Out on the ice, Peter's practice is much faster than I expected. Players fly all over the ice, doing complex, choreographed drills. And it's all strangely quiet. Peter doesn't carry a whistle, starting and stopping the drills and sprints with hand signals. After he gives the briefest of instructions, he flashes his palm to start us. Most of his drills take place in very small areas, and the drills are almost mini-scrimmages with players fighting for the puck in game-like situations.

After each drill, we line up on the blue line for short sprints to the center red line. Then we coast to the other blue line, turn around and do another set of mini-sprints coming back. I cover the crazy short distance in two or three quick strides.

Before I know it, practice is over, and I'm completely gassed. The small area drills and mini-sprints forced me to compete at game speed for ninety full minutes. It was fun and exhausting. I sure hope that I've done enough to make Peter's team.

TWENTY

On Thanksgiving the Rangers have an all day military tournament in Wiesbaden. Our first game is at 08:00. To avoid the early morning drive, Scrappy and I leave right after Wednesday's final formation. We pick up Basti and head west. We're lucky, don't hit any major traffic jams, and make it to our hotel in under four hours. We check in and meet for a late dinner in the hotel's restaurant.

I can't find *Leberkäse* with egg or Bavarian wheat beer anywhere on the menu. There advertised special is potatoes with green sauce and apple wine. "What is green sauce?" I ask Basti.

"It's a thing here," he says. "Skip it, and go with a schnitzel and a pilsner beer."

Scrappy says, "Where is my schweinhaxe?"

"Many Germans vacation in Bavaria to enjoy our special foods," Basti laughs. "Now you find out why!"

I'm hungry, so I order a Wiener schnitzel with a side of boiled potatoes and green sauce. My pork cutlet is pounded extra-thin and fried in a golden crust, keeping the savory juiciness locked inside. My bitter pilsner is a good match.

The potatoes are just the same peeled, boiled potatoes you can get anywhere, and the green sauce is chilled buttermilk with bits of hard-boiled egg and green stuff floating in it. It's not terrible, but doesn't match my Schnitzel or beer. Basti catches me looking over at his big pile of fries and laughs.

I shake my head and ask, "What is the green stuff?"

He reaches across and scoops up some with his fork, makes a show of chewing it, and swallows thoughtfully. He puts his fork down, raises his index finger, and declares, "Grass clippings!"

Scrappy laughs so hard he chokes. He takes a big gulp of beer and gags again, making us all giggle like fools. We pay, and the waitress brings us complimentary shots. We toast and Basti catches Scrappy looking away.

Basti calls him on it, "Hey, breaking eye contact gets you seven years bad sex!"

"Seven years? But penalties only last two minutes," Scrappy says.

"For you, sex only lasts two minutes!" Basti says.

THE VIKINGS' tourney is in a big old barn of a rink in nearby Limburg. Scrappy pulls up and we're the second car in the parking lot. I push through the double-doors to a dark and empty arena. The smooth ice waits for us to scar it.

I walk down a dim hallway looking for our locker room. Each step is accompanied by the soft hiss of my mechanical foot. I open a door marked "BMC Rangers" and take a breath. It's amazing, every rink smells exactly the same. A minute later, the door bursts open. My teammates file in, and our pre-game ritual kicks in.

Coach raises his hand to quiet us, "Here are the lines,

but don't get too attached to them, because I'll be testing line combinations for Garmisch all day." What ever, I'm thrilled to be starting out on a line with Joel and Basti. Man, we're going to light it up! "Both teams might come out tentative," Coach says. "Don't! These are short games. Two twenty minutes periods, running time. So on your first shift, give them hell. Get the puck in deep, go get it, and put shots on net."

I love Coach's pep talk. It's a twist on the classic "Don't think, shoot!" speech. Many players never develop a shoot-first mentality, but I've never had that problem. Kevin didn't nickname me 'Balls Deep' for no reason. Heck, I was born knowing that you need to shoot, shoot, and shoot again. Yep, when I get the chance, I go balls deep every time.

Joel loses the opening face-off, and the puck goes back to a big Wiesbaden defenseman with a "C" on his chest. I charge forward to challenge him, and he calmly chips the puck past me to his waiting winger. As the winger breaks into our zone, Danny steps up and they tangle and fall. The ref blows the play dead and makes a terrible call, giving Danny two minutes for tripping.

Coach tells me to drop back and play defense.

Wiesbaden moves the puck well during their power play. The big captain blasts two hard shots from the point. Scrappy scrambles throughout, makes great saves, and corrals loose pucks. But the Vike's goalie is bigger, calmer, and makes his saves look easier. Even though we outplay them, the game ends tied at zero.

The next two games, I play wing. Then, I play one game at defense. Scrappy continues scramble and play well, and we easily beat Stuttgart, Baden, and Kaiserslautern. This puts us in the finals for a re-match with Wiesbaden.

Coach moves me to center. Now, I can finally take control of the game, and help us win it all. But shift after shift, I'm on the ice with Wiesbaden's captain. The big bastard is never out of position and makes clean breakout passes out of his end. This makes it hard for me to generate offense, because every time he gets the puck I must drop back to help cover the attacking Wiesbaden forwards. After forty minutes, we play to another zero-zero tie.

This time, we get to break it in a shootout. Coach picks Basti, Joel and me to shoot. Wiesbaden's captain goes first, bears down on Scrappy and shoots low glove side from the hash marks. Scrappy reacts a split second too late, and the puck goes in. Joel evens things with some nifty stick handling which pulls the Vike's goalie way out of position and gives Joel a wide-open net from the top of the crease. Even Joel can't miss from there! The next three shooters all miss, and now the game is on my stick.

I swoop in at three quarters speed, keeping the puck on my forehand, showing shot. The goalie shuffles across the top of the crease, keeping himself between the puck and the net. As I cross between the hash marks, I fake a wrist shot, speed up, and pull the puck up and across to my backhand. The goalie lunges, opening up his legs, and I send a quick backhand five-hole into the net behind him. He drops to his knees and slumps over. I dance on the toes of my skates, and my teammates spill onto the ice. It's magical! For some odd reason, winning in shootout feels even better than winning in regulation.

We all mob Scrappy. He's so happy he can't speak. Drunk with the joy of winning, we collect our trophy and head to the locker room. I shower, change, and am enjoying the electric buzz of winning. Outside, I check my phone hoping for a message from Eva. Instead, I see a message from Jack.

"Got a DUI, no crash. Told the cops the car was yours, but they towed it anyway. Don't worry, I'll get it back."

What the fuck? That fat son-of-a-bitch stole my car! Suddenly my electric buzz disappears and I hate Jack for killing my game-winning joy. Instead of celebrating late into the night, I worry about my car and what kind of trouble Jack's gotten me in.

I WAKE before Basti and Scrappy, and go down to breakfast. The waiter brings a pot of coffee. I check out the *Bild Zeitung* newspaper. The sports section takes up the back half of the paper, but only covers soccer and Formula One racing. With all the color photos, including topless models, it's a weird cross between *USA Today* and *Playboy*.

Coach comes over and joins me. Breakfast is self-service, and we go check it out. On a big table in the middle they have fresh breads, cheeses and cold cuts. At a smaller table there is cereal, milk, yogurt, cakes, mixed fruit, and honey. The warm stuff—scrambled and soft boiled eggs, bacon, sausage—are on a side counter. I usually eat healthy, but this morning I opt for eggs and bacon.

I ask Coach if he was with JAG.

"Yep," he says, between spoonfuls of granola and yogurt. "I retired from active duty, and now work there as a civilian attorney."

"Can I ask you a question?"

"Sure."

I tell him about Jack and ask, "What should I do?"

"To avoid running up storage charges, get your car back as soon as possible." They'll want cash. If you get there right away tomorrow morning, it should run about two hundred euros."

"Am I in trouble?"

"No," Coach says. "Whether he had your permission or not, it's all on him."

"What will happens to him?"

"Well, that'll be up to his commander. It'll take a few weeks for JAG to get all the German and U.S. police reports together, then they'll make a recommendation. Most likely it will be an Article 15."

"Can they kick him out?"

"Yes," Coach says, taking a sip of his coffee. He explains the ins and outs of how an Article 15 can lead to a chapter.

"Even if he's pending medical retirement?"

Coach nods, "His best bet now is strong letters of support, apologizing, and asking his commander for mercy."

We go for a second round of food, and this time I opt for sweets.

Coach tells me he's deciding on who to pick for team captain. "Even though we can dress one line of civilians, for Garmisch I want a soldier. But he's got to be the right fit. The best player isn't always the best choice."

I know this, but I don't understand why Coach is considering a third-line defenseman. He seems willing to talk about it, so I ask, "Why Mick?"

"Our team is mostly trigger pullers, fighters by nature," he says. "The teams from Belgium, K-town and Wiesbaden have players from the big headquarters. They're basically office workers—"

"That's good for us, right?"

"Yes, but there's a downside," Coach explains. "When we harness our killer instinct, it gives us a tremendous advantage. When we let it run free, we lose control and play overly aggressive, sloppy hockey."

"Not good," I agree.

"Right, so I need to pick a calm, disciplined captain who can help me keep things in perspective when games get chippy or the ref blows a call."

"Got it."

"You're a great player, Will, but you're not a calming influence," Coach laughs.

I smile, "Let 'em know you're there!"

"Right, and that's exactly how I need you to play in Garmisch—but our team doesn't need a captain to fire them up, understand?"

"Sure, I get it," I assure him.

BACK ON POST, I find Jack passed out on the couch. I shake him awake. He stares at me through red-rimmed eyes, mumbles something, and takes a big swig of beer.

"Got a fucking DUI," he slurs, snot running down his face.

I want to punch him in the face, but instead sit with him. Once he calms down, I share Coach's advice.

"I can beat this?" he asks.

"Maybe," I say. "Start by getting letters of support from your NCOs."

"Dude, they ain't gonna write no letters."

"Coach said that you and your defense counsel could go on the radio to warn others about the dangers of drinking and driving," I say, trying to sound confident. But even to me, this advice sounds like the garbage they spouted at Airborne School about what to do if our chutes failed to open. "Pull your chute in and throw it down and away in the direction you are spinning. If it still doesn't inflate, keep pulling it in and throwing it down and away for the rest of your Airborne life!"

TWENTY-ONE

Before our Thursday night practice on Weiden's big ice, Basti tells me that a Czech player left the Ice Devils to play back home. After practice, I as Coach about it. As we walk back to the locker room, Coach flags down Peter.

"Hi Peter," Coach says, "Foley played in a tournament this weekend and really looked great. Any chance he can keep skating with you?"

"You heard we have an opening for a foreign player?"

"Yes, but I'm asking about practices."

"If I played him on Friday, would he be here next week? Next month?" Peter shakes his head, "No, you can't say."

"Players get hurt and come back all the time," Coach says. "Maybe let him practice only as a spare. Who knows, you might need him later."

"I'll consider it," Peter says, stepping out onto the ice.

Coach turns back to me, "If you get a shot to play, remember Peter's skepticism about depending on soldiers to show up."

ON A GORGEOUS SATURDAY MORNING, Eva waits for me next to the fan bus. The sunshine takes the bite out of the cold air, and despite the chilly December weather half of the men only wear short-sleeve FC Bayern jerseys over their Lederhosen. Eva wears a better outfit for going to the open-air game—jeans, a red sweatshirt, and a team scarf.

She gives me a hug, and asks, "Did you get coal?"

"What?"

"From Saint Nicholas?"

"Huh?"

"on December fifth, kids put their boots at the front door. If they're good, they find candy and small presents in their boots. If they're bad, they get coal, and if they were terrible, they get a visit from Krampus."

"That sounds like our Christmas stockings, but we do it on Christmas Eve."

"The Christ Child visits us on Christmas Eve."

"Who's Krampus?"

"A red demon, with vampire fangs and devil horns. He beats the naughty kids with his walking stick, or catches them and carries them away in his sack."

"Holy shit, no wonder German kids don't jay walk!"

"Not German," she says. "It's an Alpine thing, just Bavarian and Austrian kids."

"Did you put your boots out, or were you afraid of getting Krampus?"

Eva sticks her tongue out. "Of course, I got a gift," she smiles and holds out a red and white scarf. God, I love her crooked little smile.

"What is 'Mia san Mia'?" I ask.

"The team's motto, it translates to, 'we are we'."

"In Italian?"

Eva rolls her eyes.

"What?" I grin. "It sounds Italian."

"Bavarian," she punches me in the shoulder. "In German it would be Wir sind Wir, but it means the same thing—we are one family—a tribe."

Two hours later, we approach the Allianz Arena. It sits by itself in open fields and from the distance looks like a giant tire lying on its side. As we get closer, I can see its plastic shell.

"At night they light it up from inside and they can change its color," Eva says. "It's always red for FC Bayern games."

We make our way to the upper deck of the massive stadium, and the north end is already packed with hard-core fans. It's reminds me of Weiden's Fan Curve except on an industrial scale.

"They will chant the whole game!" Eva says.

The words are Bavarian, but I recognize the cadence of some from the Ice Devils' game. And just like in Weiden, when the announcer introduces the players he just gives the number and the player's first name. Then eighty-thousand fans shout the player's last name, making it rumble across the stadium.

As play starts, Eva leans over and wraps her scarf around my neck. "Here, now you look like a proper FC Bayern fan."

Huh, maybe I can get into this "Mia san Mia" stuff.

From the beginning, it's clear that Werder Bremen is no match for the mighty FC Bayern. FC Bayern plays keep away from Werder, sending as many passes backward as forward. The Bayern defensemen even pass the ball back to their own goal keeper! Throughout the game, two players really stand out—flashy Robben with his outside speed bursts, and rugged Ribery with his go-to-the-net drives. Ribery toughness is rewarded with two goals.

Damn, if he could skate he'd be one hell of a hockey player.

FC Bayern's ball-control game is effective and they cruise to a seven to zero win. Although the emotion and chants were impressive, especially after FC Bayern scored, the game was painfully slow as compared to ice hockey. Not as slow as baseball, but still way too slow for me. All the back passing reminded me of the stall-tactics in basketball before the shot clock—and sadly there's no shot clock here!

When I slip and tell Eva the game was boring, she tells me that I'm crazy.

"How can you say a seven goal game is boring?" she shouts.

"But it's so slow," I say. "Some players jog across the field the whole game."

"It could have been cold and rainy, with the game ending tied at zero!"

"That would have sucked more," I agree. "How do they break ties?"

"They don't," Eva says, "They get three points for a win, and one point for a tie."

"What about the play-offs?"

"There aren't any," she explains. "At the end of the season the team with the most points is the champion."

Whoa, boringness heaped on top of boring, I think, but wisely keep to myself.

I ride home, sipping a zoigl beer from the bottle. I reach out for Eva's hand, and think the unthinkable—is she the one? She gets up and goes over to talk with her friends. I look out into the darkness and think about Mom. I've always lived for my parents' approval. After the accident that changed, because then I only had my dad's approval to win, and that's pretty straightforward—be a man.

It was always easiest to be a man at the rink, where life is condensed and games are decided in sixty minutes. Life outside the rink is infinitely more difficult and complex.

I look at Eva and wonder, would Mom have liked her?

Hissing air brakes interrupt my thoughts. We shuffle off the bus just after midnight. I'm a little drunk and groggy, and in no condition to drive. Eva invites me to sleep over. A perfect gentleman, I accept and sleep on the couch.

The next morning over coffee, we talk about life.

"Do you ever feel there's something missing?" I ask.

"No, why?" she asks.

"You know, something to live for?"

She freezes me with a hard frown, "Are you okay?"

"Yeah, sure," I say, looking away.

She touches my cheek and turns my face back to her. Her slender hands are strong, and I can see myself reflected in her dark eyes. Sometimes I miss the important things in life, but not this time.

She pulls my face to her. We kiss, and I taste a hint of mint, ripeness, and salt. We kiss harder, and I want to conquer and surrender to her all at once. She kisses my chin. She kisses my nose. She licks the corner of my mouth. I enjoy the feeling of her tongue on mine. She drifts down, kissing both sides of my throat.

AT MONDAY MORNING FORMATION, Jack says, "Remember, I'll be on the radio this morning. I'll be the stand-up guy and warning the others about DUI."

"You?" I say. "You should tell them about your porn

collection, Operation Fat Jack, and stealing my car." Jack slumps, his eyes showing that I've scored a direct hit. "Sorry, the DJ plays hockey and is cool—he'll make you sound great."

"Thanks, Bro," Jack says, punctuating it with an overzealous fist bump.

I go to chow and eat an egg white and spinach omelet, then go to the gym to work off the beer, brats, and pretzels from the FC Bayern game. Up on an elliptical machine, I listen to Tank's morning radio show. Between songs, he says, "This morning we have special guests in to talk about the risks of driving under the influence of alcohol." After Robin Thicke's catchy *Blurred Lines*, Tank introduces Colonel McGarry.

Holy cow, the post commander. Jack is really pulling out the big guns.

Colonel McGarry thanks Tank for having him on the show. "The GTA is the Army's largest overseas training area. The locals appreciate the economic benefits we bring," he says, pausing dramatically. "But our DUI numbers are unacceptably high. We must respect our obligation to ourselves and to the citizens of Bavaria to eliminate drinking and driving from our formation."

After *Wannabe* by the Spice Girls, Tank introduces Jack's defense attorney, Captain Feldman. She says hello and gets right to the legal stuff. "Under the UCMJ the alcohol limit is point zero eight; however, in Germany the limit is point zero five."

The DJ jumps in, "That's a little confusing, ma'am. Where does it leave us?"

"Great question, Tank. Soldiers face career-ending sanctions if they violate Germany's lower cut off, and in Czech it's even simpler, the cut off is zero."

Tank plays Sammy Hagar's *I Can't Drive Fifty-Five*, gives the daily weather and currency exchange rates, and says, "Stay tuned, because at the next break Specialist Jack Martin, a paratrooper with the 173rd, will tell you about his recent run-in with the German police and what he learned from it."

My leg feels great. I continue running on the elliptical and sending positive thoughts to Jack. Maybe if he comes across as a humble guy who made an honest mistake, it'll all work out. But, if he comes across as a dumb-ass with a chip on his shoulder, he'll be toast.

Psy's *Gangnam Style* ends, and Tank voice is back. "I'm here with Specialist Martin, who fought in Afghanistan, and recently lost his driver's license. Specialist Martin, what happened?"

"Me and my friends drove to a Nuremberg dance club. We knew we'd party and stay late, so we booked a hotel room right around the corner. Everything was cool, until the next morning. We ate breakfast, checked out, and German police pulled me over in the hotel's parking lot. When I asked them what I did wrong, they said I didn't do anything wrong. My two friends are black, so it was pretty clear they targeted us as American soldiers."

"Captain Feldman, does that happen?" Tank asks.

"What everyone listening needs to know is that the Germans have different rules, and while we're here, we are subject to—"

Colonel McGarry interrupts, "Tank, why don't you play us a song?"

I stop running, hearing only dead air before Miley Cyrus starts belting out *Wrecking Ball*.

Why in the world did Colonel McGarry shut down

Jack? Is he protecting the cops who profiled Jack? If it was a bad stop, shouldn't they just throw it out?

Miley's song ends and Tank comes back on. "Stay tuned folks. At the very next break Captain Feldman will tell us how the military justice system handles its DUI cases."

I get off the elliptical and go upstairs to the men's sauna. In the dry heat I close my eyes and wonder what the hell just happened?

Captain Feldman says, "Bavaria is a wonderful place to be stationed. The food and drink are delicious. However, the beers are bigger and stronger than back home, and the legal limit is lower. If you could drink two beers and still drive back home, that won't work here."

"What happens when things go wrong?" Tank asks.

"The German police call the MPs," she says, "and the MPs call the soldier's unit. The unit picks up the offender. On the spot, the unit commander takes the soldier's license, and later the Commanding General will likely issue a letter of reprimand. Accused soldiers stand to lose rank, pay, and their careers."

"That's terrible," Tank says. "Any last words of advice?"

"Take the train. Take a cab," she says. "Specialist Martin thought getting a hotel room was a good plan, but he was wrong. Don't make the same mistake."

Oh, and don't steal your roommate's car.

TWENTY-TWO

It's two weeks until Christmas and I'm standing in formation waiting for the sun to rise. After we report accountability and are released for hygiene and breakfast, my platoon sergeant pulls me aside. Sergeant First Class Jones is a big, thick Midwesterner facing a medical discharge for chronic back pain. In his awe-shucks way, he tells me to report to Major Manning.

"At 17:00?" I ask.

"Naw, this mornin' zero-nine," he says.

At nine sharp, I report. Manning tells me my medical board will convene at Fort Bragg next week. The Army's unofficial motto, "Hurry up and wait," rattles in my head. After seven months of waiting, it now seems so sudden.

All day I worry, and long after Taps the Hoff's lecture about the medical evaluation system cycles through my brain. He said all the bad press about wounded warriors waiting forever at Walter Reed to get their disability ratings caused Congress to change the system. They may have tried to improve it, but by putting local commanders in charge of it they sure put a bull's eye on the backs of the broken. All through the night, I wrestle with the demons and doubts that come with the possibility of a medical retirement. I have a habit of making quick, stubborn judgments. Is trying to stay Airborne one that will bite me?

The weightless uncertainty, like dropping through in the sky waiting the four endless seconds for my chute to jerk open, is killing me. Everything that matters is outside my control, and this time I don't have a reserve chute on my belly. What if they kick me out? Fuck me, I hate what I'm becoming. Even before the Army, I always took comfort in my jock status. Then, the Army groomed me to lead. I didn't worry about the small stuff when I was jumping, but now my paratrooper swagger is AWOL. I didn't know how damned lucky I was until after I got hurt. Now, I have no status. That hurts more than losing my damn foot.

I THROW myself into an exhausting hockey practice with the Devils. Thank goodness I have it to keep me sane. Afterwards, I follow Peter to his changing room.

"Coach, may I speak with you?"

"No players here," he says, holding up his hand to stop me.

"I'm sorry, sir, but it's important."

"Not here," he says, stepping back into the hallway. "Okay, now what?"

"Um, next week I won't be here because I have a medical hearing in America."

"No."

"It will only be for one week," I stammer.

"No," he says, stabbing his finger at me. "Team first, always first."

I try to explain that it's not my choice. He turns and shuts the door, leaving me standing open-mouthed.

I change and speed back to post.

I call Coach, explain the situation, and ask, "What should I do?"

"About your board or Peter?"

"Hockey."

"Nothing, I'll talk to him. Just let him cool off for now."

"And the board?"

"Your GI Bill has vested?"

"I think so."

"Find out for sure. If it hasn't vested, ask for a delay until you lock it in."

THE NEXT MORNING, I meet with Jon in his office. I tell him that my board is next week.

"I've checked with my headquarters," he says. "There's only been one amputee retained in an Airborne unit." He pauses and waits for me to say something.

I cross my arms. "And?"

"And—what you are trying for is a long shot."

"I thought you were in my corner, no matter what."

Jon calmly says, "Of course, it's your life."

"So, do I take leave and buy tickets to go back?"

Jon shakes his head, "No, your unit sends you back on temporary duty. Isn't anyone working on it?"

I shrug.

Jon picks up the phone and tears into an NCO at my battalion headquarters. He hangs up, and says, "Go see Sergeant First Class Jones, he'll take you to your personnel office and they'll cut orders. You take your orders to SATO and they'll issue you plane tickets on the spot."

"Got it," I say, standing to go. "Hey, is my GI Bill safe?"

"Yes, it's vested. Oh, and save your taxi and hotel receipts, because the Army will reimburse you."

I shake Jon's meaty hand. "Thanks."

Back at the unit, Jones tells me that Fort Bragg has pushed my board back three weeks. I'm more than annoyed. After all the waiting, I know that a few weeks tacked on shouldn't really matter, but it bugs the shit out of me!

When I finally get my new itinerary, I call Kevin. "Sir, I'll be at Fort Bragg for my medical board on January second."

"You guys fly in from Germany for your hearings?" he says. "Oh, and don't 'sir' me when it's between us."

"Go with Kevin?"

"Right, when it's just us."

"Okay, Kev," I say, feeling very weird about it.

"How's your attorney?"

"Okay, I guess. I've only talked to her on the phone. She says keeping me in the Airborne as an infantryman is a long-shot, but it did happen once before."

"You could be the second," Kevin says.

"It took him two years of rehab and a lot of unit support, but they kept him in."

"It sounds like he was a senior NCO or an officer."

"Yep, he was a master sergeant," I say. "My attorney tells me I'll likely be found unfit and put out with a disability rating."

"Any chance of retraining for a new job?"

"It's my call, but I'd rather go to college than be retained as a fuel handler."

"College was always your plan, right?"

"Yeah, but I want to finish my enlistment."

"Good luck," he says. "But be ready. If you're forced out, you'll miss the Army's strong sense of mission, place, and structure."

"I already miss it," I say flatly.

"I'm being serious."

"Me too, Kev, I'm a nobody here. I'm invisible."

Kevin clears his throat, "Well anyway, my buddies who got out were out of sync for a while."

"Whatever."

"Where will you stay at Bragg?"

"I'm not sure."

"Call me when you land," he says. "You'll stay with me."

SATURDAY IS the shortest day of the year, and it's good to know that from now on the days will get longer. And, the sleet and clouds have moved on, so the sun shines from sunrise at 08:30 hours to sunset at 16:00. Then Sunday turns blurry with a fog that seems to rise from the earth itself. At 10:00, I pick up Scrappy, glad to have company on our way to practice. I cut through the dense pine forest dotted with white-barked birch. Wolf country—Little Red Riding Hood must be from somewhere near here. I shiver, glad the road to Weiden is smooth and fast.

Scrappy starts yapping about Christmas market food and how much he loves steaming mugs of Glühwein.

"Have you tried it?" he asks.

"No."

"It's a spiced wine, for adults," he laughs, "Kinder-punsch is more your speed."

"What?"

"Hey, have you tried Eierpunsch?"

"No."

"Oh man, you've got to, it's hot eggnog spiked with rum!" he says. "How about Flammkuchen? They're the thin, crispy pizza-thingy topped with cream, onions, and ham. You've had them, right?"

"They serve it in the chow hall?" I ask.

"No."

"Then, no."

"Dude, you suck," he says, "I guess you haven't tried Kartoffel Puffer, you know, the potato pancakes served with applesauce?? Or Dampfnudel, the yeast ball served with warm vanilla sauce?"

"No and no. How do you not weigh three-hundred pounds?" I say, pulling into the parking lot and getting out before Scrappy can continue his interrogation.

I rush getting dressed, hoping to sneak out onto the ice alone. Skating on the virgin ice clears my mind of everything. I get my wish and carve the ice with long, smooth strides. Cool air rushes past my face. Other players join me. Somebody dumps a bucket of pucks on the ice. Players swoop in, snatch a puck, stick handle, and shoot. Everyone's here to have fun. It's what I been looking forward to all weekend.

After practice Basti asks if anyone wants to go to the Christmas market for a Glühwein.

Most players nod, and Scrappy says, "Hell yeah!"

"What is Glühwein again?" I ask, pulling into traffic.

"It's mulled wine," Scrappy says. "It's like hot apple cider, except with red wine."

"What? That's total bullshit!" I say, smacking my hand on the steering wheel. "I'm stuck being your driver again?"

Scrappy shrugs. "Those are the breaks."

I pull into a parking garage, and Scrappy leads us to the center of old town. It has been transformed into a Christmas village by adding lights, evergreen trees, and little wooden stalls selling food, drinks, and handmade presents. Scrappy orders a Glühwein and gets me a Kinderpunsch. Even though it's the non-alcoholic version, it's warm and tasty. Someone taps my shoulder. I turn, and it's Eva smiling up at me!

"Servus," she says.

"Hi," I smile. "I've been meaning to text you."

"But your phone is broken?" she frowns.

I blush.

We talk a bit, and she asks if I want to walk around. I tell Scrappy that he's on his own getting back to Graf. He gives me a thumbs-up and a big wink.

Eva and I walk off holding hands, just like at Oktoberfest. "What's your favorite season?" she asks.

"Fall. I like the sunny, frosty days best. What about you?"

"I like when fall changes into winter, and when spring changes into summer, but my very favorite is now. I love standing outside with friends, under the lights and decorations." We stop, and Eva asks me if I want a *Glühwein*.

"No, I just had Kinder punch," I say.

"That's not the same," she teases, pushing me. "Kinder punch is just warm fruit juice."

"Okay," I say. "Let's share one."

We pass the warm mug back and forth between us. It is delicious, but in truth I'd share a warm glass of snot with her.

We finish and she asks, "Are you hungry?"

"Starving."

"What's your favorite German food?"

"Döner," I say.

She laughs.

"What?" I ask.

"Döner Kebabs aren't German, they're Turkish!" She pokes me in the ribs, and says, "Let's go get a traditional Bavarian meal."

"Sure," I say.

She returns our mug, and pulls me in to a restaurant called the Ratskeller. It takes a few seconds for my eyes to adjust. I scan the crowded room. It's full of long tables and benches, and I finally spot an open table in a prime location.

Moving towards it, I say, "Hey, here's a spot."

Eva grabs my arm and says, "We can't sit there."

"Why?"

"It's the Stammtisch." She guides us over to a corner table with two open spots at the far end. We shed our hats, gloves, and jackets. A waitress comes, and Eva says, "Zwei Zoigl, bitte."

"What?"

"I just ordered us two Zoigl beers."

"No, what's with the other table?" I ask, pointing.

"The small wooden sign?"

I nod.

"The word Stammtisch is burned into it. In most traditional restaurants, there's a table that's reserved just for regulars, and they expect it to be open for them."

"So it's like a club?"

"Sort of, friends meet at the same place each week to talk, drink, and eat. Sometimes they play cards," Eva says. "My dad's been in one for twenty-five years." Eva hands me the menu and explains that the special is a traditional holiday meal.

"You guys eat turkey?" I ask.

"Not for Christmas. At Christmas, we eat goose. My mom orders it from the Metzgerei, ah, the butcher shop. She bakes it with apple and chestnut stuffing. Here it's just Gansbraten. That's the breast and a leg, not the whole goose," she smiles, patting her stomach and blowing out her cheeks.

"What's it come with?" I ask.

"Not sweet potatoes, Pilgrim," she laughs. "It comes with Kartoffel Knoedel. The dough is made from potatoes, flour and bread crumbs, and it's seasoned with nutmeg. Rolled and packed like a snowball, it's then boiled in salt water."

"I've had them at the Kantine on post," I say. "They serve them with the pork roast and gravy."

"Yes, that's the same. Here, they'll have a special dark gravy for the goose. For a side, you get Blaukraut. That's braised red cabbage."

"That sounds great!"

The waitress brings our drinks. Eva raises her glass and we Prost, keeping eye contact and clinking the bottoms of our mugs together.

Ah, seven years of good sex for us!

The first gulp of a beer is always the best. And wow, Zoigl is a tastier, fuller version of Sammy's amber from back home. Man, the Bavarians have it all figured out: Frühlings Fests in the spring, Biergardens in the summer, Oktoberfest in the fall, and now Christmas markets!

The waitress brings our food. The goose smells wonderful. When I cut into it the meat falls apart. I cut another piece and take a swig of beer. The savory goose and smooth beer are absolutely perfect together.

"You like it?" she asks.

I nod, smile, and take another sip of beer.

"Try the cabbage."

"Wow, I didn't expect it to be sweet." I say, pointing with my fork.

"It's my favorite," Eva says. "Do you miss home?"

"I miss my dad, but me and all my friends all went separate ways after graduation. You know what I mean?"

"No," she says. "People sometimes go away to school or to serve in the Bundeswehr, but they always come back."

"Really?" I ask.

"Yes, it's comfortable here."

The waitress tallies up our check and presents it for Eva's inspection. We discuss who gets to pay, and she finally lets me. Compared to Boston, the meal is ridiculously cheap.

Outside we say goodbye German style, hugging and air-kissing. Eva tells me to call her and disappears into the crowded Christmas market. I walk around and eat a crepe filled with Nutella, Germany's chocolatey answer to peanut butter.

Driving back to post, I think about how to spend time alone with Eva. Married soldiers live in family housing, and compared to us barracks rats, they have the life! I've got no privacy, and can't bring Eva home to Fat Jack, his Cheetos, and porn!

BACK IN THE BARRACKS, my phone buzzes. It's a text from Eva inviting me to spend Christmas with her.

I call her immediately. "Thanks for the invitation."

"No pressure, it's only if you don't have plans."

"No, it's great," I say. "Should I come over on Christmas

Day to see what Santa brought you?"

"Saint Nicholas already visited. Remember my FC Bayern scarf?"

"Oh yeah, proof that you were good," I say. "So what happens on Christmas?"

"It starts on Christmas Eve. We decorate our tree, have a family dinner, and the kids go to the living room to see what the Christ child brought them. Then we exchange gifts, and go to midnight Mass."

"We go to midnight Mass too." I say.

"The twenty-fifth is spent with family. On the twenty-sixth we visit extended family and friends."

"Wow, back home we just go to midnight Mass and have Santa and gifts on Christmas Day."

"Want to come over for Christmas lunch?" Eva asks. "My mom will make her famous roast goose stuffed with apples, chestnuts, and onions. It comes with the cooked cabbage you like so much."

"Mmm, sounds great. Can I bring anything?"

"No, but my mom likes white wine or flowers," she says. "Why does your Santa come on the twenty-fifth?"

"I don't know," I admit.

"Our Nicholas comes on December sixth, because the real Saint died on December sixth and it's his feast day."

"Huh."

"In Spain, they give gifts on January sixth for Three Kings Day," she says, "because that's when the wise men visited and gave their presents to baby Jesus."

Hanging up, it hits me, this will be my first Christmas away from Dad. I wonder what he will do. The police department always has holiday parties, and over the years we had many bachelor cops over for family dinners. At least we did, before Mom died.

TWENTY-THREE

Around midnight Fat Jack stumbles in from Ed's. He's hammered, but this time it's different.

"What the fuck, Jack?" I ask.

"Fuck you," he slurs.

"Seriously, what's up?"

"The fucking VA, man. Those cock-sucking pieces of shit. Crooks! They're all fucking crooks."

"What?"

Jack pulls a crumpled piece of paper out of his pocket. "Read this bullshit. Those fuckers, they can all just fucking die. I'll kill them."

The paper is a letter from the VA. "Only fifty percent?" I ask.

His face red and fists clenched, he shouts, "Fifty mother-fucking percent. It was supposed to be at least eighty!"

"What? I don't get it."

"They only gave me thirty percent for sleep apnea. Everyone knows it's fifty! They said that's only when you get put you on a sleep machine. The doctor fucks it up, and the VA knocks you down? That's fucked up!"

"What about your back?" I ask.

"They only gave me twenty. I can't get out of fucking bed and they only give me twenty fucking percent!"

"Wow, that stinks."

"Yeah, it stinks. The fucking Army says I fail retention standards for my back, but the VA only gives me twenty. How does that work?"

"Your shoulder?"

"Dude, ten percent. I can't lift a God damned thing. I can't throw. And they gave me ten fucking percent."

"But then you get sixty percent disability, right?"

"No, the VA uses fucked up math to knock sixty percent down to fifty."

"What? I don't get it." I say.

"No shit, the VA says thirty, twenty and ten is fifty."

"You hurt your back and shoulder in Afghanistan. Doesn't that count for something?"

"Nope, not at the fucking VA," Jack sits heavily and pounds his fist on the coffee table, knocking an Xbox controller to the floor.

"With over thirty percent you still get medically retired, right?"

"Yeah, but they fuck you on that, too. I'll get about twelve hundred a month. Dude, me and Brittany can't live on that in Detroit. Fuck, we can't live on that anywhere. And the Army doesn't kick in anything!" he says. "Nothing, man." Jack goes over to his bed, passes out, and starts snoring like a buzz saw.

I sit down, and turn on the TV. The Lakers are playing, but my mind is on Jack. He hurt his shoulder and back in combat and Operation Fat Jack was his way of getting his just dues. I wouldn't take that route, but I understand why he's hell-bent on getting the Army to pay "what it mother-fucking owes." He's not a bad person. I see that now. He's just pissed that the Army broke him and now refuses to pay up.

I go down to the 06:30 formation and report Jack as accounted for. The acting First Sergeant reminds us to be on time for all of our medical and legal appointments. *Really? Thanks for that breaking news flash.* My mind idly turns while he continues with his meaningless announcements.

The opposite of love isn't hate, it's apathy.

Here, that's our daily bread. Manning's leadership is pure mind over matter. He doesn't mind, because we don't matter. I can't wait to get back to the rink. Skate! Hit! Score! Me and my teammates, the coaches, the fans, even our opponents—everyone cares.

Jack's lower-than-expected disability rating really bugs me. I do feel bad for him, but I also worry about my own rating. Can the VA really screw us like that? After the bad advice I'd gotten from the barracks lawyers, I skip all the bullshit and go straight to Jon to get the real deal.

"Hi, Jon, got a minute?" I say, waiting in his doorway.

"Sure," Jon says, reaching for his coffee. "What's up?"

"I have some disability rating questions."

"Okay, shoot," he says.

"How much does sleep apnea get you?"

"Normally it won't fail retention standards, but if it requires treatment with a CPAP device, disability is fifty percent. Without it, it's thirty percent."

"What about a bad shoulder?"

"When it makes a soldier fail retention standards, probably ten or twenty percent."

"And a bad back?"

"Is this for a friend?" Jon asks.

"Yes."

"Then, send him to see me," Jon says, lifting his JAG mug to his mouth.

"I'm just double-checking stuff he told me."

"If you want to play stump-the-chump, go ahead, but please make it quick. I don't have all day," he says, motioning me to sit.

"So, what about chronic back pain?"

"If it fails retention standards, it'll most likely rate somewhere between ten and thirty percent."

"What if the shoulder and back injuries happened in Afghanistan?" I ask.

"It's irrelevant," Jon says, shaking his head.

"My friend said VA math knocked his disability down from sixty to fifty percent. Could that happen?"

"It could," Jon says. "Everyone comes in rated at Superman level, one hundred percent to the good. With VA math, you start off by subtracting the highest rated disability. Let's take sleep apnea at thirty, shoulder at twenty and back at ten percent, okay?"

"Okay," I say.

"We subtract the highest first, and we're left with seventy percent. Then we take the next highest as a percentage of the remaining. So twenty percent off of seventy percent leaves fifty-six percent."

"If you say so."

"Yep, I say so," Jon says. "Then, we do the same for the remaining ten percent. Ten percent of fifty-six is five point six. We round it up to six. We take that off and we're left with fifty percent."

"So you're telling me that thirty plus twenty plus ten make fifty?"

"If you run the numbers like I just did, they result in a fifty percent disability calculation."

"My roommate says he'll only get about twelve hundred a month"

"Well, that's what the law says, and the VA must follow the law."

"What about me, will they knock mine down like that?"

"With an amputation, you'll be rated in a special category. You'll also get a monthly payment in addition to whatever the VA rates." Jon hits some keys on his keyboard, squints and reads from his screen. "Here, this is directly from Title 38, Section 1114, of the United States Code, 'If the veteran, as the result of service-connected disability, has suffered the anatomical loss or loss of use of one or more foot or one hand, compensation therefor shall be ninety-six dollars per month.'"

"Ninety-six bucks a month? That's less than jump pay!"

"Hold on, if you're medically retired, that's on top of disability pay. And you also have your GI Bill. Just go to school, and you'll be okay."

All the way back to Graf, I fume. I can't believe it. What a fucking joke.

After the cannon booms and we're released for the night, Jones pulls me aside and tells me I'll be pulling Christmas staff duty.

"What?" I ask.

"You're single and can handle it," he says.

"But I've got plans."

"I've got plans, *Sergeant*," Jones corrects. "Make alternate plans."

I nod. There's no point arguing, because Jones is just the messenger. This gift is coming directly from Manning. I hope that the mean little fucker chokes on a candy cane and dies.

TWENTY-FOUR

I go upstairs and bitch to Jack about being stuck on Christmas duty.

"Dude, get over it," he says. "I'll bring you some turkey from the chow hall."

"I'm supposed to go to Eva's. Her mom is making goose."

"Lucky fucking you," Jack says. "Hey, when am I gonna meet this chick?"

"She might dump me over this."

"Well Bro, I get to Skype with Brittany. She'll rant about how hard it is for her as a single mom in Detroit. Then she'll ask me for more money," he says. "Wanna swap? You take my call and I'll take your duty?"

I shake my head, grab my phone, and call Eva from the bathroom. She's disappointed, but understands that it's not my call.

"To make it up to you, I'll take you out on New Year's Eve."

"I already have plans," she says.

"Change them, you won't regret it!" I say, trying to charm her.

"I can't."

"Why?"

"I watch *Dinner for One* with the same friends every year."

"Dinner for what?"

"For one, it's an British skit about an old lady cele-brating her birthday. Her butler slips in and out of the roles of her six dead friends, toasting with her each course of a fancy dinner. Of course, he gets completely wasted."

"What's that got to do with the New Year?"

"Nothing, I guess."

"Well, if it's in English, you can bring me along."

"No," she says. "Please drop it."

———

ON CHRISTMAS, I report for staff duty right after breakfast. The sergeant I'm relieving briefs me quickly, telling me how to fill out the duty log sheets and reach Major Manning. "You only do that if you have death, hospi-talization, or anything that might generate media interest," he says.

"So I'm his glorified answering service?"

"Sort of," he laughs. He tells me I can listen to the radio, watch TV, and read. I can't leave, except to go to the bath-room, and I can't make personal calls on the government phone. "Got it?"

"Yes, Sergeant."

"Good luck, and merry Christmas," he laughs.

Absolutely nothing happens until two o'clock when I call Dad on the government phone. He sounds good and tells me he's wearing the Boston Bruin Christmas sweater that I gave him a few years ago.

"Nice," I say, "I'm sorry I can't see it."

"That's the thing about protecting and serving," he says. "Duty nevah takes a vacation."

I think back to all the birthdays and holidays we celebrated without him. Or, the times he joined us coming on or off shift. Those times he'd be at breakfast or dinner in his uniform. As a kid, I didn't notice how hard it must have been for him. Now, I know.

JACK'S HELL bent on taking me to Ed's for their New Year's Eve party.

"Come on, Will, it's Tuesday, let's ring in 2014 surrounded by boobs!"

Against my better judgement, and partly because Eva ditched me for *Dinner for One*, and I agree to go. On the way, we walk under the tower, go out gate one, and turn right into Ed's. Up front we pass through an underwhelming room with nothing going on. A narrow hallway, papered over with one-dollar bills, leads into a back room. It features a large horseshoe-shaped bar and a small dance floor. It's crowded, and men outnumber women ten to one. Behind the bar, all three women are topless.

Jack greets the one with the biggest knockers like an old friend. "We'll take two drafts, Suzy," he says, hooking his thumb back towards me.

"Hey there, cutie," she says to me. "New in town?"

"No, ma'am," I say, "I don't get out much."

"That's a shame," she says, winking at me.

Jack and I sit off to the side, nurse a few beers, and take

in the shenanigans. Everything's cool until three drunk American women head toward us, and Jack says, "Incoming."

Oh shit, the middle one is Squeaky. She plants herself directly in front of me, and asks, "Can I buy you a drink, sailor?"

Her friends crack up, and Jack's chin nearly hits the floor.

"We've got a no-contact order, Kelli.".

"Not off post," she says, stepping closer.

Mother of God, I don't know for sure if Manning's order counts off post or not, but I'm not going to test my luck. I duck around Squeaky, grab Jack, and make for the door.

Outside Jack grabs me by the arms and asks, "Who was that?"

"The officer's wife from my history class," I say.

"Damn, I'd go to jail for a piece of that!"

Church bells start ringing and fireworks go off all over the place.

"What the hell?" I ask.

"The Germans do their Fourth of July thing on New Year at midnight," Jack says.

"Why?"

"The hell if I know."

MY FLIGHT from Nuremberg to Fayetteville forces me to think about my medical board. Should I bite the bullet and retrain as a cook? I could stay in Germany, play hockey, and date Eva. Maybe we'd marry and live in Netzaberg?

Man, I'd flip burgers all day long to come home to her.

Damn, it feels like the Army has a gun to my head. I want to stay a paratrooper, but then they might put me out. Why do I need the Army to feel whole? She is such a cold, unfeeling bitch. And staying in as a paratrooper, I'd deploy all the time. Would Eva put up with it, or would she rebel against it like Kelli?

Kevin picks me up at the Fayetteville airport. As he drives us to his apartment, he looks over and says, "Remember, Willie, there are hardly any happy ex-paratroopers. We're not the same afterwards. We need our dangerous missions. We need the adrenaline rushes."

I nod, wondering if that's true. Maybe after we settle in as cogs in the big green machine, we can't find a way to settle out afterwards.

"Without dragons to slay, we drift," Kevin says.

I nod.

"No matter what happens, keep skating. That will keep you sane."

Sensing that he's waiting for an answer, I say, "Yes, sir."

Once we're at his place, he gives me the third degree. He means well, but kills me with questions about Dad.

"Have you seen him since the bombing?"

"No."

"Did you fly here through Boston?"

"No."

"Are you flying back through Boston?"

"No."

"Why not?"

"I didn't know it was an option."

"Have you guys talked about rehab?"

"No."

"Do you guys evah talk?"

"Every week."

"About what?"

"Hockey."

"Did he tell you about fan banner night?"

"What?"

"He was the fan banner captain. Bobby Orr helped him swing the banner around. They put it up on the Garden's big screen and the crowd went nuts."

I shake my head, "No, he didn't tell me." As long as I live, I will never forget my first time sitting next to Dad at the Garden. The excitement. The buzz. Being part of it. Even now, my favorite games are the ones I watched with him there.

Kevin grabs his laptop and finds Boston's make-up game. He scrolls to right after the national anthem. The camera zooms in, the crowd cheers, and my breath catches. Dad's holding the Spoked B fan banner with Bobby Orr.

"Why didn't he tell me?"

"It was right after he got hurt," Kevin says. "Ask him about it."

"I'm asking *you*."

"He was at the finish line, you know."

Of course I know, but he told me he was okay. He said it was merely a flesh wound. Fuck, I did the same thing. I let him believe I had only a broken leg when I knew it was much worse.

"What about your mom's birthday?" Kevin asks, his question hitting me like a sledgehammer.

"What about it?" I snap.

"Did you call Uncle Jimmy?"

"Of course, but please give it a rest."

"You guys got to talk, Willie."

"To share our grief? It'd kill us both. It's better when we stick to hockey."

Kevin gets up to grabs us some beers.

I sit and stew. With hockey, the pain of a loss only lasts until the next game. Death is forever. Besides, some shit you just don't share. In my family we have always found it easier to do something than to say something. We talk quietly, we grieve silently, we defend what's ours. You want to see us loose and happy? Come to the rink.

Kevin hands me a Budweiser and says, "Okay Willie, I'm not gonna beat a dead horse." He takes a long drink, looks down at my foot, and then back up at me. "You know what went wrong?" he asks.

I shrug, "Not really. I've played it a million times in my head, but—"

"Tell me about it."

I close my eyes, think back, and describe the jump in vivid detail. I see, hear, and feel everything. I guess it's what the oldtimers call a flashback.

"Shit," Kevin says, "a bad jump."

I nod.

"Hey, for the board, remembah that readiness is the Army's number-one priority."

"Yep," I agree.

"Of course, it's best to get injured soldiers back to work as quickly as possible, and the Army is hoping to get ten-thousand back that way. The other option is to speed up medical retirements and fill the slots with able-bodied recruits."

I nod.

"The needs of the Army, Willie," he says, taking another pull from his Bud, "that's what it comes down to. If the Army needs you, you'll stay. If not, you'll go. What you want doesn't really matter."

Kevin talks about the Army like a cruel mistress who

exacts a terrible price on those stupid enough to love her. I can't imagine Major Manning being as honest, and Kevin's straightforward way lets me forget his rank. It's like back in the old days, just two cousins shooting the shit.

"But no, this one time, you get a say," he smiles and raises his bottle in salute tome. "So what's it gonna be? Are you gonna hold your ground or take whatevah they give you?"

"What do you think I should do?"

"What do you want?"

"I don't know," I admit. Do I want to take whatever they give me just to stay in? Why in the hell do I want to keep jumping anyway? To be one of the guys? To chase the fleeting high? I can think of highs better than exiting an aircraft—scoring a game winning goal, or making love to Eva. Maybe I'm just afraid to cut loose from the anchor that keeps me from drifting?

"Hold your ground, Willie," Kevin says. "You didn't enlist to fold sheets. You enlisted to be a warrior. If the Army doesn't see it that way, take your college money and run."

We sit, finishing our beers in silence. It's comfortable. Neither of us need the mindless chatter.

I set my empty bottle down. "Thanks, you're right."

Later, drifting off to sleep, I'm at peace for the first time in weeks. To hell with Major Manning and the needs of the Army. It's my call.

EARLY THE NEXT MORNING, Kevin drops me off and I sit alone outside the board's chambers. Waiting for my attorney, tendrils of doubt start to work their way up from my stomach to my chest. Today something will be finished and something else will begin. Now, I'm stuck on the high wire in between. My chest tightens. If I stick to my guns and they kick me out, the blame will rest solely on me.

My attorney, Captain Lacevic, arrives in a whirlwind of motion. Petite and dark-haired, she chases away my doubts with her enthusiasm.

"Are you over jet lag?" she asks.

"I'm okay, ma'am."

"Good, your uniform looks sharp. You look great. Are you nervous?"

"Yes, ma'am, a little."

"Well, don't be. I do most of the talking." She explains that the board will decide if I can remain a paratrooper. If not, they will decide my level of disability. Their focus will be on my ability to jump out of planes, carry a rucksack, and fight. She says that I am allowed to have the last word.

"You still want to stay infantry?" she asks.

"Yes, ma'am."

"Good, okay, there are three members on the panel. Two are from combat arms, and one is medical. They won't announce any decision today. First, they send a report to the United States Army Physical Disability Agency. They usually return it approved, but may kick it back for reconsideration. Once the report is certified, it goes to your local commander to inform you. Does that make sense?"

"Yes, ma'am."

"Are you ready to go?"

"Yes, ma'am."

We enter the hearing room. It looks just like a courtroom on TV. The three members sit behind a bench like judges, except they wear dress uniforms with all of their shiny badges and awards. One is an infantry lieutenant colonel, one is an infantry sergeant major, and the third is a medical service captain. Compared to the colonel and sergeant major, my uniform looks blank.

Once the hearing starts, things go quickly. The colonel, who introduces himself as the board's president, speed-reads through a script. Captain Lacevic answers all his questions. He says because my medical records are clear, they won't call any witnesses. Captain Lacevic agrees and says she won't call any either. She asks, however, to make a statement on my behalf.

"Please proceed," the board president says.

Captain Lacevic rises and signals for me to rise. "Mr. President and board members, Specialist Will Foley stands before you today as a triple volunteer. To get here, he volunteered to enlist. That's something that less than one percent of Americans do. Then, he volunteered for the infantry. He excelled at basic training, and at advanced individual training. Then, he volunteered for Airborne school. His father, a policeman with the Boston PD, and his cousin, a West Point graduate and company commander in the 82nd Airborne Division, attended his graduation and saw him off to his first assignment with the 173rd Airborne Brigade. In Germany, Specialist Foley continued to excel and quickly made Private First Class, Specialist and Corporal. After his tragic parachuting accident, which resulted in the amputation of his right foot, Specialist Foley worked very hard in physical therapy. He respectfully asks this board to retain him as a paratrooper in the United States Army."

Captain Lacevic looks over at me, smiles, and we sit in unison.

The sergeant major raises his hand. "Specialist Foley, I have two questions. You may consult briefly with your legal counsel before answering. You may also elect to remain silent. Do you understand?"

I stand, coming to the position of attention. "Yes, Sergeant Major."

"Please, be seated. There's no need to stand, and please feel free to consult with your attorney."

"Yes, Sergeant Major," I say, taking my seat.

"Why were you reduced from Corporal to Specialist?"

"I wasn't busted, Sergeant Major. My commander took my stripes when they reassigned me to the rear detachment."

The sergeant major clears his throat, and asks, "Have you ever received an Article 15 or any other administrative punishment?"

"No," I say, flushed with anger.

Captain Lacevic stands, "Mr. President, members of the board, I can proffer that Specialist Foley has never been punished. His commander took his rank when the unit deployed and Foley couldn't go. If the board wishes to recess, I believe I can call a witness to testify to that effect."

"Specialist Foley, is this true?" the board president asks.

"Yes, sir."

"Please, both of you be seated," the board president says. The board huddles briefly, and the president says, "There's no need to call a witness, the board accepts your proffer." The board president then turns to me, "Specialist Foley, am I correct in understanding that you want to stay in the Army as an infantryman, and will not accept re-classification to other less demanding duties?"

I stand and brace rigidly at the position of attention. "Yes, sir!"

"Stand at ease, son," he says. "You understand that we

might not be able to keep you in the infantry, but we might be able to keep you doing something else?"

"Yes, sir."

"This hearing is now closed."

The Sergeant Major stands, grins, and says, "I like you Foley. You got balls."

Out in the hallway, I high-five Captain Lacevic. Seeing that she doesn't share my enthusiasm, I ask, "We won, right?"

"The sergeant major's vote," she says, "but you need two votes for retention."

"What's your best guess, will I get them?"

"Smart money says no, but I've seen stranger things happen," she says. She then shakes my hand and wishes me a safe trip home.

KEVIN DROPS me at the airport and I'm on my way back to Germany. My flight goes through Dulles International Airport, and I board the overnight flight to Frankfurt. The entire time, I think about my hearing. I wonder when I'll get the board's decision. Somewhere over the Atlantic, I realize that I'll drive myself crazy if I keep thinking about it. When we land in Frankfurt, I finally relax. With one more short hop, I'm back in Nuremberg. Focused on hockey and Eva, I get in my car and drive straight to her house.

On her front steps she gives me a hug. "I missed you," she says.

"Me too," I say, strangely feeling like I'm home.

Inside, the jet lag kicks in, and I pass out in Eva's bed. I wake with no idea what time it is. I snuggle over to enjoy her warmth. In a dreamy fog, we kiss. Eva rolls on top of me.

Then, my leg cramps. Pain pulses up from my missing foot like a ten-thousand volts and forces me to arch my back. Eva comforts me and once I'm okay, she suggests breakfast. I'm too embarrassed to stick around, and tell her that I can't because I have to get back for formation.

I dress and head for Graf. What the hell is wrong with me? Maybe I should have just lost my balls instead of my foot.

I make it back just in time to change into my Army sweats and form up in the foggy, wet darkness. As I stand with the broken, the fit soldiers move out for a formation run. One hundred pairs of feet thunder, pounding out the sound of soldiers moving with each stride and breath perfectly in sync. It puts a knot in my throat. I should be with them, not sidelined and ignored.

ALL DAY SATURDAY, I look forward to our last tune-up games before Garmisch. When I inherited my dad's wiry build and quickness, I also inherited his desire to be a part of a team. We're joiners and love to run with the pack. And with the Rangers, I'm in. I'm all in.

Out on the ice, I'm in my element and completely focused on playing well. I mess up a couple of good scoring chances, but still rack up buckets of assists, and we win both games. We're locked and loaded now, ready for our shot at winning the big tourney in Garmisch. I just hope that my scoring touch returns in time!

TWENTY-FIVE

Sergeant First Class Jones calls me over just before our weekend release formation. I do like the corn-fed Midwesterner, but I sense he's about to deliver some unwelcome news. "Manning denied your pass for Garmisch," he says.

"Why?" I ask. "He knows it's for a military tournament, right?"

"I don't know," Jones shrugs.

When Robalo cut me from the herd, and my fire team deployed without me, it hurt to see them prep, pack, and leave without missing a beat. Maybe that's not exactly how it went, but that's exactly how it felt. And now, fucking Manning is cutting me from the Ranger herd! Without me, my hockey team will push on and play well. But goddamn it, that will kill me!

WHILE GETTING DRESSED for Sunday's pickup game, I tell Basti my terrible news about Garmisch. He shakes his head, "What do you mean your commander disapproved your request to play? He can't do that!"

"He did—I'm out," I say.

Basti stabs his finger at me, "Talk to Coach!"

I shrug, again.

"Don't shrug," he says, "I'm serious! Coach is a retired colonel and can find out what the hell is going on."

During practice my timing is off. I mess up drills that I could normally do in my sleep, and when we scrimmage I fire shots wide of the net and whiff on a one-timer. Afterwards, I stay out to move the nets for the Zamboni. As it makes its slow laps, I tell Coach that Manning denied my pass.

"When did your DA Form 31 come back?" Coach asks.

"I didn't get anything back. On Friday, my platoon sergeant told me it was denied."

"Did you put in a written pass request?" Coach asks, moving his net back into place.

I nod, "That and the tournament memo you gave us."

We step off of the ice and continue talking. "Is your commander a colonel?" Coach asks.

"No, he's a major serving as our rear detachment battalion commander."

Coach nods. "You still get four-day holiday weekends, right?"

"Yes, I wouldn't miss a day of work for the tourney. I guess he just wants me to rot in the barracks."

"Don't jump to conclusions," Coach says. "It might be a simple misunderstanding. We'll go see him and find out."

I nod.

"Tomorrow ask your platoon sergeant for an open-door meeting with your commander. Be sure he knows that I'll attend as the coach of the post's hockey team."

"Will do. Thanks Coach."

Alone in the barracks, my chest tightens. Since my amputation, everything is so damn hard. I'm only at ease inside the rink. I give up on sleep, reach for my Easton, sit on the edge of my bed and twirl it in my hands.

WE GET an appointment to see Manning on Wednesday at noon. I call Coach and explain that Manning is a stickler for rules, maintains an aloof, no-nonsense façade, and hates lower enlisted soldiers, especially those who marry and move out of the barracks.

"If the Army wanted privates to have spousal units, they'd issue them to them," he'd often say. At a recent formation Manning vented his disdain for the "fake vegans" in his ranks. "Three hots and a cot, and you're not happy," he said. "Then, I see you eating Whoppers at Burger King. I'll tell you a whopper, the whopper you told me to get separate rations because you're too special to eat in the chow hall. Well, no more. All special dietary requests based on preference are heretofore denied."

Coach takes it in quietly. "Well, at least you're not a vegan or getting married." Then, he explains that the brigade left Manning behind to take out the trash and will grade his performance on whether he's cleared out the sick, lame, and lazy while the brigade is away.

Outside of the battalion headquarters, I tell Coach about the statement of charges Manning ordered me to sign.

"What? Really?" He asks.

"Yep," I say, "at the hospital."

"At the hospital? Christ! How much?"

"A nurse interrupted him there, and then Jon Hoffmann killed it here."

"Good," he nods.

At 12:00 sharp, we go inside. Forty-five minutes later, the sergeant major waves us into the absent battalion commander's large, oak-paneled office. I step forward, come to the position of attention, salute, and formally report. Manning remains seated and returns a half-assed salute. Coach joins me, and offers Manning his hand. Manning stands, and they shake.

Coach says, "Hi, I'm Jack Bradley. Thanks for agreeing to meet with me and Specialist Foley about his pass request."

Manning nods, motioning for us to sit.

"To be clear, I'm the coach of the post's hockey team. I'm also a retired lieutenant colonel, and now work as a civilian over at JAG."

Manning purses his thin lips and says nothing.

Coach presses on, "I'm hoping to clear up a couple of things concerning Corporal Foley's request to play during the upcoming four-day weekend."

"*Specialist* Foley," Manning corrects.

"Yes, Specialist Foley," Coach agrees. "Since we're both busy men, I'll cut right to the chase. I'm confused by your denial of his pass request."

"What's confusing?" Manning asks. "Foley requested permission, it's my job to decide, and I decided to disapprove it."

"All things considered, it doesn't make sense. This will be the team's seventh trip to Garmisch for the annual military championships. We won the tournament two years ago, and with Foley playing we have a good chance of winning it again. I don't understand why you wouldn't want to have a paratrooper representing the 173rd at the tournament."

"Well that's the thing, Judge, Specialist Foley is on a physical profile. His battalion is in Poland, freezing their asses off. I can't send him to the field. Why should I send him to Garmisch?"

"I see your point, Major, but that's not Foley's fault. I'm sure you have some malingerers, but Will Foley is not one of them," Coach says, and points over to me. "We both know that if he could be in Poland, that's where he'd be."

Manning sits stone-faced.

Coach continues, "Corporal Foley didn't ask to be amputated *and* Specialist Foley hates being non-deployable. While the medical system does its thing, hockey provides an outlet for him. He's with other soldiers. He's competing. And without him, we're not the same team. To run the table and win the tourney, I need him."

Manning rocks back in his chair and clears his throat. "Okay, let's say I agree with you. What about the rest of my unit? What message will approving his trip send to the eight hundred paratroopers forward deployed? What does it say when I give a soldier who can't deploy special treatment?" Manning punctuates his rhetorical question with an icy Hannibal Lector stare.

Coach ignores Manning's we-are-done-talking stare, and counters, "There is some tension there, but I know your intent isn't to punish Foley for losing his foot. Most of the other soldiers playing have already gotten their unit's support. The few denials are due to conflicts with unit missions that take priority. That's simply not the case here. Foley's sole mission is to recover, and hockey is helping him do it."

Manning leans forward, and says, "My hands are tied.

The Vice Chief of Staff sent out an email earlier this week emphasizing that the Army's number-one priority is fixing or sending non-deployable soldiers home. Did you know that we have eighty thousand non-deployable soldiers? That's twelve percent of our combat power. I have seventy-four soldiers, including Foley, pending medical boards. To get healthy replacements, I've got to move them out." Manning points in my direction, "Giving passes to play hockey doesn't help me do that."

Coach leans forward and says, "The leave and pass regulation gives you the authority to approve Foley's pass despite his current medical status, and his board date won't change based on his being absent for the weekend."

Major Manning shakes his head and reaches for a binder. "It's funny that you should bring up regulations. I have my copy of Army Regulation 635–40, *Physical Evaluation for Retention, Retirement, or Separation*, right here. It says that the system's goals are—and I quote—to maintain effective and fit military organization with maximum use of available labor, provide benefits for eligible soldiers whose military service is terminated because of service-connected disability, and provide prompt disability processing while ensuring that the rights and interests of the government and the soldier are protected." Manning closes the binder with a snap. "I see nothing about playing ice hockey. Keeping Foley here to heal or separate as soon as possible is in the best interest of the Army." The corners of his mouth curl as he turns to me, and says, "Your pass request is denied." He doesn't inflect or raise his voice. In fact, it's his calm, deliberate delivery which infuses his words with such unnatural, mechanical authority.

Coach locks eyes with Manning. "You're treating Foley like he committed a crime. Look at your arguments about what deployed soldiers would think about Foley getting a pass. Those are exactly the same reasons commanders impose restrictions to post as punishment—to make an example and show others what happens to rule breakers. But what rule did Foley break? None! He's the victim here, not the Army."

Coach pauses, and Manning stares flatly back.

Coach continues, "I understand why you are frustrated that it will take about a year for Foley to get treatment, rehab, and be boarded. But, what you need to remember is that none of it is Foley's fault."

Manning sighs, shakes his head, and checks his wristwatch.

Coach also sighs, checks his watch, and then says, "What if Foley puts in for regular leave? What if he takes four days of vacation to play? Would that maybe strike the balance you're looking for?"

"Possibly," Manning says, standing. "But no promises."

Coach and I stand, and Coach shakes Manning's hand. "Thanks for your time. Foley will put in for regular leave."

"You need to cover your travel day too, so request five days," Manning says to me, the trace of a smile creeping at the corners of his thin lips. "If your NCO chain of command supports it, I'll approve your leave."

I snap to attention and salute.

Manning brings his heels together and returns my salute. "Dismissed," he says.

Outside Coach says, "Manning is meeting us halfway, so go put in your leave right now."

"Got it, Coach."

"Make sure your NCOs know that Manning asked you to resubmit it. Otherwise, if you say nothing, they will send it up with a recommendation to deny because they know he already denied it once."

I give Coach a confused look and he puts a fatherly hand on my shoulder. "If you tell them he asked you to resubmit, they'll think he wants to approve it and will forward it back with a recommendation to approve," he explains.

"Got it, I'm on it."

TWENTY-SIX

After practice, I stay out to shoot shot after shot. Coach hits me with some quick passes and I rifle one-timers from the top of the circle. I need this. It feels good and besides hockey rewards repetition. Repeating the same movements over and over weaves smooth, automatic reflexes into me.

Bang! Wide off the boards. Crack! High off the glass. Clang! Better, but off of the crossbar. I catch the last two passes and send smooth wrist shots into the empty net. In the last week, we've won both tune up games. I had a few assists and killed a few penalties, but I missed some easy goals. I've been here before and know there's nothing I can do about it, just relax until I get my groove back. But how in the hell can I relax when I'm so out of synch?

I shower, change, and head back to my room. I read an on-line article about us:

The Bavarian News
U.S. Army Hockey in Bavaria
February, 2014

GRAFENWOEHR, Germany—Packing, moving,
and trying to find a hockey team is challenging. Now
try doing it overseas where everyone speaks German.
Such is the case for the U.S. soldiers stationed in
Bavaria. Despite these challenges, there is a group of
players who combine their love of hockey with over-
seas duty. They are the Bavarian Military Commu-
nity's Rangers.
"We share a love of country, a dedication to duty,
and a passion for playing hockey," said team captain,
Kenny Krieger, "stationed far from home, the team is
our overseas family."
Most players are combat veterans who recently
served in Iraq and Afghanistan. They represent the
BMC in an annual military championship held at
the historic Olympic Stadium in Garmisch-
Partenkirchen. The rink hosted the 1936 winter
games, and later this month will host the twenty-
third annual Military Ice Hockey Championships.
"Playing for the Rangers brings us more than
trophies. It is a great outlet for our soldiers," said
Coach Jack Bradley. "It provides a once in a lifetime
cultural experience and fosters an unbelievable level
of camaraderie."

UNDER IT, there is an old team photo with shaggy-haired Matt, First Sergeant Robalo and Professor Krieger in it. Sure, it's pure propaganda, but I love it!

I text a link to Dad, writing, "Look! Our team is famous!"

Ten minutes later he texts back, "Will your games be on TV?"

No, but it reminds me of an AFN TV spot about two

Rangers who came back from Afghanistan to play in Garmisch. The clip starts with a close-up of Major Mack in Afghanistan, wearing full battle-rattle and casually resting his hands on top of a hockey stick.

Offscreen someone asks him, "Can you tell us when your love affair with hockey began?"

"My love affair with hockey?" he says, breaking into a wide smile. "Being on the Rangers is just like being in combat. I've got to depend on the guy to my left and the guy to my right. Here, or out on the ice, it's exactly the same." The video cuts to Mick and Captain Donofrio firing pucks off of a piece of plywood into a makeshift net. In the background, artillery rockets shoot across the sky.

"Sadly, no," I text Dad, "but click on the AFN link and check out this clip."

A few minutes later my phone blings. "Proud of you. Go get 'em, Willie!"

MY LEAVE COMES BACK APPROVED. Scrappy and I leave for Garmisch right after lunch on Wednesday. It's damn cold, but the sun is out. While he drives, Scrappy chatters about nothing. He denies that he's nervous. "Just take the pressure off of me with a first period hattie!"

Yep, he's nervous, nervous as hell.

Just north of Munich, we pass the Allianz Arena. I pull out my phone, take a picture, and text it to Eva. She texts back a heart.

Huh, did she send it for me or for FC Bayern?

Scrappy slows down as we hit city traffic. We pass the BMW museum, the 1972 summer Olympic park, and a ten-story glass Mercedes-Benz building which has white

cars lined up across every floor. South of Munich,
Scrappy gets back on the Autobahn. A half-hour later, the
Alps rise in the distance. The Autobahn ends and we
drive beside a river surrounded by towering mountains.
Scrappy passes Garmisch's train station, turns left, and
pulls up at the Olympic Stadium. We grab our gear,
trudge through the snowy parking lot, and go inside to
find our locker room. A schedule taped to the door lists
our first game against the Belgium team at eight o'clock
tomorrow morning.

"Let's head over to the hotel and check in," Scrappy
says.

We show our military ID cards to the rent-a-cop guards,
and Scrappy parks in front of the massive Edelweiss hotel.
The huge lobby has a weird Alpine goat herder meets
Colorado gold rush vibe. Our double room is American-
sized big, and has a narrow balcony facing Germany's tallest
mountain, the Zugspitze. Its white ski slopes run like frozen
waterfalls through the dark pines down into the valley floor.

At 18:00, we link up with our team in the basement
sports bar. The clannish Rangers crowd together, drinking
and fueling up on pizza and chicken wings. A square-shoul-
dered, tough-looking soldier talks with Krieger. With his
deep tan, shaved head, and lots of ink, he's weathered
enough to be coming straight from a desert deployment.

"Who's that?" I ask Scrappy.

"That's bad, bad, Cameron Brown, the meanest man in
the whole damn town—" he sings. Seeing that I'm not
impressed, he pantomimes dropping a microphone and says,
"That's Cam. He comes back every year to play. This year
he flew in from Fort Bragg."

"What position?" I ask.

"Defense," Scrappy says, nodding and smiling. "And I

always feel better when he's working his evil magic in front of me."

A tall, preppy-looking guy talks with Coach.

"Who's the lanky guy?" I ask.

"That's Coach's son, Zach," Scrappy says. "He grew up playing for the Rangers and comes back from college to play."

"Is he any good?"

"If he played with Cam's intensity, he'd be in the NHL," Scrappy says.

"Shut up."

"No, seriously," Scrappy says. "He was always very good with the puck, then he grew to be six foot five, filled out, and now anchors our defense."

"Another defenseman?"

"Yeah, baby!" Scrappy laughs. "And his play is flawless. He doesn't score many goals, but he prevents a lot of them."

"Like Chara?" I ask.

"More like Pronger, very high hockey IQ and pinpoint breakout passes. The puck doesn't stay in our end when he's on the ice."

AFTER BREAKFAST, Scrappy and I meet Coach and Krieger in the lobby. Krieger sports a tie-dyed t-shirt, baggy shorts, and wool socks poking through his Birkenstock sandals.

"Morning Coach; morning Professor," I say.

"Dude, here it's Kenny," Krieger says.

We ride to the rink together and have time to kill. I re-tape my trusty Easton with blue tape hoping it will bring me some puck luck. More players arrive, and we change. A ref comes in and asks Coach for a copy of our team roster. He turns and sees me holding my hockey leg. I look away, but not quickly enough to avoid his double take. I rummage in my bag for nothing in particular, hoping he doesn't ask about my foot.

Damn, I've got to be more careful about how strange it looks.

During warm-ups it's clear that Belgium has a recreational team. Coach calls us in. "Okay boys, don't let your guard down. These games go by fast. Twenty minutes running time, switch ends, and another quick twenty. So, there's no time to recover from a slow start!"

We nod.

"We'll roll three lines with two pairs of defensemen to keep our tempo high. Joel's line starts with Will and Basti. Kenny and Danny on D. The Germans are out next, followed by the grind line. The second D-pair is Cam and Zach. Questions?" Coach asks, as the buzzer sounds.

We line up on the blue line, and raise our sticks to salute the Belgians. Kenny leads us back to our net, and we huddle in around Scrappy.

"Okay, fellas, this will be a great warm-up game," Kenny says. "Let's shoot for ten to zero. Hands in. Scrappy, lead us."

Scrappy yells, "Let's go!"

"Rangers!" we yell.

"Let's go!" he calls.

"Rangers!"

"Let's go!"

"Rangers!" we scream.

We break, and line up for the opening face-off. The ref bends to drop the puck, time slows, and Joel pulls it back cleanly. I split out wide, sprinting for the boards. From our blue line, Danny hits me with a crisp pass. I spot Joel cutting up the middle and hit him. He goes to the net and drops the puck back to Basti who fires it across to me just as I crash the net, deflecting his pass in. After ten seconds, we're up by one and my slump is over! Two minutes later, we're up by three and our shift ends.

The game ends twelve to one. After my first goal, I settles in and played my game, and my next three goals fueled my building confidence. Scrappy is pissed, because he thinks the goal he allowed was one too many. With goalies, there's an old saying: "We don't know if they're born crazy or become crazy, we just know they're *all* crazy!" Scrappy is absolutely a goalie's goalie, and I know better than to try to console him.

OUR NEXT GAME is against the GK Flyers at noon. At ten o'clock I see Cam and Danny are downing beers in the rink's restaurant.

"What the fuck?" I ask them.

"Dude, it's Garmisch," Danny says, raising his glass to toast me.

"Hydration is key!" Cam adds, joining Danny's toast.

So mad that I could spit, I storm off to the locker room.

Two hours later, we're back on the ice. I'm surprised to hear the Flyers speaking French during warmups. Kenny circles us up for his pre-game talk, "Okay, fellas, GK is Canadian Air Force with lots of Quebecois players. They are older and slower, but still pass and shoot like pros. Just play our game, and we'll wear them out."

We put our hands in, and this time Danny calls out,

"Let's go!" for us. I'm still so pissed off about his between-game drinking that I don't answer his calls.

The game starts, and Kenny's advice is spot on. We win four to two in what begins as a fast-paced game. I slap in a rebound and set up Joel's power play one-timer. Scrappy plays great but dwells on a shot from the point that beat him low stick side. It turns out that the player who took the shot played in the AHL before joining the Canadian Air Force. Still, Scrappy stays mad at himself.

In the locker room, some players undress and shower, and others sit and crack open bottles of Helles. Because our last two games are late—at eight and nine o'clock—players make dinner plans.

"What kind of bullshit is this?" Cam asks. "We get first and last games of the day, and the last two are back to back? Who did we piss off?"

"Okay, fellas," Kenny says. "Listen up. Limit yourselves to one beer at dinner, please." He looks at Cam, and adds, "And, no hard stuff."

"You looking at me?" Cam grins.

Kenny ignores him. "We get a bye in the elimination bracket if we win out. Let's do it and control our destiny."

Over in the corner, Coach watches. He stands and says, "McMouth is on the way. I don't see any reason to change our lines. I'll rotate him in as our fifth defenseman, unless someone shows up drunk."

DURING WARM-UPS, it's clear that Aviano has a mix of good and bad players. They have one standout who moves fluidly, changes speeds effortlessly, and fires the puck like a sniper. His blue breezers have white lightning bolts shooting down from each hip.

"Look, that hotshot thinks he's playing for Tampa Bay," I say.

"Nope," Joel shakes his head, "those are Air Force Academy pants."

Ouch, Air Force plays division one hockey.

The academy grad wins the opening face-off. It turns out to be a really fun game. Between whistles, players chirp and laugh with each other. Even though he's the best player on the ice, their star doesn't take shots on net. Every time he has a scoring chance, he passes. I have a hat trick and we win six to one. By my count, the Air Force guy could have had at least six.

Skating off the ice, he asks me where I played.

"Boston," I say.

"With the Terriers or Eagles?"

"High school," I say, "for East Boston."

"Oh, you're enlisted?"

"Yes, sir,"

"Man, think about green to gold," he says. "You could walk on to a D-I team."

"Sir, can I ask you something?"

"Sure," he smiles.

"Why didn't you take shots? You could have scored a bunch."

"Where's the fun in that?" he says. He notices my puzzled look. "My competitive hockey is behind me. I'm here to enjoy the games, and setting up my teammates is more fun than hogging the puck and trying to grind out wins all by myself."

It's the biggest cop-out I've ever heard, but I nod and keep my opinion to myself.

Because of our back-to-back games, we wait on the bench and watch the Zamboni cut a new sheet of ice. Stuttgart starts sluggishly and allows two goals in the first two minutes. They do recover and bounce back to even the score before the first buzzer sounds. In the second half, I score three goals in a row. For the first, I cherry-pick at center ice, catch a long pass, go in alone, deke, and slide the puck under the sprawling goalie. My second is a power play one-timer from down low. My third is an empty netter shot from half ice. When it goes in, our guys go crazy and celebrate my hat trick by throwing their helmets onto the ice.

The guys are in full party mode back in the locker room.

I like to eat, drink, and celebrate as much as the next guy, but not during a tournament. For me, the real party comes afterwards. So when everyone else goes off to Peaches and Billy's, I bow out to go back to the Edelweiss and soak in the hotel's outdoor hot tub.

Back in the room, I down two big glasses of water and stretch. I enjoy focusing our next game. When I'm in the moment like this, even water tastes wonderful. I change and look down at my fake leg. Man, I don't need the attention. I pull on sweats and go to the sauna instead. In the dry heat, my mind wanders. I don't like to drop the gloves, but brawls can be awesome. It's great when guys stick up for each other. All the best teams have at least one guy who plays on the edge. He isn't afraid to make enemies and does damn near anything to help his team win. Sometimes he's the biggest, meanest guy. Sometimes he's not.

In Boston, we have Marchand, our Little Ball of Hate. Here, we've got Bad Cameron Brown. Everyone says Cam plays his best drunk or with a wicked hangover. His off-ice excesses seem to match his on-ice bravado. I bet when he enlisted, he hoped the same would be true in the Army. The problem is that commanders like Manning view that type of aggressiveness and bravado as indiscipline and cockiness. But man, if the shit hits the fan, I want Cam in my foxhole.

JOEL AND I SKIP BREAKFAST. We join Coach at lunch. He asks about our night on the town. Joel describes the fun at the Irish Pub and Peaches.

"Please go get Cam and meet me out front," Coach says.

We go upstairs and wake Cam.

Out front, Coach is sour and starts right in. "Cam, you will not take any players out drinking tonight. If you show up late or drunk tomorrow, I will bench you."

"Coach," Cam grins.

"No," Coach wags his finger. "You can drink all night and still play, but nobody else can. If we stay focused, we'll win this tourney. Please don't screw it up."

Joel and I nod. Cam holds out his hand. Coach hesitates, then shakes.

"My word, Coach," Cam says, "I won't go out with any players tonight."

I WAKE EARLY for our big day. We are just three wins away from going home as champs. I avoid eggs, bacon, biscuits, and gravy. Instead, I choose oatmeal, yogurt and melon. Huh, do the other guests realize that the $12.95 Edelweiss buffet is nearly identical to the $2.95 chow hall breakfast? I take my tray out and sit under the hotel's panoramic front windows. The rising sun lights up the snowy Alps. it's magical and uplifting. Recharged, I'm eager for battle.

Everyone's in the locker room forty-five minutes before puck drop, everyone that is, except Cam. Ten minutes before warm-ups, Cam shows up. He grabs a bottle of beer and pops the top. Raising it, he proclaims, "The best detox is retox!" He drains a Helles in three gulps, and winks. "No players were harmed in the consumption of this beer."

I can't hold back a smile. Cam laughs and comes over to hug me.

In warm-ups, Stuttgart has picked up a few high-end players. I complain and Kenny explains that it happens every year. "When teams advance, they call ringers to come play," he shrugs, "we brought in McMouth."

We get off to an excellent start, but their goalie makes great saves and keeps us to one goal. On the bench, I'm puzzled. What's wrong with Basti? He's a smooth skater, can really control the puck, and has one of the best one-timers on the team. In our tune-up games he used slick feints and fluid moves to avoid contact. Despite our differing styles, we played well and fed off of each other. But now, the chemistry is gone.

I turn to him and say, "Next shift you better be flying! I'll chip the puck forward, you skate into it, take it to the net, and shoot! I'll follow, scoop up the rebound, and score."

"Just like that?" he asks, grinning and raising an eyebrows.

"Just like that," I scowl. "You shoot low, he'll go down like a two-dollar whore, and I'll go top shelf."

Three times we rush in on net, and three times we fail to score.

We cruise to an easy five to zero win, but my only goal

comes from a sweet pass from Joel. Maybe it's time for me and Basti to play on different lines?

I change and go watch the Baden Bruins play the Kaiserslautern Eagles in their quarter-final game. Both teams can really skate, pass, and shoot. KMC's top line looks like it could give us some real trouble. They play an ugly, chippy game and eventually wear out the Bruins. This sets them up to play us in one hour.

Coach must have read my mind when he put together the new lines for our game against KMC. To add speed he put McMouth on my line, and moved Basti back as a spare winger on the Kraut line. Basti doesn't seem too upset, and McMouth seems hungry for action.

We start sluggishly, and the Eagles control the puck for most of the opening ten minutes. Cam takes a tripping penalty, and KMC scores. We have never trailed in this tourney, and with such very short games, the pressure to score is immense. Near the end of the first half, I fly across center with the puck on my stick. As I break over the blue line, my skates come out from under me. Bam! I'm down, sliding toward the net. A whistle blows, and the ref calls a KMC defenseman for tripping.

Zach skates over and argues that I should get a penalty shot. Zach is calm, deliberate, and fluent in German. He's also a certified referee, so he's the perfect player to argue for us, but the German ref isn't buying it and the clock keeps ticking. So we line up in KMC's zone with a five on four advantage.

The Eagles win the face off and shoot the puck to our end. Joel races back and collects the puck. Looping around, he picks up speed and flies past two Eagles in the neutral zone. Zooming across the blue line, he pulls his stick back and fires a wicked slap shot on net. The rising shot whizzes past the goalie's left ear and goes in just under the crossbar. Goal!

We mob Joel, then follow him down our bench, high-fiving the outstretched hands. The period ends a minute later. We catch our breath and drink water. Coach gathers us around him. "They're a talented team, but you just scored. We've got control. Don't let go!"

"Let's go!" yells Joel.

We scream, "Rangers!"

Joel rips off two more "let's go!" and we holler back, "Rangers!"

The buzzer sounds.

We line up at center ice. Joel chips the puck forward to McMouth. McMouth surges forward, swoops in, and scores with a low wrist shot. Two shifts later, KMC comes back with a tick-tack-toe goal. With less than two minutes left, Joel fights for the puck down low and scores with a nifty backhand. The German line goes out next. If they can hang on for ninety seconds, we move on to the finals.

KMC pulls their goalie to put six skaters out. With an empty net at their end, we battle up and down the boards fighting for the puck. Before KMC has a chance to set up an attack, the buzzer sounds and we win three to two.

We all jump onto the ice and swarm Scrappy. Our fans up in the stands cheer wildly, and Eva's there, cheering wildly with them!

Back in the locker room, I grab a banana and a bottle of water. As soon as Kenny finishes telling us we deserve to be in the finals, I rush out to find Eva.

Out on the ice, the Vikings are playing GK. The Flyers now have two full lines. Every time they get control of the puck, they spread out and pass it around like a big game of keep away. It works well until the Vikes finally get possession and charge towards GK's net. The GK goalie is pretty good, but isn't able to stop every shot. As the buzzer between periods sounds, the Vikings lead one to zero.

Eva comes through the restaurant doors. "I knew you were playing today," she smiles, "and I had to see you play!"

Kenny interrupts, "Will, Coach wants everyone in the locker room."

Eva rises on her toes to give me a kiss. "Viel Glueck!" she says, rolling back down to her heels and punching me in the chest. "That means good luck!"

We assemble in the locker room. "This is it, men!" Coach says. "Playing in the Championship, that's what it's all about!" He reads off the lines, keeping them the same. Kenny goes out and returns, telling us that the Vikes won 2-0. Coach reminds us that on Thanksgiving we beat them in their own building.

In the game's first shift, McMouth hits me with a cross ice pass, springing me to go in alone on their goalie. I beat him high on the stick side. McMouth skates to me and Joel rushes in to join the celebration. I'm riding on a high tide of confidence, completely in the zone. My mind is sharp, my muscles are supercharged, and I hunger for more. We push the pace, but the Vikes push back. Their big captain scores from the point, and their bench goes wild.

"Play our game, boys," Coach yells. "Don't let them take control!"

We know he's right. Hockey is a game of emotion and momentum. Over the next few minutes, the play goes back and forth. The Vikings rush up the ice and take it to us, and we rush back and give it to them. Both goalies are solid and the first half ends tied at one.

Ten minutes into the second half, Cam battles for position in front of our net. The ref's arm goes up. When we touch the puck, he blows the play dead and calls Cam for roughing.

"What the fuck!" Cam screams.

Zach skates to the ref, "You've let both teams play physically all game. Why call it now?"

The ref shakes his head and points Cam to the penalty box.

"Will you make the same call at both ends?" Zach asks.

"That was roughing," the ref snaps. "One more word and you'll get ten minutes."

Zach skates back to the bench.

Coach asks, "Zach, are you good?"

He nods.

"Okay, Zach and the Germans kill first. Basti, drop back and play D."

They line up to take the face off to the left of Scrappy.

"The grind line goes out next with Danny," Coach says. "Derrick, drop back and play defense until Cam comes out."

Everything goes well until Derrick tries to carry the puck from behind our net into the Vikes' zone. His Bobby Orr rush falls apart on Wiesbaden's blue line. Their big defenseman fires a pass up to a breaking winger, and they skate in three on one against Danny. Danny tries to hold the middle, but a quick tic-tac-toe passing sequence leaves him and Scrappy on the wrong side of the net, and the Vikings' crashing winger taps the puck into a wide-open net.

"Fuck!" Danny yells, slamming his stick on the ice.

Down by one, with only forty seconds left, Coach calls a timeout. He puts Joel, McMouth, and me out with Cam and Zach. He tells Scrappy to come to the bench once we gain the attacking zone, and tells Martin to jump out as our extra attacker.

Joel wins the draw back to Zach, skates up the ice, and takes a return pass. Scrappy sprints to the bench, and Martin jumps over the boards to join the attack. Joel cuts to the middle, and takes a shot. There's a loud crack! Along with the fluttering puck, the bottom half of Joel's stick launches toward the net. I crash the goal looking for a rebound. Joel drops his stick and rushes to the bench. Kenny leans out and hands his stick to Joel. Martin battles for the puck in the corner, wins it, and fires a pass back to Joel, who is surging across the blue line. The Vikings aren't expecting it, and Joel is wide open. He shoots. McMouth tips the puck, and it ricochets like a pinball in the crease. As I spin away from the big Vikes captain, time slows. My stick finds the puck. I look for open net through a tangle of legs and don't see any twine. I slide to my left. Their goalie mirrors my move, and just as he lifts his skate to shuffle sideways, I send the puck between his legs and in. Score! I throw my arms up in wild celebration.

"Five hole!" Joel shouts, "You beat him five hole!"

We skate to the bench, high-fiving everyone. The buzzer sounds with the score tied at two. Coach only has about a minute to figure out who will shoot for us. He speaks briefly with Kenny, and hands a note to the referee.

I lower my head, hoping my number isn't one of the three on the note. I hate shoot-outs. The basic idea is simple: come in on an angle and look for the goalie to mess up his angles, then shoot for the open net. If the goalie adjusts well and covers the net, then look for him to open his legs and shoot five-hole. If he doesn't open up his legs, cut back and try to deke him with some fancy stick handling. The thing is, in games I play on instinct. Even when I'm on a break-away, there's someone chasing me and creating back-pressure. In shoot-out, there's no back pressure and there's way too much time to think.

Coach motions for us to huddle around him. "All right boys, our shooters are Martin, Joel, and Will. We shoot second."

The first Viking shooter skates to center and Scrappy goes to his net. The center ice ref raises his arm, Scrappy nods, and the ref sets the puck down on the face-off dot. The shooter loops back to his blue line, picks up speed, collects the puck, and cuts to the far boards. He cuts back toward the middle, carrying the puck on his forehand. In the slot, he makes a sneaky stutter-step and shoots near side. The puck zips past Scrappy's blocker and pings off the metal post. The goal ref extends his arms out, signaling no goal.

Martin shoots next. Europeans have always broken ties in shoot-outs, so he's been doing this since he was a little kid. Martin skates the same curving S-pattern as the first shooter, but instead of shooting he tries to deke. It looks like a sure goal, until the goalie lunges out and pokes the puck away. Damn, no goal!

Scrappy goes back in net to face Wiesbaden's captain. The big bastard skates straight up the middle, fakes a slap shot, and dekes Scrappy on his stick side. Shit, a goal! I knew the smart son of a bitch wouldn't waste his chance on a low-percentage slap shot, but his fake was just enough to freeze Scrappy for the deke.

Joel is up. He loops in at full speed, ready to shoot. Cutting across the front of the net, he pushes the puck forward and across to his backhand. He gets to the far post a split second ahead of the Viking's goalie. Goal! And wow, did Joel ever make that look easy!

The third Viking shooter is a short player who comes in

slowly, looking like a dumpy T. J. Oshie. Ten feet out he shoots five hole. Scrappy sees it coming and drops to his knees, deflecting the puck harmlessly away.

I'm the last Ranger shooter and have the chance to win it all. I stand at center, waiting for the Vike's goalie to get set. From a dead stop, I pick up the puck and skate slowly towards where the blue line meets the boards. I enter the zone and accelerate straight to the net. Then I slam on the brakes hoping that the goalie, having just been burned by Joel's speed, will over-compensate and continue to slide across to the far post, leaving his back door open. I shoot back against the grain, but the goalie tracks it, flashes his glove, and catches the puck. Skating back to the bench, I lose my temper and tomahawk my stick over the boards, breaking it in two. I immediately regret it—my trusty Easton didn't miss the shot. I did. Head bowed and eyes lowered, I go to the far end of the bench to sit alone.

The shootout continues in sudden-death. I stand to watch, feeling terrible, because I've put the entire game on Scrappy to come through.

Coach taps me on the shoulder. "It was a good try," he says.

The Vikes captain shoots again. He rushes straight up the middle, winds up for his big slap shot, and takes it! Scrappy stands tall, absorbs the rocket of a shot, and raises his arms in celebration. Whoa, it's normally bad luck for a goalie to celebrate too early.

Coach looks up and down our bench. "Cam, are you finished puking yet?"

Cam wipes his mouth, smiles, and says, "Sure am."

"Can you score?"

"Fuck yeah!" he says, jumping over the boards.

Cam loops around and rushes up the center. He fakes a

slap shot, fakes going five hole, and then flips the puck over the sprawling Viking goalie.

Goal!

Cam raises his hands in celebration, waves his stick around like a giant wand, and pretends to be a knight sheathing his sword. He starts to dance a jig, as Scrappy crashes into him, and we all pile on! The rest is a glorious blur! The wild celebration morphs into a rowdy on-ice trophy presentation, which becomes a crying, laughing on-ice photo session. It ends only when the scorekeeper repeatedly blasts the buzzer, and the Zamboni rolls out onto the ice.

On the way to the locker room, I see Eva. "Want to come in?" I ask.

"No, I'll see you at the dinner."

"Awesome!" I say, leaning in to kiss her.

"You stink," she says, pushing me away. "Shower, and I'll kiss you later.".

In the locker room, it's pure madness. *The Boys are Back* blares from a speaker. Everyone clanks bottles and toasts. Naked players bring the dripping trophy out of the shower and empty bottles of Helles into it. We pass the giant chalice around and chug from our championship cup.

With beer in our hair, Scrappy and I sit in the quite locker room. The angry buzz of adrenaline of battle replaced by the pleasant hum of victory.

"Dude, we did it," he says.

Ice brothers fused together by a never-to-be-forgotten weekend, we won it all and will feast together as champions!

TWENTY-SEVEN

Scrappy has yapped about the legendary team dinner for months. He pestered me constantly about packing my Lederhosen for Garmisch. That's why it's hilarious that he forgot to pack his checkered Oktoberfest shirt. He improvises by wearing a BMC Rangers t-shirt with his Lederhosen, and wow, it looks great.

The Kraut line, plus Bastian, are waiting out front and we squeeze into a taxi van with them. They all have well-worn Trachten, and their go-to footwear is high-top Converse sneakers. Like me, they love Scrappy's t-shirt combo.

It takes us ten minutes to get from the far end of Garmisch to Partenkirchen. The cabbie stops in front of a small chapel and tells us we'll have to walk the last three hundred meters to the Werdenfelser Hof. We pile out, and Martin generously pays the cab fare for all of us.

Garmisch is an Alpine resort town and Partenkirchen is more of an old-world village. The buildings on both sides of its main street are decorated with elaborate paintings; their windows framed with fancy designs and doorways bordered by Roman pillars. Some buildings have billboard-sized skiing or nature scenes. The ones from the 1936 Olympics catch my eye. Directly across from the Werdenfelser Hof, two life-sized Olympic figure skaters twirl ten feet above the street lamps.

Inside the guest house, we go back five hundred years. Heavy, waist-high oak panels cover stone walls. High arches crown doorways. At s central oak bar, a busty hostess greets us like warriors coming home from battle.

"Schatzi!" she beams, giving Mark an enormous hug. Martin, Basti and Sascha line up and wait their turn to greet the hostess. Manuela bearhugs Scrappy and me, and she turns back to Mark, "You win, Ja?"

"Yes, we are the champions!" Mark boasts.

"Soup'ah! Drinks for mein Sieger," Manuela shouts.

It's hard to tell if she's in her forties or fifties, but her radiant presence makes it clear that she's the one in charge. Her super 'Soup'ah' packs all the sincerity and joy that Santa puts into his belly laughs. The bartender pours, and Manuela hands out shot glasses filled with a clear liquid and garnished with a chunk of pear.

"What's this?" I ask Basti.

"Willi!" he shouts, giggling like an idiot.

I turn to Martin, "What is it?"

"Willi!" he says, and everyone cracks up.

Manuela puts her hand on my shoulder, and says, "It's William's Birne, a pear schnapps. For short, we call it Willi."

"His name is Willie," Mark says between laughs. When he puts the German V on the front—Villie—it doesn't sound like my name at all, but whatever.

"Then extra good luck for him," Manuela smiles, "Prost, Schatzi!"

We clink our shot glasses, keeping eye contact until we've downed our shots. She gives me a wide smile and holds up her pear by its flag-capped toothpick. We swallow our pears in unison and everyone claps.

"You toast like a real Bavarian," she says. "Only very good sex for you!"

Everyone laughs, and I blush.

The guys toast and down their schnapps, and Manuela leads us through the narrow dining room to an enormous banquet hall. Halfway there, Scrappy points up at team photos hanging high above the tables. He tells me there's one for every BMC Ranger team that has played in the tourney.

The back room has a twenty-foot high ceiling held up by massive oak beams. The white stucco walls are painted with the same festive decorations as the buildings outside. I gawk at the huge landscape painting dominating the far end of the room, until Eva steps up holding Mass Krüge of Helles in each hands.

"Thirsty?" she asks.

"Oh God, yes!"

She hands me a glass mug that's the size of a pitcher and we toast. I take a healthy drink while gazing into her dark brown eyes, and I nail it again! Things really get rowdy when Coach and Kenny bring in the three-foot tall championship trophy. I can't figure out why it takes two of them to carry it, until they hand it to Cam. He grabs the handles on either side of the massive silver cup and hoists it up to his mouth. It's full to the brim with Helles beer!

Players gather around him, chanting, "Chug! Chug! Chug!"

For the next half hour, everyone takes turns drinking, posing, and taking photos with the trophy. When it gets low,

Manuela sends it out for a refill and our wild celebration continues.

I pose, holding the cup with Eva, telling her, "I can't wait to show off pictures of my trophy girlfriend." But she either ignores it, or doesn't get my pun.

Kenny stands on a table up front, and clanks his glass with a knife. He presents Manuela with a framed photo of this year's championship team, and I already know where she will hang it!

Manuela smiles and tells us, "You are my team!" She tells us to take our seats at the three long rows of tables. With players, family, and friends, there's about sixty of us. Waiters bring menus, and take our drink orders.

Eva pushes my menu away, saying, "Champions eat *Schweine Haxe!*"

Dinner is amazing. A roasted pig knuckle and two baseball-sized Bavarian potato dumplings fill my plate, a second plate holds my cold kraut, potato and green salads, and a metal pan holds my cooked red cabbage. Eva has the same and isn't able to finish half of it. She's happy when I take a sizeable chunk of pork from her.

After they clear the tables, Manuela and her waiters bring trays filled with Willi. Everyone gets one, and Manuela leads us in a toast to our championship. We then move on to the part Scrappy has told me about at least fifty times. Before Coach gives each player their souvenir puck, each line has to tell a joke, do a dance, or sing a song. Scrappy says that Martin and the Kraut line always steal the show. Last year, they did a Chippendale skit with dancing, singing, and stripping.

Coach calls up the defensemen first. They line up and do a parody of Cam's shootout goal celebration, ending with his joyful little jig. We clap and holler out our approval.

Coach presents each player with a tourney puck and calls up my line. Joel gives Manuela a wave, and she calls in the waiters with another round of Willi. Joel leads a toast to the greatest group of guys *evah*.

"What do you think folks? No joke, no song, no dance?" Coach asks.

Joel steps forward and does a little jig, earning boos from the crowd. Coach laughs and gives each of us a puck. Next up, the Germans are joined by Basti and Scrappy. Martin reaches into a canvas bag and hands out a drum, kazoos, and a trumpet. They line up and nail an up-tempo version of *Sweet Caroline* with everyone joining in on the dah-dah-daaahs. And the good times never felt so good! Martin and his guys bow to wild cheering, which turns into a standing ovation.

The Grind Line goes last. How can they top *Sweet Caroline*?

Derrick steps forward and tries. "Have you heard the one about the old Bavarian goat herder who got sick and had to go see a doctor for the first time?"

Oh no, this could end badly.

"The doctor tells him to undress, checks him over, and says things look very bad, but to be sure, he needs a blood sample, a urine sample, and a stool sample."

Oh no, this could end very badly.

"The goat herder grabs his Lederhosen from a peg, hands them to the doctor, and says, 'They're all in here.'"

Oh no, dead silence. No laughter. Nothing.

"Does anyone know the moral of the story?" Derrick asks.

Oh no, more silence. Crickets.

Then his line mates step up beside him, and in unison they shout, "Never buy used Lederhosen!"

Maybe it's all the beer and schnapps, but everyone rolls. Coach can't stop laughing as he hands them their pucks.

Kenny announces it's time for the group photo. We shove tables against the back wall to make an elevated back row, and line up chairs to make a middle row. Everyone crowds in, with kids and some players sitting cross-legged on the floor. Manuela joins us, and with the dramatic painting of the Bavarian landscape as our backdrop, a waiter snaps a happy photo.

Afterwards, Cam circulates, recruiting guys to go on a pub crawl. He comes over to me and Eva, and says, "Come on, we'll do some Irish car bombs and then go to Peaches!"

Eva reaches for my hand, and says, "Sorry, we've got plans."

Cam's devilish smile widens, and he gives Eva a sly wink.

Eva turns to me, her eyes both playful and predatory. "Want to come up to my room?"

I follow, captivated by the sway of her hips as she leads me up a narrow staircase. She opens Zimmer Nummer Eins with an old-fashioned brass key. We go in. I close the door and she pulls me to her, firmly. She kisses me, gently. Her breath is warm. Her tongue darts in and flicks the back of my front teeth. I've never been kissed this way. It's a strange, playful, and powerful beckoning.

I kiss her back, fiercely. My hands move from her hips to her neck. She pulls back and pushes me down on the edge of the four-post canopy bed. She slips off her shoulder straps, pulls her Dirndl down, and wiggles it over her hips. She steps out of the dress, looking straight into my eyes the entire time. It isn't exactly a striptease, but is it ever sexy! My God, she's beautiful. Her face, her neck, her breasts, her hips, her perfect legs. She's curvy and feminine, but definitely not soft. My shallow breathing quickens, and my blood races sending tingling pinpricks of pain against my dead-end scar.

She smiles and puts her foot up on the edge of the bed. She unhooks two garter straps and slowly rolls down her stocking. She does the same with her other leg, bending so close that her silver crucifix brushes against my cheek.

Down to only silky white panties and a matching push-up bra, she steps back and takes off her bra. Raising her arms, she stretches and arches her back. An intricate rose tattoo circles her left breast. Her erect nipple nestles in the middle of its green thorns and blood-red petals. It's beautiful. She holds the pose, enjoying me watching her.

I blush, but can't look away.

Sliding out of her panties, she exposes closely cropped hair rising from between her legs. She reaches down and brushes her finger over a silver stud peeking out from her dark bush. Stepping forward, she leans in and kisses me.

A wave of desire sweeps away my shyness and ghost pain.

I inhale her and we kiss again. I reach for her piercing and before I reach it, she pushes me back on the bed. Climbing on top, she runs her hand down my body and strokes my erection.

"Thank goodness," she says, rubbing me through my Lederhosen, "I was afraid you were celibate."

We both laugh and she helps me out of my clothes. She turns away, and I quickly pull up the sagging flesh-colored sleeve that fits over my prosthesis and lie back. Eva unrolls a condom on me, climbs on top of me, and envelopes me in her warmth. Her crimson nipples sway above me. I relax, and she takes complete control. I come much too quickly.

We lay side by side, and I stroke her hair, wondering if I should apologize.

"Do you sleep with it on or off?" she asks.

"Off."

"Then take it off and fuck me again."

Instantly hard, I take it off, roll on top of her, and thrust my hips wildly.

"Willie," she gasps, "you're supposed to take me, not break me."

"What?"

"There's a rhythm, like dancing. Slow down and we'll find it."

I thrust slowly. She raises her arms over her head, closes her eyes, and coos. My God, she is beautiful. I thrust deeply and come, collapsing into her. I roll to my side. We kiss, and she guides my hand over to her silver stud and down between her legs.

"Kiss me," she says.

I do, deeply. Then her body tenses. A soft moan accompanies the rhythmic squeezing on my slick fingers. She pulls my hand out and kisses me.

"Danke," she whispers.

I lie awake in the early morning darkness, and listen to Eva's breathing. The memory of last night whirls through my mind. I itch my nose, and breathe in her pungent smell. It reminds me of when Kevin said a woman was ready for sex when her pussy twitched like a horse's lips reaching for a carrot. Man, did that visual ever give my sixth grade brain nightmares!

In high school, I had a few drunken hook-ups at hockey parties, but I never knew what I was doing and never remembered much about it the next morning. I bet none of those hockey groupies would hook up with a one-legged paratrooper. Thank goodness I have Eva. I roll over and drift back to sleep.

Sunshine floods in around the curtains. I jolt awake, unnerved by my new vulnerability. When Eva gets up and walks to the bathroom, her hips sway gracefully. In that magical moment, the joy of being with her eclipses all of my fears. She comes back, and we make love again. This time, we climax together.

I really hadn't realized how much I'd lost my mojo until she gave it back to me.

Downstairs at breakfast, I ask about her tattoo.

"It's inspired by a Dropkick Murphys song," she says.

"Did getting it hurt?" I ask.

"A little," she says. "Do you have any ink?"

I shake my head, "My dad wouldn't allow it."

"It's your body. You decide. That's basic Körper Freiheit."

"What's Körper Freiheit?"

"It means body freedom. Even the East Germans had it."

"So, all the commies had tattoos?"

"No," Eva laughs, "most just went swimming naked."

"Oh, then I'm all for it!"

"What would your parents think of my tattoo?"

"My dad would ask you what band you play in," I shrug. "And your piercing would blow his mind."

"Does it blow your mind?" she flashes her wicked little grin.

I look away. Then, I look back and admit, "I can't stop thinking about it."

"Just my stud?" she teases.

"No, everything."

She smiles, "But your dad wouldn't approve?"

"He'd love you. He's just not into tattoos. He's, ah... a cop."

"In Boston?" she asks.

"Yep, exactly."

"How was that growing up?"

"When I was little, I thought everybody's dad was a cop."

"What does your mom do?"

"She died," I say. "When I was twelve."

Eva asks if I want to take the train back to Weiden with her. I explain that I can't, because my gear is in Scrappy's car and my clothes are at the Edelweiss. We take a cab to the hotel; I sign her in at the front gate, and we go up to my room. Scrappy is face down on the bed.

"Scrap," I say, shaking him, "checkout is at eleven."

"I know," he says, still face down.

"That's in twenty minutes, Bro," I say, slapping him on the ass.

Grumbling, he rolls over.

Eva watches me pack and we go down to the lobby to check out. Scrappy stumbles down ten minutes later. I offer to drive and Scrappy gladly agrees, squeezing into the back seat and promptly passing out. Driving north, Eva and I listen to music, and I'm beyond happy. What a team! What a tourney! What a woman!

ON MONDAY MORNING at the chow hall, I turn to the sports section and see our team photo beside an article:

Championship Weekend in Garmisch

Stars & Stripes
February 17, 2014

GARMISCH-PARTENKIRCHEN, *Germany* —
The BMC Rangers won the 23rd annual Armed
Forces Alpine Classic ice hockey championships,
and Specialist Will Foley, who is assigned to the
173rd Airborne Combat Brigade, was the leading
scorer and tournament MVP.
At the historic stadium which hosted the 1936
Olympics, the Rangers beat a field of 14 teams from
Germany, Holland, Belgium and Italy. Undefeated
in their pool play games, on Saturday they beat the
Stuttgart Mustangs and the KMC Eagles and moved
on to an all-Army championship game against the
Wiesbaden Vikings. After a wild 4-4 tie in regula-
tion, the BMC Rangers won the tournament in
shoot-out.

HOLY COW, I've got to send this to Dad!

TWENTY-EIGHT

Coming off of my Garmisch hockey high, I struggle to settle back in to Graf's dull routines. Dreaming about my next skate and talking to Eva keeps me from dwelling on Manning's indifferent cruelty and the board's pending decision.

I wake early on Saturday, super excited about our scrimmage in Regensburg. I pick Scrappy up at 08:00 sharp and fly down A-93 in light traffic. My GPS said it would take an hour to get there, but I make it in forty-five minutes.

The Donau Arena has two indoor Olympic-sized rinks connected by a hockey shop and 50s-style diner. In the locker room, Coach tells us they have a strong program and their first team bounces between the German second and third leagues. Coach spots McMouth texting and confiscates his phone. Our team rule is phones off in the locker room, unless we are on alert for recall. In that case, Coach lets players check their phones between periods to see if their unit has called a no-notice assembly.

From the beginning, it's clear we're the better team. We pepper their goalie with shots, but he's a wall. After making twenty saves, he finally lets in an easy one. At the other end, Scrappy watches the play, nonchalantly leaning on his upturned stick like Ken Dryden. In the second period, we again play mostly in their end. Their goalie stays solid until Joel fires a hard shot up high, hitting the crossbar and ricocheting across to me. Before the goalie can react, I chip in the juicy rebound. With two minutes left, Regensburg pulls their goalie. Joel forces a turnover on our blue line and fires a shot from half ice to give us a three to zero win.

Kenny brimgs a rack of cold beer into the locker room. Scrappy brushes away the Zamboni snow piled on top, grabs a Helles, and toasts me. I flip him off, telling him next time he drives. I shower, change, and go outside to wait for Scrappy. I check my phone and see two missed calls and a text. The text orders me to report for an accountability formation that I've already missed. At yesterday's final formation they released us for the weekend, so I'm technically not absent without leave or AWOL. But because I don't want Manning to find out about my hockey, I immediately call staff duty and check in.

"One-seventy-third staff duty, Sergeant Reid, how may I help you?"

"It's Specialist Foley, I just saw a message about the recall."

"Yep, you've missed formation and need to get your ass here to sign in."

"I'm in Regensburg."

"How fast can you get here?"

"About an hour, Sergeant. What's up?"

"Some idiot jumped off the tower."

"Holy shit, who?" I ask, thinking about the pictures Jack and I took from the top.

"Can't say until the Army notifies next of kin. Oh, and

the commander ordered no phone calls, texts, or social media about it."

"Got it," I say.

On the drive back, Scrappy and I speculate about the jumper. What kind of selfish asshole does that? Was it some loser pending court-martial for using meth? Jesus, even a druggie should have the decency to kill himself in private, not put it out there for everyone to see.

I drop Scrappy off and go straight to staff duty.

Sergeant Reid says, "Foley, right?"

"Yes, Sergeant."

"Your roommate is Specialist Martin?"

"Yes, Sergeant."

"He's the one who jumped."

I stand with my mouth hanging open, shake my head, and say, "No, not possible." When Sergeant Reid doesn't answer, I say, "You're screwing with me, right?"

"No," he answers, "and I'm required to inform you that you're confined to your room until the MPs release you. They'll be back first thing in the morning."

"What the fuck?"

"Excuse me, *Specialist*."

"Sorry, Sergeant. What do they want with me? I don't know anything."

"Then don't sweat it. Maintain your military bearing and you'll be okay."

I go up to my room in a daze. Police tape hangs in a loose X across my door. What in the hell do I do now, I wonder. So I go back down to staff duty, and Reid calls the MPs. "You can go in," he says, "but don't touch any of Martin's stuff."

Upstairs I sit on the couch where Fat Jack spent half of his miserable life playing Xbox. His smell is still here; it's like he's just taking a leak, and will come back and slouch down into his hunched-over Xbox pose.

I remember my sweaty hockey gear out in my car, but I'm way too freaked out to go and get it. I look over at Jack's unmade bed and sigh. We lived together, but apart. I look around and notice that our room has been searched. My stuff's been searched too. Why would the MPs search my things? That's crazy! I didn't have anything to do with it. Jack was a grown assed man. He made his own decisions.

Why in the hell did he jump? Was he counting one-thousand, two-thousand, three-thousand, all the way down? I scold myself for being morbid and try to rein in my visions of him hitting the ground. What a fucked-up way to die, but man, am I ever glad he didn't do it here. How the hell does Manning expect me to sleep here? Is he trying to make me flip out and copy Jack's heavy drop?

I WAKE LATE on Sunday and lie in bed watching dust dance on rays of sunshine. I haven't slept much, because each time I closed my eyes I saw Jack falling.

All day I sit and wait. Nothing happens. No MPs come. Thank God Jack had junk food and beer stashed away in his mini-fridge. Darkness falls. Taps plays. When my alarm rings at 06:00, I'm already wide awake and staring at the ceiling. It's time for me to get up, shave, and go down to Monday morning formation, but I don't move. The air feels heavy with loss and loneliness. I reach down and scratch my stump, remembering my mother's death. We're all haunted, aren't we?

I'm too shaken to go down, besides Reid told me to stay put until the MPs show up. Fat Jack's smell clings to the couch. So I move over to my bed, sit, and wait. About noon, I go to get my stick and remember that it's still out in my car.

Did Manning babysit Jack to death? Every day is so damned repetitive and depressing. Is that why Jack jumped? Or did he jump in defiance? Or did he jump to surrender? Or did he jump because his life had no meaning? I sure as shit won't depend on the Army to give my life meaning—not anymore—because I don't want to end up like Jack. Huh, maybe his jump was just a good old-fashioned 'fuck you' to the Army? Maybe he left a note? I search our room and find nothing. Maybe he texted? Nothing. Facebook? Nothing.

The next morning, just before nine, a staff duty runner knocks on my door. "Mandatory accountability formation," he announces.

"I'm restricted."

"Nope, the commander said, 'La-dee, da-dee, everybody,' that means you too, jailbird."

I grab my black PT jacket, go down, and scan the crowd. Everyone seems normal. What was I expecting—grief for someone they barely knew?

The sergeant major calls us to attention and Manning goes up front. In his chilling monotone, he tells us about Jack's death. "He snuck into the Tower during a spouse club tour. Because he was in his dress uniform, they assumed he was an escort. At impact his ankles, knees, hips, and spine compressed and shattered. His body bounced and rotated, and slamming the back of his skull against the cobblestone." Manning pauses, letting his arrogance drif over us like the spray from a skunk.

At least Jack kept his feet and knees together, but I guess he wasn't trying for a smooth landing.

Manning flashes one of his empty half-smiles and

continues. "Suicide is a crime under the Uniform Code of Military Justice. When a soldier kills himself, he doesn't just end himself, he also does damage to his unit and the Army,"

No shit.

"How did his leaders fail to see the signs?" Manning lets the accusation settle in. Then, he asks, "Where were his friends?" He pauses, letting me squirm. Then he puts his cold, dead eyes on me, "Where was his roommate?" He punctuates it with a tight-lipped that stings like a slap.

Blood rushes to my cheeks. Did I miss something? Maybe, but what about the smug mother-fucker up front? Instead of helping Jack, he made his life hell. He pushed him towards suicide. Did Jack owe it to Manning to stay alive? No, Jack owed nothing to that psycho! Maybe what Jack's did was technically a crime, but come on, who gets prosecuted? Not Dead Jack, that's for sure.

Manning releases us. What a waste of time. He just wanted to hear his own voice. Thankfully, nobody asks me for the inside scoop on the way back up. For the rest of the day I wait for the MPs, getting up and siting down at the end of my bed, and tormenting myself about whether I failed Jack. I finally go get my wet gear and hang it in the shower. Man, did Jack ever hate the stale sweat smell of it!

I can finally twirl my stick in my nervous hands. Should I have seen something? What did I miss? This is crazy! Then, it dawns on me. Fat Jack was a selfish fucking coward! Look what he did to me. Look what he did to his wife. I get angrier and angrier, until guilt smothers my rage. Was there something I could have done to save my roommate?

The cannon booms, it's seventeen hundred hours and

the MPs still haven't shown up. I'm starving, so I call the CQ and ask what to do. They tell me to go to chow. I sit by myself eating pizza and thinking about Jack. Later, I lie in bed and get furious all over again. Suicide is such a selfish thing. Who benefits? Only the dead guy. Everyone else has to deal with it. Damn you, Jack! Then, I think about his situation. His enlistment. His Airborne training. His deployment to Afghanistan. That's when it all went south for him—broken body, pending medical discharge, family split apart, and finally his DUI. Unkept promises can break a man. It doesn't matter if it was a "Dear John" letter from Brittany, discharge papers from the Army, or a low-ball disability rating from the VA. They are all betrayals. They all hurt.

The next morning, the MPs finally show. They ask me if I saw any signs. They ask if I found a note. "No," I answer. As they turn to leave, I ask, "That's it?"

"Yep, that's it."

LATER IN THE WEEK, I see Robalo in the chow hall. He waves me to his table and asks me how rehab is going.

"Okay, First Sergeant." I answer.

He says he heard I lost rank. I tell him it's no big deal, but we both know it's a lie. He asks me about hockey and gets a kick out of hearing about his Rangers. When I bring up Manning and Jack's death, he waves me off.

"Not here," he says, "the walls have ears."

As we finish lunch, I ask him if he'll be at the funeral.

"I'm here to give Jack's eulogy," he smiles sadly. "We served together in Afghanistan."

Huh, I didn't know they were down range together. I'm

glad someone who deployed with Jack will speak for him tomorrow.

FAT JACK'S service is at the post chapel, just across the parade field from the barracks and only one building from the tower. I arrive a half-hour early and stand off to the side, wondering if Jack stopped at the chapel going to his last jump.

Nah, I bet he just cut across the parade field for his rendezvous with gravity.

An honor guard, wearing dress blue uniforms and carrying M-16 rifles, hovers outside. Robalo arrives and talks quietly to them, checking on his troops before their big show.

The doors open, and I shuffle in with the crowd. It is dark and warm inside. Up front, an organist plays. I wonder if I should go up and pay respects to Jack's photo, which is displayed next to his boots, dog tags, and a downturned M4. A rush of sadness hits me. Man, I just want this to be over so I can go zone out on a cardio machine. I cross myself and take a seat. The chapel fills up; I guess it will be standing room only. At least those at the back will get the best view of the twenty-one-gun salute when we move outside.

The chaplain, Lieutenant Colonel Jones, wears his dress uniform with no vestments. I guess he sees himself more as an Army officer than a man of God. A hush falls as he takes his place at the pulpit. "Dearly beloved, we are gathered here in the presence of God to bid farewell to our brother-in-arms, Specialist John William Martin." Colonel Jones' service continues with words of comfort, music, and prayers. Then Major Manning rises to speak as Fat Jack's commander. I have the urge to stand up and scream. I can't believe that I must sit here and watch the cold-blooded bastard act like he cares. I sit ramrod straight and concentrate on slowing my breathing.

Manning first acknowledges Jack's widow, Brittany, for flying in from Detroit to escort her husband home. He then says, "In our chosen profession, more than any other, we are touched by untimely death. We never get used to it, and we are not hardened by it. Instead, we cherish life more because we may be required to go into harm's way on a moment's notice. We took an oath to serve and swore to risk our lives in the defense of our nation. Specialist Martin understood this when he enlisted. He understood it when he volunteered for Airborne School. He knew it when he deployed to Afghanistan. To keep America safe, he had to deploy, go forward, and make the world safe for democracy."

Manning does it with a well-rehearsed, smooth speaking voice. But he's only regurgitating the words we use to honor our war dead, and I don't buy any of it. I've been to Boston PD funerals. They are also well-scripted, but the brotherhood and sense of loss still manages to shine through all of the formality. Here, the words don't quite fit, because there's nothing personal about it. It's all just for show.

Manning brings me back to the present with his silky voice. "I didn't meet John Martin on the battlefield. I met him here, as his battalion commander. Reviewing his military records, I know he carried out his combat duties in Afghanistan with pride."

Who is Manning kidding? Didn't meet him on the battlefield? Manning doesn't have a combat patch. He's a slick-sleeve, just like me. All my other leaders have deployed. How did Manning manage to miss out on all the fun? Why on earth did the Army ever put an untested cherry in charge of battle-hardened paratroopers?

"Today with terror attacks taking place all over the world, anywhere a soldier serves is a combat zone. It is therefore fitting that we remember Specialist Martin not as a casualty, but as a paratrooper who died doing heroic duty overseas." Manning pauses dramatically, gathers his notes, and comes out from behind the lectern. He turns, centers himself on Fat Jack's photo, and salutes. Returning his arm stiffly to his side, he does a precise about face, and marches back to his seat. A slight smirk lingering at the corners of his mouth. What an actor. He doesn't care, not about us. I can only see the back of his head after he sits, but I know that the smug bastard is gloating over his flawless performance.

Robalo stands and takes his place behind the podium. He doesn't carry any notes. He clears his throat and starts with a story about Jack in Afghanistan. "No shit, there we were," he starts, "taking fire and calling for artillery." He finishes his war story by emphasizing Jack's heroics, and turns to the topic on everyone's mind. "Let's not kid ourselves, Jack Martin didn't die a hero. He killed himself."

An uncomfortable murmur passes through the chapel.

Robalo pushes on, "It seems like the quintessential solitary act, but the impact on our community is widespread. Today when we think about the harm suicide does, we think of the psychological damage. We talk about how family and friends feel responsible, ashamed, rejected. Leaders lose sleep over the harm it does to unit readiness. All of this is true, but there's something more. There is something deeply unnatural and disturbing about suicide."

A lady near the front shouts, "Amen!"

"Twenty-two veterans kill themselves every day. And

our youngest veterans are most at risk." Robalo pauses and makes eye contact with me, "This is unacceptable."

I shift, wondering why he singled me out.

"Active-duty soldiers killed themselves at the rate of nearly one a day. In 2012, the final count was 349. That's more suicides than those who died fighting in Afghanistan." Robalo locks eyes with Manning, "Where does Specialist Martin fit in? Was he a hero or was he a casualty?"

Another uncomfortable murmur rises and falls. I have no idea about what Jack's death should mean, but I do know that what he did was wrong. I bet Manning isn't wearing his self-satisfied smirk anymore.

"I loved Jack Martin," Robalo says. "But I hate what he did to himself." With his voice trailing almost to a whisper he looks down and says, "I hate what he did to all of us." Robalo steps down, stone-faced and stoic, and salutes Jack's photo. As he returns to his seat, the organist breaks the silence by playing *Amazing Grace*. The chaplain stands stiffly and leads us in the twenty-third Psalm. He concludes with a benediction, and the organist switches to *Rock of Ages*. Everyone stands and waits for Major Manning to escort Mrs. Martin outside. She's crying and as they pass, Manning gives Robalo an evil glare.

One by one, we go up and salute Jack's photo. Eyes remain mostly down, with some bringing their heads up to take in a deep breath. When it's my turn, I salute, saying a silent goodbye to my friend. Outside, I can breathe again. The German and American flags which flank the tower hang limp. People stand in small groups, looking around and waiting. Several shoot disapproving looks at Robalo. I guess they preferred to farewell Jack as a hero and continue on with their happy lives.

The Chaplain walks over to comfort Brittany. She is

sobbing, and I wonder if she'll come collect Jack's Xbox and clothes. Just in case, I'll go straight back and hide his porn. The color guard and firing party come to attention. Sergeant Major calls out in a booming voice, "Private Smith!"

"Here, Sergeant Major!" Smith answers.

"Specialist Alvarez!"

"Here, Sergeant Major!" Alvarez answers.

"Specialist Foley!"

"Here, Sergeant Major!" I answer.

"Specialist Martin!"

Everyone holds their breath.

"Specialist Martin!"

The silence is painful.

"Specialist John Martin!"

Brittany's sobs become hysterical.

Sergeant Major nods to the firing party. They raise their rifles and fire an ear-splitting volley. In unison, they fire a second time. As the crack of their third volley fades, a lone bugler sounds Taps. Everyone in uniform salutes Old Glory.

I hold my rigid salute, thinking at least this part fits. At police funerals, the bagpipers wear Scottish kilts with their police uniform and play *Amazing Grace*. It's cool, but for a soldier's suicide a lonely bugle call fits better. When the last note drifts away, I have trouble bringing my arm down.

The crowd disperses and I head straight back to the room where Jack should still be blasting the bad guys in Halo. First Sergeant Robalo's acknowledgment that Jack killed himself lingers. Should he have left it alone? That would have been better for Brittany, but how can we prevent suicides if we don't talk about them? I unlock my door and wonder if Manning will assign me another roommate? Whatever. I pick up Jack's DVDs and magazines, and put them in my wall locker. I'd much rather be at the gym, but I can't leave until I'm sure Brittany is gone.

I call Dad on video chat, and we talk about Jack's funeral.

"Make peace with it, Willie," he says. "Don't waste your time trying to figure it out."

"I know, but..." I say.

"You know, the Church forbids suicide, but I guess people aren't so religious now-a-days," Dad says, clearing his throat.

Being in the chapel today took me back to Sundays as a kid, fidgeting in church. Do I still have faith? Did Jack kill himself because he didn't believe?

Dad breaks the silence, asking, "Did you know more people die by suicide than by homicide? The crazy thing is, when there's one, sometimes others follow. They call them clusters. Like when a popular celebrity does it, there can be a rise in suicides, and the age and gender of the copycats often match the celebrity. They say it's mostly with teens, but that's not true. Back in '86, three Boston cops shot themselves in a single week."

"Why are you telling me this?" I interrupt.

"Be smart, Willie, you don't know why he did it, and you never will."

We hang up and I'm reeling, completely lost. I know that dwelling on it is not helpful or healthy. But how can I not dwell on it? Sitting here I smell Jack. I see his stuff. If I listen hard enough, I hear his voice.

HOCKEY and the gym thankfully wear me out over the next few days. My anger ebbs, but questions still nag. Why did he do it? Did he want someone to find him? Was he afraid of going back to Detroit? Was he a coward? Or, was he punishing himself for falling short as a soldier? A husband? A father? Did he do it for the $500,000 in Army life insurance money? Man, I still can't believe the Army pays out for suicides. Maybe Jack did it to keep the Army from conquering him? Did he end up in a better place? That's not likely; the commandment "Thou shalt not kill," must include self-murder. And of sins, only suicide denies the sinner a chance to repent.

Eva texts me about meeting at Brunner's for Sunday brunch. I can't believe how happy it makes me. Fat Jack has dominated my thoughts and having something different to look forward to is a godsend.

When I arrive, Eva is at our table looking out over the pedestrian zone. She lets me go on about Jack's funeral and about how Manning stood in front yapping like a big-shot.

"Died a hero, defending America?" I say in disbelief. "Give me a break."

Eva orders cappuccinos and a bread basket. "Did you know that the ancient Greeks and Romans honored people who killed themselves for moral reasons?" she asks. "And the early Christians glorified their martyrs?"

Luckily the waitress comes back with our cappuccinos, cutting of Eva's lecture. She takes a sip, sets her cup down, and asks, "Did you know that during the Renaissance, artists and writers celebrated heroic suicides? They even romanticized love-sick suicides, like in Shakespeare's *Romeo and Juliet.*"

"So?" I say.

"Well, the Church pushed back. They denied self-murderers a Christian burial and dragged their naked bodies through the streets. We still attach this stigma to suicides, even though we now know many result from mental illness."

"Jack wasn't crazy," I say, staring at the table and letting my coffee go cold.

The waitress brings our food and Eva eats in silence.

Interrupting my dark thoughts, she says. "I don't think that I met him,"

"What?"

"Your roommate, Jack," she says. "Did I ever meet him?"

"No, he wasn't a hockey guy."

"Maybe he *was* suffering from a mental illness. The Mafia, the Army, even sports teams all share an unhealthy culture of silence. Maybe he was struggling and didn't want anyone to know."

Eva is right, it does take loyalty to build a strong team and protecting the team through silence can strengthen bonds. But do we sacrifice truth on the altar of loyalty? Manning did. That fucker pushed Jack towards suicide and then stood up and called him a hero! Manning didn't do it to strengthen bonds. He did it to show everyone what an outstanding commander he is. I wish I could explain all of this to Eva, but I can't. So, instead I sit up and say, "No, it was just a stupid, selfish thing to do."

"Everyone has the right to end their own life," Eva shoots back. "Would you want someone in terrible pain to suffer if they would rather die?"

"It's not the same," I frown. "Jack didn't have cancer. In a month or two, he would have been back home."

"But it was his life. You liked Körper Freiheit at the lake," Eva smiles.

I remain stone-faced. "It doesn't mean you can do whatever you want. What if Jack wanted to sell himself into slavery? That's not allowed. The law protects him from doing something that stupid."

"Yes, but—"

"Suicide is the ultimate selfish act." I interrupt. "What about everybody else?" I take a swallow of my cold cappuccino. "It was a permanent solution to a temporary problem. It was a theft from his family and friends. That selfish son of a bitch stole from me," I look down at my empty cup. "You know what else? He stole from himself. In life there are ups and downs. Happiness can't return when you're dead."

"Is that what you thought when your mom died?" Eva asks.

"What?" I say, my heart skipping a beat. "I was little!" I shout. I don't want to fight with Eva, so I turn my fury on Fat Jack. "Jack quit. His suicide didn't show courage; it showed cowardice. Everyone he left behind is in pain, and he feels nothing. How fair is that?"

My outburst shocks Eva. Thank goodness she doesn't rise to my anger. In measured tones, she says, "Suicide can be wrong, but it's not a mortal sin."

I shake my head. What Jack did was wrong. It was a a mortal sin. It was a crime against nature. I can feel it in my bones. He should still be here.

TWENTY-NINE

On Sunday, right after lunch, I call Dad. That's the best time, just before he leaves for morning Mass. It's funny, because when Mom was alive, she dragged him to church. Now, he almost never misses.

"Hello, Willie, my boy," he says, as his face pops up on my screen.

He fills me in on Beantown sports. I tell him about the hockey here, and that half the players grew up in Weiden. "With their chemistry they work some crazy no-look plays, like Henrik and Daniel Sedin," I say.

Dad laughs, "But in the finals, Marchand sure took it to those Swedish bathing suit models."

"He did," I agree, knowing how much Dad loved Timmy Thomas and Brad Marchand's merciless agitation of the Sedin twins in the finals two years ago.

"So you got some genuine hometown heroes lacing 'em up!"

"Yep, and they're treating me like an honored guest, know what I mean?"

"You're not German, Willie." He pauses a beat and then asks, "What's the Army got in store for yah?"

"I don't know," I say, choking up. "They're pressuring me to re-classify from Airborne to some Chair-borne job—"

"Oh, that's easy," he says. "You joined to be a paratrooper, right?"

"Right," I say, sniffing back some snot.

At Wednesday night's practice, Peter brings everyone to center ice. He calls me forward and hands me a folded jersey.

I open it. It reads: FOLEY with number 22.

A feeling of belonging wraps around me. The jersey marks me as a member of the Ice Devil tribe. It's tangible proof of my connection to them, and of them to me. It also binds me to all the Ice Devils who came before us and those who will come after. It shows the world that my teammates and I are part of something bigger than ourselves. I trust my fate to them, and they trust theirs to me. We are brothers.

Peter says, "You play Friday."

My teammates tap their sticks on the ice, and I raise my fist like I've just scored a game-winning goal. Man, I will play on Friday!

Back in the barracks, I call Dad. We connect, and I blurt out, "I got my jersey today."

"Nice! What's your numbah?"

"Twenty-two!" I say. Mom's birthday was on February second, so I always tried for twenty-two. The few times I couldn't get it, I took number two. One upside-down season, I wore number fifty-five. That's the year Mom died. I burned that jersey, and I will never wear unlucky fifty-five evah again.

"Send me a picture, will you?" Dad says.

"Sure," I say.

"Unless it looks like New Jersey's sweater. I couldn't bear that!"

"Nope, our devil looks good, and the team colors are blue and white."

"Not like the Leafs!" he says.

"Heck no," I laugh. "It has light-blue diamonds, like on the Bavarian flag."

"Huh, sounds fancy. Is the team any good?"

"Better than high school, not as good as college. Weiden plays in Germany's third league. Soon they will split the league for playoffs. The top half plays to move up, and the bottom half plays to see who moves down."

"Huh, pretty neat," he says.

"My gear's at the rink, so I'll send you pictures tomorrow. I bet you'll like it."

"I know that I will," he says, pride animating his voice.

─────────

THURSDAY NIGHT, I have to scrape frost from my windows going to practice. After a few minutes the air blowing from the vents warms, and I'm lost in hockey thoughts. I reach for the radio dial, but then leave it off because. It's so peaceful in the warm womb of my car, I don't need music to distract me from my worries.

Practice is a blast. We skate at full speed with precision. Peter uses just a few words and hand signals to run us through complex passing and shooting drills, alternating them with very short sprints. Everything moves so fast, I don't have the time to think about anything but hockey.

After practice, Peter reads off our game lines. I will play wing on the first line with the team captain! Driving back to post, I think about how lucky I am to have something to

occupy my mind and energize my spirit. Back in basic training, I stood tall at 06:30 formation waiting for the Reveille
bugle call. But I really looked forward to Taps. It sounded at
23:00, or eleven p.m. When the bugle sounded the slow 'da-
dee-daaah, da-dee-daaaaah', it signaled lights out. To my
ears, it was the sweet sound of release. It freed me from my
military duties and I could think. I could dream. I could
escaped into the seven hours of peace between Taps and
Reveille.

While Reveille challenged me to meet each new day
head on, Taps rewarded me for making it to the end. My
alpha to omega approach to military life worked at Fort
Benning and it was working for me at Grafenwöhr, until
Jack's funeral. Now, Taps is stained with his suicide.
Instead of sweet release and rest, it now brings me sadness
and regret.

ON GAME DAY it's it's cold, wet and gray. My wipers
swish by in an easy, comforting rhythm. It's peaceful and
warm, and escaping to hockey is keeping me sane.

It's surprising that little Weiden has such high-end
hockey. Back home it would all be tied to a high school or
college, where only the best-funded programs are competitive. I guess because the Germans don't have high school or
college sports, the local sports clubs have the room to thrive.

Of course, everyone in Bavaria roots for FC Bayern.
But it's still important for small towns to have a local identity, and the Devils are a great fit. Having a mix of hometown heroes with a few semi-pro journeyman players
brings Weiden together in ways that FC Bayern can't.
That, and everyone loves rooting for the scrappy underdog.

Heck, I'm a complete outsider and I'm excited to be a part of it.

I pull into the lot at just before five o'clock. The sun has set and it's already dark. In the locker room, our gear and game jerseys are laid out. I find my spot next to Thomas, and he tells me to get ready for our off-ice warm-ups. I put on sweats to cover my prosthetic. The team captain, Felix, leads us up to the horseshoe-shaped upper deck overlooking the ice. He spreads us out in a large circle of twenty-two players—all four lines, plus two goalies.

Felix leads us through casual stretching, while players talk and laugh. I enjoy the relaxed camaraderie. A few players have withdrawn into themselves. Most goalies do that, but I don't see the point. Instead, I ignore the flutters in my stomach and stay loose by talking with Thomas. When we break, he grabs my arm and pulls me over to a small group of player who stay behind. One has a soccer ball. We spread out, pass it around, and try to keep it from touching the ground. It quickly becomes a competition. Soon, we're all laughing and breaking into an easy sweat. I even get two touches with my reactive foot which feels very strange. I have enough control to get my foot on the ball, but can't feel it hit or leave my mechanical foot. As we head back to the locker room, my stomach feels fine.

We dress, and I proudly pull on my blue and white game jersey.

Thomas looks and says, "We wear the yellow one for warm-ups."

Oh yeah, I remember the yellow jerseys from the game I saw with Bastian and Scrappy. I switch jerseys and go out. Skating laps, I see Basti, Scrappy, and Kenny. They bang on the glass, wave, and give me thumbs up.

I smile and wave back. No pressure!

The Fan Curve fills up first, and Weiden's loudest fans beat on drums and chant. Thankfully we warm-up at the far end, by the Zamboni chute, so we're not directly under the relentless onslaught of sound. The arena's horn blows, telling us it's time to leave the ice. Back in the relative quiet of the locker room, Peter reads off the lines, says some other stuff, and walks out. Other than the lines, I don't understand and lean over to Thomas for help. "What did I miss?" I ask.

"You start on right wing, with Felix," he says. "Be disciplined, stupid penalties will cost us the game."

The stadium horn blares, and we rise.

Thomas looks over and laughs, "Change to blue, yellow is only for warm-ups."

I change, and hurry to catch up to everyone at the Zamboni chute. Out on the ice, flames burn low. Rock music fades and the announcer bellows, "Für die Ice Devils, nummer Sieben, Christof..." Number seven Christof Hauptmann strides out onto the ice, flames on either side of him shoot twenty-feet high, and the crowd yells out in unison, "Haupt-man!"

I get the jitters. They're almost as bad as when I hook up my static line up to jump. Three more players go, and then the announcer says, "Nummer zwei-und-zwansig, Willie..." and the crowd screams, "Fo-ley!" I freeze, and Thomas shoves me from behind. The dancing flames disorient me, and I stumble out onto the ice. I skate slowly across the dark expanse and join the growing circle of players. Above all of the noise, I hear a woman calling my name. I turn. It's Eva! In all the excitement, I'd forgotten that she rides in the convertible. She blows me a kiss and mouths, "Good luck."

The lights come up and the cars slowly drive off of the

ice. We line up on our blue line and raise our sticks to salute the visitors from Memmingen. The horn blares and I finally get to line up for the opening face-off.

I've never been more ready for a game to start.

I concentrate on the air flowing in and out of my lungs and visualize blood pumping oxygen to fuel my muscles. The referee leans in to drop the puck, and everything else fades. I see and hear the puck hit the ice. Felix draws the bouncing puck back and I surge forward with my stick blade on the ice in anticipation of a pass. I cut across center ice. Roman, the right defenseman, spots me and fires the puck straight up the middle. It snaps into place on my stick. I cut towards the enemy net, and spot a bit of white twine over the goalie's left shoulder. I snap my wrists, propelling the puck up and away, and raise my hands in celebration as the puck zips past his glove hand.

It hits the back of the net and our fans roar!

Paldi, Jens, and Roman jump into my arms. We skate over to the bench and high-five our teammates' outstretched hands. Everyone is excited for my first goal. Everyone, except Felix. I don't get it, he took the faceoff and will get credit for a secondary assist. We line up again at center ice, and I slow my breathing. The referee leans in. I become the game. The game becomes me.

Late in the second period, I break up the boards with my stick on the ice. For a third time, the pass doesn't come and I'm whistled for being offside. *What the heck?* Back on the bench, I say to Felix. "I'm wide open. Hit me and go to the net. I'll work a give-and-go pass back to you."

"Scheise! Just stay on side," he snaps and spits on my skates.

At the period break, Peter calls us over. "What is the problem?" he asks.

"I can't play with him," Felix says, pointing at me. "He doesn't stay on side."

I shake my head, "I'm wide open—"

Peter holds up a hand. "You were offside."

In the locker room, Peter reads off new lines and I'm not on one. So, in the third period, I sit next to the backup goalie, fuming about being benched. The final horn blasts, and I'm so mad that I don't react to my team's loss. I had begun the game so feisty and eager for a fight. Now I'm exhausted and defeated. But by what? A superior strategy? My temper? I don't get it. Twelve-year-olds in Boston learn how to headman the puck and work a give-and-go. Or just dump the thing in, and let me go get it. Either is better than making me wait on the blue line.

Eva is waiting for me in the parking lot. "Nice goal!" she says. "What happened in the third period?"

I shrug, "Felix complained and Peter benched me."

"Oh, sorry," she says. "Want to go to my place to celebrate your first goal?"

She gets in and I drive to her place. In her cozy living room, we hug and kiss. Her scent fills my nose. She steps back and smiles coyly. Later, in her bed, arching and tense, I explode and savor the release. For a brief, blissful moment we lie tangled together. Alive and dead. Damned and saved. Spent and renewed. Waking late on Saturday, we make love again. Eva showers and gets us fresh bread. We share a long, lazy morning over coffee, cold cuts, and fresh rolls.

———

BACK ON POST, I text Dad photos of my jersey. Thirty minutes later, I call him.

"Holy cow, are you playing hockey or driving for NASCAR?" he laughs.

"I guess we do have a few ads on our uniform. We've got them on our pants and socks, too," I say. "Oh and for warm-ups, we wear yellow jerseys that have even more corporate logos on them."

"You get any of the ad money?"

"Nope," I say. Then I tell him about my first game and goal, leaving out the part about getting benched.

ON SUNDAY AFTERNOON Basti calls to wish me luck, and I learn that Sunday games start two hours earlier than weekday games! I hang up and race to Weiden with no time to dwell on Peter's fucked-up decision to bench me. In warm-ups I'm withdrawn, until Thomas tells me that I'll be skating on his line with Paldi.

When to game starts, I'm whipped into a frenzy. I'm the alpha player, the apex predator. I will hunt the puck. I will crush people. When I get the puck, I will lower my shoulder and skate through my opponents.

Near the end of the first period, Paldi circles with the puck just inside our blue line. He waits for our breakout to form, and slips past a forechecker to start his rush up ice. As he crosses the center line, I break across the far side with Thomas trailing. Paldi's laser pass skips over the blade of my stick, and I cross the blue line chasing the puck. I squeeze between a defenseman and the boards, kick the puck up to my stick. spot open net, and send a quick shot just inside the near post, beating the goalie stick side.

The crowd screams its approval. I raise my arms in cele-bration. Paldi and Thomas skate to me. Pointing to Paldi, I shout, "Nice pass!" We skate along the boards, giving high-fives to everyone on our bench. The announcer says, "Tor! Von Spieler nummer zwei-und-zwanzig, Willie—" and the crowd screams, "Fo-ley!" The announcer continues, "Von Spieler nummer fünf-und-achtzig, Marcel—" and the crowd screams, "Pal-dow-ski!"

I'm completely in the zone. My reading, anticipating, and responding is so condensed that everything is simultaneous. I'm unstoppable. On the power play, I take a one timer from the faceoff dot. The goalie makes the initial save, but Thomas chips in the loose puck and we're up two to zero.

In the third period, a big goon knocks me to the ice. I bounce up and score. The crowd roars. When the final horn blows, we're up three to zero. We march to the locker room happy and loud. Players come over and high five me while Thomas passes out bottles of Zoigl.

I tip my beer to finish it, and Thomas grabs my arm.

"What?" I say.

"The refs leave. We dance. Come!" he says, pulling me up.

"Wait, I'm not dressed," I say, pulling on a t-shirt.

"Come!" he says, tugging on my arm.

"Wait," I say, pulling free. I sit and reattach my hockey foot, quickly pulling my sock up to cover it. I step into my breezers, slipping their wet suspenders over my shoulders.

I follow Thomas out and the Fan Curve roars. The Devils faithful cheer and pound on kettle drums. Thomas and I line up on the face-off circle with our team. Once we're in place, the Fan Curve goes silent. Then, a lone drummer booms out three rhythmic beats, and someone in the crowd yells a chant. The whole Fan Curve echoes it back, crazy with joy. I don't understand the words, making it even more chilling and exhilarating.

They chant again, and Thomas shoves me forward.

"Knock it off," I say.

"They want you! You must dance!"

They chant again, and then I hear it. "Fo-ley!" boom-boom-boom, "Fo-ley" boom-boom-boom, "Fo-ley" boom-boom-boom.

I skate out to the dot. Not knowing what to do, I freeze. My damp skin tingles with nervous anticipation. Thomas skates out to join me. He shouts out a chant, and the crowd screams it back. The players behind us clap a beat, and the crowd joins in. Thomas grabs my hand, holds it high, and we do a little jig. My sock slips, and before I can grab it Thomas shouts and we dance again. The third time the crowd gets louder and wilder, as I dance my shin pad slips, exposing my peg leg.

The arena goes silent.

My tingling skin goes clammy.

I try to skate away, but Thomas holds me fast.

A voice in the Fan Curve bellows, "A-hab! A-hab! Mein Captain, A-hab!"

The crowd and the players erupt, mimicking the shouter. "A-hab!" boom-boom-boom, "A-hab" boom-boom-boom, "A-hab" boom-boom-boom.

We sing!

We dance!

I revel in it!

Back in the locker room, I collapse into my stall. Thomas hands me a towel. "Blow your nose and wipe your face, Captain Ahab," he laughs.

We change and go celebrate at a nearby Zoigl house.

Happy and content, I look around the crowded pub. I am a hockey player and can't imagine being anything else.

Eva steps out of a sea of bodies. We hug, her perfume reminding me of our night in Garmisch. I step back. Her jet black hair is swept back over one ear, revealing a slender neck. Her silky dress stops just above her knees. Are her creamy white stockings held up by sexy garters? I sit back on a stool to hide my rising excitement.

She leans in with her crooked little smile, and asks, "Want to go to my place?"

To hell with hiding my excitement! I stand and we leave together. I drive, and in five minutes we're at her door. She fumbles with her key as I hug her from behind and kiss her neck. My hand glides down her stomach to the little silver stud hiding just below. My fingertip traces a circle around it while my other hand cups her breast. She purrs with pleasure, spinning in my arms to kiss me.

She brushes her lips along the side of my ear and says, "Let's go inside, I've got a surprise for you."

Upstairs, we kiss and she reaches up the back of my shirt to caress my neck. Her other hand massages me through my jeans. She steps back. I try to step forward, but she puts her hand up to stop me. She pulls her spaghetti-straps down over her shoulders. She wiggles her dress down over her breasts. Over her hips. Then, to the floor. She steps out of it, raises her arms. No garter. No panties. No bra. My breath catches, as I take in her curves. Her thigh-high stockings. Her silver crucifix. Her matching silver stud, standing erect, shiny, and exposed.

"You've shaved," I whisper.

She smiles. Her red lips and rose tattoo jump out in contrast to her pale skin. Her self-assured stance and wicked grin are intimidating. I blush and begin to look away, but she draws me back by arching an eyebrow.

I wrap my arms around her, and breathe her in. She tilts her face up to me. I kiss the curve of her ear. I kiss her chin. I reach down to the silver stud crowning her gorgeous, naked pussy.

Before I can touch it, she pushes my hand away and says, "Kiss it."

"What?" I say, leaning forward to kiss her naughty half-smile.

She turns her head away and pulls my hand forward, putting my middle finger on the cold metal. "You enjoyed playing with it outside—kiss it."

I drop to my good knee and air kiss. I lick and look up for approval. She tilts her hips forward. I taste her, my tentative licks becoming wet, wild kisses. She moans. I'm overcome by her scent, taste, and desire. She pulls my face deeper into her, grinds forward, tenses, and comes in my mouth.

I stand and she falls into my arms. She unbuttons my shirt. Gently, she caresses my chest. She kisses my nipples.

"Come to bed. I've got another surprise for you," she says.

I follow. My cock strains against the wet spot in my jeans. Under the covers she shows me that her mouth is as hungry for me as mine was for her. Afterwards, I spoon behind her. The bells of St. Michael's ring every fifteen-minutes, providing a slow, gentle reminder that we're all in it together.

I WAKE EXHILARATED AND REFRESHED. Lying next to Eva my mind wanders to Fat Jack and his trashy porno tapes. If Brittany was half the woman as Eva, it must have killed Jack to be an ocean away. I stroke Eva's shoulder. She rolls, and her lips drift back to mine. The tip of her tongue teases my mouth.

"I can do this for hours," she whispers. "How does that sound?"

"I'm not sure," I say. "Do it again."

She does, and rolls on top of me. We make love again.

Over a breakfast, she asks me how it felt to dance for the Fan Curve.

"Weird," I say.

"Weird? Not awesome? Not orgasmic!" she teases.

I blush and look away. Turning back to her, I ask, "What's up with Ahab? Isn't it kind of wrong to give me a peg-leg nickname?"

"No," she says. "Germans aren't so sensitive about that stuff, and it really fits."

"What?"

"You're both from New England, you lead the Ice Devils the same determined way Ahab led the Pequod, and you are focus on winning just like old Ahab was focused on killing Moby Dick."

"Huh?"

"Moby Dick," she says. "You read it in high school?"

I shake my head. "But everyone sort of knows the story," I say, making a mental note to get a copy at the library.

I go from Eva's place straight to the chow hall, hoping that someone covered for me at Monday morning formation. Joel, Derrick, and Danny come over.

Derrick slaps my back, "Ahoy there, Cap'n Ahab!"

Joel cracks, "Watch out, the Army takes rank very seriously. Keep it up and they might charge you with impersonating an officer!"

"Nah, he's good," Danny says, "Ahab was a squid, and the Army doesn't give a rip about the Navy!" We all laugh, and I appreciate their congratulations. But it quickly gets awkward, because after thanking them I don't know what else to say.

THIRTY

Thick gray clouds settle over Grafenwöhr on Tuesday. On Thursday I peddle a stationary bike, watching rain fall cold and steady against the fitness center's panoramic glass wall.

My phone buzzes; it's Eva. "Hey, what's up?" I ask.

"Can we talk?"

"Sure, what's up?"

"Can we meet to talk?" she asks.

"Ah, sure. Where?"

"At Brunner's for lunch?"

"Yeah, sure. At noon?"

"Yes, see you later," she says.

Peddling on autopilot, I wonder if maybe she has a sexy mid-day surprise for me. I arrive fifteen minutes early to a half empty café and take the same table we shared last month. I look out over Weiden's picture-book market square. The rain bounces off of the red tile roofs and pools on the granite cobblestone. When the waitress finally checks on me, I order the Weisswurst knowing that it comes with a Hefeweizen. As she brings me my oversized wheat beer, Eva arrives.

"Well, aren't you turning into a real Bavarian?" Eva says.

I stand and help her out of her wet coat and pull her chair out for her.

"I love it when you do that," she smiles.

"Do what?" I ask.

"Make me feel special," she says.

I shrug, glad that my mom and dad bothered to teach me manners.

The waitress comes with a fancy porcelain pot holding my sausages. Setting it down, she turns and talks to Eva in German.

"Did you get Weisswurst?" I ask.

Eva shakes her head. "That's not on the menu for me right now." Then she drops the bomb on me. She's pregnant! She says she doesn't know if she'll keep it, but it's her duty to let me know.

A tidal wave of emotions crash down.

Me, a father? Cool!

Me, a father? I'm not ready!

Eva and the baby have every right to count on me, but I have absolutely no idea what I'm doing with my life, let alone theirs. How could I make it work? Sure, I must be strong. That means being there for them every day without complaining or calling in sick.

Across the table, Eva tears up. What should I say? Should I admit that I'm conflicted? Damn, I have to say something. "I'm here for you," I finally say.

"Don't worry," she says, shaking her head. "I won't hold it over you."

"What!" I blurt, blushing and lowering my voice. "What do you mean?"

The waitress bringing Eva's cappuccino asks if I want

another beer. I do. Maybe ten would be better, but I shake my head.

"You should know about it, but I haven't yet decided what to do," she says.

"Catholics can only put babies up for adoption, right?"

Eva frowns, "In the Middle Ages."

"In my neighborhood," I say.

"Then thank goodness," she says, "I don't live in Boston."

I pick at my Weisswurst and decide it's not worth the effort to peel it.

The waitress looks at my uneaten food. I hand her my plate and she clears the rest of the table. When the bill comes, Eva reaches for her purse.

"No, I've got it," I say.

"Thanks, but that's not necessary."

"I insist." I say, handing the waitress a twenty euro bill.

"Thanks," Eva says. "You're sweet."

I DRIVE TO THE RINK. My head spins. When I get there, players tape sticks, sharpen skates, and think of ways to gain any slight advantage. There plenty focus, because everyone wants to make the playoffs. More importantly, we all want to avoid being in the relegation group. We are the pride of Weiden. People we've never met cheer passionately for us, and a feeling of responsibility comes with it. Man, I can't even imagine the stakes of playing for the Bruins in the Garden or team USA in the Olympics. With Garmisch behind me, my focus is very clear. Give one hundred percent on every shift with my German ice Brüder and win games for the Ice Devils.

Thomas and I talk about shootouts. I tell him about how I tomahawked my favorite stick in Garmisch. It was stupid, because like Sidney Crosby, I like a two-piece stick with a wooden blade. To me it has a better feel than the lighter, stiffer one-piece sticks. Thomas says there might be some old two-piece sticks back in storage, so we go find Ingo, the trainer. Luck is with me, and Ingo comes back with two blue Easton shafts that are exact matches to the one that I broke! I use a blow dryer to heat the open end of the shaft and the gluey stem of my spare wooden blades. When both are hot, I brace the butt-end on the floor and put all my weight onto the blade, forcing it into the shaft. Once it seats, I turn my attention to the second stick. After both cool, I tape the blades toe to heal with black friction tape and put a small knob on the butt-ends with white cloth tape.

"Perfect," I say out loud.

"What's perfect?" Felix asks.

"My sticks."

"Those antiques?" he says. "They belong in a museum."

Practice is just what I need. My new sticks feels great. Concentrating on executing Peter's complex drills clears my mind, and the physical exertion burns off my nervous energy. We scrimmage and Thomas sends me a beautiful saucer pass that I pull out of the air and tap in for an easy score from the backdoor. I point to back him, saying "Nice sauce!"

"You've won the Stanley Cup, hot-shot?" Felix says.

"You talking to me?" I challenge, skating up to him.

He pushes me away. "You fucking prima donna."

Peter comes over and separates us.

After practice, Felix showers under the nozzle next to me. As he rinses shampoo from his hair, I spot a rose tattoo on his shoulder. Its red petals and green leaves jump off of his pale skin. *Fuck me*, it matches Eva's tattoo.

THE HOCKEY GODS must have smiled on Basti and Steffi when they invited all the Devils and Rangers to their wedding, because neither team has a game. I pick up Eva at her house and am dying to ask her about her tattoo, but hold my tongue for fear of ruining our date. Besides, Eva looks so radiant in her blue-checked Dirndl. What kind of a fool would risk ruining it?

We join a large group of well-wishers at the city hall. Basti and Steffi are in the center with a photographer. In their matching Trachten, trimmed in purple velvet, they look like a fairytale couple. They go inside with a few family members for their civil ceremony, while the rest of us wait outside.

I tell Eva how lucky it is that we don't have a game tonight.

Eva smiles and shakes her head.

Thomas laughs, "Are you kidding? A German bride would never leave something like that to chance!"

Just then, the happy couple come out. The best man, Martin from Garmisch, has a table set up with fifty glasses of Sekt. He hands us each a glass of the German champagne and makes a toast. We then follow the bride and groom brightly decorated car up a big hill to a small village with a large onion-domed church.

There are more players and guests waiting at the church. We go inside and Eva steers me away from Felix and the Ice Devils. Instead, we sit a few pews back with Joel, Derrick, and Danny. Kenny is behind us with more

Rangers. After a thankfully short Mass, the priest declares Sebastian and Stephanie, "Mann und Frau."

Outside, Felix hands out sticks to the players, even me. We line up facing each other and raise the sticks, forming an arch for the newlyweds. After they pass through it, Martin leads them over to a stout log held up by two sawhorses. He has the couple take their places at either end of an old-fashioned two-man saw. Their first task as man and wife is to saw the log in half with everyone cheering them on. It takes a long time, but they persevere and cut it cleanly in half. We walk a block up the street to the Kummert Hof, the local guest house. The tables are set with starched linen, and we're seated for formal coffee and cake. Eva once again steers me away from the Devils and we sit with the Rangers.

"This is awesome," says Joel, "but shouldn't they leave for their honeymoon now?"

"No, that's separate," says Eva. "Tonight is to celebrate with family and friends. Once they clear the coffee, they'll serve beer and wine. At six, they'll serve dinner. At nine, the music and dancing will begin."

"Does it evah end?" Joel laughs.

"Most will leave at one or two," Eva says, "but close friends will stay the night and help clean up in the morning."

Things go exactly as Eva predicted. The food is wonderful. My loin in mushroom sauce with bread-crumb dumplings is amazing. Basti comes by our table to say hello, and a waitress follows him with a tray of Willi. She hands the shots out, and Eva declines. Basti looks surprised, then turns to me and winks.

Eva catches it, and says, "I'm his designated driver."

That earns me a second wink and a pat on the back. We

all toast to Basti and his bride. With all the great food and beer, the Willi is supposed to save us from a glutton's stomachache.

When people start moving to the dance floor, Eva suggests we leave.

"Are you okay?"

She shrugs.

"Is anything wrong?"

"I'm okay," she pouts.

"Why are you getting mad?"

"I'm not mad."

"Okay," I say.

"Why are you so worked up?" she asks. "Can't I go home if I feel like it?"

"I'm not worked up. You're the one getting all worked up."

"Leave me alone," she says, crossing her arms.

"Sure," I say, "but I know what's going on, and just know that I want to be there for you the same way Basti is there for Steffi."

"That's not it," she frowns.

"You wish I was German?"

"No," she says, tearing up.

"Then what?" I ask. "You're obviously upset about something."

"No," she says, "just worried, that's all."

"About what?"

"You know what," she says.

"If we get married, would you keep the baby?"

"What?" she says, with a wounded look. "I'm not trying to trap you."

"It's not like that," I press, caught between total commitment and total loss. "I would be lucky."

"And then?" she asks.

"We could move to Boston. The Army will send me to college and pays my rent. We could stay with my dad and live on the rent money."

"What would I do?" she asks, shaking her head. "Why can't you just keep working at Graf?"

"Maybe, but if my medical discharge goes through, I have to leave."

"When?"

"I don't know."

"Stop being stupid. You don't want to marry me."

"You don't want to be with me?"

"Yes," she says. "Could you see yourself staying here?"

"I don't speak German."

"You could learn and work with Basti," she suggests.

"As a plumber?" I say, shaking my head.

"Maybe the Devils will sign you to play next year."

I do love hockey and Eva. "Maybe," I say.

MONDAY'S PRACTICE is just what I need. After we warm up, Peter runs us through passing and shooting drills. He has us flying through several complex drills, alternating them with his mini-sprints.

After practice, I stop by a flower shop and go see Eva. She answers in her bathrobe and invites me in. She loves the flowers, puts them in a vase, and comes back to hug me. The lavender scent of her hair, the sight of her bare legs, and the feel of her in my arms make me feel like everything will turn out all right. She rises on her toes and I'm tempted to rub my nose against hers, but she kisses me first. She whispers, "Come, let's go to bed."

In her room, I watch her take off her robe and lie down. I realize that I would do anything for her. We gently make love and afterwards I lie behind her. I wrap my arm around her and cup her belly. She takes my hand, pulls it up to her chest, and holds it tight. I take a deep breath and think about how lucky I am to be with her.

In the morning I wake first, and head downtown to buy us rolls, cold cuts, and cheese. Eva said that when she was an exchange student, the first thing she missed was her breads and the German breakfasts. As I walk back to her place, I understand. Semmel beat donuts every damn time.

———————

THAT NIGHT I call Eva and thank her for letting me sleep over.

"Thanks for the flowers," she says.

"Did you think about my question?" I ask.

"No," she says, pausing. "Don't worry, I won't propose to you."

"I brought it up," I protest.

"Okay, but let's be clear. I am not holding the baby over you." As I struggle to control my temper, she says, "Tschuss," ending our call.

The hum of the dead line amplifies my regret—why didn't I say, "I love you."?

THIRTY-ONE

It's March. Spring's green buds of hope should already be erupting, but they're not. I should go to the gym, but I don't. Instead I hang out watching icy rain beat down on melting snow. Eva's pregnancy is really rocking my world. The last time we talked, she cried and told me she needed time to think. Now I'm stuck in radio listening silence, waiting for her to contact me. Don't get me wrong, Foley men are tough. We handle our own problems and don't ever put up our hands in surrender. Still, waiting sucks.

Boy, I wish Fat Jack was around. He was a dad, and he would have pointed me in the right direction. Or, maybe not. Maybe that's what killed him. When he and Brittany split, and Jack moved back into the barracks, he didn't have any friends. And the fat fucker didn't bother to take care of himself. He only shaved and got dressed for formations. Otherwise he just drank beer, played Xbox, and watched porn. Damn, that alone would have done me in. I should have dragged him to the gym.

I leaf through his porn stash. Most of the chicks on the covers have long bleach-blond hair and big boobs, just like

Brittany. One DVD features a raven-haired beauty who looks like Eva's twin. I sit and watch the nimble little porn-star do all kinds of sexual gymnastics, surprised that what arouses me most isn't anything I'd try in real life. I know porn isn't made to be realistic. It's made to provide over the top arousal. And man, can Eva's cute Doppelganger bring it! But I can't decide if being hyper-aroused makes me more or less lonely. For Horny Jack feeling aroused must have felt better than feeling nothing. Until he jumped.

This is crazy. Why would I let a look-alike actress get me all hot and bothered when I've got the genuine article in Weiden? I turn off the video and look outside hoping the rain has washed away the winter. My restless thoughts drift back to Eva.

Should I call her? She told me not to.

Should I call Dad? What would I say? "Hey, I've knocked up a German girl."

He'd say, "You gotta man up. Do the right thing."

Yeah, sure, but what is the right thing?

WHEN LIFE IS HARD, my refuge is the rink. I like the ritual of getting ready, stepping out on to the ice, and leaving everything else behind. I like the clarity of games, knowing after three periods who won, and by how much. And I enjoy being a winner.

The only time I'm not preoccupied with Eva is at practice. Even there, I have to pay attention and stay the hell away from Felix. On Wednesday, Peter focuses on power plays and penalty killing. Everyone is focused and serious, because our last four games will either elevate us to the top half, or send us to relegation.

Peter uses Thursday's practice to focus on defensive zone faceoffs and breakouts. I don't understand his insistence on setting up the perfect breakout, even circling back for a "second wave" if things don't form up correctly. Heck, sometimes you just need to chip and chase. A heavy forecheck can force turnovers and goals. But apparently they don't do it that way. Much like FC Bayern, they try to keep possession for the entire game. It sure is pretty when it works, but what about when it doesn't?

***

AFTER 17:00 RELEASE FORMATION, I race to Weiden for my Ice Devil game. In warm-ups, I'm withdrawn, but by the time play starts, I'm in a frenzy. In my mind, every opposing player is Manning. Every chance I have to throw my body, I crush him.

By the time I drop my gloves, I already have a goal and an assist. The giant I square off against never has a chance. I grab his shoulder pads through his jersey, getting inside and under him. With my free right hand, I throw blows into his stomach and then punch straight up, landing a blow on his chin. Sometime between my second and third follow-on uppercuts, he drops.

The crowd roars.

As the medics shuffle across the ice with a stretcher, the ref sends me to the showers. I sit and stew in the empty locker room, wondering if Peter will throw me off the team. I undress, and a few minutes later the stadium horn blows.

Players march in happy and loud. Some come over to high-five me. Thomas says that we won three to two. He hands me a bottle of Zoigl, and toasts my Gordie Howe hat trick.

Peter comes in, looks at me, and shakes his head. "You play like a devil. Good," Peter says. "You fight like a devil. Bad. Here, it gets you out, plus one game more."

I driving back to post regretting my fighting suspension. Not playing in Friday's game against Freiburg hits me hard, and Peter won't even let me ride on the team bus to watch. Just before midnight on Friday, Thomas texts me, "We lost 7–2." Damn, I hate myself for letting my team down.

ON MONDAY, Peter holds a special team meeting before practice. In the crowded locker room I can feel the tension, but don't understand any of Peter's rapid-fire German. As we put on our gear, Thomas tells me that our last four games are derby games against Regensburg, Bayreuth, and Selb. The first three are all road games, and our last one is at home against Selb. All are must-win games.

Peter runs another fast-paced, silent practice. He really pushes us, and nobody dares joke or laugh. It's all business.

Thomas, Paldi, and I go to the rink's snack bar after practice. They explain that derby games are the hardest to win, because local rivals get psyched up for the games. The arenas are always full, the crowds are more wild and louder, and the police will be there in full riot gear.

Thomas says, "We play with our entire town behind us. We don't care if Regensburg is bigger, has more money, or buys more players. Weiden is a hockey town, our stadium is our home, and nobody can come in and take an easy win from us."

Paldi puts down his knife and fork and says, "But it's the same for them. They will play harder to beat us. Only a few hundred of our fans can get tickets. The four thousand

Eisbären fans cheering against us will drown our fanS out, but they'll still be there for us." He picks up his fork and cuts his pizza, "We can win this games."

At noon on Sunday, we load the team bus for Regensburg. In a light rain we head south, riding past Weiden's train station and the chain stores on the outskirts of town. Next to the autobahn, patches of fog rise from the muddy fields.

We exit the Autobahn and Thomas says, "The Romans founded Regensburg. It's the capital of the Oberpfalz, and Pope Benedict's hometown." We go through a tunnel, exit, and cut across the river city to the Donau Arena. I remember it from the day I had to race back to post because Jack jumped. Thomas tells me each year the Eisbären seem destined to win the league and move up. This year is no different. They sit atop the standings and will start bracket play seeded number one whether they beat us or not.

An icy wind stings my face as I step off of the bus. We start sluggishly and give up two goals in the first period. In the second, Paldi and I break into the attacking zone, two against one. At the very last second, he slides the puck over to me, and I deflect it in as I whiz past the goal post. Goal! Skating, passing, and hitting are all fun, but scoring is the greatest rush of all.

I high-five Paldi, saying, "Nice pass!"

After my tap-in goal, I play instinctively and ferociously. Every shift I fly, but the Eisbären and their goalie play well. Late in the third period, we still trail. With the clock counting down, and our goalie pulled for an extra attacker, Paldi takes a pass from Felix and shoots high stick-side, ringing the puck off of the crossbar, down, and in!

Goal! Our small band of fans roar as the buzzer sounds.

We play five minutes of overtime, and stay knotted at

two, so we move on to shootout. Peter picks Paldi, David, and Felix to shoot.

The Eisbären go first. Their player comes in fast in an S-curve pattern and scores on a low wrist shot from fifteen feet out. Everyone else misses, and it all comes down to our last shooter, Felix. If he scores, he keeps our hopes alive. If he misses, we lose.

At center ice, he seems composed. The referee places the puck on the ice. There's a stillness in the air, as if the crowd drew in a collective breath and now waits together to exhale. Felix skates slowly towards the Regensburg net, carrying the puck on his forehand to show he might shoot. He crosses in front of the net and tries to pull the puck across to his backhand, but the goalie pokes his stick forward knocking the puck harmlessly away.

The Regensburg fans erupt in wild celebration, and the Eisbären players spill out onto the ice and mob their game-winning goalie. We sit. We stare. Losing in shootout feels hollow. Fake. Unfair. The overtime loss gives us one point, rather than three. That's better than nothing, but our fate remains uncertain and we ride the bus home in silence.

———

AT OUR NEXT PRACTICE, the mood is sour. We move mechanically through Peter's complex drills. We scrimmage. Everybody tries too hard to make the perfect play, and nobody will take a shot. Nobody crashes the net. I've seen this happen before. Tentative teams lose and become more tentative. We're overthinking, making everything too hard and too complex.

My high school coach used to say, "Boys, everyone thinks hockey is complicated. It isn't. Two teams. Two nets.

You win if you put the puck in their net more times than they put it in yours. There are no points for making pretty plays. Shoot, shoot, and crash the net!"

On the bench I turn to David, "You're Czech, right?"

He nods.

"Then stop fucking around," I point at the net with the blade of my stick, "Go to the net like Jaromir Jagr!"

He nods again.

The next shift he goes to the net, gets a hard pass, and the puck bounces away. But at least he tried to shoot. That's progress. With one lucky bounce, things can quickly turn and go our way.

UP IN MY ATTIC ROOM, it's hard to tell if the low rumbling is artillery or thunder. Then, lightning flashes. I pull up my bad leg to take a hard look at my naked stump. Balancing on my good leg, I hop to the open window and smell the rain. Lightning cuts across the sky in jagged bursts. Each thunderclap rumbles in my chest. After a bright flash, I swear I see Jack on the couch.

Did his doubts drive him crazy? Is that why he jumped? The questions linger, mixing with the smell of ozone and rain. The storm grows stronger. I shut the window and go back to bed. Each flash and each rumble stirs my uneasy thoughts. Focusing on the storm's sound and fury, I pray it isn't a violent echo of Jack's death. I hope it's the beginning of better times.

It blows through, the rain stops, and Taps sounds with sadness and finality. I struggle to think about hockey instead of Jack and Eva. But they are a part of me, citizens of my thoughts and dreams.

I ache for Eva. For our casual talks, our walks through the old town, and our lazy mornings spent exploring each other's bodies. I haven't told her, but it's there—I love her.

SUNDAY IS GAME DAY. Just after 14:00 on a sunny spring afternoon, we pull up to Bayreuth's big metal barn of a stadium. When our logo-covered bus stops, we spill out and gather in small groups to collect our bags and sticks. We have three hours until puck drop, leaving plenty of time to stretch, warm up, and dress. Felix moves our warm-ups outside and into the spring sunshine. The change feels like a good omen. Our players, especially those who grew up playing their youth derby games in Bayreuth, look forward to playing in the old, airy metal-shed of a stadium.

In the game's opening minutes, the Bayreuth Tigers bottle us up in our own end and pepper our goalie with shots. On the bench, I try to catch my breath. I say to Paldi, "We've got to chip and chase! Get after the puck! Forecheck and hit!"

"No," Paldi replies, "we've got to set up our breakout, skate, pass, and score."

The next ten minutes look as bad as the first ten. The Tigers play like they're on an extended power play. At the buzzer, we're lucky to be down by only one goal.

I turn to Paldi, "We can't sit back. We've got to be aggressive, kick some ass!"

"They pushed the pace," Paldi agrees. "But we must slow things down, control the puck, and set up our rush."

"We don't need to control anything! We need to chip the puck off of the boards and go after it!" I snap.

"Nein," Paldi says. "Good hockey is possession, passing, and shooting."

"Not when the other team is dominating," I argue.

"We need to set up, get open shots, and score."

"You guys think too much like soccer players. You want to make a few fancy moves and back passes. But if you spend all your time on razzle-dazzle plays, somebody's gonna knock you on your ass, take the puck, and put it in the back of your net."

"No, you win by keeping the puck on your stick, passing it to open players, and taking good shots."

Peter holds up a hand for silence. Everyone looks at me. Peter says in English, "No dumping the puck."

As we line up to take the ice, I tell Paldi, "You're impossible. Back home when we're up against a faster team, we simplify and go north-south, none of this east-west nonsense."

Paldi shakes his head, "If you want to play that way, go home."

In the second period we battle back and get a few shots on net, but their goalie makes timely saves. We start the third period still down by one. Late in the third, Paldi hits me with a pinpoint pass as I'm breaking across the middle. The backward-skating Bayreuth defenseman shifts, lining up his shoulder with my chest. I keep coming. When he leans forward to hit me, I chip the puck off the boards and spin my body in the opposite direction. He turns to follow the puck. In one stride, I pass him. In two strides, I pick up the puck. In three, I'm breaking in alone on their goalie. I pull the puck to my right, left, right, and wait for him to move. When he shifts sideways, I shoot an inch to the inside his left skate. Goal!

The ecstasy of scoring on a breakaway is almost indescribable. It all happens so fast, and so slow, at the same time. So focused on scoring, I forget that I'm alive. At the same time, I've never been more alive. This same magical separation of mind and body happened when I jumped. As I looked over the toes of my boots at the earth a thousand feet below and waited for my chute open, time stood still. The roar of the plane was replaced by the silence of falling through the sky.

Our fans break my Zen-like scoring moment with their rhythmic chant: "A-hab!" boom-boom-boom, "A-hab!" boom-boom-boom, "A-hab!" boom-boom-boom.

The game's last two minutes are a blur. We take a tripping penalty and Bayreuth throws everything at us. We somehow keep their power play to the outside, and our goalie, Victor, turns away shot after shot. Then they set up a beautiful tick-tac-toe passing play, and score. The buzzer sounds and we lose, leaving with none of the points we so desperately need.

Our team bus rolls into the Weiden parking lot a few minutes after one. We unload our gear and put it in the locker room. Most players must get up for school or work in just a few hours. When I get back to Graf, I only have about three hours before PT formation. I decide to stay up and flip through the six channels on AFN. Bored, I switch to watching Jack's porn. Man, when she flashes her crooked smile, that sexy little hottie looks like Eva.

I go back to bed after the 06:30 formation. When I wake up, it's mid-afternoon. During our 17:00 formation rain falls, clearing away the lingering fog and making it feel a little less dreary. I eat dinner at the chow hall, go back to my room, dial Eva, and hold my breath. I just need to hear her voice. She answers and seems happy. I carefully avoid the topic we both want to discuss and we chit-chat about nothing.

Finally, I ask, "Why do you want me to stay in Germany?"

"You make me feel special," she says.

"You are special."

"You hold doors open for me. You pull out my chair and help me into the car. German guys don't do any of that. We meet at a place, I open my own door, and if he's already there he doesn't even get up. Afterwards, we split the bill but he still wants sex."

"Really?"

"Yes."

"You make me feel special, too." I say, wondering if she loves me.

After our call, I daydream about moving into one of the Netzaberg houses with her. If I stayed in the Army, and we married, they would assign us a house. Man, I'd have to be nuts to turn down that deal.

MONDAY AND WEDNESDAY night's practices are mechanical. Nobody wants to take a risk or make a mistake. At Thursday night's end-of-practice scrimmage, Felix slashes the back of my good leg. Later he drives me into the boards with a dirty hit from behind. As I get up, everyone watches Felix circle me with his chest out and jaw clenched.

I'm clearly the outsider, but anger quickly replaces the sting of exclusion.

Saying nothing, we know it's time to fight and drop our gloves.

After a few tentative punches, we close in. Nobody moves in to stop us. I reach inside to grab Felix's shoulder pads through his jersey, but I can't reach. He's taller, has longer arms, and keeps me away by grabbing the collar of my jersey with his left hand. He uses it to hit me in the face with quick jabs, like a boxer hitting a speed bag.

I crouch low and rabbit punch his body until I can go high and smash my fist into his arrogant German chin. We spin, jockeying for position, and slam into the boards. Finally I land a hook and his mouth bleeds red, like his fucking rose tattoo.

He reaches over me and pulls off my helmet, and hammers blows down on my head. It's an ugly fight, and Peter finally pulls us apart.

Felix spits blood at me and says, "Fick Dich."

"What?" I shout, surging forward.

Thomas rushes in to help Peter.

"What?" I shout again.

Felix wipes blood away with the back of his hand. "Fuck you, Prima Donna, Es ist meines!" He picks up his gloves and stick, and heads to the locker room.

He leaves me standing there like a fool. Peter points me to the bench.

Thomas brings me my helmet, gloves, and stick.

"What did Felix yell?" I ask him.

"He shouted an accusation, like you took something from him."

I sit watching the practice. What the does Felix think I stole from him? His team? His fans? His girlfriend? Whatever, that's his problem.

TAPS SOUNDS. Most nights I have trouble sleeping; this is one of them. Why did Felix come after me? There's no clear answer, and other destructive thoughts line up to take a shot at me.

Why did Jack jump? Tortured by the same damn question, I pray for Jack. Maybe he had PTSD? I met him after he came back from Afghanistan. Brittany had already packed up and moved back to Detroit. Jack always had a joke about why it was the Army or the VA who was so completely fucked up. But what thoughts nagged his troubled mind?

What about me? I never went to war. Am I even worthy of having PTSD? I sure didn't earn it the old-fashioned way. Does that make me a fake? Fuck me, this isn't about me. It's about Dead Jack, that fat fucking quitter. Man, he would have been a horrible hockey player, unless he played in goal because in goal he would sure have covered a lot of net!

I finally fall asleep.

"How's your German coming along?" my dream Eva asks me.

"Good," I say.

"Really? I heard the best way to learn is with your teacher on her back." She caresses me, her fingernails drag across my chest causing sparks to fly. Her magical touch causes every part of me—every fiber—to vibrate and climb to an exquisite, elevated pitch. I roll on top of her, and she arches, tilting her hips up to help me bury myself deep inside her.

My zero-six-hundred alarm rings, and I get out of bed with an aching piss hard-on. It passes, but by noon I can't take the silence. I call Eva. Her phone rings and rings. This time she doesn't answer.

THIRTY-TWO

Our last two games are against Selb and our entire season hangs in the balance. On Friday afternoon, we board the team bus for a forty-minute ride north to their cement and steel icebox. I can't imagine an uglier arena, and its inside is as cold, hard, and industrial as its outside.

The crowd's hostility is clear during warmups, and when the game starts it grows. The Wölfe get carried away battling for position in front of our net and take a stupid roughing penalty. They clear the puck twice. Then, with both sides changing on the fly, we set up in the attacking zone. Thomas and Paldi are down low near the goal line, Schoppi and Mark are up high on the points, and I'm skating free in the slot, taking away the Selb goalie's eyes. Selb struggles with their one-man disadvantage, and twenty seconds into the shift Schoppi takes a wicked slap shot from the left point. Their goalie makes the save, but gives up a juicy rebound.

I find the bouncing puck and slide it under his outstretched glove. Goal! Our small but mighty band of traveling fans scream, "A-hab!" boom-boom-boom! And our slim lead holds through the third period. With three minutes left we take a too-many-men penalty and give up a power play goal. The clock ticks to zero, the horn blares, and we move on to overtime.

Felix loses the opening face-off. Selb enters our zone and works the puck back to a defenseman. He fires a low shot, which Felix blocks, sending it out over our blue line. David sprints forward and collects it. A Selb player trips him from behind, and the referee signals a penalty shot.

A hush falls over the stadium. All eyes are on David as he picks up the puck and sprints toward the Selb goalie, who had aggressively come out to the hash marks and now tries desperately to adjust to David's speed. Backing up, he tries to poke the puck away but David leans in and protects it with his skates. The goalie's stick whacks into the skates, and David falls as he shovels the puck one-handed into the open net.

We win! But in this league an overtime win only earns us two of the three points we badly need. Next week, we can't leave any points on the table. In front of our own fans, we must win in regulation.

———

AFTER TUESDAY'S PRACTICE, I push through heavy double doors into the damp night air. As they shut with a metallic crunch, my Eva and Army troubles start to pierce my hockey happiness bubble.

I set my bag down on in the cement steps and consider going back in to find a place to sleep. A hidden place where I'd be calm and at ease. I'm about to do just that, when Peter knocks on the narrow glass window and waves me back inside. He leads me to his small office. His rigid, stoic demeanor doesn't hide his discomfort. He hands me a letter.

"We have problem," he says, pointing. "From German Hockey Federation."

I yank the letter from its flimsy envelope. I can't read it, but I can see that it's addressed to the Ice Devils, with my name buried in a sea of twenty letter German words.

Focusing on two words I can read, I ask, "Mechanische Augmentation?"

"Selb files complaint for advantages from mechanical foot."

"My foot makes it possible for me to play, but there's no advantage. It's me who plays. It's me who hits, shoots, and scores."

"Yes," he nods. "But they demand technical answers," he says.

"There's no advantage. I have a disability!"

"Technical answer back this week, yes?" he asks.

I turn, leave, and drive straight to Eva's. The trees lining her street are still winter skeletons and offer no shelter from the bitter wind blowing in from Poland. As I cross the street, I soak my good foot in a puddle the color of motor oil. Eva sees something is wrong. She reads the letter. Her mouth tightens. Before she can say a word, I know I'm toast.

"Oh, Will," she says, reaching for my hand. "Selb says your foot is an unnatural augmentation and the DEB must decide if gives you an unfair playing advantage."

"Being an amputee gives me an advantage?" I say, thinking back to all the pain. The pain of losing my foot. The pain of gait training. The pain of my first failed Rangers practice. My on ice success is fueled with cardio and strength workouts, hard work in practices, and a lifetime of playing hockey the right way. "It's complete bullshit!"

Tears run down her cheeks as she reads on. "They ask if your prosthetic has any moving parts or a motor."

I'm caught off guard by Eva's unchecked emotions. Her tears show that she loves me. But, the stinging injustice of the letter destroys the moment. I can't live without hockey. How could anyone dare to take it from me?

Eva sets the letter down. My angry fire burns out.

"It isn't fair," I say, with my voice trailing off, "I was just starting to—" I can't figure out the right words, but I feel it in my gut—I am being violated.

"You think you're the only one who's ever been treated unfairly?" Eva asks.

I shake my head, but can feel my dreams slipping away. What about the Devils signing me for next season? What about Eva and me? What about our baby?

"Come on, let's work on a response, A-hab," she says, adding three claps.

"What's the point?"

She puts her hands on her hips. "Stop feeling sorry for yourself."

We go to the kitchen and talk about my options. I leave in a daze, knowing only that I need to reach out to Coach. Back in the barracks, I call him. He teases me about my new nickname, but stops as soon as he hears the news.

"They want what?" he asks. I explain that the DEB wants the design specifics.

"Jon Hoffmann will need to jump through some medical red tape to get that information," he says.

At lights out, I think back to Landstuhl. Gait training was a bitch. Every muscle in my body begged me to stop. The one time I collapsed and blurted out, "I quit," Jill cut me off. I remember the feel of tears welling up. Unacceptable, I thought, because paratroopers don't cry! I forced myself up and learned to walk again. How can anyone now accuse me of having a mechanical advantage? How!

I can't lose my Eis Brüder. They are my tribe! My team! My Mia san Mia! We're all hard-wired to be connected. We spend nine months in our mother's womb and then take comfort and nourishment from her. Our families sustain us, and later school brings us classmates and friends. Sports morph these early relationships into something we call teamwork. The Army builds on all of this, transforming groups of strangers into cohesive units.

As I fought back from the isolation and loneliness of rehab, hockey found me. I again became a part of something bigger than myself. And now, Selb wants the DEB to take it all away from me? It hurts, and it's no damn wonder.

ON MONDAY MORNING, Coach and I meet at Jon's office. Jon can't believe the Germans are investigating my hockey foot. He and Coach talk about privacy laws, HIPPA, and some other legal mumbo-jumbo.

Coach turns to me. "We're war-gaming how medical privacy laws might stall their investigation."

"Will it work?" I ask.

"Back home it might buy us some time, but we don't think that the Germans will let us play that game," Coach says.

"What's your deadline?" Jon asks.

"The club has to answer this week," I say.

"When's your next game?" Jon asks.

"Our last regular season game is this Sunday."

"Okay," Coach says, "Turn the response in late Friday, because it's unlikely that the DEB will work on Saturday."

"Unless they've already decided," Jon says.

"What?" I ask.

Coach shrugs, "They might have already decided that motors and moving parts are a no-go, and just need to verify how your foot actually works before they rule."

"Can they do that?" I ask.

"I'm not an expert on sports law," Coach says, "but the world has seen similar issues."

"Like Oscar Pistorius?" I ask.

"Sort of, but he races in the para-Olympics," Coach says. "Maybe more like the African runner who was winning all the women's eight hundred meter races until she was tested for testosterone and banned."

"Caster Semenya?" Jon says.

"Right," Coach says. "They found male testosterone levels and ruled that it gave her an unfair advantage over female athletes who had normal levels."

"What's that got to do with me?"

"The battle lines are similar," Coach says. "Semenya argued that God made her that way and banning her is discriminatory. The track and field officials argued that their discrimination was necessary, reasonable, and proportionate in order to preserve the integrity of female competition."

"And she lost?" I ask.

Coach shrugs, "At first, but it's still going back and forth in the courts."

"Didn't the Olympics ban speed skaters who used hinged blades to get more push?" Jon asks.

"Yes, but that's a little different. Those skates were designed to improve times. The DEB could only rely on that case if they found Will's foot was designed to give him an advantage."

"So, I'm screwed either way?"

"Maybe," Coach says, "but you've got some equities going your way."

"Like what?" Jon asks.

"Will is technically handicapped, so he might find some protection under German disability law," Coach says, "and we can argue that the moving parts only mimic the natural foot he lost. It just puts him back to where he was and doesn't give him any advantage over two-footed players."

"Huh," Jon says, taking a swig of his coffee. "We should ping Jimmy about the foot's design."

"Can you call him now?" Coach asks.

Jon puts his phone on speaker and dials. On the first ring we hear, "Hello, Jimmy's pizza and spare parts store."

"Hey Jimmy, it's Jon in Graf."

"How's the weather?" Jimmy laughs.

"Fuck you," Jon says. "Hey, I've got you on speaker with Colonel Jack Bradley and Specialist Will Foley."

Dead silence, until Coach says, "Hello, this is Lieutenant Colonel *retired* Bradley. I'm Will's hockey coach. He's playing in a German semi-pro league, and the league wants the design specs on his hockey foot."

"Sir, what for?" Jimmy asks.

"They want to know if it gives him a competitive advantage. If they find it does, they'll likely ban him from the league."

"They know he didn't lose his foot on purpose, right?" Jimmy says.

"Sure," Coach says, "but what we need is something that says his prosthetic only mimics the foot he lost and doesn't give him any advantage. Can you do that?"

"I think so," Jimmy says, "but prosthetics range from very simple to very complex. Will's running blade and hockey foot are the perfect examples. The blade is simple with no moving parts, and the hockey foot is very complex, motorized, and Bluetooth enabled. Plus, it's titanium rod is harder than bone and never gets tired."

"Can you downplay that?" Coach asks.

"No, not really. Without the sensors and electric motors Will couldn't properly dig in his blade and skate."

"Skate like he did before losing his foot?"

"Yeah, sure," Jimmy says.

"And just like other players?"

"Yes, exactly."

"Okay, that's exactly what I need you to write up," Coach says.

THIRTY-THREE

Hockey is an emotional game, and I've never played it with patience. I've always brought the game to my opponents. With the Rangers, my instinct to seize the momentum was reawakened. With the Devils, I am even more aggressive. Every shift, I precipitate the action. I don't just hold my ground. I pick fights. Partly, I do it to vent. My anger towards Manning is bitter, but not a blind. My anger towards Selb is newer, and white hot. I know that I can't hit Manning. But if I play, I will hit Selb.

It will feel great and the Fan Curve will love me.

I shave and look into the mirror, knowing that my passion and dedication fuel my success. I'm in the best shape of my life. It's not my foot making me play better. It's me.

If I play on Sunday, I will hit. I will shoot. I will score. The fans will chant, "A-hab!" clap-clap-clap, "A-hab!" clap-clap-clap, "A-hab!" clap-clap-clap. We will win. I will dance.

AT FIRST FORMATION, Jones tells me to report to the commander at 17:30. Why doesn't Manning just send the board results to me through Jones? Why does he make me wait to get them? I bet the sick fucker is just torturing me. He must want to personally rub my nose in it. At least when I'm out, I won't have to answer to that grinning psychopath.

All day long I speculate. Did the board keep me in? The board president liked me. The sergeant major loved me. But after all the abuse, why do I want to stay in? For Eva and the baby, of course. And besides, if they really put me out, I'll be labeled as a failure.

After release formation, I go wait in the commander's hallway. Just like the other times, I'm stuck riding in the caboose of Manning's night court pain train. Do I really want to stay in as a paratrooper? Fuck me, it's hard to know right now.

An old-timer sits waiting in his dress uniform. Below his gold staff sergeant chevrons, I count four service stripes. That means he's spent two years in combat. The shiny badge on his breast pocket shows that one of his tours was at the headquarters in Baghdad. His rack of medals has three rows, and includes a Purple Heart.

Then, it hits me.

Fat Jack must have sat in this hallway on the night he died. That explains why he was in his dress uniform when he jumped. Just like the staff sergeant sitting across from me, Jack wanted Manning to see all of his awards and decorations from years of serving in the shit.

The staff sergeant is called, and goes to face the music. I silently wish him luck. Alone in the hallway, I'm pissed. I'm pissed about what Manning did to Jack. I'm pissed about what Manning is doing to me. I'm pissed about what getting kicked out of the Army will do to me, Eva and our baby.

The strutting rooster of a sergeant major sticks his head out and waves me to my feet, saying, "Come on, Foley, you know the drill."

I knock, enter, and report. Before I even know what I'm doing, words spill out, "Sir, I volunteer to retrain. I'm even willing to reclass as a cook to stay in."

"What?"

"Sir, I have a baby on the way—"

With the trace of a grin flickering across his cruel face, he says, "You're pregnant."

"No, sir. I—"

"Who's the baby-mama?" he interrupts.

"She's a local, sir, and—"

"So, you're married?" he asks, enjoying my discomfort.

"No, sir. It was an accident."

"An accident?"

"Yes, sir."

"She was walking down the street, tripped, and fell on your dick?"

"No, sir."

"Then it wasn't an accident," he says, in a terrible monotone.

"Sir, about changing my MOS?"

"Foley, that ship sailed at Fort Bragg," he says, a crocodile smile signaling that my time to talk has expired. He reaches across his desk, picks up a single sheet of paper, and hands it to me. "At ease, Foley, read it."

As ordered, I read.

The board found that I'm no longer fit to serve as an infantryman. Even though I expected it, I'm shaken. In this room, Manning took away my status as a corporal and leader; now the Army is taking away my identity as a soldier and paratrooper. "Corporal" and "Airborne" are now just fancy words that once described something I was before I lost my foot.

Manning interrupts my thoughts, asking, "Any questions?"

"No, sir," I say. But before saluting, I change my mind. "Sir, one question."

"Yes?"

"Did you have Specialist Martin here the night he jumped?" I ask.

Manning's face remains almost as dead as his eyes. Almost, except for the nervous tic at the corner of his left eye. In a monotone that approaches a whisper, he says, "You are dismissed."

I stand fast, looking into the eyes of Fat Jack's killer with pure contempt.

Manning's nervous tick kicks into high gear.

The sergeant major steps between us, and says, "Get the fuck out of here, Foley!"

I execute an about-face and leave without saluting. Rocking Manning's world by asking him a question he will never have the courage to answer is small potatoes compared to finally knowing the truth.

Back to my room, I call home, and pour my heart out about everything, everything except Eva and the baby. "How can I be too broken to stay in the Army, and too fixed to play hockey?" I ask.

"Sometimes life ain't fair," Dad says.

Not impressed with his cop wisdom, I say goodnight and hang up.

Like Ahab being dragged out to sea by Moby Dick, I'm drowning in the folly of my life. But, thank God, I still have hockey. It's my only slim chance to stay in Bavaria and provide for Eva. I have to make it work!

I give my DEB packet to Peter at quarter to five on Friday. Handing it over, I tell myself that the DEB will give me a fair shake. They just need to know more about my foot, that's all. They'll understand that I didn't scheme to gain a competitive advantage. Besides, Germans rule followers. I didn't break any rules, so they won't punish me. They can't—I've got to sign with the Devils and play next year. That's what I tell myself, but I'm not convinced, because in deep in my gut I doubt that it will work.

Despite my misgivings, I am certain about one thing. If I get to play on Sunday, those rotten motherfuckers from Selb will pay.

THIRTY-FOUR

Selb thrashed me badly in their ugly, concrete arena. But I held up, and banged in a goal. Peter appreciated it, but that's nothing new. My coaches have always encouraged me to play mean, praised my killer instincts, and loved my knack for scoring nasty, greasy goals.

My ability to read the game, fight for position, and change directions quickly separates me from the rest. When I fight for rebounds, I know the puck doesn't always glide, it can bounce. Down low in the slot, quickness is more important than top speed and hand-eye coordination is more important than brute strength. My eyes find and track the puck, my muscles react automatically, and my twisting, spinning moves come naturally. Getting the blade of my stick on the puck first is the key. Once that happens, my hands take over and I bury the puck in the back of the net.

PETER CALLS me on Saturday afternoon. He says that the club didn't get a suspension letter, and German mail doesn't run on Sunday. So, I can play!

I call Eva and then text my dad to share the good news.

I see Joel in the chow hall, and he says he wouldn't miss it for the world.

It's impossible not to get caught up in how important the game is to the whole town. The connection between Weiden and its Devils is beyond symbiotic. When the region's booming porcelain industry collapsed, what gave people hope? The Ice Devils. They gave the town something to cheer for.

Home games are a salve. No, a salvation. The light, noise, and excitement break up the dark and cold winter. Sixteen-hundred blue and white true believers gather, chant, share in the ritual of game night, and pray for their Devils to dance. Tomorrow, we'll dance for them. We'll dance for us. I'll dance for me.

SUNDAY MORNING I wake with fire in my belly. I have a sense of purpose like never before. Our arch-rivals, our hated neighbors, the bastards who ratted me out, will be in our house. With a win, we will qualify for the play-up bracket and avoid relegation.

I arrive early for what will probably be my last game as an Ice Devil. Walking through the empty arena, I can already feel it—something inside me will die here tonight. Looking up at the scoreboard, I think, has there ever been a player who loved the game as much as me? I go into the locker room sad that my season will soon be finished. Damn, I'm just not ready to hang up my skates. Nothing equals the joy of winning and tonight might be my last chance to dance.

I will wreck Selb. I will go out a winner.

Felix takes us upstairs to stretch. I can't figure him out, and am very glad that I won't skate on his line tonight. As we loosen up, the Selb bus pulls into the parking lot below us. Their players enter our arena loud, like a bunch of thugs. Their mob of fans must stay outside. They stand together, smoking and drinking between two team buses, while police in riot gear keep an eye on them.

I vow that tonight, they will ride home sad and silent.

I skate my first lap, and look up into the stands. The fans are young and old, men and women, rich and poor. Dad always told me, "The Bruins allow us to be a part of a black and gold tribe—something bigger than all of us." It's true here, too. We unite our fans, allowing them to forget what divides them. Outside they might not agree on much, but inside they agree on everything. How many places are like that today?

The pre-game hoopla and opening face-off are a blur. By my second shift, I'm playing completely in the zone. On my third shift, I fight for position in the slot. I find the puck, it leaves the blade of my stick, ricochets off of the goalie, and lands to his left. I spin and send the bouncing puck into his skates. He kicks it out. I shoulder a defenseman out of the way and shovel the puck up between his knees and into the net. The red light snaps on, a horn blares, and the arena erupts. Howling, "Balls deep!" I raise my arms in triumph. The crowd, our bench, and my line are all bound together by overwhelming joy.

Right away in the second, Selb goes on a power play and scores on a deflected slap shot from the point. Their fans, bunched up to the right of the Fan Curve, celebrate wildly. We must respond to take back the momentum. Instead, we grind through the period, fighting for the puck along the boards. With the long change, I get caught up ice while Paldi and Thomas change on the fly. A big defenseman drives his shoulder into my jaw and visor. My head snaps back, bringing my stick up. The copper taste of blood fills my mouth, but I concentrate on finding the puck. I feel it on my left skate blade, kick it forward off of the boards, and skate to where it will be. Before the defenseman knows what is going on, I fire a laser-beam pass to a Devil streaking toward the net. Felix redirects it in, raises his arms, and curves towards me in a victory lap.

"Danke," he mouths, turning up ice to our bench and high-fiving the outstretched hands. The period ends with us up by one.

Between the second and third periods, my bad leg aches. Accepting physical punishment from the Selb defenders is the rent paid for going hard to the net and battling in the corners. The mean fuckers push, hack, grab, and whack me. They target my prosthetic leg. Whatever, bring it on!

In the middle of the third period, Selb's center carries the puck into our zone, Thomas darts across and lifts his stick, collects the puck, and speeds in the opposite direction. The closest Selb winger takes a swipe at the puck, misses, and trips Thomas. The ref whistles the play dead, and Peter calls a timeout. He waves us together, and diagrams an umbrella power play, putting Paldi on point to quarterback it, and me down low to screen the goalie.

Paldi turns to me and says, "Play big, like Chara."

"Bigger," I grin.

As we form up, I chatter, "All right boys, low shots, hard shots, look for rebounds. Balls deep, boys, balls deep!"

Thomas, as a right shot taking the face-off on the left, uses an overhand grip on his stick. The linesman crouches to drop the puck. Thomas anticipates it and spins his body clockwise, pulling the puck on his backhand to Paldi. Paldi cheats down to the high slot, looking for an open shooting lane. He reconsiders and backs out to set up our umbrella formation. He plays catch with our players on the half-boards. The short-handed defenders have to shift from side to side to track the puck's movement, while I battle for space in front of the net, trying to stay between the goalie's eyes and the puck, staying ready to deflect a shot or pounce on a juicy rebound. As everyone settles into the rhythm of the perimeter passes, Paldi sends a hard pass towards the net. The streaking puck deflects off a defenseman's skates before it makes it to me.

Everyone collapses in to fight for the loose puck. In the mad scramble, I maintain clarity. Through a forest of sticks and legs I track the puck, lunge forward, and poke it with the tip of my outstretched stick. The goalie dives forward and crashes into me. Players fall onto us. Again, I taste the metallic tang of blood in my mouth.

I watch the puck trickle through the goalie's splayed legs and cross the goal line. I scramble to stand. I rise and run on the toes of my blades like Gretzky. Halfway to our bench, my teammates mob me. We all go down in a tangled, happy pile. We are bigger and more powerful than gods. We are invincible!

Peter is the only calm in our storm. He calls a line change and commands us to settle down and defend our lead. We frustrate Selb's relentless attack for five minutes. With just over two minutes left to play, Selb pulls their goalie to gain an extra attacker, but are disorganized and can't gain our zone.

The horn sounds and we spill onto the ice as winners. Victory fills us with electric joy. Our post-game locker room is no longer a home for silent pain. We yell and sing, strip off our jerseys and shoulder pads, and toast with bottles of Zoigl.

Someone grabs me by the elbow. I turn, and it's Peter.

"Brilliant game!" he says.

I hand him a beer. We touch bottles and say, "Prost," grinning like fools.

"Have this time with your team," he says to me, and saluting everyone with his Zoigl before leaving.

Equipment clatters and beer bottles clink as we celebrate and get ready to dance for our fans.

"We won, Willie!" shouts Thomas, slapping my shoulder.

"Three points in the standings!" adds Paldi.

"Get your shoulder and elbow pads off, it's time to dance!" Thomas yells as he throws gear into his stall.

Felix goes to the door, and motions for us to follow. The joyful Fan Curve noise echos through the arena. I savor it. I want to remember these sights, sounds, and emotions. In my gut, I know this is my last dance.

The crowd chants. We chant back. I am so damn lucky to be here, doing this, with my team. I'm caught in their grip and never want to leave. Their go-to chant makes my chest vibrate. "A-hab!" Boom-boom-boom! "A-hab!" Boom-boom-boom! "A-hab!" Boom-boom-boom! I skate out, turn back to my teammates, waving for them to join me. And together, we dance!

AT THE ZOIGL AFTER PARTY, I can feel my time with the Ice Devils slipping away. And after winning, I want Eva's attention. I scan the cheerful crowd, and can't find her. So, I leave. Back in the barracks, I watch my faux Eva skillfully simulate sexual pleasure. Masturbating before her, I blow. My orgasm soothes me, until I think about the real Eva. I feel sorry for her, pregnant and trapped in a small town with Felix.

I can't sleep and obsess about the Army finding me too broken and the Germans finding me too fixed at the same fucking time. Even though their conclusions are exact opposites, they end exactly the same way—with me forced out.

I don't know how I'll be able to pack my gear and go. The Ice Devils are a part of a long line of teams that have made me so happy for so very long. They are my ice brothers and losing them might will destroy me.

THIRTY-FIVE

After a loose Tuesday night practice, Peter hands me the DEB decision letter. He says we lost, shakes my hand, and tells me that I'll always be an Ice Devil.

I take the letter to Eva and watch her face cloud over with concern, shock, and then anger. She sighs and says, "They write that your motorized prosthesis is a mechanical augmentation which gives you a distinct playing advantage."

"Mechanical augmentation gives me a distinct playing advantage?" I shout, thinking wow, those fuckers at the DEB really have a way with words.

"They say no DEB players may have mechanical enhancements," Eva says with tears staining her cheeks. "Wait, they are more specific. Playing competitive ice hockey in Germany with a motorized prosthetic foot is forbidden."

After all I've been through—amputation, gait training, and rehab—being banned from ice hockey is the worst. "It isn't fair," I say. Hockey gave me the best times of my life. I learned to skate the same winter I learned to walk. I played pond hockey before I understood the game's basic rules. I spent my entire childhood playing, and it gave me the chance to travel, compete, and win championships. It introduced me to great people and gave me unbelievable experiences. It introduced me to the BMC Rangers and the Ice Devils. Without it, I wouldn't have met Eva. It seems impossible to simply pack my gear and say goodbye to it all.

Eva pulls me close. We go back to her room and lie down. I wrap my arm around her and cup her belly. She pulls my hand up to her chest. For a time, neither of us speaks. I soak in her warmth and comfort, take a deep breath, and think of how lucky I am to be with her.

AFTER WEDNESDAY MORNING FORMATION, Sergeant First Class Smith tells me to report to the commander. I can't believe the he wants to see me after last time, but whatever. I go straight there, knock, enter, and give him a crisp-ass salute.

Without a word, he hands me a single sheet of paper.

It's the orders sending me home. Why does he keep fucking with me? Why didn't he just give my orders to Smith? He waits. I look back at him with the unflinching stoicism Robalo displayed at Jack's funeral.

Manning stands and reaches to shake my hand. "Thank you for your service," he says.

Thank you for your service? Really? I ignore his hand, execute an about face, and leave without ever looking back.

After Taps sounds, I lie in the dark considering my life. Coach said the decisions about me were apples and oranges. That's not true. They are apples and apples—the Army says

I'm apple sauce and the DEB says I'm apple strudel. Who am I kidding? They really both say that I'm disposable.

EVA CALLS and asks if I can come to her place today. The tone of her voice crushes all my hope for something good.

If she can't say it over the phone, maybe she's decided to abort our baby. I break the speed limit racing to her house. She buzzes me in, and I meets her on the steps. "Come inside. I made us coffee," she says.

We sit and before she can pour, I blurt out, "You not going to kill it, are you?" I don't wait for her to answer, and immediately tear into a speech about why abortion is so very wrong. I see the unhappiness harden on her face, but I keep on speaking.

When I finally stop, she says, "I'm not having an abortion."

I exhale, "Thank God."

She remains silent.

"You okay?"

"No," she says, "sad, angry, guilty."

"Eva, I'm sorry."

She wipes away a tear. "Weiden so small," she sighs.

"I love you."

She doubles over and cries into her hands.

I lean forward and rub her back. "Please don't, I'm here for you."

She pulls away and straightens up. "It's not yours," she says, very deliberately.

I shake my head, unable to process it.

"Felix is the father," she manages to get out, between sobs.

Like nerve gas, her words attack every fiber of my body. Felix is the father! I want to cry, but even my tear ducts are frozen by the shocking news.

"I wish it was ours," she sobs. "I wish more than anything it was yours."

I sniff back snot.

"I'm sorry," she says, reaching for me.

I pull back. "It's not true!"

"It is," she whispers.

"Then how can you wish it was mine?"

"I told you before," Eva sobs. "You make me feel special."

"Bullshit!"

She looks, her eyes are full of sorrow, waiting for more from me.

Emotions collide inside me like freight trains. I want to strangle her. I want to console her. But her betrayal is too painful for words. I stand and put on my jacket.

She stares with her mouth working soundlessly, like a fish gasping for air.

I turn away and feel guilt before committing my crime—leaving her without saying another word.

To hell with her, I fume while driving away. Felix can have the cheating bitch. To drown out the pain, I sing *Walk this Way* with Aerosmith, and *Back in Black* with AC/DC. Then the Dropkick Murphys start in with *Rose Tattoo* and I kill the music. The image of Felix and Eva's matching tattoos almost makes me drive into a tree. Fuck me! How could I have been so blind?

Somehow I make it back on post, park and stare at nothing. Stupid. Cheated. Relieved. Angry. Confused. I still love her. I pound the steering wheel. Holy shit, Felix has known for weeks! He knew it when we fought! He said it was his!

Upstairs, I open a beer. Eva still loves me. Despite everything, I want to lie beside her, kiss her, smell her, taste her. Instead, I watch porn. This time I skip my dark haired beauty in favor of blond lesbians with huge silicone tits. After I blow, I decide to forgive Eva. Why do tender thoughts always follow sex? It must be biological. My stupid dick doesn't know that I've been cheated, and sit here empty and alone.

I sleep badly and wake feeling numb. I imagine Dad's cop wisdom on fatherhood, "Nobody thinks they're ready, but men of character step up." But that was before. Eva's revelation freed me from having to step up. It comes along with some survivor's guilt over dodging the fatherhood bullet.

I'm pretty sure I would have stepped up, but heck, that's Felix's problem now.

ON SUNDAY, I'm overwhelmed by emptiness. Ghost pain shoots out from the hole Eva left in my heart. I lie in a fog between being awake and asleep before my bladder forces me up. Hopping across the cold tile, I'm wracked by remorse. Back in bed, bone-deep weariness keeps me down.

The Army abandoned me.

The DEB took my Eis Brüder.

Eva betrayed me.

Now, whether I stay or go doesn't matter. Nothing matters, because I'm a ghost. Other than at accountability formations, I'm invisible. I'm a nobody. I shudder, because hopelessness can be deadly.

Why has life turned so hard against me? Somehow, I must have brought this on myself. I see my Easton resting in the corner, but have no desire to pick it up. Then, I see my dress uniform hanging in my wall locker. It still has gold Corporal stripes stitched on each sleeve. I get up, dress, and inspect myself. My sky blue pants are bloused smartly into my shiny black jump boots. My navy blue coat is decorated with shiny gold buttons, silver jumps wings, and a row of colorful ribbons. A light blue infantry cord snakes around my shoulder and under my arm. Everything fits a little looser now, but still looks great. I put on my maroon beret, with my unit flash and regimental crest centered over my left eye.

Damn, I really was something. I wonder if Fat Jack felt this way when he inspected himself on his way to night court.

I look over at my copy of *Moby Dick* laying on the floor.

Ahab was a stupid nickname. Even after Eva explained it, it never sat right with me. Then I realize, I'm not Ahab. I never was. I'm the poor damn whale. Battered and scarred, swimming alone in a vast ocean of loneliness. I lie down and think about Squeaky. I wonder if she still has the key to the water tower and suddenly, I'm at peace.

MY PHONE BUZZES. I ignore it.

Jack jumped.

My phone buzzes. I ignore it.

It would be so damn easy.

My phone buzzes. I answer.

"Hey man, you skating?" Scrappy asks.

"I'm banned," I say.

"Not from the Rangers, Bro. I'll drive. See you at eleven?"

"Eleven?" I echo and hang up.

I take off my uniform and lay down. Maybe I can sleep away the rest of my time in the Army. Maybe I can sleep away the rest of my miserable life.

A sharp knock startles me. "Dude!" Scrappy yells from the hallway.

I open the door.

"Come on, let's go."

"I don't have gear," I mumble.

"Basti can talk to the Zamboni driver. He'll let the legendary Cap'n Ahab get his stuff."

At the rink, I get my gear. In the more compact locker room out back, Joel chats with Kenny Krieger. Basti comes over and sits beside me. Out on the ice, Coach divides us into teams. I'm glad to be here, but don't feel like trying too hard. Then I remember the Air Force guy and decide to play for assists. I set up some nice goals and smile. I tell shaggy-headed Andy to go to the net with his stick firmly on the ice, and throw him a beautiful waist-high saucer pass. It lands right on the blade of his stick as he charges toward the far post. In! He scores!

There's yelling and pounding on the glass behind me. It's Thomas, Paldi, and Peter. They chant, "A-hab!" Smack, smack, smack! "A-hab!" Smack, smack, smack! "A-hab!" Smack, smack, smack!

I wave and they smile.

Back with my tribe, I'm getting the fast-paced group therapy I need so badly. In our icy sanctuary, I forget all my problems and just play. It's glorious. After practice, we drink Zoigl. On the way out, Scrappy and I watch the Devils whizz through their complex, silent drills. I see Felix.

He's just three feet from me, on the other side of the glass. I'm not angry. In fact, I silently wish him luck.

Scrappy drives us back to post. I look up at the suicide tower and shake my head. It's too bad that Jack didn't have hockey. I look over at Scrappy. As long as he has my back, everything will be okay.

THIRTY-SIX

Like a man going over Niagara Falls in a barrel, I'm swept up in the rush and speed of leaving. On April first, I sell my car. The next day packers arrive and box up my stuff. I'm not sad, but I'm not happy—the absence of one doesn't automatically give you the other. Anyway, I set it all in motion and am now powerless to stop it.

I go with Scrappy to Weiden's spring festival. He parks and we walk to the city center. The town is nestled in a wide valley, surrounded by green hills and dense forests that thrive in the mild summers and are hardened by the harsh winters. Today the sun is out, and the buds on the trees add a happy glow to everything. Yellow Easter flowers blossom along the old city wall. There is the sweet smell of new life in the air.

We take an ancient footbridge over a small stream, and enter the old town through a narrow pedestrian arch. The cobblestone streets are swept clean. The smell of grilling bratwurst and pork steaks makes my mouth water. People we pass say "Gruss Gott," and we answer with the same polite Bavarian greeting. In the town's main square, hundreds of people sit in the sun. Many sip cappuccinos. I look up at the Brunner Café. Man, I'll miss their Weisswurst.

Scrappy leads us toward a large stage set up at the base of the old city hall. Church bells chime, reminding me of my first night at Eva's. I realize too late that Scrappy is heading toward a group of Ice Devils. They stick out in their colorful team jerseys. We exchange the more informal "Servus," greeting that Bavarians use with their friends.

All these small things are so natural now. Back home, I'll miss them.

Felix and Eva stand together in back, and my chest tightens. For a moment, I'm jealous and mad. Then it passes, and I feel some measure of respect for Felix. Respect, and maybe something like understanding. I don't know if he'll be a good husband, but I'm pretty sure he'll be a good father. I wave, and Eva gives me a small wave in return.

There's an announcement over the loudspeakers. The crowd quiets and the Ice Devils go up on stage. Scrappy and I step off to the side.

Thomas says, "Catch," and throws me a jersey.

"Come on," Paldi motions, waving me forward.

"Don't be stupid, go," Scrappy says, giving me a push.

Weiden's Burgermeister says a few words, and calls us forward. The crowd claps, and it turns into a standing ovation. After, I take off the jersey and give it back to Thomas.

"No, keep it," he says. "It's a gift."

Scrappy and I stick around and listen to a local rock band from Troglau. The Bavarian rockabilly is great, the sun is warm, and the Zoigl is tasty. The people crowded around our table are happy, close-knit, and traditional. They love nature, festivals, and their Ice Devils. I don't know how ice hockey found its way into their hearts, but it did and they are a little better for it.

THAT NIGHT I call Dad from my empty barracks room. Even the corner where I kept my trusty Easton is bare.

"Are yah ready to go, Willie?" he asks.

"Pretty much, I'm going out for a last round of beers in Graf tonight."

"You're not twenty-one," Dad laughs.

"The cut off here is sixteen!"

"Oh Christ, don't bring those bad habits back here. We got standards," he teases. "Hey, I've got the weekend free. I'll pick yah up and we can drive ovah to the Marathon remembrance."

"Let's wait and see," I say.

"Bobby Orr will be there. What do yah say?"

"Maybe."

"Okay," he says. "I'm just looking forward to seeing yah."

"Me too, Dad."

I walk under the tower, past Ed's, and go to Zum Adler for my last Zoigl. The Biergarten in back is lively, and it takes me a minute to find Joel and Danny. We toast like pros, laugh like fools, and they wish me luck in Boston. Joel promises to look me up the next time he gets back home.

Back in my empty room, I think of her. Most would agree that I'm lucky Felix was the sperm doner, but I'm not so sure. I know it wasn't meant to be, but I miss her.

ON MY FLIGHT HOME, I have time to think. Looking back, the year went by fast. I made corporal, led paratroopers, lost my foot, lost my rank, and lost my identity. Hockey found me, and I found new brothers at the rink. Jack killed himself, and the Germans took hockey from me. Eva's pregnancy threw me for a loop, and then fate robbed me of a chance to start a family with her. I guess I should be grieving, but I'm not. Grief and disappointment killed Jack, and it won't happen to me.

As the fasten-seatbelt light comes on, I thank God that Scrappy called the morning I stood looking at myself in the mirror. I have to keep those crazy thoughts away and remember that I'm a Foley.

In Baltimore, I switch to my connecting flight to Logan. There's a huge "Welcome to America" sign. I'm moving into the unknown, and this time around it feels good. At the immigration counter, a TSA agent flips through my passport and asks me where I've been.

"With the Army, in Germany," I say.

"Thank you for you service," she says, handing back my passport.

That phrase rings hollow now. When I enlisted, I was truly patriotic. Returning home, not so much. I guess in America's thank-you-for-your-service culture, everyone in uniform is seen as a hero. Well, one thing's for sure, I'm not a hero.

An hour later, I'm in Boston. Automatic doors slide open to the crowded main terminal. My dad waits front and center. He waves. My eyes leave his good hand and focus on his mechanical hook.

The man I am today is miles away from the boy I was just a year ago. The boy would have felt betrayed by his father's deception. He would have returned his father's stony silence with his own stony silence. Of course I have every right to be furious, but instead I choose to forgive.

I laugh and point, "We're quite a pair."

He smiles.

We hug.

"What would Mom think about her two bionic men?"

"She'd be happy we're together," he says.

We laugh.

"Can you open a bottle of beer with that thing?" I ask.

He smiles and holds it up, "That, and lots more, Aaarrrhhh!"

We laugh again.

Dad drives us straight to the Boston Commons. He picks up backstage passes at the first responder table.

"Here, you're my plus one," he says, handing me my pass.

Despite my protests, I end up on the stage with Dad as the mayor recognizes the Marathon bombing victims and first responders. When he comes down the line pinning hero's medals and shaking hands, I step back. He turns to the crowd, and says, "Please welcome our heroic native son, just back from overseas military service."

Still blushing as things wrap up on stage, I weave between roadies who are setting up drums and musical equipment. Robert Gordon Orr stands over to the side talking with the Dropkick Murphys. I can't believe my eyes! There is Boston's beloved numbah four, the best player ever to lace up the skates. Heck, even fans of snipers like Gretzky and Jagr concede that Orr was the best defensemen of all time. And there he is, in the flesh, wearing his black and gold Bruins sweater.

Later, when the band stops playing and thanks the crowd, they wave for everyone backstage to come up and take a bow. I'm nervous, and my nervousness doubles when I find myself shoulder to shoulder with Bobby Orr.

As the cheers die down, Mr. Orr turns to me. "How's rehab going?"

"Good, sir," I nod.

"Will you run another Marathon?"

"I wasn't hurt at the bombing, sir," I reply, breaking eye contact.

"Oh gosh, I'm sorry, I just thought..." Bobby says.

"That's okay, that's happened a lot to me today," I smile.

Bobby smiles back, and asks, "May I ask, what happened?"

"I was an Army paratrooper, hurt in a parachuting accident."

Bobby waves to someone and motions like he's signing something. A staffer comes over and hands Bobby a Victoriaville stick and a marker. Bobby thanks the staffer and turns to me. "May I sign this for you?"

I beam, feeling like a kid with Santa. Well, almost like that, if Santa was in the Hockey Hall of Fame for winning two Stanley Cups with Boston.

"How should I make it out?"

"To Will Foley, Mr. Orr."

"Here you go, Will," Bobby says.

DAD DRIVES US HOME, and we enjoy the comfortable silence. At home he admires Bobby's stick with its single stripe of black tape on its blade. He asks if I want to share a pizza.

"Ham and pineapple?" I suggest.

"That's different," he says.

"In Germany, they call it pizza Hawaii."

He calls in our order and says, "Oh, one of your Army buddies texted me. Let me find it, yeah here it is. Sergeant Leonard says he'll start at UMASS Lowell in August. Here's his email address," Dad says and hands me his phone.

I forward the message to myself thinking, damn, I really dropped the ball and should definitely write her.

Dad notices my wrinkled brow and asks, "How yah doing?"

"Good," I lie.

"Been through a lot. Yah at peace with it?"

Peace. It sure isn't something you get by sorting out the stuff between your own ears. It's linked to the people around you and what they expect. It's also linked to what you expect from them.

My mom? Her death was an accident and she's not coming back.

Dr. Dennis? When he amputated my foot, he cut away my naïve belief that the sun would always shine on me.

Jack? I won't ever forget him or forgive Manning.

Eva? We never had a chance, because her place is in Weiden.

And me? I'm not Ahab. And I'm not that cursed whale. When the rink calls to me, I'm an Orca looking for my pod. Just like those beautiful black-and-white killer whales, I don't like to swim alone. Huh, who knows, maybe UMASS Lowell has a team.

"Will, yah okay?"

"Yeah, but I'm not quite at peace yet."

"Why not?" he asks.

I tell him about Eva.

"Sounds like a great gal."

I tell him about the baby and Felix.

"She sounds like a smaht cookie."

I nod.

He hands me a fresh Sammy as the third period starts. The boys win and noticing my lack of excitement, he says, "Still thinkin' about that German girl?"

"Nah, that ship sailed." I say. "It's the remembrance ceremony."

"What's the matter?"

"The part when the mayor called me a hero."

"What's wrong with that?"

"Everyone has these crazy expectations. That I'm brave. A great patriot. Wise beyond my years," I say, staring off at nothing. "I'm none of it."

Dad clears his throat and waits until I look him in the eye. "Willie, a hero is just someone who sacrifices for someone else. You did that when you enlisted. You were doing that when yah got hurt."

I shake my head. "I was just a doing my job."

Dad points at Bobby's stick, "If you asked Mr. Orr if he was a hero, he'd probably say the same damn thing, but to you and me he's the biggest hero around."

I nod.

Dad then hands his remembrance medal to me and says, "The world needs heroes. People look up to athletes, movie stars, and sometimes even regular guys like us."

I smile and shrug.

"Listen, if it gets us better seats at the Gahdin, I'm all in," he says, standing to give me an enormous bear hug.

As he squeezes me tight, I say, "Me too, Dad, me too."

The End

ACKNOWLEDGMENTS

Writing a novel is a solitary act, but leave it to a hockey guy to turn it into a team sport. Many, whether they knew it or not, helped me to write and publish my debut novel, *AHAB*. Throughout, my family gave me loving support and candid feedback in equal parts. The Bayern Rangers, the Weiden Blue Devils, and the Boston Bruins provided fertile ground for an idea that grew into a compelling story. And, their colorful players and passionate fans gave the story its sporting soul.

AHAB plays out in Bavaria and Boston, against the backdrop of the U.S. Army and professional sports in 2013-14. I diligently worked to ground the story in accurate historical references and settings. My research was jump started by three books: *Care of the Combat Amputee* published by the U.S. Army Medical Department Center and School, *Grafenwöhr Training Area, Yesterday & Today* by Gerald Morgenstern, and *Stay: A History of Suicide and the Philosophies Against It* by Jennifer Michael Hecht. Later, knowledgeable subject-matter experts reviewed my technical, medical, and military references for accuracy and authenticity. For that I owe Dr. (MAJ) Matt Noss, D.O., Dr. Kraig Hays, Ph.D., Dr. Debra Davidson, Ph.D, and SFC (Ret.) David Guenther huge debts of gratitude. Of course, any mistakes that leaked through my five-hole belong solely to me.

I drafted many chapters of *AHAB* as a student in the University of Tampa's MFA program. This special writer's community was led by Lynne Bartis and Dr. Erica Dawson. Each semester knowledgeable faculty mentors and enthusiastic workshop partners critiqued drafts. Stephan Kiesbye led my first workshop which included James Aaron Buchanan, Abigail Smith, and Michael Phelps. My next semester, Jessica Anthony and Corinna Vallianatos led the workshopping efforts of LindaMarie Tonn, Michelle Crespo, Lakeisha Matthews, Marilyn Duarte, Catherine Fahling, Hannah Benefield, and Carolyn Warmbold. In my third term Kevin Moffett guided the efforts of Justin Herzog, LindaMarie Tonn, and Martha Manfried. Bringing it all home, Jeff Parker mentored fourth term students Perry Authement, Hannah Benefield, Dee Perkins, James Ryan, Aysia Torres, and Carolyn Warmbold. Jeff Parker and Jason Ockert were the readers for my MFA thesis—a complete second draft of *AHAB*.

Family and friends, including Ute Huestis, Sarah Huestis-Mitchell, Michael Jetton, Connor Davidson, LTC (Ret.) Alison Tullud, Jim Neumiller, and Sofia Caulwell, gave me valuable feedback on subsequent drafts. As *AHAB* moved towards its final form, my prose greatly benefitted from the skillful editing of Kevin Huestis, Genie Hughes, and Carolyn Warmbold. A very talented graphic designer, Lee Elliott, came up with a brilliant concept cover, and Robin Johnson of Robin Ludwig Design Inc. turned Lee's artwork into a stunning book cover and jacket.

Justin Herzog helped me bring everything together. A talented writer, savvy self-publisher, and truly generous friend, Justin opened self-publishing doors I was too inexperienced to open myself. Which leads me to you—my readers. I hope you enjoyed reading *AHAB* *as much as* I enjoyed writing it.

Brad Huestis
    Tampa, Florida
    February, 2021

ABOUT THE AUTHOR

Lieutenant Colonel (Ret.) Brad Huestis grew up playing pond hockey in Iowa and Canada. He is Airborne and Ranger qualified, and served as a U.S. Army paratrooper, artilleryman, and judge advocate. Twice deployed, he received the NATO medal and a Bronze Star medal. His award-winning debut novel, *AHAB*, grew out of his love of soldiers, hockey, and storytelling.

www.bradhuestis.wixsite.com/website

www.facebook.com/brad.huestis.author

www.linkedin.com/in/brad-huestis-a61a7273

www.amazon.com/author/brad.huestis

Made in the USA
Columbia, SC
09 January 2024

29336864R00224